The Narrow Cage

The Narrow Cage

An American Family Saga

BY KATHLEEN STONE RYAN

THE BOBBS-MERRILL COMPANY, INC.
Indianapolis/New York

Designed by Bob Antler
Manufactured in the United States of America

First printing

Library of Congress Cataloging in Publication Data

Ryan, Kathleen Stone.
    The narrow cage.

I. Title.
    PZ4.R9913Nar   [PS3568.Y367]   813'.54   80-687
    ISBN 0-672-52655-7

For BARB, LINDA, AND TERI,
without whose help and encouragement
this book would never have been written

I. THE VOICES
November 1884–February 1885

Ride a cock horse
To Banbury Cross,
To see a fine lady
Upon a white horse.
With rings on her fingers
And bells on her toes,
She shall have music
Wherever she goes!

—*Nursery rhyme*

The great house was stirring, but barely. Breakfast had to be put on the table, fires lit, sleepy children roused.

Letty crept from the bedroom. She cherished the peace; her slippered feet were mouse-quiet, lest she disturb her husband, deliver the day into his hands before she had savored it.

Her morning room waited in the pale dawn light. She tugged the wool of her robe around her and reached for an old tartan shawl, comforting as the nanny of her childhood. She threw it about her and stood by the cold hearth, regarding the pair of high-backed chairs that still delighted her. Lemon silk, tall as tulips, they stood out against the severity of the blue and white striped wallpaper. Yellow defying the chill of November.

She shivered. It would be Thanksgiving in three weeks. Next Wednesday Albert would be ten. How time passed! To think it was almost eleven years since she'd come to this stern house that Nathaniel had built for them. How different she'd been then!

Yet little of it showed. She turned to stare into the oval mirror over the mantel, her brown eyes looking back at her with strain. Yet her hair remained ungrayed, springing away from her high temples, smooth as bird wings. It fell undressed at this hour, in a river, dark as teakwood. The cold winter light molded high cheekbones as if they were marble. She saw that in spite of four children, her figure remained trim, the lines of her breasts firm. "I wish I were taller," she said aloud, wistfully frowning at her slenderness, the narrowing of her shoulders beneath the old shawl. Vulnerability enfolded her like a cloak.

She slipped into the depths of one of the chairs, willing herself to feel safe. She felt surrounded by the fortress of the house. Its solid strength should have encouraged her. Instead, its massive walls and encompassing parkland had always been oppressive. She had lied the first time Nat showed it to her, agreeing with him that it was magnificent.

With window eyes, lidded by deep shades, the house had observed her coldly, too impressed with its own grandeur to grant her any welcome. It was of course Nat's creation, a dwelling that became him. The young architect had followed his orders, replicating a granite "cousin" that had stood on the Scottish moors for a hundred years. Of native stone, its gray walls and haughty turrets defied vining creepers to have any softening effect, while slate roofs rebuked the sunshine, preferring mists.

Letty's children had been born here: Albert, Amelia, Polly—and the poor, stunted Brett, her baby.

Today the household needed little direction from her. She closed her eyes, her mind exploring the house's chambers and crannies: Phillips in the dining room, setting the table for breakfast. Taft, an eagle peering from the aerie of his pantry, his taloned hands repolishing the already gleaming silver; missing nothing. Phillips, after two years, was shaping up, but it took a long time to train a good houseman. As for Taft . . . they were all a little afraid of Taft. All, that is, except Nathaniel. Taft was Nat's man.

Letty shivered suddenly and pulled the tartan closer.

The others she could feel comfortable with. Betsy, the parlor maid, had been with her from the first. Now Betsy would be going over Nat's den, sharp with male odors—splashed whiskey, cigars, aromatic pipe tobacco. Betsy would persuade the full draperies to let in light, to flow over the oak-paneled walls. The den nullified most efforts to illuminate it. Nat liked it that way.

It wasn't a room in which Letty felt welcome. Betsy would flee it quickly too. She would move on to the elegant parlor, fragrant with rose-petaled potpourri. Picture frames of silver and gold-enclasped mirrors enhanced the cucumber coolness of muted satin, casting back light and loveliness so that chairs and Dresden shepherdess, gilded clock on the mantel—all were more than they might have been without each other. The china girl dancing in an eternal froth of frozen lace.

Norah would join Betsy to open up the salon, not for the difficulty of the task, but for the enormity of its responsibility: six windows to unveil, each draped in crimson velvet, corded and tasseled. The sunshine—what there was for November—pouring in like a thief and stealing away the shadows.

Letty pictured Norah and Betsy talking in soft syllables, unobservant of the patient chairs, grouped like guests waiting for the party to begin, the maids weaving between them as they went about their task; footfalls swallowed in the thick pile. Not taking time—for familiarity breeds unconcern—to pause, even for a moment, before the immense portrait of Governor Mackenzie, the first Nathaniel, seated next to his wife, Sarah, while beside them were two of their ten children, caught in the offense of boredom. Letty had often stared at the painting above the stone mantel and wondered, Was she living up to the Mackenzie traditions?

Nat's illustrious ancestor, gazing down with supercilious arrogance, never bothered to give her a reply. Letty would have relished asking Sarah whether husbands were kinder to their wives in Revolutionary times.

Letty sighed. A glance toward the bedroom door assured her, thankfully, that Nat was still asleep. She looked about the morning room. The fire was long out, but Norah would stir it to life when she brought Letty's tea.

The tea couldn't come soon enough. Letty shivered—unwilling to pull the bell rope, disturb the routine of the servants. Norah knew her habits. She would be up soon with the tray.

Letty's eyes fell on the pile of books Mother had brought over yesterday—delivering them as a bishop confers confirmation on a flock of supplicants. "It's time you began reading to your daughters, Letty." This with an expression of duty done on her long face.

Letty had stared at the books, recognition disturbing her. "Why, these are Hitty's and mine! Where've you been keeping them?"

Mother had not answered directly. That was Mother. "No sense giving them to you until my grandchildren were ready to have them. You ought to begin to teach Amelia and Polly, Letty."

Teach. Mother had never taught. The books had appeared in the nursery, one at a time and sporadic as showers. Letty had looked at the pictures first; shared them reluctantly with Hitty. Five years younger than she, the fat little girl in flannel dresses and stockinged sturdiness had tugged at her, whining, "Hitty see—?"

Letty knew that what was in the books was a part of her childhood she'd sooner leave behind. Yet, terrible and compelling, the books were there; she would have to open their pages.

This morning, her fingers moved over to slide under the first book, to set it, battered cover, dusty smell, corners curled as dead leaves, on her lap. And to go back in time.

"Nanny, why are they burning that lady?"

"Gracious me, what are you talking about, Miss Letty?"

"See here, in the picture, Nanny—?"

"Oh. That would be Joan of Arc." Lips pursed.

"But why are they setting fire to her?"

5

"You ask your mama about it next time she comes up to the nursery." Which could be days. Emma Benedict was careful to whom she gave away her time.

When she did appear, Letty flung herself at her. "Mama, that book you left here—?"

"Yes, Letty. Its about great women in history. I thought it was something you should read."

"Why did they burn Joan of Arc?"

"Joan of Arc?" Mother's face took on its guarded look. "Well, Letty, she forced them into it. You know she wore men's clothes and led an army into battles. She must have known what to expect."

"Why did she do those things, Mama?"

"Read the story for yourself, Letty."

"I have but I don't understand it."

"Letty. This is why I dread coming up to the nursery—so many questions. I should think you'd be able to teach yourself. It's all there in the book. Oh, I'm beginning a migraine—"

"What does it mean, she heard voices in her head telling her to save France?"

"You see, that's it. She was a witch, or else crazy—very probably she was both. People like that come to a bad end."

Letty turned to the well-remembered page. There was Joan of Arc, unfaded by time, a girl in boy's clothes tied to a stake. The flames that wreathed her were burning her into a poppy's stamen, candlewick black against the crimson petals.

Letty shuddered. Was it appropriate that she read this story to the children? To Albert? He could hardly be interested. These were stories about women. She riffled through the musty pages: Lady Jane Grey, her head on the block; Flora Macdonald who'd helped Bonnie Prince Charlie make his escape; Elizabeth Fry comforting prison inmates.

Where was she among all these women? She showed up pale. A knock on the door startled her. Norah at last, with the tray.

"Good morning, ma'am. I trust you rested well?"

"Thank you, Norah. The tea will be nice. It's chilly in here."

"No wonder. The fire's gone out." Norah fussed with the logs and coaxed the fire with newspaper and fresh kindling to get it to burn. "There, ma'am—you'll soon be warm now."

"Thank you, Norah. Have the children had their breakfast yet?"

"Katie was just taking the trays upstairs when I come up, ma'am. Was there something you wanted with Nanny?"

Another nanny . . . Letty and Hitty's nanny was long gone.

"Just to remind her, Mr. Mackenzie's taking Albert with him to his club today."

6

"Oh, she wouldn't forget that, ma'am. The boy's had his bath already. The whole nursery's in an uproar."

"It is a special treat, I know. Tell Nanny I'll try to get upstairs later to read to the girls."

"Yes, ma'am." Norah's eyes telegraphed her anxiety to be gone. It was Monday. There were more fires to light, more beds to change. Norah's nine years with Letty had taught her how it went.

"That'll be all then?"

"Yes, Norah. You may go." Letty poured her tea into the fragile cup, cradling it, a dove protected against her breast. She should begin to read to Polly and Amelia regularly. It was what she'd wanted her own mother to do. But what if Amelia asked questions that Letty couldn't answer? Was that what Mother had meant—slipping away from them under the cloak of a headache, the muscle twitch in her cheek conveying displeasure?

Letty sipped her tea thoughtfully. Children must be taught, of course. But what did one teach them besides obedience and diligence?

Perhaps they were too young to be read to? Polly, at four, would wriggle, ask to get down from her chair. Amelia, at well past eight, could be made to listen—but at the thought of Amelia, Letty's heart turned. The child's gray eyes would watch her, not disclosing the thoughts that lay behind them.

Letty leaned toward the leaping fire. Out of her childhood came other stories stored in that pile of books: The little girl who couldn't stop crying; her eyes fell out of her face and floated away, like paper boats on the river of her tears. "You see what happens!" warned Emma. "Mustn't cry, Letty."

The boy who ate only sweets. A dentist, as tall as the page, came after him, extracting his teeth with pincers larger than the man's legs. "So!" said Emma. "This is what happens."

Worst of all was the girl who played with matches. Dress afire, she runs screaming; each picture leads to the last—a heap of ashes. "Children must learn in any fashion they can be taught, Letty. Pay close attention to the pictures. See what happens when you are naughty!"

Pay attention? The pictures were etched on Letty's mind; they were her nightmares.

Had Hitty been as terrified by the stories? Letty had always been an obedient child. Was terror really an important ingredient in bringing up children—as everyone seemed to agree?

Letty straightened in her chair, pushing away the fantasies, the ancient, edgeless fears. Nat was stirring in the bedroom.

He opened the door and stood there glowering. His muscles, lightly hidden beneath his silken robe, were coiled so that it seemed, were he to stretch, he could not help but become the tall man one supposed him to be. Yet he was really short, bull thick, his little feet remarkably small and light. His dark hair, tousled now, was only touched with gray, yet his profile had sharpened with age, the hawk nose that came to meet the full, drooping lips, a shock unalleviated by kindness in the sullen, charcoal eyes.

"I trust you slept well, Nat?"

He muttered something, scratching at the pelt of his chest through his gaping nightshirt. He walked past her, clearing his throat, and opened the opposite door. In his dressing room she could hear him expectorate into the china slopbowl, hear the splashing of his urine as it hit the side of the toilet receptacle, imagine she could smell its ammonia, acrid and distasteful.

She set her tea aside. It was upon her now and needed to be faced —the day. Nat, as usual, had begun it for her, stealing her privacy while he spoke no word. He did not need to. She had long ago endowed him with authority.

She got up and rang for her maid to help her to dress.

2

Amelia sat in the high-backed nursery chair, cupping the mug of milk in her hands. Avoiding Nanny—if Amelia was to carry out her plan today, that was what she must do at all costs.

She had purposely picked today. With Albert going to lunch at the club with Papa, Nanny would have her hands full. Amelia took another look at the milk. Its creaminess reflected back up at her, turning the silver of the mug's inside ghostly. How she detested milk! Would she ever be old enough not to be made to drink it? She stared at Nanny, fussing with Albert.

It had been a mistake. At once, Nanny's blue eyes were turned on her.

"Get it down, Miss Amelia! You know it'll put roses on your cheeks."

Amelia forced her mouth to the mug, restraining the need to gag. The ruse worked. Nanny went back to clucking over Albert.

"You mind your manners now, young man"—brushing crumbs off his best suit—"I don't know why your hair won't lie flat"—tugging at his brown curls with the tortoise-shell comb, then stepping back to appraise him. "Now you look nice. Your papa'll be proud of you!"

Albert stared at her, his father's coal eyes in a younger Nathaniel's face. But the personality was wrong—as if something hadn't come out right in the mixing bowl. A spaniel glance that said he expected reprimand, even when he hadn't done anything. "Oh Nanny, do I have to go?"

"Of course you do." Nanny's lips pursed. Then on impulse she leaned forward and hugged the boy. "There, there, lovey—it'll be all right. You'll see. You got to move out into the world, you know. You'll be ten next week."

He shrugged. Miserable.

"Sam'll be there. You like Sam—even if he is older'n you are."

"No I don't. Sam always talks about beating me up." Albert's lower lip trembled. "Oh, Nanny, I don't feel well. My throat"—he put a fine hand to his collar—"it aches."

"Go on with you now. It was your head this morning, then your chest—it'll be your big toes next," Nanny scolded, her face kind. "You know when your papa sends for you, we don't dare disappoint him." She propelled the boy toward the door, removing an invisible thread from his good gray coat. "We got to get you downstairs before you dream up some more aches and pains, eh." Her hand automatically went to the high, thin forehead. "Oh my, you do feel warm. We'll tuck you to bed with some hot milk as soon as you get back."

Albert turned, hope in his eyes. "If you were to say I was sick—?"

But she shook her head. "Best go through with it, darlin'. We all know how your papa is." She bent and whispered, so low Amelia could scarcely catch the words. "Courage, lovey."

With slow feet, Albert began to descend the back staircase.

Nanny turned back to the nursery. As soon as she'd helped four-year-old Polly clamber down from the table, the child ran to the great rocking-horse. Nanny followed her to wipe face and hands, then lifted the little girl into the saddle.

"Whee!" Polly screamed, her hilarity bouncing back from the walls of the room. She hurled herself into a rocking motion, the scarlet reins tight in her hands, her white-stockinged legs thrust out stiff in the stirrups, her blond curls bobbing.

The horse's eyes stared straight ahead, hard and unblinking. Its wooden nostrils flared as three-year-old Brett dumped the contents of his cereal bowl on the table.

Amelia's nose quivered in disgust. "Nanny, Brett's done it again."

"Lor', Master Brett, you'll be the death of me." Then, as Nanny began to attack the mess with the always handy cloth, "God love him, he don't know no better. Do you, angel? But I must say, he does provoke me. Where's Katie?" Nanny straightened her back. "She should be here to help me—and me with so much to do this morning —Master Albert going downtown—there's just more than a body can see to." She shook her head wearily. "You finished your milk yet, Miss Amelia?"

The eight-year-old gazed back at Nanny. "Do I have to?"

"Now, Miss Amelia, you know better'n to ask that. Drink it up, dear. Then you can get down, like Miss Polly. Ever such a good girl she is. Cleaned her bowl and off to play already."

Amelia took another swallow. It took every ounce of will to get it down. She tasted it, sour in her throat. A tiny trickle escaped from the side of her mouth.

"Have a care now!" Nanny picked up the checkered napkin that matched the breakfast cloth, swiped at Amelia's mouth, then glanced inside the silver mug with its dented bottom, victim not only of Amelia's earlier childish protests but of abuse in the pantry. "Almost gone. One more mouthful will do it, there's a nice girl." Nanny's rules were made to be kept.

At last it was finished. Nanny took the mug from Amelia. "You can get down now. When Katie comes up, she's to clean your hands."

"I can do them for myself." Amelia's voice was sharp with dignity as she lowered herself from the tall chair.

"Oh my," Nanny was cheerful now, with breakfast almost over, "it's growing up that we are today! Then let her at least help you with it. Katie!" The stocky, red-haired girl entered the doorway. "Where you been, my lass? Gone all this time, just when I needed you most. This day of all days!"

"Norah sent me below with a tray of dishes, miss." Katie spoke with more than a hint of a brogue. At fourteen she had been apprenticed to the Mackenzie household after catching the attention of Mrs. Mackenzie. Katie's "Mumma" had been laundress to the family for years.

As Katie picked up an embroidered linen towel to wipe Amelia's hands, she reflected it was probably one that Bridey Maloney had recently stood at the old ironing board to press. Katie sighed. She was grateful for the chance to bring home wages, but her days in this big house were long. She was officially attached to Nanny, but the others seemed to forget that. Whoever needed her, that's who called her. "Haven't you finished that polishing yet? Hurry up about it, girl. There's the back stairs to be swept."

Katie watched Amelia towel her hands dry, her movements meticulous. What made a little bit of a thing seem so much older than her years? The dove eyes that could stare without blinking were not what you'd expect of an eight-year-old. And her manner, even when she whirled about so that the brown hair moved from its straight lines down her back to fly in brief childish pleasure, was self-contained. You knew she was aware of exactly what she was about, her comments oddly quaint, while the gray eyes watched everything, forming what secret, dark judgments? Katie wondered what it would be like to be Amelia? To grow up in this household? Folks said that to have money was everything. Katie wasn't so sure. Recalling her own childhood, the rough-and-tumble existence, Katie didn't think she would choose to change places with one of the Mackenzie children.

Wealth, though it might assure one of a meal and a bed to oneself, truly kept one a prisoner. Katie pictured her own family hearth of an evening—brothers and sisters huddled together to share the warmth and hear Mumma or Auntie Mary tell of the old days back in Ireland. The Maloneys might go to bed hungry for bread, but never for love. With the Mackenzies, you could almost say it was the opposite way round. If it weren't for Nanny, these children might never know the meaning of a kiss or a hug.

"I am finished, thank you, Katie." Amelia startled the Irish girl out of her reverie, handing the maid the now damp towel.

"I can see that you are, miss." Katie took the piece of linen, her voice sharp. Covering her absentmindedness. It was hard not to treat Amelia like one of her own sisters. For all her ladylike manners, the child was still just a child. This was true of all the Mackenzie brood. Airs and graces they might have, but scratch the surface and they were not much different from the Maloney children.

All except Master Brett. Poor love, thought Katie as she brought a blue and white china basin filled with warm water for Nanny to use. Master Brett's never been right. All the wealth in the world wasn't going to restore Master Brett his brains to him, if indeed he ever had any. Nanny knew this, the entire household knew this, but it was never spoken of openly.

"Think he'll ever learn to talk?" Katie asked Nanny.

"Shouldn't wonder, one of these days." Nanny wiped Brett's cheeks, the slobbery chin always wet with saliva. "There, there," she said to the little boy. "Master Brett, you do get into a fair mess, no doubt about it. Katie, if you'll fetch up another bowl of cereal, I'll try to get it down him now the fuss is over." She nodded meaningfully toward the doorway. "Glad Master Albert isn't sent for every day of the week. Don't know if I could weather it."

Katie smiled understandingly. But Nanny was already busy with other matters.

"While you're about it, Katie, that mug's empty. Take it down to the kitchen along with the rest."

"Yes, miss."

Katie hefted the round tray philosophically. Another trip to the kitchen while Mr. Taft was even now looking about to see where the last of the breakfast dishes had got to. Washbowls to empty, towels to stow in the hamper, sheets to change—well, it would all get done somehow. It was amazing how many people it took to keep a large house like this running. Even at that, they had to hustle themselves to keep up.

Amelia watched the departing Katie. It was a sight she was familiar with, but she liked to see all the activity nonetheless, to feel herself almost a part of it. It must be lovely to have so many important things to do. She wondered why Katie sighed so often.

Amelia wandered over to her doll trunk and inspected her dolls. There were nine of them, lined up just where she had left them last evening. Their rag faces beamed at her.

"Have you been good?" she asked them. Painted smiles gave answer. All but Sophie's. "Sophie! You must have been wicked again! I know you have. You are going to be punished."

Sophie still smiled.

Amelia picked her up and spanked the cotton-clad body vigorously. It was always this way. Sophie was the worst. Wouldn't learn. She set the doll back, arranging her white apron, the calico dress.

Nanny's voice reached Amelia. "Do ye be getting on with some needlework now, pet. Your mama may visit today and we'll want to have some work to show her, won't we?"

"Yes, Nanny." Amelia groaned, but she knew enough not to argue. That might spoil her plan. She glanced at Nanny under the cover of her long lashes. Soon, very soon now, Nanny would take Brett into the night nursery to be changed. Would bring him back, to coax and plead with him to swallow a few bites from the cereal bowl that Katie was even now fetching. Katie, returned, would lead Polly off to have her pinafore changed. Those few minutes would give Amelia her chance!

Not that there wasn't great risk involved. But she'd weighed it all and decided the planned venture was worth the gamble.

Extra time could be had by announcing to Nanny that she, Amelia, had to "retire." Nanny took great interest in the bodily functions of her charges. Elimination at this time of the morning was not only expected, it was regarded as part and parcel of the nursery routine. Any child who failed to provide Nanny with satisfactory effort over the china chamber pot could count on being reprimanded and dosed with Nanny's special concoction of crushed calomel, a white powder that wasn't always served with the compensation of jam. Hard to get down, it was choked on and spluttered over while Nanny's eagle eyes observed that it was "all gone." Washed down with a cup of water.

Of recent weeks, Amelia had augmented her scheme by insisting to Nanny that she was old enough to "retire" alone. Today, she would just have to face the possibility of calomel—or worse, castor oil—by restraining herself.

"Nanny." Amelia laid aside the sampler she had fetched from the drawer where all the nursery sewing was kept. "I have to 'retire' now."

Just as Amelia had guessed, Nanny's mind was on other things. "Well, what are you waiting for? Be off to the receptacle with you," she said sharply as she spooned another mouthful for Brett.

As Amelia tiptoed by, she could hear Nanny talking to herself. "—do hope he'll be all right, the lamb. Know he was coming down with a cold—maybe the fever. But when Mr. Mackenzie asks, what's a body to do? Poor Albert—and him so frail. But I got to mind my own business, just like Mrs. Mackenzie keeps saying to me. 'They can't remain babies forever, Nanny,' she says. I know that's true. But, dear Lord, I worry about that boy—going with his father."

Nanny was well into it. Amelia smiled secretly. She'd been right to pick today! Brett's protesting wail followed her into the hallway, diminished as she picked her way to the closet, with its slit of a window, that was considered suitable for the chamber pots.

Amelia's nose wrinkled as she pushed open the door. No matter how often Katie scrubbed down the closet, the odor of excreta was not to be eliminated. Amelia's sensitive nostrils quivered. She pursed her lips. Stared, first at the row of pots, some of them discreetly covered with linen towels, others empty and waiting. Stared too at the lavender bag that hung on the far side of the room. Filled anew with aromatic blossoms this summer, it still could not compete with the room's stench.

Amelia stood by the doorway, which she had prudently closed. Touching the fingers of each hand lightly—twice through—she counted to twenty. Then, taking a deep breath, she threw her small shoulders back and reopened the door. Softly.

No one in sight. She heard Nanny crooning to Brett, Polly talking to Katie. She was safe! Safe to carry out her adventure.

She pulled the door to behind her and with the smallest of steps, crossed the narrow hallway. She slipped along the bannister that guarded the terrifying hole formed by the stairway. Below it she could just barely glimpse the distant reaches of the downstairs hall. Two floors to negotiate. Would she succeed?

With muscles tense, ears alert to catch the least sound, feet feeling for the rough nap of the carpet that covered the staircase, she gained the top step and began to make her descent.

They were so steep, these stairs! She felt a momentary spell of giddiness as her eyes followed the expanse that dropped before her. She was already clutching the bannister, but now she held on to it more tightly. Should she turn back? Abandon her plan? It was unthinkable. For how long had she dreamed of doing just this very thing that she was faced with now? An uncertain but explorative step brought her to the second stair from the top.

She was on her way! She swallowed convulsively and then, hearing Katie's voice scolding at Polly, ceased her hesitating and began to walk gingerly but determinedly down.

Before she knew it, she had gained the second floor. Far more elegant than the third, it held out many objects that tempted her to linger. An enormous gilt-framed mirror hung on the wall between the doorways to Mama's bedroom and her morning room. Beneath it an ornate marble-topped table stretched its carved splendor. It was on this that the wonderful music box rested. Amelia had heard its playing only once. She had overheard Norah telling Nanny, "Its a pity Mrs. Mackenzie doesn't like it. Ordered it from Germany for her, he did—the year of the Centennial. You'd think, a lovely thing like that, she'd play it more often."

And Nanny had replied, with the wisdom of nannies, "Ah, but what did the gift mean to her? Him dallying about while Miss Amelia was expected."

Amelia had pricked up her ears at the mention of her name. "Nanny? What's 'dallying'?"

Nanny had turned to Norah, eyebrows raised. "Lor', I never realized the child was paying attention. It's not a word you need to know, Miss Big Ears. Get on with your sampler, there's a love."

Amelia, stubborn, had persisted. "But, Nanny, you said it was when I was 'expected'? Did Papa present the music box to Mama because of me?"

"God love you, it could have been at that. Now what did I say about the needlework? You've only done one row of stitches and the morning's slipping away."

Now, bent on her adventure, Amelia paused to stare at the marvelous box. The one and only occasion she'd heard it playing was when a visiting grandmama had begged. "Letty, you never let us hear it. Surely you could wind it up occasionally?"

Amelia, watching from her secret perch by the third-floor bannister, had heard Mama's voice murmuring, "—hate the thing. Reminder of Nat's indiscretions." And Grandmama's, "Now, Letty. You know it's just a part of marriage. The main thing is not to let on publicly that you know."

Mama had turned the key in the box. There was a crystalline tinkling as the magic of the music was called into life. Amelia could have listened to it forever; she held her breath, willing it not to end. But, like happiness, it wound down. Mama had replaced the key beneath the box and it sat there to this day, unused.

Amelia would have stood there longer, thinking. But the sound of Mama's voice caused her to jump. Mama was in her morning room, giving orders to Cook. Mama's voice was so pretty; like a song. But Mama might be close to finishing with the menus, and Cook might come out any minute. Amelia braced herself to begin the last flight of stairs, down to the gleaming hallway that led to the front door and gave access to the rooms she wished to visit. It was for this that she had dared.

The sound of her small feet was muffled by the richness of the carpet that covered this portion of the stairway. Deep blue it was. Like walking down a waterfall—if such a thing were possible. Or stepping into shadows. The smell of polish, candle wax. It was another world from the nursery—and as far away.

Amelia's heart pounded in excitement. She was almost there.

3

She was down! Furtively, Amelia peeped about her. Never, except under the strict supervision of Nanny and then only at the rarest times, had she been in this part of the house before. Certainly not alone. The nursery was the province of the Mackenzie children, just as the world beyond the baize-covered doors that led to the kitchens was the servants'. No one wandered about this house unless they were bidden.

Amelia had received no invitation. She tucked in her stomach tensely. Heard her breath come shallow and fast. It was important to find a hiding place, somewhere she could introduce her small body, should necessity arise. An unwary maid, bent upon dusting; Phillips burdened with logs for the fireplaces; even and almost worst of all, the terrible Mr. Taft—tall as a giant and so imposing in his footman's livery—could force her to take immediate cover. She glanced around. Her eyes fell on a large umbrella stand topped by a heavy mirror. She tiptoed over to it, examined the space between it and the hall's corner. Yes, there would be just enough room for her to squeeze herself in there. With the hallway's darkness, she would stand a good chance of not being seen.

This much decided, she turned about. It was the moment she had been waiting for. On soft feet, she began to go up the vestibule. Papa's study first. Cautiously she approached the door and opened it, silent as twilight.

The room smelled like Papa. A rich odor of leather, the sharp tang of the golden liquid in the cut-glass decanter that Mr. Taft always placed in readiness, cigars. The distant figure who was Amelia's father was usually hidden behind the wreathing smoke of a cigar. Amelia,

17

certain now the study was empty, stepped through the doorway. If the hall was dark, this room was even darker. One window behind the leather couch sufficed to let in light. But red-shaded lamps on every table waited to be lit. Miraculously, on Papa's rolltop desk stood a great glass bottle with a ship inside! A sailing ship, complete with masts, spars, portholes. Amelia would have given much to have had time to really look at it, to be able to ask how the vessel had gotten in there. But she dared not linger. With one last look around the room, she left, careful to pull the door to behind her, to leave everything as if she had never entered.

Now the parlor. Mama's stiff, horsehair-padded chairs very nearly matched the settee. Her tea table stood folded against one wall, and a large Chinese bowl of potpourri emitted its rose-petal fragrance beneath a portrait of Letty herself. The picture, done in pastels when Mama was very young, seemed to fit the delicacy of the room. Mama had been wearing a dress the color of leaves, and her bouquet of rosebuds held the same coral tone as the watered silk of the upholstery.

Amelia thought she had never seen anything so pretty. She wished she might have some little snippets of the fabrics to take upstairs with her, to make cushions for her dolls. She stared at the potted ferns on their high stands and thought them lucky to be able to grow in such a lovely place. Even the walls were beautiful. Mama had had them covered with some kind of paper that was ivory satin, striped with red velvet ribbons. Amelia would have liked a dress of it! She glanced down at her own frock. Its plain gray flannel contrasted poorly with the elegance of the parlor. She sighed.

Across the hall from Papa's study was the dining room. Here she had been before. As soon as they were deemed old enough, the Mackenzie children were summoned to appear here for Thanksgiving and Christmas dinners, to sit mouselike at the end of the enormous table. Yet not so far away that they could not feel themselves to be under the surveillance of Papa. His withering gaze found them out whether they wriggled or spoke to each other, no matter how hushed the tones. At the same time the grown-ups had rules of their own. They laughed and cavorted and carried on the sort of incomprehensible conversation that seemed peculiar to adults.

Amelia, as she stared now at the solemn row of chairs set on either side of the terrifying expanse of table, felt as if she could still see it all: Cousin Athena with her many chins, her gargling voice, and her way of shaking all over like jelly on a plate whenever she spoke. Uncle Pratt, a white rabbit with his fur-ball sideburns, his little pink mouth that seemed to be always saying the world tasted bad. Grandmama, proud and erect, watching them all while her hand turned knuckle pale on the handle of her ebony cane. Watching until she could stand it no longer —rapping for silence—telling them what had been on her mind, the small curls on either side of her face bobbing in time with her mouth movements. Papa laughing at her or getting suddenly, inexplicably angry. Pouncing on the children for something they didn't know they had done. Grandmama flushing, trembling, her eyes hot and embarrassed. Indignant. Mama trying to make it all smooth again. Peaceful. Sometimes being silenced by Papa, whom nobody reprimanded. Oh, how terrifying—how utterly terrible—was Papa!

One time, Amelia had caught his attention. She'd been too fascinated by everything that was going on to be able to eat. Had Nanny been there, she'd have given a gentle reminder: "Eat up, pet, there's a good girl." But on Christmas Day, Nanny, as became her station in life, was having her meal served on a tray in the nursery.

Papa's voice had reached down the table. "Amelia! There are poor children all over the world who would give their all to be seated before a plate of food such as you have. Why haven't you touched it?"

Startled. Tears coming unbidden to her eyes. "I—I'm sorry, Papa."

"To be sorry is no excuse. Clean your plate or be sent upstairs at once, miss." Papa's gaze had burned, like the rays of the sun.

She'd stuffed herself. Bolted it down. A great, leaden weight, it had lingered wherever it had been sent to when you swallow things. It wanted to come up. Amelia had felt its protest as she endured the after-dinner kisses of Aunt Athena, the embarrassing jokes of Uncle Pratt, Grandmama's acid comments. Until at last she was free!

"Nanny—oh, Nanny—"

Nanny's concern had followed her to the room with the chamber pots. "What on earth, Amelia—?" Then, as the entire meal had come up, "Oh, dear. What happened? All that nice turkey."

"Papa—Papa had to scold me for not eating."

"Ah," said Nanny, understanding.

Amelia stared now at the high-backed armchair that Papa always sat in. Its red velvet covering seemed to hold his imprint. The way he leaned his stocky body forward allowed his powerful arms to rest on the oaken surfaces, his slightly bowed legs thrust beneath the seat, as if readying him to leap forward into action. Yet Papa never had to take action. All he had to do was to look. Even the imposing Mr. Taft was deferential.

Yet Amelia secretly admired her father. She held the knowledge to herself like something alive and warm. Why, she was sure, if he wanted to, that he could even vanquish the ghost in the attic.

The attic was on the same floor as the maids' rooms. A locked-away place under the eaves, it was the subject of great speculation in the nursery. Albert seemed to know most about it.

"It's not a ghost. It's a monster."

"How do you know, Albert?"

"Because I seen it once. I was outside and I seen it staring out the window. You should've seen its teeth."

That had brought Nanny into the act. "Master Albert, I won't have your sisters frightened. You stop that."

It had stopped Albert's talk, but not the memory. Yet, decided Amelia, gazing at Papa's chair, her father could demolish that ghost or monster—if he wanted to. That was another matter. Then, too, Papa wasn't home very often. Amelia was glad the attic was locked.

She crept out of the dining room. The salon was adjacent to it. Above all, it had been the salon that she had come down to see.

She entered its doors with a fast-beating heart. She had only glimpsed it once or twice before, at times when the children were being passed about from relative to guest, like objects to be sampled and savored—ears tweaked, noses assaulted with the pungent odors of the old, the eccentric. What Amelia wanted was to be able to wander about the room alone, to savor its wonders.

It lay before her now, like a jewel winking in the sunshine. The heavy draperies were drawn back to reveal the pale green silk that relieved the darker tones of mahogany and teakwood. These tones were repeated in the collection of priceless china displayed at varying points about the room, china brought with a commingling of luck and care by Mackenzie clipper ships some thirty years earlier. These same ships had placed a firm seal upon the Mackenzie fortunes during the early 1800's. Amelia's grandfather had founded a fleet whose dimensions were gradually expanded to include not only trade with China but also with European countries. The delicate porcelain held a double meaning: it had its intrinsic value, and it stood for Mackenzie doggedness and ingenuity—the family will toward financial success.

The salon was like a giant seashell. The teakwood tables, also relics of clipper voyages, sparkled with inlaid ivory depicting strange figures, animals, blossoms. The china itself had been prepared for royal use. This was not the entire collection—Letty and Nathaniel did on occasion eat off its plates—but it was unquestionably the best part. And even among the best, one enormous bowl stood out from the others. Supported by a specially devised stand, it was tipped by four bronze dragons' tails to just the right angle for viewing its interior. Within, and on its sides, as they had done for centuries, the graceful figures moved in an eternal, formalistic dance. Underwater green gave a background to tangerine flowers and leaves of pale gold, while in and out this fantasy, butterflies of orange and crimson wove their own rhythm.

It was this bowl, above anything else, that drew Amelia's eye. But as she made her careful way toward it, she passed before the fireplace over whose marble mantel hung the portrait of Governor Mackenzie. She stopped to stare, not so much at the first Nathaniel, as at his lady. Sarah Mackenzie, by no means a beauty, had strength in her face. A firm chin, direct eyes. Her dress, a deeper green than the china, was softened by a creamy fichu to which a single rose had been pinned. The baby leaning against her cushioning bosom had eyes that seemed old before their time.

Amelia's gaze went from Sarah to Nathaniel. How like Papa he was! The same long nose, stern eyes looking out from either side of it. Amelia had seen a picture of an American eagle once. Both Nathaniels were like that. Staring out, as if interrupted in tearing prey. The painted lips were like Papa's too: full and with a small twist, mouths not accustomed to speaking gently.

Amelia shivered. Grown-ups could be scary. She supposed it was because they were so terribly important, so far removed from the world at their feet. Well, they didn't have to be concerned with it, that was true. Not like Nanny and Katie did. Things like Brett tipping up his cereal bowl, Albert's having a fever, whether the chamber pots had been used—it was these matters that were beneath their gaze. Giving a small sigh, she moved on toward the bowl.

It rested on an impressive carved table. On either side, and tilted on similar stands, stood two great plates, their silk blue surfaces decorated, like the bowl, by brushes centuries stilled.

Amelia sucked in her breath. Her toes curled in the soft house slippers. Dare she lean forward, the better to see these marvels? How she wished she were taller. But the table's edge came up to her waist. There was nothing to climb on, not even a footstool. Nor did she wish to risk leaning, letting her body touch the teakwood. She bit her lip, rising just as high on her feet as she could.

She could see inside! "My, how pretty!" she said to herself. The ladies on the plates seemed to smile back at her. The flowers nodded. The butterflies darted before her wondering eyes.

To be able to come in here and see these wonders whenever one wanted! She was amazed that Mama and Papa didn't stand here all the time. Like the music box that went unplayed, these treasures seemed to be standing here unappreciated. Oh, if she were older, she would visit this spot every day.

She leaned forward a shade more, her gripping toes tense against the carpet, her hands clasped behind her back to balance her. Then it happened.

She was falling—falling forward against the table. The unimaginable was taking place. Even as she watched, restraining her need to cry

21

out, one of the great plates tipped violently. Under the table's rocking, it slid off its stand and fell at her feet. One of its smooth edges had knocked against the teakwood, a blow sufficient to remove a pie-shaped wedge from its graceful contours.

"Oh!" said Amelia, hearing her voice as if it belonged to someone else. It had to be another person this was happening to. It couldn't be her. She quickly knelt beside the plate, contemplating the damage. She picked up the small triangle that lay so incriminatingly on the carpet, but the piece would not fit back again. Not to stay.

Dry-mouthed, she stood there. She wanted to run and hide! to make off as fast as her legs would carry her, back to the nursery. Oh, why had she ever left its comforting confines?

She could pretend to know nothing about it, escape from the scene and make up some tale if she was discovered to have been missing. But Amelia knew that someone in the house was going to catch the blame for this mishap. One of the maids? Phillips? Could she stand by and see this happen? Already she could hear Nanny's voice, coming with gentle probing to assist Amelia's conscience. "I believe I know a little girl who has an odd look on her face. Did you overhear something about this plate getting broken, lovey? Come on, darling, you can tell Nanny." Amelia knew she would be unable to resist such persuasion. She would tell, if only with her eyes.

Her thoughts were going helter-skelter—a jumble of alternatives and excuses following one after another, like mice at the sight of a cat. Amelia sat there, kneeling back on her feet. They were turning to pins and needles. She fingered the triangular piece of china again. In panic, she tried once more to see if it would stay in the spot from which it had fallen. No good. Even if it would stick in place, there were the telltale chips of pale blue frosting the carpet's surface. She could never cover this up even if she were able to restore the plate to its resting place.

She resisted the impulse to cry. There was a tight quivering in her throat, and she wanted to burst into sobs. But she must be brave. Wasn't that what she was always telling her dolls? "Now, there's no use in your crying. You must take your punishment quietly. After all, it's deserved!" But what punishment would she deserve?

Suddenly she heard voices in the hall—Papa talking to his friend Mr. Abbott, Sam's father. They hadn't left yet! She'd been sure they'd gone, that the carriage had taken them into town.

She'd imagined all sorts of people catching her, but never once had her fears allowed her to think it might be Papa! Frozen with fright, she instinctively crouched over the plate, as if it were possible to hide it with her body.

"Albert, we've a few minutes before going into town. Why not show Sam the salon? Someday he may be coming here to a party. He might like to see what the place looks like without too many people around."

Papa's voice had that odd quality it took on when he was speaking with someone he liked, admired—as if he felt kindly. Amelia hadn't heard him talk that way very often.

Amelia heard footsteps, then Albert's voice. She knew it at once, though she had her back to the doorway.

"Papa? What's Amelia doing down here?" It was his best blame-placing tone. The one that said, "Nanny-come-see." All the children did it. "It's Polly's fault." "Albert did it, the mean boy!" Nanny would sigh and come to intervene.

This wasn't Nanny coming into the room; it was Papa. Amelia felt a sour taste rise up in her mouth. Her stomach lurched. She swallowed spasmodically, fighting back the vomit.

"I don't know what Amelia's doing down here," said the nasal voice of Nathaniel Mackenzie. "Get up, girl, when you're spoken to." The words were like drops of icy water when snow melted on a roof —stabbing, forming a mound of ice.

Amelia tried to rise. Her pins-and-needles legs would barely support her.

"Stand still!" thundered Nathaniel. Then, catching sight of the fallen plate, "What the devil—?" He leaned forward, pushing his eldest daughter aside so that he might have a better look. His face had turned puce.

"Well, miss, you had better start talking."

His drooping mouth had begun a nervous twitch. His hands shook. Little as Amelia knew her father, she knew enough to recognize these as the very worst signs.

So did Albert. Instinctively he moved back, after gliding up to see what was beside the table. He exchanged glances with Sam. The other boy was regarding the scene with curiosity. Almost a head taller than the stocky Albert, Sam was a handsome boy. Now, he, too, shook his head as he saw what had happened.

Kindly John Abbott felt a sense of impotence. He gestured to the two boys. "Why not go out and wait by the carriage, son? Take Albert. We'll be out before long."

Amelia faced her father with all the courage she could muster. "Papa, it was an accident." The gray eyes met his levelly.

"I do not accept that as an explanation. What were you doing down here in the first place?" Nathaniel tapped his riding crop impatiently across the gloved palm of his hand.

"I tell you—it was an accident."

"Accident be damned!" Nathaniel exploded. He wheeled about,

looking around him as if expecting to see somebody. But John Abbott, following his advice to the boys, had also retreated. There was no one in the room. Nathaniel strode with his short, muscular legs to the double doors.

"Letty! Letty, I demand you come down here immediately," he bellowed.

Amelia could hear running feet, then Phillips' startled voice. "Was there something, sir?"

"Get me my wife. At once, you hear? Something monstrous has happened."

When he returned to the room, Amelia stood where he had left her—a small, brown-haired girl in gray morning frock and white pinafore trying to make herself invisible. It was not to be achieved.

Nathaniel saw her differently. He observed with fury the straight back, the determined lift to her chin. Had she no shame for what she had done? To destroy a priceless heirloom that had been transferred from house to house, family to family, son inheriting from son. Nathaniel's eyes bulged with rage.

By God, she must be made to pay! To learn she could not lightly damage Mackenzie property. What was Nanny thinking, that she had let the child wander down here? And Letty? Nanny might have direct charge of the children, but in the end it was his wife who must bear the responsibility for anything that went wrong in the house.

Letty! His mouth curled in a sneer as his bewildered wife entered the room, her face pale at so peremptory a summons.

"Nat, what is wrong? Phillips told me I was wanted at once." Her gaze passed over the room, coming to rest almost at once on her daughter and the broken plate. "Oh," she said, her voice quiet with understanding. "Oh—oh my. How did this happen?"

"You tell me, madam." The riding crop played a drumming tune against Nathaniel's leg, as if impatient to be used. "You tell me, Laetitia, if it is not my express order that the children are to remain in the nursery at all times?"

"Yes, Nat."

"Unless I give instructions otherwise?"

"Of course, Nat."

"Then how, may I ask, does this impudent miss happen to be down here? To say nothing of what she has caused to happen!"

"Nanny knows—" Letty's hand had gone to her throat—a nervous gesture. She fumbled with the high ruff of her collar. She needed air. "Nanny knows—" she repeated softly. Was she going to faint? She knew what she was saying and yet she did not. Why was Amelia standing there so self-contained! If the child would just cry—beg for mercy —he might let her off more easily. It was asking for trouble to provoke him.

24

Nat's anger flowed over her. "Nanny—Nanny! Am I to have excuses from you as well, Letty? You know full well that the children are your ultimate responsibility. What have you to say for yourself?"

She stared at him, momentarily speechless. Of all things she dreaded, a confrontation with her husband was the worst. To avoid it, she went to great lengths. Why, only this morning, she'd marveled at how well everything went. Was that only an hour or so ago?

"I'm sorry, Nat. I do try—we all try. But accidents will happen, no matter how many steps are taken—"

"Accidents! I've just heard about accidents from your daughter— now you give me the same lame excuse."

"Oh no, Nat, I hadn't meant—"

"Enough. The child must be punished. Letty, do you have your household keys?"

"Of course." She showed him the embroidered bag that hung from her waistband. Did he think she'd be without it? "I always have them, Nat. This morning I have to give the servants fresh table linens —we are entertaining tonight."

He waved away her words. "All I asked for was the keys. Not an accounting of your time. If you will come with me, madam? Your daughter too." He strode toward the double doors, his back stiff with indignation.

They followed.

From the entrance to the study, John Abbott watched them climb the staircase. It was hard for John to understand what his friend was feeling. True, Amelia had shown disobedience, and a very valuable piece of porcelain had been damaged. But Nathaniel's handling of the situation was so different from what his own would have been.

John lit his pipe thoughtfully, then strode toward the door. He needed fresh air. Gesturing to the hovering Taft that he would let himself out, he opened the entryway and passed through it to stand on the front steps.

The two boys were cutting up. Playing the fool. By God, Sam was growing into a good-looking devil! If poor Evelyn could become aware, she would be proud of her son. The thought of his wife, confined to the prison of her specially designed chair, drooling and helpless from the incomprehensible malady that had struck her early on in their marriage, both saddened and infuriated him. When they had so much to share, it was cruel it should have worked out so. Even now, he treated Evvie as if she could understand everything that was said to her. He ignored her pathetic gyrations, her slack mouth, rolling eyes. The children, too, visited their mother regularly. Livvie brought her garden flowers and filled the bowls in the bedroom with perfuming posies. Sam treated his mother with courtesy, almost as if she were still the same woman he'd known when he was a little boy.

25

For his part, John tried to make it up to the children. Perhaps it accounted for the closeness he experienced with them. Sam traveled with him frequently. Olivia waited impatiently for their return; she understood without explanation that sometimes, in spite of his love for their mother, he simply had to get away.

So, he'd spoiled them, Sam and Livvie. Wasn't it better than the fuss he'd just witnessed? He'd a feeling the little Amelia was in for a pretty stiff punishment. It was none of his business, but in a family that had known no tragedy such as had struck him and poor Evvie, there was so much room for things to be different. He sighed to himself. His pipe had gone out.

He lit another match. It flared and died in the slight breeze. He turned into the doorway and, sheltering his pipe, got it going again. His pleasant, craggy face was lighted momentarily in the glow. He puffed on the Meerschaum—one of his favorites. Waited for Nathaniel. Waved cheerfully at the boys.

He tried not to speculate on what was going on upstairs.

Amelia longed to ask where they were going. She dared not.

Past the second floor—her mother's morning-room door stood open. Next, the third floor—Nanny, her hands nervously plucking at her apron, stared from the nursery entrance, biting back exclamations and questions. What sort of trouble had the child gotten herself into? Nanny felt the burden of responsibility fall upon her like an enormous tent, collapsing in under its own weight. Suffocating. Would she lose her job? She'd hear about it, soon enough. Meanwhile, best to tend to her duties.

The highest floor of the Mackenzie house was sharp and clean. Amelia could see into the maids' rooms as she followed Papa and Mama down the corridor. Under the eaves, they were. She knew from hearing Norah and Katie talk that these quarters were freezing cold in a Philadelphia winter, insufferably hot during the summer; they offered iron bedsteads, rough cotton blankets, and pillows made of coarse ticking. Washstands with crude pottery basins and pitchers completed the decor. A single chair for each room, simple chests to hold clothing; it wasn't much to provide a home away from home.

But Amelia found the maids' domain to be as fascinating as every other part of this house. If Nanny had let her, she would have been up here, inspecting and asking questions, wanting to know it all. Until now. Now she realized she had reason to feel dread. For they were passing the maids' chambers. As the uncarpeted expanse of the landing met their feet, Papa's making an even, heavy clomp, Mama's a lighter tread, Amelia knew without a doubt where they were heading. The attic!

The same realization hit Letty. "Nat, you're not going to put the child in there? You couldn't be so cruel!"

He had paused, the locked doorway before him. "Your keys, Letty." His hand extended. Impatient.

"Nat, must it be the attic?"

His lips twisted. "Letty, you really amaze me! After what has happened, can you imply that this lesson is too great? Give me the keys at once. Or do you wish to be shown up before your daughter as weak —vacillating?"

Her fingers found the least used key in her collection. While he waited—a hooded crow, alert to pounce. He had the authority. Unquestioning authority. This was his daughter. She, Letty, was his wife. She stared, conscious she was breathing heavily.

"Well, Letty, do you have the key, or don't you?"

The brass felt heavy to her fingers as she placed it in his palm. Coldness seeped from it.

She seldom came up to the attic. Away from sight, it tempted her to forget it. This highest floor, where the maids squirreled away their privacy, their pathetic little remnants of pride.

He thrust the key into the lock. There was something intimately familiar about this action—his right to open all doors. It was a farce to hand him the key; he had a copy of every housekey in his desk.

"I know it needs cleaning—"

"Cleaning!" His dark eyes probed the disorder. Trunks, blocky and sullen as fortresses; valises gray with dust. In the light of the single window, they all melded together. The peculiar smell of mice was everywhere, the floor peppery with their droppings. Spiders had festooned what was, after all, their kingdom. "Letty, when was the last time you inspected this place? Never mind. It will do for now." He pushed Amelia before him.

"It's so dark, Papa. Do you think I might have a candle?"

"What, and set the house ablaze? Amelia, you don't seem to have grasped the fact that you are in deep trouble. No special dispensations for you, my girl! You stay here till I come and fetch you—"

"Nat, how long will that be? Is she to have no meals? What will she do if she has to use the toilet?"

In the dimness, his eyes glowed. Anger stoking the fires. Nat would brood on this, as he did the smallest transgression. Taking it as a personal affront—unwilling to let it be expunged in forgiveness, expiation. He could be sullen now, for weeks.

"She may have a chamber pot. Water to drink. One of the maids can see to it. Not Nanny, mind. Undoing any good this lesson might bring."

Amelia shivered in her cotton dress. Hands clasped before her, she peeped about for Albert's ghost. Her teeth were chattering.

"Amelia!"

"Yes, Papa?"

"You will stay in here until you are really sorry. Understand?" He licked his lips. "I must say, Amelia, your impudence astounds me more than anything else. You seem to have no shame. None whatsoever." He stared at her. In the poor light, he could see the gray eyes staring back. Obdurate. Unrepenting. Well, she would learn, or his name wasn't Nathaniel Mackenzie! He growled in his throat, turned about, inadvertently faced his faltering wife. Her face rose before him, moon-like in its pallor. Her brown eyes unhappy, evasive of his own.

As he motioned for her to leave the attic, Letty looked down. "Nat, Amelia shouldn't walk about too much. The floor isn't fully finished in several places."

He gave an exclamation of disgust. "Where is she going to go without a light, Letty?"

"I merely thought—"

"A faculty you exercise poorly. Now move out of my way. I have already caused my guests to wait too long." Without so much as a backward glance at his daughter, he left the attic.

Amelia could hear the big key grinding in the lock . . . footsteps retreating. So this was to be her punishment. She hugged her shivering body with her arms, staring about her. The question of whether there was a ghost or not had become of much greater immediacy than before. As she tried to make out the contours of the attic, the scuffling sounds began. A large mouse scampered across the field of her vision. She bit back an exclamation. It wouldn't do any good to cry out—no one would hear her. The footsteps of her parents were her last link with humanity—until someone came with the chamber pot and the water.

She'd have to make the best of things. With small, cautious steps she made her way the length of the attic, pausing briefly to bend down and examine a box or a carton that took her interest. Gained the window with its streaked surface, its veiling of cobwebs. A fat spider sat in the middle of one. At eye level, it seemed to regard her. She gave it careful space.

She leaned forward to peer through the dirty glass. To her surprise, she could see all the way down to the driveway. Bates had the carriage waiting by the front door. Mr. Abbott was leaning against one of the posts of the portico, his pipe in his mouth. On the browned out winter grass, Sam and Albert were playing the fool. Feinting and tumbling. Papa would be angered if Albert tore his clothes. Mr. Abbott didn't seem to care. It was so hard to understand the differences among grown-ups.

Now she could see Papa arriving on the doorstep. Hatted, his coat buttoned about him. Gesturing toward the boys. As she watched, the four of them got into the carriage. Such an elegant carriage! Like a fairy tale; the horses' heads coming up, being reined about toward the gates. A flick of Bates' wrist and they were off, in a swirl of gravel and a clatter of hooves. Gone now.

Amelia felt a sinking in her middle. She realized it would be lunchtime soon, and she was to be allowed no food. The sensation felt like hunger. But more than that. A lonely ache, as if there were a place inside her that wanted to be filled yet could never be, because she did not know what it hungered for.

She sat there staring at the spider. Who would move first? It was to be a long and lonely day. She'd have given much to have had one of her dolls with her. Even the incorrigible Sophie!

Nothing was turning out as badly as Albert had anticipated. Much as he stood in awe of his father, he couldn't help but notice the mellowing effect Mr. Abbott had upon Nathaniel. Papa's eyes took on a sparkle, and he was even able to laugh once the carriage had borne them away from the house. The affair of the Chinese plate wasn't mentioned as the vehicle sped them through country lanes whose high hedges and shadowing brick walls afforded large estates the privacy money could buy. They joined the main highway after a while and then skirted Fairmont Park on the banks of the Schuylkill, where eight years before the Centennial Exposition had mushroomed. Most of the buildings were gone now, but Nanny had told Albert what a grand sight it was. Mama and Papa had met President and Mrs. Grant and had shaken hands with the Emperor and Empress of Brazil. Papa was so important!

The sun had come out now to glint back at them from the watery ribbon of the river. The carriage reached Market Street Bridge at last and crossed over. Albert could see the banks cluttered with storage sheds for ice, lumber, and coal. A dark barge slid down the grayed, glassy surface of the water, pulling ripples and a flock of seagulls after it. He watched them dip and wheel as the carriage clattered to the far side, entering the city of Philadelphia.

They made steady progress down Market Street until they came to Penn Square, where Papa leaned forward to ask Sam, "What do you think of our new station, boy?" Sam stared at the heavy stone of the lowest arcade, all they could see from the windows, and said, "It's very fine, sir." So much bustle and movement, people hurrying everywhere!

"And that's City Hall," said Papa, pointing to its columns, its high

31

tower glimpsed as they turned down Walnut Street. The colonnaded front of the Dundas-Lippincott Mansion on the northeast corner of the intersection seemed somehow left behind by progress, the shielding arms of great winter-bared trees and a dormant walled garden unable to protect it. "That'll be gone too, someday, I shouldn't wonder," Papa told Mr. Abbott.

"Seems a shame," said the Virginian.

"Ah, but our city has to grow with the times," Papa said meaningfully. As he began to talk of banking, of new investments he'd been able to make, John Abbott's face lit up with interest. They scarcely noticed when the wheels of the carriage stopped before Papa's club, a stone building of marble steps and fluted pillars. A liveried attendant in tall hat with red cockade stepped forward to help them out.

Until today, Albert had only heard about the club. Now he was to eat his lunch here! They entered a darkened hallway flanked by deferential waiters, then passed by elderly, bewhiskered members who gossiped over sherry or marsala. Forthwith, they found themselves ushered into a paneled dining room, chairs drawn out for them at a table set with heavy napery, shining silverware. Hovering waiters, napkins over their wrists, deftly brought plates, filled thin-stemmed glasses with wine, heaped before them generous portions of food. Albert, bewildered as to which of the array of forks and knives he should use, watched his father carefully. Nanny had not prepared him for this.

At the thought of Nanny, Albert suppressed a sigh. Exciting as all this was, he ached to be home with the solicitous nurse. The sore throat he'd awakened with developed to the point where he was finding it harder and harder to swallow. His head felt like a suet pudding, his limbs heavy. By turns the room felt insufferably warm, overwhelmingly chilly. While he knew that his cheeks flamed, he shivered.

Fortunately for Albert, Nathaniel's attention was centered elsewhere than on his son. If pressed, he might have admitted that he had included Albert only because John Abbott was bringing Sam. Nathaniel had expectations of Albert, but so far he thought of them as somewhere in the future—"When the boy is grown." Only John's habit of focusing on his own son had caused Nathaniel to give Albert a second thought.

Nathaniel felt expansive in John Abbott's company. The man was easy to get along with. Knew when to tell a story, when to sit back and let the conversation take its course. John's large frame and lanky stature might have placed the shorter Nathaniel on the defensive. In fact, they did not. In John's company, Nathaniel would chuckle, set aside his dignity, and grin at the repartee like a small boy smoking behind the barn.

"You know," John was saying, "the longer I know you, Nat, the more I'm amazed at the diversity of your interests. You've an empire, man!"

"Shipping," Nat replied, "was good enough for my forebears, John. But with the country opening up, I'd be a fool not to see the opportunities."

"The rails paid off," said John cautiously. He liked his host, but in business it was a chess game, where enthusiasm marked naiveté. "You're going to have to tell me more, my friend," he said, sipping his wine.

"The profits go up with the control, you see. Surely you can visualize it, John? If you have the mines, you have the coal. If you have the trains, too, textiles cannot help but pay off."

"Put that way," John said, "it's very persuasive. You think Matt Frogge will go along with us?"

"He's going to be here today, so you'll have a chance to ask him yourself."

John sat back. Nat always had something new in the works, an almost uncanny feel for successful ventures. A pity he didn't have the same facility with human relationships. Nat's bluntness put people off, walling him away, though one could sense his loneliness. John was one of the few who could reach through in friendship, willing to accept Nat on his own terms and ignore the pretentiousness, the fussy martinet. Nathaniel could put on that front for others if he wished. John would have none of it. As a result, a casual camaraderie existed between the two men. A relationship that could in no way hurt John Abbott, involved as he was in banking concerns.

If Nathaniel failed to notice his son's lack of appetite, Sam Abbott was not so unobservant. Very much his father's son, Sam took in details about those around him. He saw that "old Al" was a bit off his feed. Sam inwardly shrugged. If Al wanted to pass up a good meal, that was his business. Sam nodded as his father refilled his glass with wine. At almost twelve, Sam—under his father's tutelage—was learning how to drink.

Albert was ill. It was increasingly hard for him to sit at the table. The meal seemed interminable.

At last it was over. The boys followed the older men to the Members' Lounge on the second floor, where coffee and brandy were to be served. Nathaniel led the way, climbing the stairs slowly. Feeling the weight of the excellent meal.

Bringing up the rear, Albert stared at Sam's back. His thoughts, when they were not centered on how unwell he felt, teased at the relationship between John and Sam. Their easiness with each other was so utterly different from anything to be experienced with Papa. Sam's ability to be at ease with his father filled Albert with astonishment. True, Sam was almost two years older than he. Yet the gap in age hardly seemed to account for the difference.

Albert reached for the bannister and gripped it with a tense hand —sensing vertigo. He was behaving like a girl! At least, walking behind the others this way, there was no danger of Papa seeing. But he'd have to watch himself. Illness made him teary—vulnerable. While there was only Nanny to see, to chide, "There, there, lovey—tell me all about it," he was safe. There were no such safeguards now.

Coffee and brandy were served. Sunk into the depths of a leather-covered chair that held him, womblike, comforted, Albert fought the desire to sink into slumber. The wine he had sipped had numbed his brain. He yawned, then reached for his coffee cup with a hand that trembled from rigor. Nausea washed over him.

His appearance caught Nathaniel's attention. "Albert? Yawning? I should have thought you'd have more concern for our guests. Does this luncheon bore you?"

"No, Papa." Struggling to put on a bright mask.

"Then let's see you sit up, take some notice. Tell you what, when we've finished our brandy, we'll go down to the gym. Spar a little. It'll settle the meal, start the blood flowing."

"Excellent idea," said John easily. "What about you, Sam?"

Of course it was all right with him, Sam said. Albert realized in a flash that he hated Sam. Hated him for his friendly good looks, his casual manner, his self-confidence. Most, he hated him for something about his father. Hot tears hit Albert's eyes. He envied Sam. Would have given his soul to have John's hand on his back, to hear him say "son" in that casual way.

Albert stared at his father, covertly. Nathaniel's mouth was at his brandy glass, tasting its last drops. The long, cruel nose dropped away to the drooping lips. Inexplicably, the nose, the mouth, the set of the head were Albert's own. Could he have but seen his own profile, he would have known that he shared this with his father. He was, in every aspect but one, a Mackenzie. The one difference, his personality. He had inherited that from his mother. A sensitive Benedict. It was his greatest misfortune.

It was also Nathaniel's misfortune. He longed for a son he could be proud of. Not a molly-coddled nursling, still wet behind the ears. Nathaniel had a halfhearted plan, which now was taking full shape. Down in the club's basement, in the well-equipped gymnasium, he drew John to one side.

"I'd like to try something with Albert, my friend."

John looked up. "With Albert, Nat?" He tried to sound casual. He had observed the boy's quietness during the meal, but wasn't certain how to interpret it. Was it fear of being around Nat, or just the unfamiliar surroundings—the club's atmosphere—that made the boy uneasy?

"I have been unhappy about Albert for some time now, John." Nathaniel's long face had grown tense. "Too much with Nanny. A boy can't be wrapped in swaddling clothes forever. Agree with me, John?"

"Albert's nearly two years younger than Sam, Nat. I think you've got to give him some time. Let him feel his way."

"Two years—two years. It's not what I'm talking about and you know it!" Nathaniel had begun to scowl. The twitch at the corner of his mouth was acting up. John knew the signs.

"Dammit, John. Listen to me. The boy's too effeminate. It scares me, John." His hands were trembling. "You know how that can turn out."

"Nat." John put his arm about his shoulder. "I really think you're looking for trouble. Albert will grow into a fine man, one you can be proud of."

"Will he, John? Will he? He's too like his mother, John. Oversensitive." He spat out this last. "Girlish." His eyes moved across the gym. "I want to put the boys in the ring, John."

"In the ring? Nat, I don't think that's fair. Sam's at least a head taller than Albert, and heavier. The boys have been pals. It's asking Sam to do something he may not be happy with."

"Mind if I ask him?"

John didn't know how to answer. But he'd made it a point to let Sam make up his own mind about things.

"I don't mind your asking him. Just so long as he doesn't feel he can't turn you down, Nat."

Nathaniel found Sam at the punching bag, Albert gloomily looking on from one of the wooden chairs that lined the walls.

"Sam? A moment of your time, boy."

"Of course, sir."

"You done much boxing?"

"A little. Father and I put on the gloves."

"Excellent. I want you to spar with Albert."

"Albert? He's a head shorter than me, sir. Younger. Would it really be fair, do you think?" Sam's face was flushed.

"My boy," Nathaniel spoke slowly, easily, "I didn't ask you to give him a pasting. Merely get in the ring with him. My boy hasn't been exposed to the ways of a man's world enough. I'm asking your help, Sam. Your father and I talked it over."

"You did, sir? What does Father say?"

"He assured me you would do everything you could to come to my assistance." He smiled encouragingly. "After all, I'm making this request for Albert's own sake. I should think as his friend—? You two have known each other a long time, Sam. Right?"

"Very true, sir."

35

Nathaniel laid a paternal hand on Sam's shoulder. "My boy, I know you won't let me down."

"Try not to, Mr. Mackenzie. Albert ever been in the ring before?" Glancing at the boy, who sat with his eyes closed.

Nathaniel's eyes followed his glance. Shrugged. "Has to be a first time for everything, Sam."

"I suppose you're right. Well, if Father says it has his blessing, I'll be pleased to go a round with Albert." He tried not to remember his own baptism, John helping to bathe the bruised face, the even more wounded feelings.

As the elder Abbott approached them, Nathaniel said, "This is a wonderful boy, John. Sam's promised to introduce Albert to the ring."

"You feel all right about it, Sam?" John's eyes probed his son's. Sam seemed comfortable enough.

"Mr. Mackenzie says it's just an introduction, Father. He's asked me to help Albert out."

John nodded. But he still felt a twinge of concern.

Albert was gotten to his feet and made to change into boxing shorts.

Nathaniel threw him a towel. "This is a chance now."

"Yes, Papa."

But it wasn't. From the first Sam was aware that something was gravely wrong. Not only did Albert not know a thing about sparring but he wasn't even behaving properly. He staggered about the ring, leaving himself wide open to punches. It was understandable that he had no idea how to hold his hands, yet he couldn't seem to follow instructions even when Mr. Mackenzie got in the ring with them. To make matters worse, some of Nathaniel's friends had gathered at ringside to cheer the boys on and, eventually, to make some fairly tasteless remarks.

Old Al heard these. They seemed to make him frantic. He started hitting out in every direction, almost losing his footing on the slippery canvas. All the while Mr. Mackenzie was shouting at him and telling him what to do. Al acted as if he were deaf. Flaying about in all directions, often a mile away from Sam.

Finally, Mr. Mackenzie had enough of the remarks from the on-lookers. He mentioned in threatening tones that it was old Al's first bout. That if they didn't like it, they could take on Albert's father. That shut them up for a while.

"Go on—have at him, Sam." Mr. Mackenzie had stopped yelling at everyone else and turned his attention Sam's way. Like he'd never mentioned a word about not giving Al a pasting.

Sam had the ugly suspicion that that was what Mr. Mackenzie had meant all along. Sam, looking at Albert's face with its curious flush, deliberately gave him the advantage. Left his jaw wide open for a blow.

Albert took a wild swing. Missed. He almost lost his balance and wound up hugging the ropes. Like he was dying or something. What on earth was wrong? Sam walked over to Albert. The boy's shoulders were shaking. God, he wasn't crying, was he?

Sam was pushed aside by Nathaniel. "Get out of here, Sam." The man's voice was terse.

Sam stared at Mr. Mackenzie. His face was white with rage, shame. To make matters worse, Matthew Frogge called out, "Your boy doesn't seem able to live up to your reputation, Nat."

"He will, Matt, he will," said Mr. Mackenzie. He turned to his son. "Put your hands up, Albert."

Albert's hands in the padded gloves went up—but not high enough.

"Before your face, fool. Protect yourself from me. You'll never make a champion if you're not willing to defend yourself." He said something low to Albert.

The boy began shaking, trying to turn away, crying out that he couldn't help it. Just to let him alone. "Please, Papa—"

Mr. Mackenzie's voice was taunting now. "At least try to hit me. Up and at it, boy! For Christ's sake, act like you mean it. Or are you a girl, to run screaming from the ring?"

Sam exchanged glances with his father. John Abbott shared his son's feelings. Sam was glad he'd gotten out of the ring when he did. He was afraid of where this farce would end. Sam could see that his father was considering jumping in—to try to stop what was going on. But by the look on Mr. Mackenzie's face, that was doubtful.

To Albert, the room swam in a hazy fog. Dimly he heard the voices of the men watching at ringside, Sam's limited remarks. It was as if they didn't exist. There was but one reality for Albert—his illness. Out of it, the face of his father emerged, like a sea monster rising from the deep, jaws dripping to devour him. It was a nightmare from which he willed to be delivered, released from the entire situation, allowed to crawl back into his clothes and be taken home to Nanny. His skin was on fire one moment, chilled as if packed in ice the next. His eyes burned, he had no control over the tears that fell unchecked. He feared that his father might kill him, then despaired that he might not.

"Swing at me, boy. Addlepated ninny. What are you, a baby or a man?"

As if in a dream, Albert mustered the last vestiges of willpower and swung. He missed by a mile.

Nathaniel felled him with a vicious punch. The man was sick of it. Sick and ashamed. He knew with the clarity of hindsight that the whole thing had been an error. His wish, that Albert could be roused into at least putting up a brave effort, goaded by pride into showing he was made of good stuff, had failed.

"Nat!"

"I'm sorry John, Sam—everybody. The boy was just too scared, I'm afraid. Next time, he'll do better. Here, let's get him under a cold shower."

But John, leaning over the unconscious Albert, was saying quietly, "Nat, will you listen? The boy's not just knocked out. I'm afraid he's ill. Feel him, will you? He's burning up."

Reluctantly, Nathaniel placed a hand on Albert's skin. "We better get him home," was all he said.

So, in the end, it was Nanny to whom Albert was committed. The sick child had his wish. All Nathaniel's ideas of weaning him away from the nursery were to no avail. As he sat drinking whiskey with John before the study fire, the sight of Dr. Henry Porter being escorted upstairs by Letty did little to improve his temper.

"Nat, he'll show up differently next time," John said. "Have a little patience. Boys change remarkably, this time of life."

"Patience! There's a word I've always had trouble with. No, John, old friend, Albert's going to let the family down. He's enough of a disappointment as it is. Takes after Letty's side, you know."

"Is that so bad?"

Nathaniel shrugged. "The Benedicts aren't Mackenzies, if that's what you mean. The old lady, Letty's mother, is a dragon. But Oscar Benedict is a pussycat." His drooping mouth curled in derision. "Poor blood in Albert's veins. Blame myself I didn't see it before I married his mother. Inheritance is far more important than we think, John."

"Nat, you're making too much of this incident. For myself, I've always liked your boy. Believe in him."

Nathaniel stared, astounded. "You like Albert?" he said slowly. "You like Sam, don't you?"

Nathaniel dropped his eyes. "Sam's different. He's a son any man'd be proud of." He refilled their glasses. "Letty calls that damned Henry Porter anytime there seems to be the slightest thing wrong with the children. I swear he only comes here to drink my best brandy."

"Nat, really!" John at least got him to smile.

But in this matter Nathaniel was correct. Or close to it. Letty had already given instructions that Dr. Porter's brandy tray be brought to her morning room. As the physician bent over Albert, he found his thoughts straying to the glass that would be awaiting him. Excellent brandy. One hardly needed the excuse of a winter's day's chill to lend pleasure to it.

The boy was ill. No doubt about that. His fever was elevated, his pulse thready, his breathing harsh. He was going to need the best of care if he was to survive. Henry Porter wasn't prepared to come forth with a diagnosis, but he had a shrewd suspicion he was dealing with rheumatic fever, complicated by pneumonia. Time would tell.

He set the boy's burning wrist back on the coverlet and examined the swollen skin that had almost totally closed Albert's eye. "How did he get this shiner, Letty?"

She cleared her throat. "I am informed he was in a fight."

"A fight? Dear me. One would think that being this ill—who did he pick a fight with? One of his sisters?" Henry gave a forced laugh.

"Nothing like that, I assure you." Letty's cool voice hid her anguish. "Nat took him with him to his club for lunch and Albert got into the boxing ring."

"Ah. The club. The boy wanted to put on the gloves. How old is he, Letty? One sees so many come into the world, an old duffer like me loses track."

"He's nine, Henry. Next week is to be his tenth birthday."

"Hmm," said the doctor thoughtfully. "Ambitious little boy, isn't he? But too frail for that sort of thing, Letty. Ought to tell Nathaniel to keep an eye on him. Not let heroics take over. Though," he wagged his head importantly, "boys will be boys, eh?"

"Is he going to get better, Henry?" The question burst from Letty's taut lips. Her hands were white as she clasped them before her.

Dr. Porter avoided her eyes. "We'll have to wait and see, won't we?" He straightened his back, which ached now when he had to bend over a patient. "Going to need careful nursing, Letty."

"Oh yes. The staff are all prepared to take turns."

"Good, good. I want a steam kettle going at all times. Mustard plaster on the chest—the things you are already so familiar with. I should speak to Nanny."

Letty nodded.

"He shouldn't be left alone. That young girl you have who helps Nanny—?"

"Katie?"

"Well, someone like that must be here all the time. We are going to be in a crisis, Letty. Next two or three days should tell us—" He stopped, seeing her distraught face.

"Oh God!" she said. "Is my boy going to die, doctor?"

He patted her on the arm. "It takes courage to be a mother. I sometimes think you ladies have it all over us gentlemen when it comes to endurance. Let's have a word with Nanny, shall we?"

She nodded dumbly, then went to the bell pull to summon Norah.

In her morning room, the brandy tray waited. It would be there often in the coming days.

When the door had closed behind Dr. Porter, Letty stood uncertainly before the entrance to the study. She could hear the murmur of male voices within its paneled walls. She had just raised her hand to knock when the oak door opened.

"Nat, I am come to tell you—"

He ignored her words. "Do you have your keys, madam?"

"My keys?" She clapped her hand to her mouth. How could she have forgotten Amelia? Until they had brought Albert home, her thoughts had been almost constantly on the little girl shut away in the attic. Yet for the past hour or so—oh, how could she have been so remiss?

"Come, madam, your keys." Nathaniel's face conveyed his annoyance. "Unless you think your daughter should remain in the attic all night?"

"Oh no, Nat." She hastened to undo the embroidered bag, to retrieve the large brass key. "But I do need to speak to you—most urgently."

"About Amelia?" His gaze was haughty. "Oh, I suppose this has to do with Albert."

She returned his gaze. "Your son is gravely ill, Nat."

He looked past her. "He did poorly today, Letty. Put me in a bad light with the fellows at the club."

"Oh, Nat!" She let her impatience creep into her voice. "The child was sick, desperately sick. I blame myself—Nanny is chastising herself —that we let him go with you at all."

"The boy needs to learn to become a man, madam."

"And he will, Nat. But no boy, no man for that matter, can be at his best when he ails. Is there no warmth or compassion in your heart? First you punish Amelia most cruelly, then you expect Albert to—"

He interrupted her harshly. "Letty, your business is the running of the household. But when you fail so grossly in your duties—"

"Fail, Nat? How have I failed?" Her hands gripped the embroidered bag that held the keys.

"By not giving me adequate offspring. Your elder son is a lily-livered ninny, and your daughter Amelia defies me, thumbs her nose at my authority. Yet you have the audacity to ask me how you have failed?"

She swallowed painfully. "I just thought you should know that Albert may not survive this illness, Nat."

He took her news in silence, his eyes on the wide, sweeping staircase. At last he said, "Is this what Henry thinks?"

She nodded. Tears had begun to splash on her cheeks. On an impulse, she leaned toward him, tried to take his hand. "Oh, Nat, be with me in this. We may lose our son—our son. I don't think I can bear it alone."

He regarded her sternly. She might have been Amelia. He made absolutely no move to respond to her gesture of appeal. "Your God will make the decision, Letty."

"He is your God too, Nat."

"You know I don't hold with such claptrap."

She shook her head in anguish as she watched him tread the staircase, his heavy body causing it to creak as he mounted to the floors above. At the second landing he left her sight, but not her awareness. First with her ears and then with her mind, she followed him to the top. Did she imagine she could still catch his footfall as he crossed the bare floors that led to the attic door?

But there was no doubt in Amelia's mind as to who was unlocking the door. Every nerve and sinew strained, she had first caught the voices, raised as they were, in the lower hall. Finally she'd heard the stairs crack and groan. As the sound came nearer, she braced herself.

"Papa!" Spoken softly.

"Well, Amelia?" His thick frame was outlined in the corridor's yellow gaslight. His face was shadowed in the glow of the small oil lamp Mama had had Norah bring to the attic.

At the sight of her father, Amelia rose from the trunk that had been her perch for the past few hours. She had moved back from the window, feeling night's intense cold reach through its panes to clasp her. In self-defense she had found a torn, mice-chewed robe and

41

wrapped herself in it, fighting back her distaste for its smell, its obvious filth. She had to keep warm.

Her legs had become numb, hands stiff. She stood up clumsily.

"Who brought that lamp? I gave no orders for a lamp!" His brows made a thick line as he frowned.

She gave no answer. But his nose had led him to the chamber pot, which Amelia had tried to cover with some tattered magazines. He made a face of disgust.

"They can bring you lamps, yet they cannot bring their lazy bodies to empty the pot. It stinks in here, miss."

"I know, Papa."

"Have you thought over your conduct?"

"I have tried to, Papa."

He wet his lips. Cleared his throat fussily. "Have you decided to say you are sorry for what you did?"

"I have always been sorry, Papa."

"You omitted to say so before."

"You didn't ask me, Papa. You gave me no chance." The gray eyes were unwavering. Only the lamp flickered.

"And a change of heart, Amelia? You would venture out of the nursery again—without permission?"

"I cannot lie, Papa. I would certainly do so, were I to find the opportunity."

"Pah!" he exploded. He strode forward and hit her across the cheek.

She gave a small cry but suppressed it at once. Only the movement of her hand, raised to finger the bruise, betrayed her pain.

"Why, Amelia? Why are my rules of so little importance to you?"

"It's not that, Papa. I respect you, indeed I do. It's only that I wish to see. It is, after all, a very splendid house." Her eyes flashed. "All but this attic. I do not care for the attic, and I think Mama should send someone in to clean it more often. If I ever have my own house, I'll not tolerate spider webs or mice in any corner of it."

"By God!" he said and then, in spite of himself, he laughed. The girl had spunk. Perhaps he'd gotten himself one true Mackenzie after all? It was a pity it had to be a girl.

"May I go downstairs now?"

"Yes," he said, lifting the lamp to blow out its flame. "Go to the nursery. But I should tell you, your brother is very ill."

"Albert? He was ill this morning. Nanny said he was 'working up for something.'"

"She did, eh? Well, see that you behave yourself while there's extra work to do. Your mother will have every servant under this roof scurrying around with bowls of soup and mustard plasters. You be a help to Nanny. You could get whipped yet, you know."

"I know," she said solemnly. "Do you think Albert might die, Papa?"

"Why do you ask that?" he growled.

"It might be better if it were Brett. He's such a nuisance."

He laughed again. "Don't say that to your mother, Amelia."

"Oh, I wouldn't. Or to Nanny. But I do think babies are quite dreadful. They smell and cause nothing but trouble. When I grow up, I'm never going to have children."

This time he laughed loudly. "Children are a part of a woman's life, Amelia. Better make up your mind to that. Any woman who doesn't have a husband and a family is either a spinster or a whore—and I'm not sure which is the worst."

"What is a 'whore,' Papa?"

His face closed up. "Never mind about that. Enough questions out of you. Get down to the nursery as fast as you can. And for heaven's sake, tell Nanny to give you a bath."

His distaste for her was evident. She sped away from him as fast as her small feet would carry her. It had been unnecessary to tell her she needed cleansing. Perhaps that was why the ghost had left her alone.

She felt dirty and somehow sad inside. When Papa laughed, why wouldn't he smile at her? Why did he despise her so?

Yet he was a very strong person. Immensely brave. She had the oddest thought: What would it be like to touch Papa? Just once to hold his hand, to talk with him? He was really a marvelous person. But so dreadfully, frightfully important. That was it, of course. He had so little time for any of them.

43

By Albert's tenth birthday it was determined that he was going to live. The crisis had come and gone. The boy would get better, but slowly.

Letty received Dr. Porter in her morning room. "You do really find him better?"

Henry Porter nodded. "But there is something I think you should know. I wish Nat were here. I would like him to hear this, too. When will he be back?"

She glanced needlessly at the green and gold clock on the mantel. It could tell her nothing she didn't already know. "Nat's at the club, doctor. He will not be home until late."

"Ah. Then I might as well address my remarks to you, Letty. The boy's had rheumatic fever. And with pneumonia on top of it, it's a miracle he's alive."

"But he's over the worst?" Her eyes defied him to take away her hope.

"For now, yes." He was cautious; cleared his throat ominously. "There are, however, complications."

"Yes," she said slowly, "I have always heard. Fanny Nunn's boy —it left him with a weakened heart." She turned on him suddenly. "Are you trying to tell me, Henry, that my son has been affected in the same way?"

He was silent. Played with the long gold chain of his watch.

"Look, whatever it is I have to face, you must tell me. I must know the worst. It's the only way I can help Albert."

"Very well. Almost always, in cases like these, the heart is left impaired."

Her hands, clasped in her lap, became knuckle white against the blue wool of her dress. "So, it's his heart. Just what does this mean to Albert?"

He gestured with an air of futility. "I wish I could promise you a return to perfect health for the boy, Letty. You know, you see a baby into the world, you watch him grow. It's hard to remain unmoved. Medicine—I've devoted my life to it—but it's still a very inexact science." He shook his head. "We just don't have all the answers, much as we'd like to think so. Of course there are tonics we can give him, elixirs to build up his health—"

"But—?" She pressed him, knowing he was holding back the full implications of Albert's condition. And she must know. How else was she to take every precaution, institute every safeguard? She struggled with impatience as he requested her permission to light a cigar, extracted one, and after applying the match, watched the smoke curl about his head.

"Caution," he said finally. He puffed. "Limited activity, even after he regains his strength. A rest every afternoon. No strenuous endeavors."

There was a tap at the door. Phillips had arrived with the brandy tray.

"Ah," said the doctor, a gleam in his eye as the silver salver with its cut-glass decanter was placed on the table beside him. "How thoughtful of you, dear Letty." He set down his cigar and poured himself a glass of the amber liquid.

Letty watched. Waited. It all took such time. Always, when it was Henry. Well, that was one of her failings—impatience. She knew she needed to work on it.

"Wonderful stuff." He lifted the glass to the light, admiring its color. Then placed it to his nose, sniffing the fine aroma. "I suppose Nat won't reveal its source?"

She forced herself to smile sweetly, then tried again. "By 'strenuous,' would you mean physical activities?"

"Oh"—he took a taste of the brandy, savored it—"the sort of nonsense boys indulge in. Sports—hard riding, long hours out of doors—anything that would tax the heart."

"I see. Would you include schoolwork in your cautions?"

"Anything—anything that would cause him to become overly tired." He sipped once more. "Letty, we still know so little about the body's secrets. We physicians do our best"—he wagged his finger at her—"but nature is a harsh taskmaster. She almost always has the last word, my dear."

"Would you say, Dr. Porter—Henry—that the choice of a tutor would become all important in a situation like Albert's?"

45

"A tutor? I'm afraid I don't understand."

She wet her lips. "You see, Nat has a man already picked out—a military man. I've not met him yet. There were to be further discussions after Albert's birthday."

Thoughtfully, Henry Porter turned the brandy glass about in his hands. "If by 'military' you mean cold baths, excessive discipline—"

"And enforced rules, extra effort—oh, Henry, you know the kind of man Nat would pick out. He wants a son he can be proud of. And until now, I've had no say in the matter."

He understood. Slowly he said, "It wouldn't do to put your boy into the hands of a man such as you describe."

"Would you be willing to speak with Nat?"

"But of course—any time. There should be no problem."

She stared into the fireplace, where the flames crackled cheerfully. "I hope you are right."

"Come, Letty. Nathaniel has always seemed a reasonable man."

"Yes." She sighed. "Yes, he might just listen to you."

"To you too. After all, you are his wife." His tone reproved her.

"Henry, more than anything in the world, my husband wants to be able to boast of at least one of his sons."

"Letty, no one could blame you for Brett. The midwife told you how the cord was wound around his neck. We were lucky to save him."

"For what?" she said bitterly. "He'll never be a normal child."

Henry's tone was soothing. "I think you are taking all this too hard. After all, my dear, you have just come through considerable strain."

She shrugged. "A little more brandy before you go, doctor? The late afternoons are growing so chilly. But then, with Christmas just around the corner, what can we expect?"

He thanked her. Poured himself another glass. It was indeed excellent brandy. Nathaniel had good taste. Not only in wines but in women. Henry glanced appraisingly at Letty. For a woman her age, she had weathered well. Indeed, she was remarkably handsome with her proud head, her wealth of brown hair as yet unstreaked by gray. Her skin was clear too—as smooth as a young girl's.

It was understandable that she should be a little unhinged right now. Women got tied up in knots when it came to the welfare of their children. It threatened them when the time came for one of their brood to be released from the nursery. But a boy had to move on and out. He shook his head when he realized that that could not now be the case with Albert.

Unfortunate that the rest had turned out to be girls. One couldn't count Brett. The child wouldn't survive into puberty, anyway. No use telling her that yet. Plenty of time to prepare her. After the business with Albert was settled.

Henry finished his brandy. He had just enough time to get home before dinner. All in all, it had been a satisfying day.

8

Letty remained in her chair, staring at the fire. Despite her pleas that the physician speak with Nat, she knew that in the last analysis the matter rested with her. She would have to broach the subject. But how to do so in a way that would get Nat to take her seriously? That would avoid having it end in accusations that she was trying to undermine his authority, to encourage a lack of manliness in her son?

Seated there, she thought of Henry Porter. The families had long been friends. In the ordinary way, the Mackenzies would not have been receiving any doctor, family or otherwise, on a social basis. Doctors did useful work, but they could not be regarded as equals. Indeed, it was unusual for a boy of good family, such as Henry Porter, to be attracted to medicine. Nathaniel's mother had known Amy Porter and had shared her dismay when the young Henry took up his training as a physician. There were so many more elevating endeavors in which a boy might become interested. As Letty realized, that had all been such a long time ago! Henry, at least ten years Nathaniel's senior, would be retiring before many more years. Meantime, it was comforting to be able to turn to him when the children were ill.

It would be unreasonable for her to expect that Henry see Nat as she saw him. No one could know the real color of their relationship. She gave a deep sigh. The sentimental girl who had yearned to marry into the illustrious Mackenzie family was buried under layers of disillusion.

She was a woman who had disappointed her husband. Had he in turn disappointed her? The question jumped from her hand like an escaping moth, fluttering away to singe its wings against the white heat of her doubts. Did any wife have the right to expect more of her husband than that he support her—uphold her as the mistress of his house, the mother of his children? Well aware of Nat's wanderings, Letty parried the thrusts of their hurt by reminding herself of the double standard. Men lived in one world, women in another. It had always been the case. If a man spent his time elsewhere, it had to be the wife's fault. If she were attractive and accommodating, he would stay at home.

A noise in the hallway. Nat's voice? He'd come home after all? His comings and goings were often unpredictable. That made it hard to plan meals, to tell Cook what to prepare. But, there again, it was all part of the role of a wife—to be adaptable. She knew—because Nathaniel had explained it to her—that his own activities could turn on such trivia as a meeting being canceled, some arrangement coming up that he had not foreseen.

She got up from her seat by the fire. It was time to change for dinner. Perhaps if she wore her green moiré tonight, and had Nanette arrange her hair with special care, she might be able to appease Nat? She was considering her dresses when her French lady's maid entered.

"You rang, madame?" Then, after a glance at her mistress, "Madame looks tired tonight. Is there something I can do?"

Letty plucked at the fabric of one of her elegant frocks. "Make me look nice tonight, Nanette. Mr. Mackenzie has come home to dinner unexpectedly. I would like—" She sighed, unable to finish.

But Nanette understood. Her French background gave her the capacity to grasp the unsaid. It was one of the reasons the young émigrée was so valuable to Letty. With the twist of a comb, the pinning of a collar, Nanette could transform her mistress from a wilting mess into a lady of poise, dignity. Letty gave herself up to the maid's ministrations thankfully.

One sight of Nathaniel at the end of the long dining table was enough to dispel any hopes Letty might have had of passing a pleasant meal. He was his usual self—dour, withdrawn, with little but terse criticisms to offer. She heard her own voice echoing down the long expanse of the table, bright and cheery in a forced kind of way.

Nathaniel's growled responses left her feelings to curl, like caterpillars shaken from their perch. Exposed, craving shelter. Nat had this way with him.

Her small talk was for the servants. Else, she'd have let the silence rest undisturbed between them. But Taft and Phillips must think that all was well between them. Momentarily, chasing buttered peas with her fork, she wondered what "well" might mean. She had never known it different from this, even on their honeymoon. Only when others were present—people Nat needed to impress—did he manage to be affable.

Had Nat ever sought to impress her? She remembered their courtship. He had presented his case to her parents like a business arrangement. And she? She had been too naive to see it.

In spite of her efforts, dinner was completed in an almost total lack of conversation. Nodding at Nat as they left the room, she bade him good evening and signaled that she would repair to her own suite.

It was his habit, almost always, to go out after dinner. She had no idea where he went and felt it none of her business to ask.

She closed the door to her morning room behind her, then took up her accustomed chair beside the fire. She sat there, a novelette to hand. But she was not in the mood for the exploits of the innocent young heroine, besieged as she was by a suitor with evil intentions. She picked up a copy of *The Ladies' Home Journal,* the magazine that had been established but two years earlier, and thumbed through its pages.

A half-knock on the door startled her. She turned about to see Nathaniel standing there. "Why, Nat!" she exclaimed, surprised. "I had no idea—" She indicated the chair before her. "I had thought you were out. Will you have a seat?"

He sat down, leaned back in the high-backed chair, and removed a cigar from his pocket. He stared at the glowing tip with lidded eyes. "It looks as if our son is going to recover," he said at last.

"Thank God," she said fervently. "It seems my prayers have been answered."

He glanced at her. "I am not so sure, on looking back, that you were well advised in asking for his recovery."

"Nat!" She could not hide her astonishment.

He looked away, smoking thoughtfully. "Has it not occurred to you, Letty, that it might have been better if neither of your sons had survived?"

"You can't mean that!"

"What do you take me for—a sentimental woman?" His rage whipped out at her, catching her where she was. Vulnerable in her sense of failure. "Surely you cannot expect me to rejoice in sons who are hardly liable to make me proud to be their father?"

"Nat, how can you be so cruel?"

"Come, Letty. How long are we to keep up this pretense about Brett? The boy is an idiot. A driveling, drooling idiot. I don't know about you, but I for one don't like to think of the future he may have." He blew a smoke ring. "I had thought at least one of my boys—Has Henry Porter spoken to you?"

50

She nodded quietly, feeling the muscles of her throat tighten. "Last evening. He was here to see Albert. He said he would be talking to you too."

"Caught me at the club. The man is a fool!" This last, bitterly. "First he tells me there's little that can be done to help Albert. Then he warns me that the only thing I can do may endanger him. I say, if that's the sort of life the boy's going to have to lead, better not to have brought him through the illness in the first place."

"You can't mean that!"

One look at his face told her he did. The cold eyes stared at her. "With a no-nonsense tutor, Albert would have at least had a chance. Sports—taking him with me to the club's gym. I know now he was ill the day John and I took the boys there." He scowled. "I had hopes. A boy like Sam Abbott"—he rubbed one square hand against the other impatiently—"a man is entitled to his hopes."

Letty was seeing the snuffing out of his hopes. She had known that he had them but had tried to close her mind to them. They spelled out too clearly her own role: her failure to give him a Mackenzie worthy of the name. She groped for something to say.

"Albert is intelligent, Nat. He can still have some sort of a life."

"Can he?" His gaze was withering.

"In time—when he has recovered. I think he can."

"If you believe that, then you are as big a fool as Henry. What sort of an existence can there be for a boy who must be taking to his bed every five minutes? Not to overtax his strength? Pah!" His mouth twisted, the small twitch at its corner beginning. "Albert is going to be forced to live like a woman!"

His disdain. The very way he said "woman"—as if it tasted bad to his tongue. She pulled herself up in her chair, unconsciously defending her own position, knowing it was not possible for a man to appear any way but "manly." Yet for those who must be categorized as otherwise, it was a possible fate. Endurable, at least. Why then did men, full-blooded men, regard it as a shadow existence?

She offered, "Nat, is it possible you exaggerate? Albert's recovery might leave him stronger than Henry has predicted?"

"Exaggerate? Letty, are you so superior tonight, you can guarantee me a son? One who won't fall below my expectations of what a Mackenzie should be?"

"No, of course not, Nat. I was only trying—"

"Then try in another way, madam. Perhaps you can yet bring a boy into the world who will do for me what the other two have failed to do, eh?"

"Another child, Nat?" At thirty-eight, she had begun thinking of herself as old, her womb desiccated, like the inside of a peach pit.

Shriveled and useless. He wanted to get her to conceive again?

"Dismiss your maid early tonight, Letty. If you mean you sincerely wish to try? We shall make one more attempt to see what kind of offspring you can produce. At least the Mackenzie name is owed that."

"Nat, you seem to think I have power over childbearing. That it's in my hands to determine what sort of infant I bring into the world. Yet I cannot even assure you it will be a boy."

His laugh was mirthless. "You remind me of that? I who have to stand aside and watch Benedict traits come forth to distort the Mackenzie heritage?"

"Ah," she said softly, "now it is out. But if you didn't want your children to be part Benedict, why in God's name did you marry me?"

"I have asked myself that, often. Let us say, it was a poor decision —one I have had to learn to live with."

Her cheeks were flushed. Her hands had tightened into fists in her lap. "And what is so wrong with the Benedicts? Or Mother's family, the Hydes, for that matter? I would have you remember that we were on this continent before any Mackenzies set foot on it. Just because your family used the Revolution to acquire political power—why, some of the Hydes went back to England. Preferred to remain loyal to the Crown."

"So?" he sneered. "As an American, are you proud of that?" A flicker passed over his eyes. Distant lightning. "You put me off, Letty. I came here to tell you that I would require you tonight." He rose from his chair. So that had been his intent all along. The talk about Albert had merely been a way of leading up to his determination to awaken her fertility. The way he might have had Bates breed the gray mares.

She twisted her hands. His decision, the acts it would necessitate, demeaned her. As they always demeaned her. Lately she had allowed herself to breathe more lightly, to regain her sense of wholeness, almost to hope that the times of violation were at an end. It seemed that they were not.

"Be ready," he said darkly. "I will be up in an hour or so."

She nodded. Drowning in hopelessness. To be faced with yet another bout of childbearing. With all that that implied! She picked up a scrap of embroidery that lay beside her chair and stabbed at the fabric, drawing a needleful, blood scarlet, through the linen's coarse surface.

Blood and fire. Odd they were the same color—when the flames rose up, hot. Joan of Arc again. She wondered what the symbol had to tell her—that a woman who refused to bleed like a woman was a woman to be burned? The ancient traditions of men weren't to be questioned, challenged.

52

She shook her head. How foolish she was being! She was a female, a wife. Nathaniel's wife. He had every right to expect her to lie with him, to let him get her with child.

She filled her needle with cool green silk. It was dangerous to indulge in such fantasies—a sign of instability. She suppressed a shiver as she worked diligently on her embroidery, glancing up ever so often at the enamel clock. Keeping an eye on the time.

The copulation of Nathaniel Mackenzie with his wife Laetitia was a precise operation not tinged by any sentimentality. Nor slowed down by anything except Nathaniel's need to take time to bring himself to ejaculation.

Letty had dismissed Nanette early, as instructed. The maid had been concerned that her mistress' neck muscles were "terribly tight, madame. You will have one of your headaches unless you let me massage them." But Letty had waved away her kindness. If she was going to have a headache, then a headache she would have. Perhaps after it was over, she might call Nanette back. Often the maid could soothe with deft fingers where all else failed.

Nathaniel knocked and then entered without waiting for an answer. He was clad in a silk robe, its tasseled tie barely closing it. Beneath it she could see that he was naked. But not ready for her. He sat on the bed beside her, the weight of his body curving the mattress downward. He loosened the sash of his garment. In the light of the one lamp she could see the familiar contours of his barrel chest, its covering of dark, flat curls.

"Well, Letty?"

"I am ready, Nat," she said. She supposed that she was. As he had trained her. She remembered, as she did every time, the fear she had had on their wedding night. Well, at least now she knew what to expect. She watched him pull the covers back. Lift her nightgown to her thighs.

Exposed. I am exposed and bare as a forest in winter, she thought. Tried to forget the thought. Naked in its disloyalty. She must please

54

him. He waited for her hand. To tease, caress his manhood. Bring him to be interested in her. For thus had he explained it, from the first time onward.

She took him between her fingers, softly lured him into becoming hard and erect. Preparing him for the moment which, ironically, she dreaded as much as he sought it.

"Now, Letty."

She lay back, as he expected her to. He stroked the inside of her still firm thighs. As a woodsman examines the trunk of a tree, before laying an ax to it. Then, casting aside his robe, he rolled on top of her, found her opening, and went in.

Deep. Cruel.

He moved back and forth, rippling her inner flesh with his insistent rhythm. His breath became quicker and more panting. He moaned several times. Then he quietly ejaculated, filling her with himself, his hopes for a child. Let it be a son.

To be so close and yet so distant. As if they inhabited different universes. Separated by more than their skins.

When he was through, he pulled away. "You must have some sort of calendar? You always did."

"A calendar? Oh, yes—if I am late."

"Inform me as soon as you feel yourself to have conceived. In the meantime, we will renew our efforts."

Dumbly, she nodded. Lay there as he had once suggested she do. He'd said it crudely: "When the whores want to avoid getting caught, they get up and wash as soon as they can. I'm informed the opposite is true. Conception is more likely to take place when the hips are elevated."

She longed to wash the stickiness out of her interior. It always made her feel so dirty. Odd, when it could lead to the miracle of growing a child, that she felt soiled. She placed a pillow under her thighs and counted to fifty. Nat had already left her.

When she adjudged it time to get up, she lit another lamp and made her way to the washstand. Bathed her assaulted tissues with clean water. Dabbed at herself tenderly with a very soft towel. Then, from a drawer in her nightstand, she extracted a pot of salve. On its side, written in purple ink, were French words, long ago faded and blurred to a state where they couldn't be deciphered even if she had understood enough of the language to read them. Something Nanette had obtained for her.

"If the tissues are bruised, madame—"

"Oh, Nanette, I shouldn't even be talking of this—"

"Pardon me, madame. A lady's maid must know many things if she is to serve her mistress well, yes? In France we talk more easily of such things than you in America. Madame Mackenzie, the application of a certain ointment can be of profound help."

"A help, Nanette?"

"For lubrication, madame. Forgive me if I speak of matters that are delicate. Madame must understand, in order to get the best use out of the ointment."

"Use, Nanette?"

"If one is excessively dry, madame, one has pain."

"Ah!" At last she had understood. Fully.

"It is possible to apply the salve internally, before the husband—that is, before the act—"

"Yes, yes." Hastily. Embarrassed—but so relieved. To hear that there was something. It took the French, with their unabashed understanding of such matters. Thank God for Nanette. But then a thought. "Suppose my husband—that is, could it be something to make him angry?"

Nanette had shaken her head, smiling. "One does not tell all one's secrets, madame. It is something the most famous of the courtesans knew—centuries before you and I."

Did she want to emulate a courtesan? But the ointment, when tried, proved of such profound effect that she had decided such scruples were unimportant.

Nanette had said, "Lubrication both before and after. Not only will madame find it most soothing but it can, some say, assist when the *bébé* is, how shall we word it, not yet desired?"

Which was why it would have done no good to use it tonight. Until afterward.

IO

Fate conspired with Letty when it came to resolving Albert's immediate future. She had gotten Nathaniel to half agree that the man he had in mind for Albert's tutor would not fit Henry Porter's strict regime. The matter had hung in limbo, partly because Nathaniel would not let it appear as if he were giving up and partly because no solution had presented itself—until the visit to Green's Drapery Store.

Letty was making her semiannual expedition to replenish household linens. The yearly renewal of maids' uniforms was at hand. Supplies were running low on dust cloths, sweeping sheets. Tea towels were wearing thin. Mrs. Crocker, the Mackenzies' seamstress would soon pay her month-long visit to cut and snip and put in hems. Letty arrived at Green's with a long list of necessaries.

"—and then we shall be needing twenty-five yards of percale, if you please." Letty was seated atop the high-backed chair that Green's provided for customers whose patience was going to be tried while Brenda Green measured and remeasured, bouncing the bolts of cloth about in her pudgy, capable hands. As if they were rolling pins and she was flattening out pastry. Letty was glad to be able to sit, though the tall chair was stiff and little more than a perch. She'd been weary these past weeks—an ache in the small of her back, a tendency to malaise. Was it possible, she thought wearily, that she was with child? She was but three days "late" and that was hardly enough to go on, but perhaps—? She withdrew her thoughts from such speculations to answer a query from Mrs. Green.

"Oh, it's the white percale I need. It's for sheets and pillowcases. I find linen altogether too chilly in the winter months. I don't care if it's fashionable."

Brenda Green gave no friendly smile as she hurled the fabric across the counter, restricting its rolling at the exact place by her flattened palm. Letty couldn't help but suppress a sense of irritation. It was tiresome enough to have to go through this kind of shopping. But dealing with Brenda! Letty and her mother had often spoken of it.

"If only she could be more like Painter," Emma Benedict had said. "That man is a saint! But his wife acts as if she is doing us a favor, not the other way round. After all, we don't have to shop at Green's."

But they did. It was easier. It was always easier where one was "known," where they could be counted on to have the same supplies year after year. It was why they would never try the newer shops.

"Mother, may I have a word with you?" A young man Letty vaguely recalled having seen before tapped Brenda on the shoulder.

She scarcely paused as she answered him shortly. "Can't you see I'm busy now, Freddy? Mrs. Mackenzie's order comes before any of your nonsense." Her voice, like her personality, was harsh, abrasive.

"Mother," this time the youth's tone was demanding, while remaining courteous, "you remember we agreed that next time Mrs. Mackenzie came into the store, you would speak with her?"

Letty was intrigued. Aware that she might be allowing herself to become drawn into some sort of family argument, she nonetheless asked, "Is there something I can help with?"

"It's nothing," said Mrs. Green sharply. The terrible scissors continued to eat their way through the cloth.

"It may be 'nothing' to you, Mother." The young man seemed undaunted. "It's very much 'something' to me." He reached across the counter and extended his hand to Letty. "May I take the liberty of introducing myself to you, Mrs. Mackenzie, since my mother won't do it for me? I've often seen you here in the shop. I feel as if we were already friends. I am Fenichel Greene, only son of Painter and Brenda Green."

The scissors stopped. "Freddy!" Brenda's mouth opened and closed in exasperation. "Freddy, you got more cheek than any three boys your age." With a loud snort, she began folding the material she'd cut, pushing bolts out of her path with an anger to fire her energy. "He has always been like this, Mrs. Mackenzie. His father's spoiled him rotten. All the thanks we get. Even the name we gave him isn't good enough for him."

Letty had taken the proffered hand, not knowing what else to do. To refuse would have been to have made an issue out of nothing. Besides, she found the youth amusing—more, he was unexpectedly charming. She stared at him, sizing him up. He'd be about eighteen or nineteen. In contrast to his parents, he was immacu-

lately dressed. Was that what had attracted her? Or his brashness—
for it was surely that? Or his poise? She was aware of the strength
of the brown eyes upon her, their self-confidence—at the same
time an unvoiced plea. That was it. He seemed to convey the message that she could help him.

The idea appealed to her. It took her mind off her slight nausea,
the ache in the small of her back, even her lassitude. What could he
want of her? When the answer came, she was taken aback.

"I'm looking for employment," he said simply.

"Employment?" Immediately, she felt trapped. "I really don't see
how I can be of any assistance." She felt the alive eyes seeking to hold
her own.

"You see!" muttered Brenda.

The young man leaned on the counter. Familiar—yet perfectly
discreet. That was the annoying part of it. "I thought you might know
of some place where I could apply," he said.

Letty noticed he had a wide, generous mouth. She wished she
didn't find him likable. It would have been so much easier to have
withdrawn, to have acted with dignity—even with outrage at his boldness. But there was something about him.

"Got ideas above his station," said Mrs. Green sourly. She had
begun to make a neat package of the percale, whipping string about
the lumpiness the brown paper concealed, tugging the twine from a
spindle below the counter.

"Nonsense, Mother. I am remarkably well read for a man of my
age. I've studied extensively—history, geography. Composed no less
than four works in poetic essays. I should think—"

"Poetry!" Brenda sniffed. "That's what you call it. Personally, I
find it trash! You get in the back and start putting away those boxes
of shoes like I told you to."

"No, wait." Letty heard herself say it, as if it were someone else's
voice. "If you don't mind, Mrs. Green, I'd like to hear what your son
has in mind."

Brenda sighed. "Very well, Mrs. Mackenzie. But be quick about it,
Freddy. She didn't come all this way into the city just to hear out the
likes of you."

He came around the counter and perched on a stool next to her.
An elf with a roguish smile. That extraordinarily fastidious manner of
dress.

"I want to become a tutor," he said with a lift of his eyebrows.
"Oh, not forever, don't you see. Just to start with. I shall be a writer
eventually. A scholar too, I shouldn't wonder. But that sort of thing
takes patronage."

"So you want to be a tutor. May I ask why you've selected that?"

"I thought I said. It's the kind of work suited to me. That is, to my talents."

"Ah, you consider you have talents?" Letty marveled at his self-assurance. Coming out of a drapery shop?

"Of course," he said easily. He curled his feet around the legs of the chair. Again the impression of an elf—astride a toadstool. Letty found herself smiling. He had enchanted her. Surely he was a weaver of spells.

"So you compose poetry. What else do you do?"

"I make work seem like play."

"Ah."

Mrs. Green interrupted. "Better ask him what kind of work. Put him to cleaning out the shelves—sorting the stock—you'll find him under the counter with a book, the goods piled up around him. Like he'd never been asked, let alone told! I tell you, Mrs. Mackenzie, we'd be well to be rid of him. Hire a decent pair of hands—give me some help here I could count on."

To ease herself out of the situation, Letty said, "Come and see me, young man. One day next week." As his brown eyes widened, she asked, "What did you say your name was?"

"Fenichel. Fenichel Greene. I spell it with an extra *e.*"

"Oh."

"He made it up," said Brenda darkly. "You're not to feel obligated to do anything for him, Mrs. Mackenzie."

"Oh, I shan't," said Letty easily. But inside her a small plan was beginning to form. Albert needed a tutor. Could she persuade Nathaniel? And if she could, would this strange boy be the wisest choice? Somehow his puckish qualities made her feel cheerful—a useful quality around an invalid. Yes, this odd boy might be a real answer.

Her feet trod lightly as she left the shop. Beside her, Bates bore her purchases in their brown paper wrappings. Stowed them on the carriage seat opposite her.

"Would you be going home now, ma'am?"

"No," she said on an impulse, "Drive me to my mother's house. I believe I'll drop in on her for tea."

He touched his hat. Set the grays in motion.

60

II

Hitty Benedict was seated at the small table in her bedroom, writing in her journal, covering the blank paper with lettering that was purposely cramped and stilted. It was hard to get fresh books to write in. Mother always wanted to know what they were for, then scoffed at their use, claiming that Hitty was again showing how easily she wasted time and money.

But what am I saving them for? wrote Hitty. *In May I shall be thirty-three, and my hours are precious to no one but myself. Even Mother admits that my chances of marriage are now over and I am good for nothing. Well, she didn't exactly say that, but I know what it means when she looks at me that way.*

Hitty put down her pen, stared out the window. A poem was coming. She could feel it, as when a sneeze is building. Except this was a pleasant sensation. She looked down at her journal, sensing incompleteness. She took up her pen once more:—*As to my wasting money, I have none, so it is Mama and Papa's money I am putting to ill use. That's hard to resolve, since I feel such pressure to write. Without paper, pens, I cannot do so.*

There, it was finished—the thought. She felt a responsibility for words. They were like her children, the only ones she would ever have. They deserved all her attention, her loyalty. Well, not quite all. There were still Mother and Father. Why couldn't she give up the childish names for them? "Mama" and "Papa" sounded infantile in a woman approaching thirty-three. She supposed it was habit.

Inside, she wasn't Henrietta Hyde Benedict, a dumpy spinster. She was willow lithe, with a mind like a pool, spread out to its edges, to reflect life. Mother said she was stupid. That was because, once she

61

had captured her impressions, she didn't know what to do with them. They floated, like errant leaves, down to the watery depths of herself. Lay there for long-legged crabs and monstrous mayfly larvae to clamber across. Useful to none but herself. In moments of great concentration, when she was stringing words together like bright beads on the ribbon of meaning, she could reach down into her interior, fish out a phrase, a flash of color, and know that it had been there all the time. Lying in waiting. It was her sole pleasure in life.

She tapped her pen against her teeth. She had a problem—a "something" she wanted to write about. Couldn't risk Mother—or any of the maids—finding. She pushed her plump body away from her desk table. Wished fervently, for not the first time, that she might be allowed the choice of her own furniture. She'd have a real desk of course. Like Mother's—and like Letty's. One with neat pigeonholes and drawers in all sizes, for papers, envelopes, sealing wax, and stamps. For letters received—if there was anyone to write to her. Once she'd dreamed of writing to a poet or a writer, but she imagined their derision when they received a letter from a silly woman in Philadelphia. Besides, how would she find the address even if she did get up the courage to write?

She pulled a fresh piece of paper from the slim drawer that hung beneath the rickety table and dipped her pen in the inkwell.

He stood beneath the window, the light on his hair turning it into fire. Was he an angel? I think not. But to me he came from realms of flame. His eyes would have seared me, had they met mine. It was well that they did not. She paused in her writing, setting the pen down momentarily.

She was being silly. Yet he had attracted her—the new young curate that was suddenly there, assisting the Reverend Mr. Evans in church last Sunday. You would have thought that they'd have had intimation of his coming. Especially all the way from Mr. Evans' native Wales. Speechless of course, except in the utterance of soft phrases, to answer the minister in his questioning of the congregation. "Lord have mercy—Christ have mercy—"

She'd stared from the pew where she sat. Knowing it to be ill advised. Her eyes should have been lowered—her mind locked away in a closet of disinterest. He was so young! Why are the beautiful always so young? She knew her own body would be motherly to him —had he bothered to glance her way.

The Reverend Mr. Evans had introduced him at the church doors. "This is Michael—Michael Hughes. His real name's Idris, but we thought it too foreign for Pennsylvania tongues. His middle name's Michael. He'll get used to it yet, won't you, Mike?"

So, he had the appellation of an angel! She had felt the phrases borning in her even then. She peeped up at him from under her bonnet, shy as a girl. He had great dark eyes. Some said, when the

Reverend Mr. Evans came to take over the parish, that it was the way of the Welsh. Liquid tones and black hair.

Michael was too young for her. He could not be more than twenty-nine. His age and his station placed him so far away from her that she could think of him without discovery. No one would have dreamed that she could be that foolhardy. A curate!

He'd muttered something to his superior about its being all right to call him Michael. But she could see that it wasn't. He wore it like somebody else's clothing, lent to him because he appeared poorly clad. A proudness was on him, the way his head tilted back, his soft eyes gleamed. She'd woven that, too, into her dreams.

She dipped her pen into the inkwell once more and was about to write when her ears caught the sound of horses' hooves on the drive-way. Now who could be coming at this hour?

A maiden's dream, rushing up unbidden from the depths of her being, was melted in the daylight of reality as she went to the window. Her sister's trim carriage with its enviable grays was below, parked before the weathered Colonial dwelling that the Benedicts hadn't been the first to enlarge. But the essence of the house Revolutionaries had once camped in had been retained. Its polished floors reflected warmth, its white shuttered windows were neat as a Quaker girl against the gray of stone and roof line. In summer, azaleas flamed, replacing the froth of dogwood and crabapples' coral around the terrace; daffo-dils, iris, and ruffled peonies embroidered the flagstone paths.

Letty waited for Bates to help her down, her feet careful on the steps as the man gave her his arm. His livery stood out like a stain of plum juice against the snow. Letty, in furs and neat woolen coat.

Letty! So who had she expected to see? The minister surely wouldn't presume to call unless invited, at Mother's precise invitation. Yet it was appropriate that they invite him, along with the new curate. Michael—of the angels! Here, in this house. She felt the blood rush to her cheeks. She was becoming what they said was the fate of an unmar-ried girl—a deluded old spinster. She sat down before her table once more, picked up the paper on which she had written of Michael, and crushed it between her hands.

The fire was dying. She strode over to it, lifted the logs with a poker, placed the paper with its telltale writing between two glowing spars. At once it burst into quick flame, cleansing her of evidence.

Watching it, she found her mouth dry, her loins curiously tense. She glanced away from the charring paper to her hands. Was it her imagination that they were turning clawlike? As Mother's—wrinkled and veined with the inevitability of age? If only she could stay it all—drop back, say, ten years, to the period of her life where there was still hope. Hope that some man would find her desirable as a wife. Fill her body with children! Give her a house to manage and a name to take on like a new, fine bonnet. Spinsterhood. She knew the stories. Was it inescapable that she become odd in the head, eccentric of manner? Would she be avoided by the rest of society—except in pitying looks and acts of charity?

A young man had stirred her. It wasn't fair. She, who was bereft of hope. She turned as Hooper tapped on the door.

"Come in."

Hooper stood there—a dried-up woman who had become old with Emma, she hid her wrinkles beneath her maid's uniform. Like a tree in which the sap no longer rises. She gazed at Hitty as if she didn't see her, so used had she become to the accustomed sight of this unmarried daughter about the house. Colorless as hall furniture.

"Your mother sent for you. It's Miss Letty. She's stopped by."

Hitty met Hooper's eyes. Blank as marbles. "Thank you. Tell Mother I'll be down directly."

It was an order disguised as an invitation. Hitty looked at her journal. It would have to wait till later. Maybe there would be something worth writing in it.

Patting her blond hair in place, Hitty glanced in the mirror. A face to be overlooked, round of cheek, snub nosed with a sensitive mouth that had a tendency to droop—it would easily be passed over in a crowded room. Her blue eyes gazed back critically. If only she were like Letty! Hair dark as a robin's wing—and handsome. It was evidence of Letty's beauty that she was married to Nathaniel Mackenzie!

The tea table was set in the parlor. Mother presided, like a tattered raven, too old to take flight. She had her hand on the teapot as Hitty entered. A cup for Letty sat under its covering of an enormous tea strainer. The leaves lying caught in its silver mesh were wet and brown. As those that carpeted the lawn in the fall, after several rains.

"Ah, Hitty." Mother looked up, peering as if she had her glasses on, which in fact she did not. "You took your time. Your sister came to join us."

"Yes," said Hitty needlessly. She nodded at Letty, seated now, her coat removed, her hat on a chair beside her. Its feathers were brushed with moisture. Then it had begun to snow? Letty reached for her cup, taking it from Emma with warm, sure hands. A mien Hitty envied—always.

"How are you, dear?" The question conveyed that Letty wanted to know, was desirous beyond pretense of knowing how things sat with her sister.

"Thank you, well." Hitty waited for her own cup to be poured. Watched Mother's trembling hands—liver splotched—naked over the tea tray, except for one magnificent diamond which she wore constantly, whenever she was "dressed." It caught the dim light that flowed in from the tall windows, amplifying it into something more. To Hitty it appeared cold—greedy to take what illumination there was, keep it for its own. Would she ever wear such a diamond? She thought not. The finest of Mother's jewels would go to Letty, who already had her own to match them. Letty, as the married daughter, would merit preference. Or so Hitty assumed.

"Now tell us, Letty—" Emma's eyes sparkled. She was waiting for something salacious. They were bidden to bring her titbits thus, for it was on such that she thrived. Like a bird of carrion that watches until the lions are done. Sups hungrily on morsels scorned by mightier creatures. "—tell us what you have been doing."

"I have engaged a tutor," said Letty. Something about her expression, the lift of her head, told Hitty that all was not well.

Emma sat up a shade straighter. Touched the ornate silver tray before her with fingernails that were hard and curled. "A tutor? For Albert, I presume?"

"Its tentative," said Letty, retreating from her former position. "I interview him next week." She crossed her feet under the soft woolen frock, demurely. "I rather think, though, he will do."

"Who is he?" asked Emma. As if licking from a cooking bowl.

"You're going to be surprised." Letty didn't look at them. She picked up her spoon. Held it, as if choosing the exact point where it would enter the brown liquid. "I am, myself," she said. Laughed lightly.

"Letty, you are outrageous!" Emma exclaimed, her hands moving together until their fingertips touched. "Stop teasing and tell us who it is."

"The son of Painter Green," said Letty quietly. She had ceased stirring. Replaced the spoon with finality. Waiting. Waiting for Mother to say it.

"Painter Green?" Emma's face wrinkled as she searched her mind. "I don't recall—" Then, with a look of sheer astonishment, "Oh, you couldn't mean the draper! As a tutor for Albert?"

"Mother—wait. I said it was the son."

"I know, but Letty—surely you couldn't be serious."

"Perfectly serious, Mother. He's a studious young man. Quite a character, once you get to know him."

"And you, I take it, feel you know him?" Emma's disapproval showed in her whole body, not just the lines of her face.

Hitty, watching it, sighed. There would be trouble. It was unavoidable. Why had Letty brought this to Mother? And before it was even settled? It was always unwise to tell Emma anything before the loopholes were closed up, the contracts sealed. Even then, she could find a way to get in there, to make small problems larger.

Emma leaned forward in her chair. "Does Nathaniel know anything about this?"

Letty colored. "I plan to tell him after I've seen the young man again."

Emma wagged her finger at her elder daughter. "Letty, you are asking for trouble. You know that, don't you?"

Hitty tried. "What was there about him that struck you? I mean, he must have had some qualities—some appeal—for you to have considered him in the first place."

Letty looked grateful. "Yes, you're right. He has—how to put my finger on it?—he has charm."

"Well," said Emma enthusiastically, "at least that's something! Though whether it'll appeal to Nathaniel . . . Letty dear, how often I've asked myself why we allowed you to marry that man." She shook her head, causing the small silken curls that hung like elaborate frosting on a cake to dance. "But how could we know? Such a difficult, self-absorbed man."

Letty didn't answer. Her face had taken on a closed look. "Nat has placed the choice of a tutor in my hands," she said simply.

"Well, that's a change!" exclaimed Emma. "I suppose on account of the boy's illness. Is he still upset about that?"

Letty didn't answer them for a minute. Then she said softly, staring at the rug by her feet, "For a man of Nathaniel Mackenzie's pride, this has been about the bitterest blow he could sustain."

"Ah," said Emma. "Well, it at least shows he's capable of feeling." The thin old lips pressed together.

The silence of the room was broken only by the snap of a log as it fell to the bottom of the hearth with a shower of sparks. Hitty glanced at it without seeing it. Saw instead the face of the curate. The words "young man" had brought forth Michael. She licked her lips, finding them quite dry. Her breath came shallow, suppressed.

"Now, Letty." Emma had taken up the issue of Albert's tutor again. "Charm is all very well. But what other qualifications does he have? What's his name, anyway?"

"Fenichel."

"Extraordinary. Nathaniel will never go for a boy with a name like that." The hands folded smugly in the lap.

"It is his name. But Brenda calls him Freddy."

"Freddy. Well, Frederick would be better. I must say, Letty, I cannot see it. Painter Green's son—and that awful Brenda! Surely, the young man can't be intelligent?"

Letty smiled evenly. Hitty could see that she had suddenly made

66

her mind up about something. Her manner was changed. She appeared sure of herself.

"You like him, don't you?" said Hitty.

"Yes. I rather think I do. It's not just that, of course. He has one quality Albert is going to need rather a lot of."

"What's that?" asked Hitty, curious.

Letty spoke slowly, as though she had made an important discovery. "Devotion. Albert will require devotion. I know we all do, but he more than the rest of us."

Emma snorted. "I do not think that I need devotion. Letty, you make people sound like helpless victims, forever leaning on one another for our sustenance." She pulled herself up straight in her black lace dress, drawing her Shetland shawl about her. "I, for one, pride myself on my independence."

Hitty tried. "Mother, come. Here we are, surrounded by servants. We do not make a bed or cook a meal for ourselves. How can you say we aren't dependent on others?"

Emma gave her younger daughter a withering look. "Why will you always take me up on my statements, Hitty? I merely wished to say that I think I do very well for myself, considering my age and my rheumatism."

They bowed to what was recognized as an unanswerable argument. These two daughters, so very different, yet bound by their common knowledge that this woman who had given them birth would always have the last word. Or else punish them for it. Robbing victory of its savor.

Even now, Emma wasn't finished. "Letty, while you are thinking of young men as possible tutors for Albert, have you considered the nice Welshman who has just come across the sea to assist Llewellyn Evans?"

"Mother." Letty tried to disguise her impatience. "The new curate is here only because Mr. Evans has need of him. Otherwise the bishop would never have given consent for him to come in the first place. Surely you can understand that?"

"I understand nothing of the sort. What sort of work would keep two able-bodied men busy in a parish the size of St. Stephen's? It's only on Sundays they are required to put in time."

"Oh, Mother. They have to call on the sick—see to the orphans, to say nothing of holding services, marrying, burying the dead."

Emma was stubborn. "Mr. Hughes would be a fine influence on Albert. And I'm sure he needs money. It's the only way he can afford to bring his wife over."

"He has a wife?" It burst from Hitty before she could prevent it.

"Of course he has a wife," said Emma tartly. "He showed me her picture when I was over helping the Altar Guild this week. Rowena, a lovely Welsh girl who will join him just as soon as there are funds adequate to their needs."

Rowena. Hitty said it to herself as if it were the missing word in a verse—the only one that would rhyme. It fitted. *Michael and Rowena.* Twin flames that mingled, searing whoever came too close. She felt the deadness in her spreading like a rot under the ground.

Letty and Emma talked on, wrapping the topic of Albert in their concern. While Hitty sat there. Turned to stone. Amazing that she could swallow tea, even ask for another cup.

At last Letty rose to go, pulling on her hat, draping her fox furs around her, thrusting her fingers deep inside her enormous muff. The odor of violets filled the room as Letty's clothes were moved about, caused to emit their fragrance. She was given to French soaps, French sachets. Hitty imagined her sister sitting at her dressing table in her boudoir—the owner of a husband, peering at herself in the great oval mirror, preparing for him.

"You're oddly quiet this evening, Hitty," said Emma sharply after Letty had gone. "Sickening for something?"

"Oh no, Mother. I'm quite well."

"Hmm. I hope so. I need you to write some letters for me later. Perhaps after dinner."

"Yes, Mother."

"You can ring the bell now. Tell Hooper we've finished with tea. Perhaps you ought to rest before the meal? At your age, Hitty—"

"I'm not that old, Mother."

"You're past thirty. The women of our family tend to disease unless they take care of themselves. As an unmarried girl—" Emma sighed. "I've never known whether to believe the old wives' tales. Still, there is wisdom in what's been handed down for centuries."

Hitty had heard it before. "May I go upstairs now, Mother?"

"Not before I've finished." It was useless to put her off. "There is something about marriage—the contact with the male—that keeps a woman younger. Some secret of nature that prevents her from drying out."

"So what am I to do, Mother? As you observe, I am unattached."

"My poor Hitty. It is a cross I bear for you—that you weren't sufficiently attractive to manage to marry. Never mind, I am sure life has other compensations."

They were interrupted by the door opening. Oscar Benedict had returned from his afternoon at the club, the same club Nathaniel frequented. Emma proffered her face for a kiss. The merest touching of wrinkled cheeks.

68

"Its snowing quite heavily," he said. Then to Hitty, "How's my best girl today?" His eyes sought hers. Cheerful from the brandy he had drunk.

"Letty was here," said Emma severely before Hitty could answer.

"She was?" Conversational. His pink face, framed by the aureole of white hair, turned to his wife. He was like a kitten, easily distracted. The lump in Hitty's stomach, formed since she had consumed her second cup of tea, grew. She felt awash with it—miserable.

"Hitty was going up to rest," said Emma, dismissing her.

"Ah," said Oscar. He extracted his gold watch. "Just time for a nap before dinner. Think I'll go to my den."

Hitty fled. She gained her room on the second floor without drawing another comment from her mother. Sometimes, just getting free was like finding one's way out of a forest in the dark. Each person represented a fallen log—to trip the unwary. Papa, for instance. So needful of love—yet when it was given, he had already turned elsewhere. Distractible as a child. Brett's features rose before Hitty's face. Yes, that was what Papa was like. Innocent and responsive—infinitely more so than Brett, who couldn't control the simplest movement. Yet their needs seemed the same—their span of attention.

The fire was almost out. She would ring the bell for fresh wood, but she knew they'd all be at their busiest now. Chaplain, the underbutler, would be setting the table. Cox, the head of the staff, checking over his silver, working at it with a chamois leather, singing tunelessly under his breath.

Everyone had something to do. It was the hour Hitty hated most. She wished she had a bird—a caged bird. Someone to talk to. Perhaps, if she asked Papa, he might prevail upon Mama to permit her one. She'd like that. The cage could hang in the window.

12

"Nat, I have something to tell you."

"What?" She had caught him, spoon poised over his morning egg, his eyes scanning the paper. It was one of those rare days in February when the sun shone, casting indigo shadows across the brightness of the snow. In spite of her nausea, her blanket fatigue, she felt her spirits lift.

"I believe we are going to have another child," she said. Gazed at him, keeping her voice steady.

Nathaniel's mood, though characteristically dour, lifted enough to permit him the glimmer of a smile. "When will the boy be born?"

She refrained from reminding him that there was no guarantee the baby would be a boy. "In late August, I believe."

"Ah." It was his only comment. He wiped his mouth thoughtfully, returned to his newspaper.

She sipped tea. Her stomach was protesting, but she fought the impulse to reject food. She stared down the long table, over her husband's head, to the world beyond. If only all winter days could be like this! Blue skies—clouds like bubbles on a swift moving stream, a slight breeze moving the barren tops of tall trees that would be clad in heavy greenery by the time the child came to term. She felt herself to be brooding, like an old hen in a farmyard, settled down upon her task of bringing life into life.

Nathaniel's growl broke into her thoughts. "See that you take better care of yourself this time, Letty."

"I have always taken good care of myself. I don't know what you mean."

"The mind, Letty—the mind. Talked to a fellow in the club yesterday. Said the outcome of a woman's confinement could stand or fall upon her humor. The influences she allowed to come her way."

"Nat, you know I go nowhere. I try my best to keep occupied, content."

He nodded, munching. His jaw moved rhythmically. Then he gesticulated with his knife. "A very good thing. Read the Bible—fellow I spoke with said the Psalms, religious tracts, all that sort of thing, worked toward the child's being strong."

"Yes, Nat." She knew how easily he could be influenced by "some fellow at the club." Yet ask Henry Porter to talk with him— they might as well have been arguing with the wind. Nat heard what he wanted to.

He caught the slight sarcasm in her tone. "Letty, it's not becoming to see a wife fail to take her husband seriously. I should think you, of all people, would be open to suggestions."

"I—?" An unwise rejoinder. She should have bowed her head submissively. But she didn't feel submissive. She gazed at him down the expanse of the table. The corner of his mouth twitched. She was stepping into dangerous waters.

"You of all people, Letty. Surely you don't need a reminder of Brett."

She started to say that Henry Porter had reassured her, over and over, that nothing could have prevented the cord's having become wound about the baby's neck. What was the use? Nat was determined to make her responsible for Brett's condition.

"Keep the spirits elevated, Letty. This may be our last chance to have a normal boy."

She could have hit him. He'd gone back to his soft-boiled eggs. He was starting on the second, after neatly decapitating it with a sharp knife, cutting the calcium white of its shell in two. Now he spooned its liquid yellow into his mouth. A drop clung to his lower lip, and he ignored it while his eyes perused the newsprint. She watched it suspended there like a fat yellow pearl. It disgusted her, even while she was fascinated.

"Then you'll not be going with me to the inauguration?" he asked.

She'd forgotten. Grover Cleveland was to be sworn into office on March 4. As one of Philadelphia's more prominent citizens, Nathaniel Mackenzie would automatically be invited.

"I don't see how I can. By March, my condition will have begun to show."

He grunted. "I won't be coming straight back. John wants me to visit with him at his place in Virginia."

"Ah," she said, thoughtful. It would make the new tutor's first days in the Mackenzie household easier. By the time Nat returned, a routine would be established.

She ventured forth into heavy water. "I engaged Albert's tutor yesterday." She held her breath. Waiting—for what? He had already said she could hire whomever she wished.

He scowled. "Seem suitable?" he said, without looking up from his newspaper.

"Oh, very. And Albert likes him."

He looked up at that. "That may not be the best test of whether the man's the most favorable choice."

She went along with him. "Oh, I agree. But when one is satisfied that the other criteria have been met—surely it is fortunate they took to each other?"

He shrugged. "You had made up your mind on the matter. I am merely surprised you took until this morning to tell me about it."

She crumbled the remains of the dry toast between nervous fingers. "I would have told you at dinner only you were out."

"You think I didn't know till now?" His eyes mocked her.

She stared at him silently. "Who would have told you?" she said at last.

He put down his paper. Laid the palm of his hand flat on its surface. "Letty, your naïveté astounds me. Do you really think you can do anything in this house and not have me informed of it?"

She felt the room closing around her, " 'Informed,' Nat? That is an odd word to use. Have you set spies on me?"

"Call it what you wish, Letty. Taft is loyal. He tells me anything and everything he feels I should know. Nor do I ask how he obtains his information. The man serves me as he is supposed to—that's the only thing that concerns me."

"You talk about me to Taft?" She could hear her voice, shrill. Unpleasant in its panicky overtones.

"Are you going to have hysterics, Letty? If so, be good enough to leave the table before you indulge yourself. I want to finish reading the paper. I have to go into town in an hour. I wish a few moments of peace—"

"I'm sorry, Nat." She spoke bitterly. "Perhaps if I had known you were already aware I'd engaged the tutor, I should not have troubled you." She paused, feeling the anger flowing over the edges of her eyes, down her cheeks, flaming them. It was one thing to exercise his rights as head of the household—quite another to discuss her with the servants! "My condition," she said sarcastically. "Did Taft tell you about that too?"

He didn't even look up. "I didn't need to hear it from Taft. That came from another source."

"Another source! So, I am surrounded by informants! Nat, I am your wife—not a prisoner in this house, to be watched and talked about behind my back! It's monstrous."

This time he glanced up. "I told you I didn't wish hysterics. While you are going on about this very trivial matter, every detail is being carried through those doors"—he pointed to the entrance to the pantry—"straight into the kitchens. You complain of Taft. You feed the servants gossip by your own behavior. Is that how a Mackenzie should act?" His lower lip curled. "I think not. Now, we will have no more talk about it." His gaze threatened her. "Ever. You understand?"

She rose in her chair, pushing it back as she did so. She wanted to run, but it wouldn't have been dignified. Above all, she must not let on how much he'd hurt her.

She left the dining room, aware that he'd already dismissed her. Gained the staircase. She felt faint—nauseated by more than her condition. She wanted to weep, but tears would not flow. Because they had been forbidden. Brave girls, Emma had often told her, do not cry. Not for any reason.

She wasn't brave and she wasn't a child. She opened her morning-room door, wondering how its prettiness had turned so swiftly to drabness. The yellow silk of the two chairs by the fire looked like old lemon skins. Thrown away after they'd been squeezed, to lie in the gutter, for ants to feast on.

She walked over to the window. Who would have told him she was with child? Nanette? Surely the kindly French girl wouldn't have betrayed her? Norah? Both Norah and Betsy had been with her for years, ever since she had first set up housekeeping as a bride.

The point was, who knew her secret? Of them all, only Nanette had access to Letty's bureau drawers. She would know, not only of the calendar, but of when and for how long her mistress would have need of the towels every woman wore, to protect her clothes from staining. It had to be Nanette! Yet she trusted Nanette!

She turned away from the window. Should she question the girl? Wasn't it safer to act as if she didn't know? Try to set some trap for her?

She sat at her desk, but not to write. To still the trembling of her hands. Perhaps after all, it wasn't Nanette. Sharing a bedroom, Nat himself could know. Take out her calendar—count the days. He wasn't above it.

She laughed aloud. Surely this was the answer. He didn't know everything, but he wanted her to *think* he knew! She was safe with her household. She could behave with them as she'd always done—cautious, dignified, but not wary. She lifted her pen idly. The nausea was ebbing.

But what if he had set spies on her? Disquieted, she dipped her pen in the ink, pulled scrap paper toward her. She scribbled, as she so often did when perturbed. It seemed to ease the inner tension when nothing else would do. Not that she was an artist, but she'd shown some promise as a child. Her governess had urged Emma that an art teacher be found.

"What nonsense! Expose one of my girls to an artist. Surely you must know, Miss Sprules, that artists are immoral."

Miss Sprules had flushed. "I hardly think that is a fair statement, Mrs. Benedict. I believe Letty to have talent—"

"You are not paid to have opinions, Miss Sprules. Merely to see that my daughters have an education."

Miss Sprules had lost. But she had secretly bought paints and paper for Letty out of her own slim purse. Encouraged the girl to develop her ability.

Encouragement had been a hothouse flower in the frost of Emma Benedict's house. It had been the central point around which the issue of Miss Sprules' employment had revolved. Devolved.

Letty still recalled the day they had said good-bye. "But must you go—?"

"I'm afraid so, dear. Now keep on with your painting—"

Letty's pen sketched. She'd thought it would only be patterns— flowers, perhaps the long stems of birches against a brick wall. But in the end it was the same symbol.

She always drew a cage. A cage without a door in it.

II. THE CRADLE WILL FALL
August 1885–December 1886

Rock-a-bye baby
On the treetop,
When the wind blows
The cradle will rock;
When the bough breaks
The cradle will fall
And down will come baby,
Cradle and all.

                —Nursery rhyme

I

Letty's time was come. All afternoon, she had sat in the shade of the immense elm tree that cast its cooling over the lawn. An umbrella against the August sun. She had taken to spending much of her days out here. For short periods of time, Brett would be brought to sit beside her. She'd had a special chair made for his sagging body. As long as he had his rag to chew on, he'd be content. Sometimes, his strangely opaque eyes seemed to follow the dance of the butterfly, to be caught by the swoop of a bird over summer's faded flowers. Then again, Letty could never be sure how much he saw.

Everything was suffering in this heat. She mopped her brow for the twentieth time and moved the batiste of her loose dress away from her damp breasts, unable to bear for long any constriction. As one of the contractions with which her body was preparing itself for the task ahead hit her, she held herself perfectly still. Like a pointer that eyes a quarry in the bushes. She breathed intentionally lightly, noticing, as from far off, the soft curling of hair on the nape of Brett's neck.

A footfall behind her, displacing stones on the pathway, signified someone's approach.

"It's Norah, ma'am—with the lemonade." Katie, sent to oversee Brett so that he was not too great a burden on Letty, stretched for the sodden mass that was the child's "rabbit." Gave it back to him. "There you are, love," she said kindly.

"Ba-ba," said Brett. In the past few months he had acquired a few sounds. To Nanny and his mother they were signs he was talking at last.

Phillips set up the table close to Letty. Beyond the reach of Brett's sticky fingers. Betsy came forward with the tea cloth—embroidered in a Parisian *atelier,* edged with lace. She spread it over the polished surface with a deft movement. Norah put the tray down. Ice chinked in the tall pitcher.

"My, that sounds cool!" said Letty appreciatively. "How did you manage to find any ice?"

"We've been saving it, ma'am," said Norah. Her compassionate glance took in the strain lines that had appeared in Mrs. Mackenzie's face, the enormity of the bulge beneath the sheltering dress. It wouldn't be long now, Norah thought to herself.

Letty started to say, "Please see that the children have something to drink," when a sudden, unexpectedly sharp spasm took her. She stopped in mid-sentence. Bit her lip, fighting back the desire to cry out.

"Mrs. Mackenzie?" Norah and Katie spoke with one accord. Phillips maintained respectful silence. The bearing of children was women's work. It wouldn't do for him to make a comment.

"I think—" Again the bitten lip as she tried to rise, then sank back as the spasm repeated, this time in greater strength.

"Shall we send for Dr. Porter, ma'am?"

"Yes, perhaps we should. No, on second thought, let's count to ten. The last time, we got him here too soon. But perhaps the midwife—?"

Everyone knew that Dr. Porter's presence at a delivery was merely a precaution, in case something should go amiss. It was Mrs. Parsons who would supervise all the stages of labor, as she had with every Mackenzie baby from Albert on.

Letty often wondered what became of Nellie Parsons between deliveries. Each time her calm voice, capable hands were there to guide Letty and the baby through difficult waters, she vowed in her gratitude that she'd get to know more about this woman. "It's as if we place her on a shelf till we need her," she would think, as she gasped between contractions. Yet it was always the same. Once the infant rested in its cradle, Mrs. Parsons would gather up her things, smile at the new baby, and disappear till the next time.

Would this time be any different from the others? Unthinkable to dream of having anyone but Mrs. Parsons attend her. As Norah hastened up the path to alert Bates to carry the message, she felt comforted. Nellie—Nellie would see her through. She always had.

Yet there was apprehension in her gestures as she got herself out of her chair. This, too, was nothing new. Having a baby was like going on a trip. A trip no one could take for you, even though they could stand by your side, wipe your brow, and tell you when to bear down. It was a voyage in which there was no guarantee that one would reach the opposite shore. Over and over, a woman faced it, feeling the security of her existence menaced by the depths of the waters as she was tossed to and fro on the swelling seas of pain.

A man could know nothing of this. Strange how nature arranged it. Never a question as to how it should all be divided up. The point was, it wasn't. Impossible to think a man suffered when he performed the act that would start a child on its growth. Where was the equity in it? Of course there was none.

She took her time as she moved up the pathway. Aware of the solicitous gaze of Betsy and Phillips. Katie had borne Brett away to Nanny and the nursery, hushing him with her soft, Irish tones.

Such a long walk! How had she ever believed it to be but a few steps from lawn to terrace? Even then, she was only up to the house. There were the stairs to climb. Dear God, would she make it? As another contraction seized her, she motioned to Betsy to bring the chair. She needed it to lean on—rest a little.

Through the haze of panic that was doing its best to defeat her, she saw everything as if it were far away. Yet highlighted so that the smallest deed held great importance. Polly being given a ride in her bright yellow wagon by the undergardener. Amelia chasing after a hoop, trying to keep it rolling upright on the bumpy turf. On the terrace, book in hand, Albert lying in a long chair, his eyes heavy in the sultry heat. Fenichel seated beside him, a wiry figure, like one of those marionettes connected to strings, his attention fastened on the chess board.

It seemed to Letty that it was important to know what each member of the household was doing. To see that it all ran—that the children were taken care of and Nat's arbitrary needs met. She took a deep breath and felt the spasm loose its hold—temporarily. She could move on, a few more steps.

She gained the terrace. Felt the hardness of the bricks, warm from the August sun, beneath her thin soles. Fenichel and Albert stared at her. Their faces swam, like the reflection of twin moons on a lake. Pain now. She fought pain.

"Mama, are you sick?" Albert's voice, high with fear.

"It's all right," she said, reaching out in her tone to comfort him. An automatic reaction. He was one of her children. But she need not have worried. Fenichel was there, preceding her.

"I think your mother's time has come," he said low.

Albert sank back. "Oh—" Embarrassed.

They were beyond her periphery, even if she wanted to be concerned. Phillips' strong arms were under hers. Betsy now, and Taft— anyone but Taft—forming a chair with their arms. Telling her to lean back, to let them carry her. How foolish of them to think they could bear her burden. She alone could have this baby. She felt her lips quiver into a smile, which turned into a tremulousness. Dry sobs.

From across the lawn, like a duck coming in to land, a small figure flew. Screeching into her awareness. "Mama—oh, Mama! Mama, don't get sick and die!"

It was Polly. Flinging small arms about her mother, the usually pretty face contorted with fear. Where had the child got the idea that she would die? Letty put out her hand, stroked the blond curls. "Darling—it's all right. Go to Nanny."

"I don't want Nanny. I want you."

It was the first time any of them had ever said that. Letty gazed at Polly in astonishment. She would have drawn the child to her, but the tightening in her back warned her that another pain was close.

"Somebody take her—please?" she pleaded.

"I'll take Polly," said a prim voice.

Letty turned her head to see the figure of Amelia approaching. Composed and together, though she had been chasing a hoop but moments before. So cool. How did the girl stay so cool?

Had she, Letty, ever been like that? Slim, her figure undistorted, lithe in her movements. Her own person? If she had, it had been so long ago as to seem unbelievable. She envied Amelia with a fierceness that surprised her. Envied all of them—because they were pain-free. At liberty to belong to themselves.

She let them carry her up the staircase. She knew that the part of herself that belonged to her had of necessity retreated into a small corner of her being. For the next hours, she would be owned, as she was never owned except in labor, by the emerging being. She was nothing but a pathway down which a restless human would crawl, reaching for an external existence. Inexorable as the role was, it permitted her merely to watch, as a spectator. Yet, incongruously, it spared her none of the mindless agony of giving birth.

"We must undress you, ma'am." It was Nanette, helping her to remove her clothing with hands that knew their task well. Even so, it wasn't easy. Layers of perspiration-soaked garments, the constricting shoes, stockings peeled away like fruit skins.

"Oh, *la pauvre petite,* why is it that the *Bon Dieu* makes so much misery for women, when *les bébés* come?"

"Nanette," Betsy said quietly, "it would be of the greatest help to Mrs. Mackenzie if you would see to the straightening up of the room."

"*Oui,*" said Nanette, lapsing into her native tongue in her anxiety.

Letty lay back against the sheets, counting the moments until Mrs. Parsons should arrive. Not until then would she feel safe. These good, consoling women didn't have her skill. They couldn't take charge, bring order and direction to it all. She felt herself caught in a space in time—an opening that left her vulnerable to dammed-up emotions. Naked to terror.

The "supposings" began. Supposing the pain should never end? Supposing the baby got trapped somehow, not to be released except by being torn from her flesh? Her life ebb away in a dark floodtide of bleeding? The baby—the baby be born defective—or turn out to be a girl? How would she face Nathaniel?

"Coming along nicely, are we?" Nellie Parsons had arrived! In matter-of-fact tones she took charge, bustling into the tense bedroom, calming not only her patient but the female members of the Mackenzie staff. They could go to their duties now. Mrs. Mackenzie had ceased to be their responsibility.

Nellie Parsons took out the steel-cased watch that Letty always forgot between her visits and consulted its dial. "Pains about a minute apart. Shouldn't wonder if it isn't going to slip out of you easy as melted butter on a warm pan, m'dear."

The wrist next. A frown of concentration on her wide brow. Replacing Letty's hand beneath the light covers, "You can look forward to an easy time, love. Heaven knows, you've had enough practice." It was a joke she dragged out, the second or third time. "Ready to have something to hang on to, are you?"

Letty nodded, speechless. The strong cotton pull they had fashioned for her out of old sheets had been secured to the bedpost. She felt its roughness placed within her hand.

"Oh!" She let it slide away, out of her fingers. Pain had struck.

"There, there—it's hanging on that's needed." The rope was put back in her grasp. This time Letty clung to it with all her might. Translating agony into muscle tension, arm strain.

A cool cloth on her forehead. Unaccountably, she could catch the rise and fall of childish prattle from beyond the open windows. Nanny's voice bidding Polly and Amelia come dress for their supper. Had it been that long she'd lain here? The soft tread of feet on the stairs. Nanny shushing them. Polly's querulous tone, "But why is Mama ill?"

Then it all faded out again. Hidden beyond the fog that swirled at the farthest edges of her awareness was Dr. Porter's rumbling baritone. "Going well, eh? Just thought I'd inquire."

Would Phillips remember to bring him his brandy? Another spasm washed over Letty, taking her in its swift tide, creeping up her body and down her extremities until it had all of her in its drowning depths.

2

She had been in labor for hours, much longer than with any of the others. At one point it had all stopped momentarily. She found Mrs. Parsons bending over her.

"Bear down with all your might, missus, dear. Bite on the rag— but push with everything you've got in you. There's a love."

She did as she was told. Seconds passed. Here was Mrs. Parsons again. "Tell me, missus, has the baby been active?" Her face coming into Letty's vision. High starched cap, badge of her office, sitting flat on her gray hair. Her tidy body hidden beneath the long gray dress that was her uniform.

Letty struggled with the question. "What? What did you say?"

"Has the baby been active? Kicked a lot?"

Licking dry lips. "Why do you ask?"

"No reason, dearie. Just a mite curious."

"Something wrong?" Gotten out slowly. Enormous effort. Another wave, striking her, carrying her out toward the open sea. Was she, in fact, to drown?

"Wrong? Not as I can tell yet. There now, you're really pushing, aren't you? I can see the head—oh, the precious darling, it's the crown all right."

"Something—?" Something wrong? No more strength to ask it. The head—ah, dear Lord, the head at last.

Voices talking. Remembered now. Betsy was here to help. Like at those other times. Betsy had a knack.

Mrs. Parsons saying, "The child should've come more quickly. Not enough there to let it fight. Reason I asked her about the kicking."

Betsy's voice. "Thought this time was different."

"Next few minutes should tell."

"Something wrong with the baby—?"

"Save your breath for pushing, Mrs. Mackenzie. We're almost there, dear. One more shove. I can see the shoulder—"

"Aaah—"

"It's a fine boy! Look at the little angel. A boy for Mr. Mackenzie —my, my, won't he be proud. See, missus?"

Too quiet. A bloodied figure held upside down by the feet. Mrs. Parsons sat quickly on a chair, slapped once, twice—across the tiny buttocks. Silence. Slapped again. Letty didn't dare to breathe. All that for—but what was this?

"Waah—awah—awah!"

Letty's tears scalded her tired cheeks. "A boy, you say? Really a boy? May I see?"

Mrs. Parsons held him up, displaying the infant's maleness. "But you mustn't hold him. Not before he's cleaned up. Oh my, no."

Betsy bore the newest member of the Mackenzie clan toward a waiting bowl, fluffy towels, the accoutrements of childbirth.

Under Mrs. Parson's able hands, Letty expelled the afterbirth.

"You're torn quite a bit. But it'll mend soon. Couple of weeks in bed, you'll be right as rain. Glad it's a boy?"

Letty smiled weakly.

With the baby in her arms, she asked, "Why did you want to know about his kicking? He is beautiful." The most beautiful baby she'd ever had. Peach bloom fuzz on his pale skin, eyes like a china doll's, enameled, staring. She gazed from the infant's head to Mrs. Parsons, starched cap now stored away in its hatbox, her other implements, private necessities of her profession, packed into the worn carpetbag she always carried.

Mrs. Parsons understandably looked tired. Not happy. What is it? Her question, asked almost out of idle curiosity, now that the baby had been safely delivered, took on a more ominous note.

"He's all right, isn't he?" Letty asked the midwife sharply.

"Oh my, yes. See for yourself how lovely—" The response was too ready. Mrs. Parsons didn't meet Letty's eyes.

"But strong? You said something about him not having much fight?"

Mrs. Parsons touched the small head with a hand roughened as an old stick, gentle as a new leaf. "When the milk comes in, missus—he'll strengthen up. You'll see how quickly."

"You frighten me," said Letty abruptly. Her heart had turned to ice.

"Some don't reach for life the way they should. But see, his eyes are open. Put him to the breast right away—it's my best advice."

"Mrs. Parsons, will you come back and see me?" There! After all these deliveries, she'd finally said it.

"Bless you, Mrs. Mackenzie, you don't need me." Nellie Parsons' fine eyes bathed her in compassion. "There's a good nurse engaged." She touched the baby's downy head again. "My work's done, missus."

"Oh please," said Letty, "I have so much faith in you. If you could just look in on us—you know, tell me how you think the baby's doing?"

"You're both going to do very well. But yes, if you like, I'll stop by. At least to inquire—" She glanced toward the door. Dr. Porter would be wanting to see her. She'd better tell him what she thought of the child. That way he could begin to prepare the family. Mrs. Parsons had seen many babies. Often it was the color gave them away. This one had a chance, if only it took the breast. "I'll come by in a few days."

Letty's exhausted eyes lit up. "Oh, thank you. It will be such a comfort knowing you are coming."

"You did right well, lovey. I was proud of you," Mrs. Parsons whispered.

The high praise brought a flush to Letty's wan cheeks. Kind—so kind. Letty drifted into sleep.

Dr. Porter was waiting in Letty's morning room. "Everything went well, I take it?" Phillips had remembered the brandy tray—sandwiches.

"Fair enough." Nellie Parsons dropped her voice. "It took longer than it should've. But I'd say the infant has a chance."

"Is the baby sickly? Deformed or damaged?"

"Not so as you'd see it. Color's poor. All depends if he'll suck."

"Ah." Dr. Porter twiddled his fingers in his lap, gave Nellie Parsons a shrewd glance. "What's the trouble, do you suppose? His heart?"

"You're the doctor, sir. I was only giving my impression."

"To be sure." Placatingly. "I've learned to value your impressions, Nellie. Anything else I should know?"

"She ever mention whether the child was very active while she was carrying it?"

"Now, Nellie, you know I couldn't discuss something like that with my patients."

She lowered her eyes. No, of course he wouldn't know. Not him. They never did. "I told her to put him to the breast just as soon as she could. Well, doctor, it's been a long afternoon and evening. Think I'll be on my way."

He nodded. "Mrs. Frogge's getting close. Be waiting for them to call you."

"Very good, sir." What, more Frogges in the world? Weren't

there enough—and that woman so pale, so worn out as it was?

Nellie descended the back staircase. Softly, so as not to disturb. But most of the household were still up. Perspiring in the clammy heat of the August night.

"Going to be all right, is she?" asked Norah.

Nellie nodded. "Just wish the child were a little more husky."

Mrs. Bowker, known as "Cook," a kindly, obese woman, her leg flesh rolling over the tops of her shoes, arms like hams, interrupted. "You mean there's worry about the baby?"

"Not so you could put your finger on." Nellie began to button her coat. "But in my business, you get a feeling."

"The carriage's waiting to take you home." Betsy knew Mrs. Parsons' habits. Liked to get back to her place just as soon as a case was over. The team of starched nurses would be here to take her place. She preferred to leave before they arrived.

"Then I'll not be lingering," said Nellie. She could see already the little bit of pork pie she was going to heat for her supper. A dish of tea with it and she'd be able to have a nice sitdown in front of the fire. Let sleep drop over her, smoothing out the concerns of the day. Such a long day.

The baby did poorly from the first. He was too quiet, slept much, and when he was brought to suck, didn't seem to have enough hunger to push him to reach for the nipple.

Letty held him close to her breast. She stroked persuasively on his cheek with her two first fingers.

"Never get his attention that way, Mrs. Mackenzie!" Nurse Schmidt had a sharp voice that made edges for the shapelessness of her guttural accent. "We have to make him wake up proper. Like so!" She flicked cruelly at the infant's face with her thumb and forefinger.

The little boy moved away from the blow, but feebly. His eyes opened to the merest slits, then closed again.

"Oh, please don't hurt him." Letty's voice was a cry.

The nurse stared at her with nostrils flared in disgust. "You no wake him up, you kill him."

"Kill him? Oh no, I have enough milk for two babies and—"

"Enough for an army—it makes no difference. We have to capture his attention or he sleep his life away. Right into the grave, *hein?*" She bent over the baby and unwrapped the cocoon of coverings, exposing the tiny feet. As she'd done with his cheeks, now she flicked at his soles.

The baby moved ever so slightly at Nurse Schmidt's touch. She gripped his foot tighter, flicked once more, her nails clicking. The child gave a sharp cry.

"No!" said Letty. "You are hurting him!"

"You rather he starve, Mrs. Mackenzie?" The nurse shrugged. "If he were mine, I would do this over and over again. It has to be done. Else, will die."

"I don't want him hurt," Letty repeated.

Nurse Schmidt gave her a look of scorn, picked up an empty glass from Letty's night table, straightened three books that lay to hand, and strode arrogantly away.

"Please, please darling—" Letty whispered. But the baby slept on. Peaceful, sculptured in repose, his skin clear and unmottled, totally unlike the other babies she had borne, he summoned swift tears to her eyes. She pushed the nipple into his face, attempting to get him to mouth it. She was heavy with milk. She longed with all her being to enfill him, that he might open his eyes to life, might prosper.

The rosebud lips fastened about the nipple but made no effort to suck. Mouth closed once more, the baby rested quiescent in her arms. What dream was he dreaming? From what realms had he come that he hesitated to move forward into this present life?

Letty tried to communicate to this baby her longing. *This baby.* She must find him a name! Perhaps that would encourage him to live. She realized that she and Nathaniel had never once discussed what the child would be called. She must have something picked out by tonight when, most likely, he would visit her.

Warren, she thought. It had been Nat's mother's maiden name. Amelia Warren Mackenzie had died before Letty and Nathaniel had met. Surely he would consider, maybe even like, the name. She tried it out on the baby softly, whispering it. "Warren—Warren, darling." Then, "Oh, please live—please live for me."

Warren lay small and unresponsive in her arms. Not as Brett had done. Brett had taken the breast, cried overly much. He had rebelled at a life his damaged brain couldn't cope with. Warren lay passive, peaceful—ignored it all. Waited.

Nathaniel had been puzzled by the child. At first he had dandled him on his knee, as was expected of a new father. His cold eyes had regarded this latest of his progeny, and he had said to a still exhausted Letty, that first morning following the baby's birth, "May I congratulate you, Laetitia."

"Thank you, Nat." She had received it as it was intended: a tribute to her obedience.

Later that morning, the other children had been allowed to troop in; even Brett, borne in Katie's arms. Nanny had cooed and made faces at the baby, who lay as if in deep slumber. Polly had skipped over to her mother's bedside. "You aren't ill after all, Mama? But if you're not ill, why are you in bed?"

"I have to rest, precious. Have you seen your new brother?"

"Oh, yes. He's dull."

"Right now, Polly, yes. You see, he's very little. He has to sleep a great deal. But bye and bye—"

Polly's attention was lost. She wanted to know all about the vase of flowers sent over from the Benedicts' hothouse. Carnations that filled the room with their heady, nutmeg odor. "From Grandmama and Grandpapa?"

"Yes, darling. And from Aunt Hitty."

A nosegay of pansies had come from Hitty. Dear Hitty! How like her, so unassuming as to be irritating. Why couldn't Hitty have done something about her shyness, her overweight? It was now too late for her to attract a husband. What was to become of her?

Letty glanced once more at the pansies. Velvet-eyed and startlingly lovely floating in the green glass dish, they seemed to speak for Hitty as she couldn't speak for herself.

"Mama?" Amelia's voice broke into her thoughts. "Why doesn't he open his eyes?"

"He's so little—" she heard herself say, defending him. Yet she waited for Dr. Porter's visit with impatience. Anxiety.

The children were herded back to the nursery. Nanny, squeezing Letty's hand, had murmured, "I told you he'd come into the world safe." It reminded her of the day she'd allowed herself to share her doubts with Nanny. Holding Brett. "Nanny, do you think this next one—? I mean, we don't know why Brett is the way he is. Or at least we can't be sure. I hardly think I could bear it if it happened again."

Nanny had comforted her. "Oh, I don't believe you should fret yourself, milady. The others were all born perfect. Master Albert's illness came later. You carried him well. No, you oughtn't let it press on your mind. Try to set it aside, will you?"

Nanny had helped. But waiting for Henry Porter Letty felt a rising tension, like a mist coming up out of the river on a fall evening. Cloying. Was the baby really all right? Why didn't Henry Porter get here? She was in a fever by the time he arrived.

"Well, Letty, doing nicely this morning, I'm glad to see."

"But what of the baby? He doesn't seem as active as the others."

Henry had shaken his head. "Much too early to tell." His tone reproved her. Womanlike, she was worrying too much. It could have an adverse effect on her milk. "Been put to the breast, eh?"

Letty blushed at the frankness of the discussion, but the efficient Miss Schmidt nodded.

"Fine, fine. Look in on you later," was all Henry would say.

Did she imagine significant looks between him and Miss Schmidt? That their conversation in the hall was of matters they wouldn't tell her?

It was close to dinnertime when Nathaniel returned. The sound of horses' hooves on the gravel had roused her. She tried to raise herself in the bed. How long had she slept? The frigid Nurse Schmidt was seated beneath a pool of light, reading. As Letty moved, she looked up.

"You are awake. I think we put the child to the breast, yes?"

Letty nodded. She was bathed in sweat. The sun had gone around to the other side of the house, but the afternoon's heat had collected in the room and made it well nigh insufferable.

The nurse was standing over her with the baby, her face set in lines of disapproval. Waiting for Letty to tell her she didn't want her help in rousing the child. The look said, "Your baby is as good as dead. Why do we bother with this farce?"

Letty took the bundle, seeing her son's face contorting as the light poured in on him. Away from the sheltering bassinette he was like a naked nestling, torn too soon from the egg. Unfinished and afraid. Yet he remained so perfect—the tiny hands that clutched at the air feebly, the small mouth making motions of soundless mewing. Letty opened her nightgown, preparing to entice him to take suck, then closed it quickly as she heard Nathaniel's footstep on the stair.

Nat was drunk; flushed and aggressive, he strode into the room. He came forward, peering at the blanketed cocoon, pulling a corner of the coverings away with a finger that trembled ever so slightly. Liquor had been doing this to him of late. When had it begun? The small changes that were so minuscule from day to day that she hadn't noticed.

"Not awake yet?" he asked. As if he'd given the matter much thought. He turned to Nurse Schmidt. "This what you meant by my wife not being willing to work with you?" Nurse Schmidt evidently was to be an ally.

Letty felt she shouldn't have been surprised.

"When the baby won't take nourishment, we must force it to. This child is very lazy—" The guttural voice whined on. "Where I come from, we do not allow this sort of behavior. The infant must arouse itself—or die." She shrugged, glancing for affirmation from her patient's husband.

Nat grabbed one of the delicate feet. "Show me. Show me what you mean."

She used her nails then. They were hard and sharp, reminding Letty of the pink claws of a crab. The nurse made flicking motions, and when this didn't produce more than a stir from the baby, she pressed the nails deep, making half-moon arcs on the newborn skin.

The baby howled. His eyes tight, umbilical in their unwillingness to see. Blind to the world beyond the womb, he cried loudly, the typical hiccuping protest of those freshly delivered to life.

Nathaniel grinned. "It's working," he said. "Try it some more."

"No! Please, no!" Letty attempted to pull the child to her. Not sure if he were hers to claim, if by taking him away from them, she were condemning him to starvation.

89

Nathaniel stared at her. "She's not to be listened to," he said bluntly. "Go ahead, nurse. See what you can do to wake the little bastard up. Henry Porter says we don't get him to feed, we're going to lose him." He licked his lips. "You want that on your conscience, Letty? You want to remember that for the rest of your life? That you let my son die because you were having hysterics over what we had to do?" He glared at her, his rage searing the edges of her being.

Numbly she shook her head.

Nurse Schmidt's voice was sure now. She had an ally. "Dr. Porter is a good physician—he has had much experience. If he speaks up for these approaches, you can know they are justified."

"We've known Dr. Porter for years," said Nathaniel. "My mother knew his mother long before he decided to disgrace the family by going to medical school." Affability. It was another of the signs that Nat had consumed a lot of alcohol. It reversed his normal terseness, turning it inside out, like an orange rind, exposing his need for closeness. Yet even under the influence of drink, he could reach out only to strangers. Miss Schmidt, for instance.

He touched her on the shoulder lightly. Patted her. "Come on, Gerda. What do we do about this baby?"

His use of the first name prodded under Letty's eyelids, arousing her from torpor. Nathaniel knew so many women. Was this haughty German one of his choices? With Nathaniel, one never knew.

Nurse Schmidt said, "There is one last resort. It is based on country ways—yet in the villages it has been known to work."

"What's that?" Nathaniel's face was flushed from the effort of trying to will his son to respond.

"We place a small amount of honey on the breasts and a drop or two of whiskey on the child's lips. This will make him wish to do something about the stinging. When he opens his mouth to protest the whiskey, we introduce the nipple—covered with sweet food. You follow?"

I am like an object, thought Letty as she lay there. Taft had brought a tray of whiskey to the door. Betsy had fetched the honey. What must the servants think?

"Letty, uncover yourself. What are you being so squeamish for?"

Before either of them alone, it wouldn't have mattered. But when they were here together, it made baring her breasts obscene. She was nothing but a section of meat on a butcher's slab. To be ogled at—weighed and examined.

Her breasts burst forth, purplish and pressed to their skin's limit with milk. Her nipples, which should have invited the child, oozed bluish milk. Her nightgown was already soaked from their plenitude.

"She has enough, you see!" said Nurse Schmidt reprovingly.

"You butter her up with the honey," said Nathaniel. "I'll be ready with the whiskey. While Nurse Schmidt put some of the dark treacly goo on her index finger, he poured himself a shot glass, tipped his head back, and drank.

The experiment was a failure from the start. When Nathaniel had gone, Letty washed her breast free of the stickiness. Some of it had gotten on the infant's face. Where she dabbed with the cloth the skin came up mottled, angry to be disturbed. The baby whimpered.

Left to herself at last, she held Warren close. Miss Schmidt was getting on her coat, peering at her watch. Her ten-hour shift was over. The relieving nurse was expected at any moment.

Nurse Barker was a much younger woman; she was kind, solicitous. Letty wished she could have had her for all the hours. She came over the expanse of carpet between the door and the bed, questioning, "Shall I take the baby now?"

"Can't I have him just a little while longer?"

There was no reproof on the young girl's face. She spoke clearly, revealing herself to be of middle-class origin. "Mother always keeps them alongside her." She smiled kindly.

"Oh? How many children does your mother have?"

"There'd be twelve, but only seven have lived." Nurse Barker's brown eyes held sorrow. She peered at the small Warren. "He's so pretty, Mrs. Mackenzie. My word, you have beautiful babies!" As if she had seen the others.

Letty felt comforted suddenly. "If I sleep—you know—roll over on him—?"

"Of course," said Nurse Barker. "I'll be right here, watching. Hasn't he taken to the breast yet?" Lightly, but with concern.

Letty shook her head, trying not to show that her eyes were brimming with despair.

She slept propped high on her pillows, to give her enormous breasts full freedom. When she felt hands pulling the baby out of her grasp, she came up from a deep sea-bottom. The waters parted and she stared into the dimness, only alleviated by the lamp by the nurses' chair.

Startled, she saw Nurse Barker swiveling in her seat, as if caught in a still picture. "Oh, sir, I didn't hear you come in."

Nathaniel now reeked of drink. He had his flask out and was trying to feed liquor to the baby as if it were milk.

Nurse Barker was on her feet. She had none of the self-possession of Gerda Schmidt. She wheeled around the drunken Nathaniel, a puppy dog puzzled by the antics of its owners—unhappy but unable to intervene.

Letty screamed.

91

Her calls echoed through the house. Finding them in their beds —kneeling at their prayers—stoking the kitchen fire for one last time before the night.

Betsy turned over and whispered to Norah, "What should we do?"

"We can't interfere," said Norah, her eyes wide in the moonlight.

The screaming went on. It was Mrs. Mackenzie's voice, high and hysterical. Something about killing the baby? Taft banged on Phillips' door.

"You're going to have to get him to bed."

"But, Mr. Taft, sir, I can't go in there. Not in their bedroom."

"Wait with me in the hall. We'll ask the nurse."

A small figure had preceded them. In the shadows it was hard to recognize Albert. He turned about as Taft and Phillips approached.

"I knew he was going to make trouble. He was working up for it during dinner. You saw it, didn't you, Taft?"

The footman coughed lightly. "It's not for me to say, Master Albert."

Some action was called for, but they stood about outside the door, the three of them, joined by a drowsy Fenichel, uncertain what to do.

Albert, with surprising determination, stepped up to the door, turned the knob, and threw the entranceway open.

The scene that met their eyes should not have amazed them. Yet it did. A chair had been thrown on its side, the baby's bassinette toppled. A distraught Mrs. Mackenzie was half out of bed, the young nurse frantically pulling on Mr. Mackenzie's arm.

The baby was mewing pitifully—held high in the air by his father.

Phillips and Taft paused in the doorway. Then, as one, they approached the drunken man. Yet they did not touch him. Awed by the setting, they held back.

Albert rushed to his mother. "Mama, what is he trying to do?"

For answer, she sobbed, "Get the baby. Don't let him kill your brother."

Taft spoke now. "Sir, if we might have a word with you?"

"Eh—?" Nathaniel staggered and Phillips steadied him.

"The baby, sir. The nurse would like to take the baby."

Nathaniel looked at the younger butler as if he didn't hear him. He tried to tug his arm away, but Phillips hung on, obdurate.

Taft said pleasantly, "The nurse needs to change the child, sir. She's asking for you to hand him over to her."

"Wet, eh?" Nathaniel laughed, his mouth loose and slobbery. Eyes unfocused. He allowed Nurse Barker to take the infant.

"What was it you were wanting of me, Taft?"

"Sir, isn't it time for you to be in bed? Bates is ordered for early in the morning."

Nathaniel seemed to consider the information while he swayed gently back and forth. Then he took a step forward and almost lost his balance. "No good sons—all I got is girls."

Taft and Phillips led him away.

"Mama, are you all right?"

She clung to Albert briefly. Then her eyes were only for the baby. "Nurse, is he unharmed? Oh, thank God. Thank all of you for coming." Now that she had been rescued, she was embarrassed. She pulled her sacque around her to hide what she felt.

Taft knocked on her door. Spoke without entering. "He's to bed, ma'am. Would there be anything else?"

Letty glanced about, reassuring them with her eyes. "No, thank you. Albert, darling, get back to bed before you take cold."

On the upper landing, Betsy and Norah huddled. Nanny, her hair plaited and loose down her back, filled the doorway to the night nursery, like an animal that guards her lair.

Betsy called softly to Phillips. *"Pssst.* Mrs. Mackenzie all right?"

Phillips nodded. He'd catch it if Mr. Taft caught him talking. He whispered, "Drunk as a lord. Don't say I said so, eh?" He shook his head, went on down the back staircase.

Inside the night nursery, Polly was asking with a sleepy voice, "What's wrong, Nanny? I'm scared—all that shouting."

Amelia said primly, "Go to sleep." She turned over, reaching for Sophie.

Polly's arms went up to Nanny. "I'm so scared."

"Hush." Nanny rocked her.

In his crib, Brett slept soundly.

On his back, in the bed made up for him during Letty's confinement, Nathaniel snored. His breath was foul.

In the morning the baby was weaker. Letty had refused to give him up all night. Nurse Barker's pleading, "You need your sleep, Mrs. Mackenzie," had brought only a shake of the head.

Once, when the morning was too new to waken the birds, Letty had opened her eyes. The lamp on the table at the end of the room was the sole illumination. "What's the time?" she asked.

Nurse Barker had turned about, startled at her patient's voice. "Why, its a little past three, I think."

"I believe I'll try to get him to suck." Letty pushed her nightwear aside, exposing the dribbling breast. "Darling, please—"

Warren's lids fluttered. He stared at her steadily, with the old look of those who have not yet awakened to the reality of this existence.

"Warren—live for me." So low, her plea was no more than a rustle in the curtained room, leaving the night air unmoved.

Her nipple brushed his cheek. His head on the frail neck wobbled, eyes shut against her. She had nothing to offer him. Her tears touched his face.

"Shall I take him, Mrs. Mackenzie?"

"No, not yet."

What was she waiting for? The nurse's eyes asked the same question as she withdrew to her chair by the lamp. There was a sour taste to this hour of the morning. Unreality. As if they'd no right to be pushing aside the veils of darkness. No wonder the baby had scorned them.

Nurse Barker looked up, satisfied herself that all was well. She pulled a light wrap about her shoulders. The day would be suffocatingly hot later on, but now it presented a dew chill. With gratitude she heard the first sounds of the household awakening. Tea. She'd been promised tea.

It came on a large tray, half an hour later. Norah brought it, her eyes seeking answers that hadn't been hers to receive the night before. The little nurse gave her a smile.

"Did you—did they—manage some rest after all?" Norah asked.

"Mrs. Mackenzie's been asleep off and on. Poor dear, she's exhausted—but won't let me take the wee one."

Their eyes went to the pair on the bed. The child was invisible, wrapped in its coverings. Letty lay with her chin at an awkward angle—sharp, contorting her neck, her head tipped as if wishing to see what was beyond her. Her dark hair, touched as by a fine-tipped brush with gray, fanned out over the white pillow. Her skin looked sallow.

Their voices had awakened her. She tried to sit up, her arms still clutching the baby. One hand went out, tentatively, pulling aside the sheltering blankets.

"Let me have him, Mrs. Mackenzie, while you drink your tea."

"My tea—?" Letty's eyes looked puzzled, stared at the cup Norah was proffering. "You brought tea? What time is it?"

"About seven o'clock, ma'am. Cook thought the nurse would be partial to something hot."

"Of course." From a long way off.

"Let me take him, Mrs. Mackenzie. I'm sure he must need to be changed."

Letty let the nurse take the baby. She sighed, breathing out on the morning air all the doubts of the night before. The dreams—the wild, crazy dreams.

"Norah—?"

"Yes, ma'am?"

"Norah, you must do something for me." The tone was urgent now. Voice sure and crisp. "Before Mr. Mackenzie is up, you must send Bates on an errand."

"Bates, ma'am? He was to be ready early. The master had an appointment early."

"Phillips, then. I must get a message to the minister." She fixed Norah with eyes that were both sad and fierce. "My baby is dying. I want him christened—right here in this room. He must be blessed, and he must have a name before he goes."

"Oh, ma'am." Norah's compassion flowed over Letty like a rebuke. "You'll see—there'll be time to take him to the church."

Letty shook her head, as if it cost her effort she couldn't afford to expend. There was anger on her voice. "Norah, please listen to me.

95

Why won't anyone in this house listen to me—?"

"Oh, ma'am, we always listen. We do try, I'm sure."

"Never mind now." Wearily. "I'm tired this morning, Norah. I haven't much patience. If you don't think you can carry a message, then send Betsy to me."

Betsy came. "Is there something I can do for you, ma'am?" Her face saying she'd been told nothing. Letty felt irritation rise up to cover her naked feelings. "I told Norah—I want someone to go for Mr. Evans." Tears, hot and scalding, pushed under her eyelids. "Won't anybody believe me? My baby is dying!"

Nurse Barker moved forward to take Letty's wrist. Consulted her watch with a frown. Why couldn't they listen? Letty pleaded. Heed her call for help? "I want to see the baby christened—"

"Yes, ma'am. You'd like for us to send for him *now?*" Betsy's stare told Letty what she already knew. They thought her mad. Her confinement had deranged her. Well, they'd have to accept that.

"Right now."

Betsy looked at Nurse Barker. There was a rustle at the door.

"What goes on here?" The clear, German voice made them move guiltily. "How is my patient?" Nurse Schmidt moved forward into the bedroom. "Slept well, I trust?" Her tone accused them.

"I've written the report," said Nurse Barker.

"Fine, fine. I think we get her washed now." The way she was removing her coat told the others they were dismissed.

"No, wait!" cried Letty. She pushed the teacup she'd been clutching, its remains of tea cooled to a tan-colored pond, on to Betsy, "I have sent for the minister. We've got to get ready for that!"

"The minister?" Nurse Schmidt's question curled about them like a whip, derisive, mocking. "Does Mr. Mackenzie know this?"

Letty stuck her chin out. "No. Mr. Mackenzie slept poorly last night. He has an early morning appointment, I'm told. It is *my* wish that we send for Mr. Evans."

"I see." Nurse Schmidt's expression warned her. There'd be trouble—possibly a great deal of trouble. Yet it was, after all, none of her business. She was merely an attendant.

Letty leaned forward, forcing Betsy to pay close attention. "The other children—they are to be dressed—prepared to come downstairs. All the servants—a real christening, just as if it were in the church. You understand?"

No one had thought to tell Nathaniel, as he ate his sullen breakfast, that the minister was coming. No one wanted to break in on that cloud of gloom, arrest the trembling fingers in their effort to cut open an eggshell.

Taft could not avoid the obligation. "I think you should know, sir, that Mr. Evans is expected."

"Ridiculous. I sent for no minister."

"It was Mrs. Mackenzie's wish."

Nathaniel wheeled in his chair. "You are informing me that my wife sent for a minister?"

Taft nodded. Braced himself for the inevitable.

"She's gone mad, eh? Hasn't she, Taft?" Nathaniel glanced at the clock on the mantel. "Why, it's not yet nine. Is she out of her senses completely? Was Bates dispatched without my knowing?"

"Mrs. Mackenzie was very insistent, sir."

"Why wasn't I told?"

Taft's years of experience stood him in good stead. "It seemed wisest, sir, in view of the importance of this morning's meeting, that you be allowed your rest. If you recall, last night you expressed the fear you were sickening—?"

"Did I indeed?" Nathaniel's eyes widened. "I cannot think why. Did I say as much to yourself?"

"To Phillips, sir. When he assisted you to bed."

Knowledge that he would just as soon not know pervaded Nathaniel. He turned and pushed the half-eaten egg away. "Is there any need for me to meet with the minister?"

"In view of your appointment—"

"Yes, you're right. Tell Bates to bring my carriage about in five minutes." Nathaniel peered at the mantel clock again, as if it were veiled in fog. His eyes were bloodshot, obviously paining him. He gestured at the breakfast things. "And take this goddamned stuff away. Bring me whiskey."

97

5

The clatter of horses' hooves on the driveway announced that the Reverend Llewellyn Evans was about to arrive. Nathaniel, brooding in his study, shook his head and downed one more shot of liquor.

Llewellyn Evans strode into the hallway. His step was strong, his mien sprightly. "My good man, where is your mistress?"

"She's upstairs, sir. She's not able to leave her rooms yet."

"When was the child born?"

"Three days ago."

"Ah. Well, show me upstairs."

The household was waiting, like eyes in the forest. As Llewellyn Evans mounted the staircase, his ascent was followed. Servants hovering until just the right moment. On the third floor Nanny was putting the finishing touches on her charges.

"Katie, Brett's face has got to be wiped again."

"I tried, Miss Dove." Only Katie—and that when she was upset—called Nanny "Miss Dove."

Nanny chose to ignore the appellation. "And take a rag with you. He'll be a mess afore it's over."

Nurse Barker could have gone home—to her mother and her morning egg—but she elected to remain. She felt somehow linked to this baby. And to Mrs. Mackenzie. She hadn't been able to get the sight of last night out of her mind. She'd tell her mother about it later. Mother would cluck her tongue against her teeth, shake her head. "—awful when the drink's on them. Janie, never marry a tippling man." Yet, how could you tell?

Norah had indicated there would be breakfast. "In the servants' hall, miss. Cook says if you'd oblige her by coming downstairs."

"Oh, I don't have to eat. I can wait."

"It's only a bit of oatmeal, miss. But it'll stick to your ribs." Norah's expression said she was grateful Nurse Barker was to stay for the christening. It was very considerate. They all knew she was tired. But ah, the young had resilience. Norah paused for a moment on the back stairs to massage her veiny legs. Why did they always swell—just when she needed them? Ache fit to tie one in knots.

The breakfast was swallowed in staccato fashion—by stops and starts. One ear for the carriage, the opening of the front door. Dishes hadn't been cleared from the nursery when Betsy gave the signal.

"It's him. Mr. Taft's gone to let him in. He'll want to have a few words with the mistress. Best be ready, though."

Llewellyn Evans approached Letty's bedside. "I came just as soon as I got your message. The child is poorly?"

She nodded, her voice thick with sorrow. "I don't think we'll have him long, Mr. Evans. Thank you for coming on such short notice. You will have to excuse my appearance."

He waved her protestations aside. "Under the circumstances, dear lady, it was wise to send for me. It was christening you had in mind?"

"Oh yes," Letty answered fervently. "It's very much what I want. I'm afraid if I waited till I was able to come to the church myself—" She let the words go unsaid.

He patted her hand, his eyes eloquent with understanding. "Then let's do it. Just the three of us to be present?"

"Oh no," she said hastily. "I want it to be as nearly as possible like the real ceremony. I have summoned the servants, asked the children be present." She stared at him earnestly. "I want Warren to be remembered."

"Warren?"

"It is the name I've chosen. It seems proper—Warren Benedict Mackenzie. Warren was my husband's mother's maiden name, Mr. Evans."

He bowed. "Then it would be very proper." He glanced about. "I take it Mr. Mackenzie is out of town?"

She could feel Nurse Schmidt waiting. Waiting to hear what answer would be given. Letty wet her lips. She sighed lightly and then proceeded, as if walking through thick mud, "He appears in church from time to time, but Nathaniel doesn't hold with God."

There was a silence. The carnations in the vase seemed to feel it as they emitted their heavy fragrance on the morning air. Had she shocked him? Letty lifted her eyelids, enough to be able to tell that he was considering the statement. Unsure of how to respond.

He took her hand, pressed it within his own warm ones. "That being the case, we must include him in our prayers, Mrs. Mackenzie."

"I think so," she said deliberately.

Nurse Schmidt spoke up. "Should Mr. Mackenzie at least not be given the chance to be present?" Her voice echoed in the room, bouncing off the heavy draperies, the mahogany furniture. Shaming them—that they were planning a clandestine act.

Letty answered wearily. "Nurse Schmidt, if it is any of your business, which I assure you it is not, my husband already knows."

Mr. Evans patted Letty's arm. He stood up, placing his strong figure in its flowing cape between patient and nurse. An intervention. "Do we have something to serve as a font?" he asked.

"A font? You mean some kind of a bowl?" Letty's brow wrinkled as she considered the question. "Perhaps Taft could find us something suitable."

Nurse Schmidt was asked to ring the bell pull. Betsy, who had been hovering in the hall, came at once.

"If everyone could come in, please?" Letty was trying to raise herself up on the pillows. "It may take a few minutes before we are ready, but I don't want to waste any time. And Taft. I have to see Taft, Betsy."

"I'll pass along the word, ma'am." Betsy retreated, the bow of her morning apron lying like a nervous butterfly on the small of her back.

Taft came to the door. In the meantime, Mr. Evans had taken his black bag, opened it expectantly. He reminded Letty incongruously of a peddler about to display his wares. She felt guilty for the image, suppressed an hysterical urge to giggle.

"Come in, please, Taft."

He had been in the night before. But today was different. He opened the doorway, but stood holding it between his face and the sight of his mistress abed. He coughed gently and spoke to the air before his eyes. "Was there something, madam?" ·

"Taft, Mr. Evans requires a bowl. I assume it should be quite a large bowl? For use as a christening font."

Would you have any idea of what kind of bowl, madam?"

Mr. Evans said abruptly, "It matters not what sort of bowl."

Taft cleared his throat fussily. "Would madam have in mind one of the Chinese bowls—as fit for the occasion?"

"No," said Letty sharply. "I have it. Let us use the silver bowl we keep potpourri in. The one that stands beneath my portrait—in the downstairs parlor."

He straightened his back, adding at least an inch to his stature. He showed his displeasure by looking straight at her. "If it is the one I think it is, it has not been cleaned recently."

"I can't imagine that it will matter," she said impatiently. "Just bring it upstairs."

He withdrew. Meanwhile, the others were outside the door. The servants, as bidden. Nanny, one hand on Polly's shoulder, the other prodding Katie, who held Brett. Amelia, keeping her own distance. Albert and Fenichel, emerging from the schoolroom.

Before she would give the signal for them to come in, Letty wanted to hold Warren. He had been replaced in his bassinette at the arrival of Mr. Evans. Nurse Schmidt brought the child to her, handling him as if he were already something inert. Letty reached up her arms for the baby, letting him lie within their circle. He had all the appearance of a statue carved of marble on a tomb. Sweet and apparently perfectly at peace, he slept. The small mouth parted, breathing as shallow as the movement of a petal opening to the sun.

Mr. Evans had approached. Letty pulled aside the corner of the blanket. "I'm not giving up yet," she said fiercely.

He patted her on the shoulder. "No, you should not."

The doors were opened. They filed in, solemn, crowding against one another, trying to find their private space within the bedroom that was alien to most of them.

Letty held the baby close. She hadn't looked at him for a long time now—minutes or hours? Was it her imagination that he had grown even more still? Fear, like an icy wind, blew around her, chilling the sense of expectancy the Reverend Mr. Evans had managed to invoke. Was Warren—? Her mind refused to form the thought, clutching for security at the knowledge the blankets gave out warmth. The blankets alone—or the tiny body through the coverings?

She searched the milling faces before her until she found Nanette's—the only one who would know instantly where to find what she needed. "My mirror!" she said to the lady's maid.

"Your hand mirror, madame?"

"Yes, yes. Oh, please be quick—"

She held it over the small mouth. Her hands trembled, slippery with panic. She turned the reflecting surface about, to see. There was a misting. The barest suggestion, as if a single flake of snow had landed upon its glass, melted to a fluid drop, then dried, leaving only the impression that it had been there. Warren lingered.

"Hurry!" she said to them.

The Reverend Mr. Evans looked up, caught midway in his preparations. "I need the bowl," said the minister, his eyes on the door.

"Yes, yes. Phillips, go and see what is keeping Taft!"

"Mr. Taft is on his way, madam. I can hear him on the stairs."

"Thank God!" She pursed her lips, stared at her infant.

Taft was in the room, extending the bowl.

Betsy had placed a small table close to Letty's bed, yet not so close as to lose its island quality.

"Put the bowl here," Mr. Evans said, motioning to Taft.

Mr. Evans had taken a flask from his bag, a vial with a silver top, attached to the neck by a short chain. He undid it with a flourish, poured a stream of water into the bowl.

There wasn't much water, but it was holy. It lay there like a lake, its surface broken by the dusting of broken rose leaves, a single lavender bud culled from the previous summer—Letty's potpourri, which she had gathered with her own hands.

"Who are to act as the child's godparents?" Mr. Evans asked.

Letty sighed. In her panic over having the ceremony take place before it was too late, she hadn't once given thought to the need for godparents. She stared up at the minister, her eyes distraught.

"How many shall we need?"

Mr. Evans answered her. "Two of the same sex, one of the opposite."

"Albert?" She called him forth from the crowd. "Would you be willing to stand as godfather to your little brother?"

"I, Mama?" His pale face flushed up. "If you would like it, surely. But am I old enough?"

"It's all right," she said wearily. "Everyone will think you are a fine choice."

Her mind was already on her next choice. Father! She'd tell him he'd been selected. He would be pleased. She should have sent for him —for Mother and Hitty! Guilt grabbed at her but she pushed it away. Someone must stand in for Father.

"Fenichel, would you mind helping us out?" she asked. "We need someone to stand in for my father."

He came forward as if he'd been expecting it. His green suit clung to his body like folds of moss on a downed tree trunk.

Without waiting for his nod, she called Amelia.

"Me, Mama?" Almost as surprised as Albert.

"Yes, darling. I haven't had time to ask Aunt Hitty to be godmother. You will have to act as if you were she. You won't mind, will you?"

"What am I to do?" The gray eyes challenged, as they always challenged. The head with its fine brown hair, smooth as a wing in flight, lifted to gaze at Letty.

"You will have to hold him. Just come over here, darling. Put out your arms—he's not very heavy."

Seeking reassurance, Amelia stared about her. It was not to be had.

"Mama," she called, frightened. "I do not wish to hurt him."

102

"Its all right, darling. Mr. Evans is ready to take him anyway."

The liturgy began. The ancient words flowed over Letty, giving her leave to be moved. "Dost thou, therefore, in the name of this child, renounce the devil and all his works, the vain pomp and glory of the world, with all covetous desires of the same—?"

Albert, having no clear idea of the questions, led the responses. Would it, after all, make so much difference that the soul of Warren Benedict Mackenzie, having renounced all that had to do with this world, reenter the heaven from which presumably he had sprung, clothed in these promises made for him?

Letty wished she knew.

6

The baby lingered.

Letty, awakened at noon with a tray of food, toyed with the soup Henry Porter had ordered for her, the omelette. She made a face at the glass of ale.

"But it will make milk, Mrs. Mackenzie." Nurse Schmidt shook her head in disapproval.

Letty waved her away, too weary to argue. Of what need had she of milk, she whose breasts dripped with it? The nurse brought her a fresh binder, attempted to help her expel the rich liquid that bubbled and seeped from her nipples.

"Too bad," said the nurse. "Such a waste. A poor woman would sell it." Her tone implied Letty was at fault for not having need of the money.

Letty lay back. Her womb, emptied of its burden, closed down upon itself, shriveling like a walnut that has lost its dewy sweetness. Cramps plagued her body. Afterpains, they called them. She tried to get comfortable. At last, she slept again.

The chiming of the clock on the mantel aroused her. Or had that been it? She sat upright, feeling with frightened fingers for the baby's warmth. Finding it, she touched his tiny arm with her hand. Warren was still alive! She peered at the clock's dial. Only three! The warmest part of the afternoon. She sighed.

She heard someone coming up the stairs—the scuffling sound of dresses caressing the treads, hands on the bannisters. The soft ripple of laughter. Laughter seeking to enter into this room! It was monstrous! Letty sat upright, pulling her discarded sacque about her.

Nurse Schmidt came to tell her what she already knew. "Your mother and sister would like to see you."

"Oh," said Letty, conscious of her dishevelment. "But my hair isn't combed, and I must change my gown."

"Nonsense!" said Emma, pushing her way into the room. She made her hobbled progress from door to bedside. "Ridiculous to feel you must dress up for your mother, Letty. I wanted to see you, that's all." The smell of her oldness permeated the room as her carnations had done the day before. She paused, resting on her cane, and stared down at her grandson.

"You had him christened, I hear," she said slowly.

"Mother, I would have sent for you—" Letty tried to raise herself in the bed.

Emma's voice was surprisingly soft. Uncharacteristic of her. "It's all right, Letty. I understand." She looked away from the baby, her sharp old eyes wet.

Emma wheeled about, commanding a chair. Nurse Schmidt produced one, while Hitty took the vacated place by the bassinette.

Hitty spoke up. "He's beautiful," she said delicately. "You are calling him Warren?"

"Warren Benedict—"

"For Nathaniel's mother," said Emma calmly. She was breathing stentoriously.

Letty realized with a pang of remorse that the stairs had been a real effort for her mother. We take our parents so for granted, she thought, and then suddenly they are old. We wonder where they have gone, the strong guardians of our youth. It crossed her mind that someday her own children would see her thus. Aged hands curled and ineffectual, breath labored, heartbeats numbered. Would her offspring treat her kindly? The idea made her feel vulnerable.

Emma's voice cut through her thoughts. "Was Nathaniel here?"

"For the christening?" Letty shook her head.

"Just as well," said Emma heavily. "He's a godless unbeliever. He would be a far easier man to get along with if he'd take some of it more seriously." She glanced at the crib, its tiny occupant so still. "I shouldn't wonder if God's taking your baby just to punish him. Nathaniel doesn't deserve to be a father."

"Mother, please," Letty begged. "Besides," she argued softly, "what you are saying implies that God wishes to punish me, too."

"Not at all," said Emma smoothly. "He is merely asking trust of you, Letty. Trust He knows best." She folded her hands on her lap, having set her cane carefully against the arm of her chair, "We all have to trust God. You know that."

Hitty said, "Would it be all right, do you think, if I picked up the baby?"

They all stared at her. Nurse Schmidt, at the end of the room, laid down her sewing—watchful, alert.

Emma cleared her throat noisily. "Hitty, how could you even ask it?"

"I'd like to." Hitty had reddened. She seemed like Polly suddenly, with her blond coloring, her rounded cheeks. But her eyes were serious. "I want to be able to remember him. This is the only way I know how."

"Yes, of course," said Letty quickly. She leaned over to pull the covers back from the pale form in the crib. "He's so terribly weak, I'm afraid," she said almost in apology.

"He's lovely," said Hitty. She raised the small head until she could touch it with her own soft cheek. "Perhaps he's too lovely for this world—"

"Nonsense!" said Emma in a small explosion. "Letty was too old to have another child. Laetitia Mackenzie, I hope you are going to let this child be your last."

Letty pressed her lips together. Nurse Schmidt had taken up her sewing again. If only Mother wouldn't talk this way in front of the woman! But there wasn't any stopping Emma. There never had been.

"I think the decision must rest with myself and Nathaniel," she said, trying to sound dignified. Failing miserably.

Hitty had Warren crooked in her arm and was humming to him softly. The sight upset Letty, for reasons she couldn't put her finger on. She wanted to snatch the baby away from her sister.

"I think he ought to be put back," she said, struggling to keep her voice even. "Here, give him to me."

"Of course," said Hitty, startled. Hiding hurt.

As she took the child back, Letty heard a soft tap on the door. Nurse Schmidt got up to answer it. Betsy was there, coming into the room with a large vase of roses.

"Ah!" said Emma, "I wondered where they had gotten to. Now where would you like them, Letty? Surely those carnations are ready to be thrown out?"

She had taken over, directing Betsy where to place the newer arrangement. As Betsy removed the first vase, a shower of petals dropped to the night table's surface, lying there like miniature pink canoes, thrown every which way by some unseen tide.

"They're lovely, Mother. Thank you for bringing them."

"Hooper wanted me to have some for the parlor this morning. But I told her, no, I wanted them saved for you. All of them." She fixed

Letty with a stern eye, defying her to miss the depth of the self-sacrifice.

Letty could hear a fly buzzing against the windowpane. She knew she should ask Betsy—someone—to serve refreshments. Mother liked her afternoon tea, even in August. But it was all too difficult to undertake. She felt her eyelids flutter.

"Letty, you're tired!" said Emma sharply. "We'll be on our way. Hitty wanted me to come over." She always said it this way when she felt the least bit guilty. "I was waiting for you to send for me, but when Mr. Evans came, I could see why you hadn't. Nevertheless, Letty"—she paused, taking her cane in her curled hand—"I would like you to remember that I am your mother. If anything had happened without my knowing—"

"I'm sorry, Mother." Weakness enveloped Letty like a fog. "I really meant—but you see, we've been trying to get the baby to take nourishment and—" Her voice sounded as if it belonged to another. She clenched her fist under the sheet. Must hang on, at least until Mother left.

Emma stood over the bassinette one last time. She stared briefly. "Now Letty, don't have another one," she said reprovingly. "It's not fair to a child, bringing it into the world without its having enough strength to live." She straightened herself up on the cane. "Well Hitty, get your things together. We're going home. Letty needs her rest."

She came painfully around to the other side of the bed and planted a light kiss on Letty's brow. A benison, a signal of her regard, bringing with it her right to say anything. To hurt, to judge—and then to step neatly sideways, knowing she had done her duty. Unaware of the havoc she left. If she had known, she'd have snorted that it gave sign of weakness. Weakness to Emma was a moral lack. The odor of inner decay. She made her slow way down the length of the bedroom, nodding to Nurse Schmidt, scarcely seeing her against the background of the wallpaper.

Hitty gave her sister a sad smile. She'd felt the baby's unresponsiveness. It had communicated itself to her arms. Once she'd found a cat dying in the garden. She'd picked it up and loved it—willing it to take some of her own strength, open its eyes, and leap away. The creature had no sign of injury. Yet it merely lay there, its soft flanks panting in the warm sun. She'd carried it into the kitchen, in search of more adult help—for she'd been quite young at the time.

The maids had shaken their heads. "It's done for, Miss Hitty—can't you see?"

"Oh no!" she'd protested. "It isn't really! We can make it live—I am certain." But the cat had been taken away and Hitty led back to the nursery. She'd screamed, protesting, "Let me see! I don't believe you."

Now it was a baby. Hitty knew they could do nothing. She saw that her sister realized it. Nurse Schmidt would go on doing the necessaries, carrying out Dr. Porter's orders until the last. Nurse Schmidt's job didn't involve "knowing."

Hitty and her mother were met in the hall by Henry Porter.

"Ah, Henry—" said Emma, as if he'd appeared there because she'd wished him on the doorstep.

"Emma—delighted to see you. Hitty too." Dr. Porter's pink face beamed. "How did you find our patients?"

"Henry, don't be evasive with me!" Emma snapped. "That child is dying. I think you should prepare Letty."

His face sobered instantly. "She knows," he said solemnly. "The child was weak to begin with. The midwife reported a slow delivery."

"When are you going to make Nathaniel understand there are to be no more children?" She pounded on the floor of the polished hallway with her cane. Her eyes flashed.

"Now, Emma, I hardly think Nathaniel needs to be told how to manage his affairs."

"That's where you're wrong!" Emma was breathing heavily. "The man is impossible—inconsiderate and utterly selfish. Oh, you needn't glance about like that. Nathaniel's out. In any case, I'd say it all to his face if he were to come walking in that door right now."

Henry drew forth a silk handkerchief, mopped his brow eloquently. "My dear Emma, I hardly think this is the time or the place—"

"I can't think of a better one! As you know, I believe in speaking out."

"Mother," said Hitty mildly, "don't you think we should let Dr. Porter go upstairs and see Letty?"

"Are you trying to tell me that none of this is any of my business?" While Henry Porter and Hitty looked unhappy, avoiding each other's eyes, she plunged on. "It's very much my business. That's my grandchild lying up there too weak to move into life. It's not just an individual matter when something like this happens, Henry. There's a whole family affected—two families." They could see she was trembling, her veined hand taut on her cane.

"Emma." Henry licked his lips nervously, toyed with the gold watch chain that hung across his chest. "You are allowing yourself to get worked up. I agree that this whole thing is very distressing, but—"

"Distressing!" She interrupted him. "A child is carried for nine months, brought into the world with all the labor that involves, is too frail to live—and you call it distressing! Henry, sometimes I think the world would be a better place if we were allowed women doctors." She stared at him. Her look said there was little more that was worth saying. "Go to your patient, doctor." She moved across the hall, beyond him, staring straight at the door. She said to the hovering Taft, "If my carriage is ready—?"

"It awaits, madam."

"You may help me out to it." She motioned for him to take her elbow.

Henry Porter breathed heavily, as if trying to exhale the memory of the words she'd spoken, the things she'd said. He felt anger. They all seemed to think a physician could make miracles happen. He knew it wasn't true.

Henry Porter didn't stay in the house long. There was little for him to do. Letty, it seemed, was recovering. He received the nurse's report in the silence it deserved. Nodded. Folded his hands across his stomach. Gazed down at the bassinette, then at Letty.

"There's no hope for Warren, is there?" she asked.

"Dear girl, there's always hope." But his eyes fell away.

She sighed, feeling his evasion, his wish to depart. "I have so much milk," she said.

He straightened himself. "The nurse knows what to do. It will dry up in a day or so."

"Yes, I suppose so."

"Lovely flowers. Some from your own garden?"

"No. From Mother's."

"Ah," he said, his expression suddenly baleful. "The capable Jaspar—he wins all the prizes for her. My wife talks of it incessantly."

Letty didn't answer him. She wanted to tell him she was angry. That he didn't help her. That while her baby was dying, he spoke of flowers. She willed Henry to leave. Violently willed it.

After what seemed like a long talk at the door, Nurse Schmidt's back expressing satisfaction, he began his descent down the stairs.

"Call me if, you know—"

"Very good, doctor." They were a team, sufficient unto themselves.

Letty pretended to have fallen asleep. She could stand no more.

Nurse Schmidt nodded in her stiff, upright chair. A book threatened to slide off her lap. Every so often she pulled herself upright, glancing quickly around the room to see if her delinquency had been observed. Seeing that it had not, she would clear her throat forcefully, causing Letty's eyelids to move, but not open.

At last the heat overcame Nurse Schmidt's efforts at self-restraint. The book slid from her relaxed fingers, and she dreamed of cool streams in her native Germany, heard her father's voice telling her she might travel far, if only she had courage.

The August garden panted under the sun's inexorable rays. One of Emma's roses—the most fullblown—responded as did its sisters still growing on stiff stems in the flower beds beyond Letty's windows. As the clock on the mantel chimed five times, a single petal fell from the dark red blossom, to lie in china stillness on the mahogany surface. At the same time, a bird flew by the window, its wings clapping in startling sound.

The noise wakened Nurse Schmidt. She rubbed her eyes furtively, as if thereby she could cover her humanness.

Letty moaned. "Something happened—" she said distinctly.

"It was nothing." Nurse Schmidt got up, tidying her long starched apron, pulling at the skirt of her dress.

"You can't make me believe that!" Letty frowned at the nurse. "Through the open window—something left."

"You had a dream." The crisp voice reproved her, deciding it all for her in terms that could be understood.

Letty paid no attention. Leaning sideways, she tugged at the coverings over her child. Then screamed. "He's dead! My baby is gone!"

"Let me see," said the nurse. She bent, felt the small cheek with one competent hand. Held the minute wrist momentarily. "You are right," she said shortly. She began to pull the sheet over Warren's head.

"No, give him to me."

"Mrs. Mackenzie, the child has expired!"

"I want to hold him one last time."

"Very well." Nurse Schmidt's lip curled in disgust. "We must notify the undertakers." She handed the lifeless body to Letty and left the room.

Nathaniel was informed of his son's decease as he entered the front door. "Ah," was all he said. He handed his hat to Taft. "Is there whiskey in the study?"

"Yes, sir."

"Tell Cook I shan't be home for dinner."

"Very good, sir. The staff would like to offer their condolences, sir."

"Thank you, Taft. Mrs. Mackenzie, is she very upset?"

"I believe she's taking it hard, sir."

"Someone better notify the Benedicts. The old lady'll raise hell if she isn't told. Claim we tried to keep her in the dark."

"I'll see the information is sent, sir."

After he'd had three drinks, Nathaniel left. Letty had heard him return. She had lain there waiting, wondering if he would mount the stairs to see her. But no. She had disgraced him. Her efforts had been in vain. She stared at the spot where the crib had stood, wishing she could cry. Her eyes ached, but the tears remained unshed. She reached for her Bible. In a trembling hand she added a few words to the flyleaf. Next to Warren's name: *died, August 17, 1885.*

7

As Letty regained her strength she tried to fill the empty places of her heart by turning more to Brett. She felt linked to him by more than motherhood. Their birthdays fell on the same day. On October 14, as Letty became thirty-nine, the little boy turned four.

They took walks outside under a shower of golden leaves, Katie pushing the thin-wheeled wicker perambulator while Letty kept pace beside her. Brett's eyes seemed to take in the movement of the red and lemon benison, for he would reach up a chubby arm to gurgle his astonishment or his pleasure. They were never sure which.

"Katie, what do you suppose he thinks about?" Letty asked idly, more to hear the sound of her own voice than Katie's answer. For they couldn't know. Brett was his own enigma.

"If one could say that, ma'am, sure an' one would have the answer to many riddles." Katie maneuvered the pram around a sharp bend in the path. They were strolling in the gardens of the great house. It loomed behind them, impressive as an animal that lurks among trees, waiting to gobble them, should they foolishly come too close. It was an odd analogy, thought Letty, considering that the house gave all of them shelter, warmth from the chill of winter that was coming.

Letty found herself wishing she could remain forever out here with Katie and Brett, the world stopped at autumn, embroidered by purple asters and the lemon stars of chrysanthemums cascading from their own weight to arch over the pathways. She found being with the Irish girl soothing. Katie had simplicity coupled with native wit. She told tales of a home life that was so different from anything Letty had ever known as to make it sound unreal. Yet Katie's enthusiasm gave it a reality. An odd world where people cared about one another—touched bodies as they lay snuggled under one blanket, huddled before the fire. Somehow, although she invited Katie to carry on in her entertaining way, the pleasure Letty felt would sometimes turn to irritation. Nothing could be that idyllic. On one such occasion she interrupted Katie sharply.

"We'd better be turning back now. It's getting cold."

"Yes, ma'am," said Katie, catching the note of displeasure, though not understanding what it was she'd done or said. But Mrs. Mackenzie was like that. Moody, they called it in the kitchen. Since the baby's death, it had surely gotten worse.

As they rounded the corner, there was the sound of a carriage. Katie was aware of her mistress' stiffening. Another few steps, however, showed them it wasn't Bates.

"It's Mother," said Letty quietly. "A good thing we were coming in. She'll expect to have tea."

It wasn't Emma. Seated in the parlor, like a stout fieldmouse, sat Hitty. Undivested of her coat and bonnet, she was waiting to be invited to make herself at home.

"I hope you didn't mind my coming," Hitty said at once. She toyed with her gloves, gray and soft in her lap.

"Of course not," lied Letty. She never had anything to say to Hitty. It wouldn't do to let on. Her visits must be suffered through, like Mother's, but of course they were different. Hitty tugged at one, like a cat begging to be let inside on a winter's night. If one gave in, then it was there forever, curled on the hearth.

Hitty, thought Letty with annoyance, should have her own home. It was too bad of her not to have had it all arranged by this time. She disliked the guilt she always felt when Hitty looked around the house with obvious envy, wanted to go upstairs to visit the children, asked to read to them.

"Were you expecting someone else?" asked Hitty sweetly.

"As a matter of fact, yes," said Letty suddenly. She had not known on what day he would come, but Henry Porter was sending a new doctor—a physician who would look at Brett.

"He's doing so well, Henry," Letty had protested the decision, feeling the ice about her heart creeping up in great slabs to enclose its palpitating. "Surely you cannot be suspecting anything? He has learned so many new words."

Henry had looked down at her from his great height of superior knowledge, patted her hand. "Letty, Letty—don't put words in my mouth. I simply want Dr. Grey to have a look at him."

"But why?" she had persisted, sure now there was something

wrong. "Who is this Dr. Grey?" Said it harshly. "We are content with you, Henry."

"I know, and I appreciate your confidence. Sometimes," he'd stroked his chin, forming his goatee into a point, "one likes to have one's judgment confirmed."

"Then there is something wrong!"

"Letty, dearest girl—"

She'd allowed him to notify Dr. Grey. Why, she couldn't now imagine.

Hitty was staring at her. "Then I should go?"

"Oh heavens, no!" Letty tried to say it lightly. "As a matter of fact, you might be interested to stay. If he comes, that is."

"Who are you expecting?"

"It's a consultant. Someone Henry wants to look over Brett."

"The baby is ill?" Alarm in Hitty's face.

"No. At least, I don't see it. He's made such strides of late. I was quite surprised at Henry—" Letty stopped abruptly. "Let's have tea in my morning room."

"How nice," said Hitty accommodatingly.

It was the day Dr. Grey had chosen. Whether Letty had forgotten or whether he had not said, it mattered not. She and Hitty had just begun the afternoon repast when his carriage drove up.

Dr. Grey was a man to inspire confidence without overwhelming. Pink cheeked, with blond hair fading at his sideburns, blue eyes that regarded them kindly, he came into their midst more as a friend than a physician. None of the fussy clamor that always seemed to proceed Henry. A very slight odor of ether entered the room with him. Exceptionally clean hands, a black bag—these were the only clues to place his visit outside the realm of a social call.

"May I offer you tea?" asked Letty. "We were just sitting down." She glanced at Phillips, who'd shown the good doctor in. "Another cup, if you please."

"Perhaps if I might see the child first?" Dr. Grey set down his bag. As he moved, the smell of ether increased. How did he stand it? Possibly one became accustomed to its acerbity?

Letty addressed Phillips once more. "Ask Katie to bring Brett down."

"Very good, ma'am."

"It will only take a moment," she said to Dr. Grey pleasantly. "Oh, by the way, this is my sister, Miss Benedict."

He bowed. To Letty's embarrassment, Hitty flushed.

He agreed to take a seat. The weather was discussed. It was fine for a fall day—though it wouldn't be long before winter would be upon them.

Abruptly he asked if there were some place he could examine the child. A flat surface would be needed. "—such as a bed? The boy's own bed."

"That would mean going up to the nursery."

He rose from his chair. "I wouldn't mind. I need to talk to the person who has charge of the child."

Letty colored up. "Nanny would be the best one. Though there is an Irish girl—"

"Where is the nursery?" He appeared impatient.

Letty rang the bell pull. Then, because of his manner, she opened the door and called, "Betsy?"

But Katie was coming down the stairs. The heavy weight of Brett, clad in his sailor suit, dragged down her arms.

"Go back up," Letty called to her. "This is Dr. Grey. He wants to examine Brett in the nursery."

Katie wheeled about, using the bannister for balance. Brett saw his mother and cried to her, his small arm reaching, his hand red and swollen from being chewed. His mouth was slack with drool.

"You see!" Letty exclaimed to the doctor. "He is beginning to talk. He couldn't have recognized me a year ago. We are so encouraged by his advances." She defied the doctor to tell her otherwise.

He annoyed her by ignoring her statement and began to follow Katie up the stairs. "I'll find my way," he said shortly.

"We'll wait for you here," said Letty. She mightn't have bothered. His departing back gave no indication of his having heard her. Letty retreated to the morning room, meeting Betsy on the landing.

"When Dr. Grey has finished with Brett, please see he is brought back here," she said.

Betsy's eyes widened. "Dr. Grey, ma'am?"

"Yes, yes," said Letty impatiently. "Just wait outside the nursery door. I don't want him to leave without talking to me."

"Very good, ma'am," answered a bewildered Betsy. It was the first she'd heard of any "Dr. Grey."

Letty was wringing her hands as she sat behind the tea tray. Hitty perched, watchful, on the edge of one of the lemon silk chairs. Almost as confused as Betsy.

"If Henry doesn't think Brett's ill, why has he brought this man here?"

"I don't know!" Letty spat it out. She didn't like what was going on. His manner—so pleasant at first. Then that odd air of dismissal. She was, after all, the child's mother. She wanted to go upstairs, to be present while Brett was examined. But to have done so would have been to intrude on Nanny. He'd said it so bluntly, "the person who has charge of the child." If he'd wanted her, surely he would have said so?

She jumped as he returned to the room. "Please come in. I am sure you found Brett to be improving remarkably. You'd like some tea, wouldn't you? I had a cup brought."

He nodded slowly and took the straight-backed chair he'd occupied before. As if he had little intention of lingering. He placed his hands, palms together, and bowed his head until the tips of his fingers caressed his brow. "How much has Henry prepared you?" he said at last.

"Prepared me?" Letty half rose in her chair. "Prepared me for what?" The hammering of her heart was so loud, she could barely hear his voice. "What is it that I should know?"

The blue eyes looked at her. Hitty noticed they were kind eyes, much kinder than when he had first reentered the room. She decided she liked him in spite of his odd manner. A man who needed taking care of, she thought. Wondered, briefly, if his wife did this.

Letty was staring at him, white-faced.

"You are going to have to explain what you mean, Dr. Grey," she said firmly.

"You must forgive me." He passed one of those large, clean palms over his face suddenly. "I am too much around the very sick—hospitals—other medical men. I never did have much skill with social graces. Mrs. Mackenzie, your son is gravely ill."

Letty gave a little cry. She dropped her hand, causing teacup and saucer to clatter, rattling the silver spoon. "You are sure? Oh, how can you be sure? You've only just seen him. I was certain Henry told you the great progress Brett's been making these past months."

His face looked enormously sad. "It has nothing to do with that, Mrs. Mackenzie. I wish to heaven I were not the one to have to break it to you. I was fully under the impression Dr. Porter had kept you informed of the condition from the beginning."

"Condition? What condition?"

"Tuberculosis of the bone. It's fairly far along, I'm afraid."

"Tuberculosis—I don't understand. What are you trying to tell me? Doctor, I'm afraid you are going to have to be very specific. I don't understand what tuberculosis of the bone means to my child."

His eyes were kind as he spoke. "It means he has only a short while to live. We do not exactly know how long. But we can tell you this. It would be as well to prepare yourself."

Letty lifted her hand to her mouth. "Oh God!" she said, muffling the statement with her fingers. Her lace-edged cuff trailed out from under the soft blue of her sleeve.

"My sister has already lost one child this year!" Hitty said haughtily, as if by reprimanding him she could get him to change his mind, to deliver another, kinder verdict.

He couldn't, of course, oblige. "I'm so sorry," he said, looking first at one of them, then at the other. "I'm afraid this has been a fearful shock." His eyes seemed to widen, caressing Letty with their warmth.

"It's all right," she said quietly. "Now you've gone this far, you must tell us what to expect."

"He'll get weaker. Subject to ill health. Pneumonia may take him." He received his refilled cup from her hands. "It sounds harsh, but it would be merciful in the long run. The disease cripples."

"I see." Letty pressed her lips together. "So, another of my sons is not to survive."

"Care should be taken in handling the boy. I've given the nurse instructions. Your other two children—"

"I have three," she said crisply. "Albert has a damaged heart. He keeps pretty much to the schoolroom—being almost eleven."

"Ah," he said. "We must hope none of the others is so afflicted."

She looked at him with an odd expression. "The girls will survive," she said simply. "It is only the boys of this family who are cursed. Or so it seems to their father."

"I would like to speak to you of something else," he said, ignoring her statement. "Your sister tells me you recently lost another child."

"Warren lived but a few days," Letty replied simply.

"How long ago was this?"

"He expired on August seventeenth of this year."

"A little over two months ago." He seemed to consider the matter. "Many physicians make the mistake of concentrating on their patient without paying much attention to the family." He spoke slowly, giving the impression of weighing each word. "But the relatives suffer. Mental anguish can lead to complications—even physical illness." He reddened slightly. "Not all my colleagues would agree, of course. Yet it is something I've observed."

Hitty said, her eyes shining, "I never heard a doctor speak so before. Have you, Letty?"

He ignored Hitty. They were learning it was a characteristic of his, to concentrate on one issue at a time.

"When we talk of the family," he said carefully, "we have to speak primarily in terms of the mother. After all, she is the one who gives birth, who experiences the greatest sense of loss." He stopped, appearing to gauge the effect his words were having on Letty. Then he went on. "My practice has been confined mainly to children. But more and more, I have to treat the mothers."

"I am perfectly all right," said Letty evenly. "If you can save my child—?"

"We cannot save your child. It isn't in our power. You, on the other hand, I can provide with sedatives, calmatives to help you to bear your trial."

"He's not gone yet!" she said fiercely.

"Letty," urged Hitty, "please listen to Dr. Grey. Dearest, he's offering to help you."

Had Letty heard anything that was said to her? She gazed at the physician, her eyes childlike. "I keep telling you, it's not I who needs your help. Make my boy well."

He got up, patted her hand. "I want you to promise me something."

"What?"

"If you should need me at any time, you've only to call." He was gone as quickly as he had arrived. Without fanfare.

Hitty got up and went to her sister. "I'm so sorry."

"How am I going to tell Nathaniel?"

The question lay between them, naked and tremulous. Seeking to be covered by the clothing of an answer. There was none that would suffice.

"If you just said—" tried Hitty, her round face troubled.

"No. Listen, you don't understand Nathaniel. None of you do, except perhaps Mother. He's a difficult man—drinking far too much lately." Then bitterly, "Well, I suppose it's easy really. He despises Brett. He won't care."

"You can't mean that!"

"Hitty, you are so naive. Brett's presence embarrasses Nat. It would be a relief to him not to have the child around."

"You've both still got three lovely children, Letty."

"You don't understand. You don't see any of it. I think you'd better leave now."

"Yes, of course. What shall I tell Mother?"

"Tell her all of it. You were here. You heard."

"You're sure you don't want to break it to her yourself?"

"Hitty, stop being sentimental. Mother wants to be kept informed. She doesn't care who does the telling."

It was November. The trees were leafless, the gutters choked with sodden masses of decaying vegetation. It rained incessantly, and the skies were full of dark, scudding clouds.

Letty had found a way to ease her sorrow. Once or twice a week, when Nathaniel could spare his services, Bates would bring the carriage to the front door and drive her to the cold churchyard. A dreary place even on a summer's day, it afforded little comfort or beauty as it lay soaked from the showers. The yews with which it was planted offered an impenetrable wall beneath the gray trunks of the elms. Here was a place set aside for grief. Letty knelt by the new grave that lay alongside those of Nat's parents—Warren's grave. She knelt on the damp earth, paying small heed to the discomfort or the stains left on her clothing for a distraught Nanette to sponge away.

Head bowed, she did not pray. Instead she hoped to do penance for all she imagined she must have done, to have incurred the anger of the God she believed in.

Those who went with her to the churchyard stood apart from her. Sometimes it was Katie, often it was Amelia. Bates, as always, stayed with the horses.

Katie would hold flowers. There were none in the gardens now, but a brief stop at Emma's would elicit a posy or two from the hothouse the able Jaspar maintained. Katie, at a signal from her mistress, would approach, handing over the blooms. Together they would pour fresh water into the crystal vase, remove the blackened sticks that were all that remained of the last batch of geraniums or camelias.

119

Amelia's presence wasn't helpful, like Katie's. "Mama, do I have to come?"

"Yes, you do."

"But why?" The gray eyes demanded an answer. "I don't like graveyards. They're dreary."

"Amelia, it is important for a girl to learn to control her feelings. We aren't supposed to give up just because we find something distasteful."

Amelia, sulky, sitting opposite Letty in the carriage, her hands hidden in a muff of rabbit fur gray as the sky. A tippet of the same fur about her neck itched her, causing her to withdraw her hands from the muff and scratch surreptitiously.

"Amelia, stop it! You're raising red marks on your skin."

But one had to scratch. It was unbearable. Amelia tried to will her neck to become narrower so as not to touch the fur. It didn't work.

While Mama was in the churchyard, Amelia would wander into the church, sit in one of the shiny pews, and stare up at the multicolored window over the altar. A picture of God coming down, his hand hovering over a dove. God was coming out of a cloud. Only his shoulders and head were visible—his muscular arms. Would he crush the dove? God must be very terrible.

Letty's voice sought her out. "Amelia, I asked you to stay with me. Why are you always running off?" Letty's face was pink from the cold, damp pearls clinging to her beaver coat, her enormous muff. Her eyes had an odd look. She was different now—ever since Warren had died. Amelia didn't want to look, but her mother caught her about the shoulders, making her face her. There it was again—that expression —veiled. Someone peering from behind curtains.

Amelia attempted to pull away. "Shall we go, Mama?"

"Why are you always in such a hurry? I like to sit and say a tiny prayer."

"May I go out to the carriage?"

"Oh, I suppose so. Don't talk to Bates. It upsets the horses."

Letty sat where Amelia had and stared at the same view of the window. The afternoon was waning. Purples and blues were more somber than in the morning. It was why she chose to come at this hour. It wasn't right to feel uplifted, even by something as glorious as a stained-glass window. God wanted her to feel sadness, pain. She sighed.

Mr. Evans had assured her that God cared. "Not a sparrow falls to the ground, Letty—"

She wondered about caged sparrows. Voices from a narrow cage. Could they still sing?

She hadn't wept for Warren. She wouldn't weep for Brett. Her tears were too selfish—too insistent upon mercy.

When she got home, Nathaniel was waiting for her. He glowered at her as they met in the hallway. Amelia had gone with Bates to the side of the house so that she might enter by the kitchen entrance and mount the back stairs to Nanny.

"Letty, a word with you."

"I must get warm—"

"Go on up to your morning room. I'll join you there."

She sat by the fire, crouched over herself. Surely God would respect her offering? A pure and a contrite heart, it said somewhere? Where had she heard it? She stared at the flames, seeing them lick about the form of Joan of Arc. That again! She'd thought herself rid of the specter.

"Letty, you're asking for trouble." Nathaniel's voice behind her made her jump. She tasted fear, hot in her throat. Heart pounding.

"Trouble, Nat? I don't follow you."

He took the seat opposite her. Brooding, dour. "All this driving off to the graveyard, dragging Amelia with you. It's not a good sign, Letty. Shows instability. It's got to come to a halt."

"You can't mean it?"

"Never more serious about anything in my life. Been talking to Henry about you, Letty."

"What right did you have to do that, Nat? I'm not ill."

"Just the point. Think you may be."

"It's outrageous!" She gathered her indignation around her like a blanket, feeling it thin, inadequate to cover her needs. A quiver of fear passed through her, delicate as a feather, yet strong enough to cause her to set her teeth to stop their chattering.

She heard him going on, dully. "—your time of life—often after the loss of a child—Henry said you were to be watched—"

"Watched! Who is to watch me? Am I then to be a prisoner in my own house?"

"If necessary." He said it evenly, his small mouth moving over the words. She was the condemned—he the judge and jury. Yet what had she done?

He wished to punish her for his sons. One by one they were going —letting him down. She lowered her gaze to her hands, saw them as bound. She realized she would like to let blood from her wrists—see it flow—a dark river from the center of her being.

"I am forbidding you to go to the churchyard, Letty. Bates has already been told to disregard your orders." He crossed his legs, sat

121

back in his chair—or was it her chair? She'd always regarded this as her room. Was there to be nothing left her?

He had taken a cigar out of his coat pocket and was holding it before his nose, inhaling its aroma, as if only the small, meaningless matters of life had existence. She had disappeared. She felt a cry of protest in her throat. She panicked. She longed to reach out to her husband, beg him to take her hands, hold her back in some kind of reality. Any reality.

Instead she sat there, looking self-contained. Her oval mirror was behind Nat's chair, giving her back the room, her own dead face in its frame of hair, the lemon silk chairs and the gentle lap of the firelight upon the shadowed walls. The stranger who gazed at her from the mirror—having her own eyes, her own chin—would tell Nat nothing. Nothing but that she was chilled from the graveyard. The woman in the reflection tilted her head to one side, her thoughts drawing across her face like veiling. Weren't Eastern women disguised that way, only their eyes showing?

He broke in on her thoughts. "Letty, I want you to return to normal."

"Normal?" Perhaps she hadn't heard right?

Impatient, he puffed on the cigar he'd lit, gesticulating with the match before he shook it out. "I've got plans—Christmas plans. You're to pull yourself together, try to take hold. It's not that far away. Lot of things to be seen to."

"Why, Nat? What is happening at Christmas?"

"A party," he said as if he'd mentioned he wanted roast duck for dinner. "John Abbott will be coming to stay—and his two children of course. There'll be the usual meal on Christmas Day. But I told them I'd give them a real party—orchestra, dancing, all that sort of thing. Pick your day, so long as it's the week after Christmas. They can only stay till New Year's. John wants to be back in Virginia by then. Livvie's getting old enough to attend the balls."

"Livvie?" Her eyes widened. He'd hesitated just a shade over that name. "You mean little Olivia's growing up."

"Certainly," he replied. His lids came down, narrowing his vision so that he could look at her through slits. Remain unreadable. "Quite the young lady now."

"How old would Livvie be now?"

He moved the hand holding the cigar through the air, describing a half circle. "I have no idea. You'd need to ask John. Shouldn't matter to you anyhow. Take it from me, she's old enough to be seated with the adults." He pointed his finger at her. "So don't go placing her with the children. Embarrassing her. They're my guests, Letty!" He shouted it.

She could see his large ears, flat against his head, showing pink under his hair. His locks were thinning. She wasn't the only one to be growing old. Forty—she'd be forty next October. When would it all begin to hurt, as Mother hurt?

"So you see why you have to stop all this grieving, Letty. This— I don't know what to call it—but it's disturbing." He frowned, puffing violently on the cigar, a steam engine taking a steep grade. "Yes, it's frankly upsetting."

"I thought I was very quiet about my feelings. I haven't cried— carried on. Not one tear have I shed for Warren."

"Warren!" he said nastily. "The child was only alive a day or so, yet you give him a name, a personality, as if he'd lived a real life."

"He was real!" she cried.

"Come on, Letty. He was practically a miscarriage. You can't have living children anymore. Henry said so."

"Henry?" She felt her lips move over the name. Henry had judged her as faulty, told Nat so, asked that she be watched, not allowed to give orders to Bates or take flowers to the graveyard. Then who would assure Warren that, even in death, he was loved—longed for?

"Letty!" Sharply. "You have this way of not paying attention. It's part of what I'm telling you. You've got to pull yourself together, madam. Play the part of hostess, whether you feel up to it or not."

"Why?" She asked flatly, aware that she was sounding like Amelia. If a child could question, surely so could she? But what was it she had told her daughter? We must learn to endure? Suddenly it seemed too much, that she suffer through a party, with house guests she had not invited. Who were they to invade her house, anyway? Just because Livvie Abbott was growing old enough to go to balls.

Nat was gazing at her curiously. He had opened his eyes wide, was examining her as though he'd never seen her before. "Letty, did I hear you right?"

She lifted her head. Haughty, though her heart was beating a wild rhythm. "I asked you 'why.' Why do I have to give up my mourning simply to please you and your friends? I don't care if it's Christmas. I've suffered a tremendous loss. My baby is lying out there in the earth—" Suddenly she wasn't questioning anymore. The dignity had fallen away, a cloak that had never really belonged to her. She was trembling and exposed. "You can't make me go through with it," she said feebly.

"It's as Henry described. Letty, I'm going to try to be fair, to give you your chance to become normal. Cease this brooding self-pity. Show me you can go out of the house and call on friends again. Buy some new dresses." His face indicated deep disgust. "Else I shall be forced to see it as melancholia."

123

"What do you mean, Nat?" Her hand went to her frilled collar. She was terrified, disbelieving her ears.

"I'm determined to be generous with you, Letty. But there are limits. I can have you put away, Letty."

She stared at him. Joan of Arc. So that was what she'd been fearing all along—the unprotested disposal of women, especially women who couldn't be gotten rid of any other way. Servants could be dismissed. Poor women, or so she'd heard, saw their men merely walk away. But women of her kind were like the ones in history. They couldn't just be sent into the night. Mary Queen of Scots was kept a prisoner for years because she represented a threat to her half-sister, Elizabeth. She must have known that death was inevitable.

He got up from his chair, his motion heavy and awkward. Not a very tall man, he'd always had power. How long had it been since she'd known he had power? The first time she'd laid eyes on him, she'd imagined what it would be like to enter a ballroom leaning on the arm of Nathaniel Mackenzie. Had Joan of Arc played with power, mustering her army of men to lead France? Women were fools to invite distinction. Their safety lay in not being noticed. All those poor creatures burned as witches back in Salem. If they'd hidden their talents . . . She tried to will herself to become one with the chair.

Nat loomed before her, glowering. "It's possible to get you put away. Henry would certify you insane."

"Henry's my friend," she said numbly.

"Henry Porter is employed by this family—more particularly by me—as our personal physician. He'll do as I say."

She thought he was about to leave and sat frozen, waiting until the moment when she could be alone. Think it out. The wall had come sooner than she'd believed possible. Flattening.

He wasn't quite finished. "About Brett." His finger wagged before her face. "You've got to let that child go, too."

"Then Henry told you."

"Oh, I've known," he said carelessly, "ever since the brat was a year or so old. Henry was sure. He only wanted the consultant because you were insistent there'd been a change. We had informed Nanny."

"You knew? Nanny knew? Yet it was kept from me—the mother of the child!" She was on her feet. Faced him. "Who am I to you—your wife or—?" Rage prevented her from finishing it.

"It's because of your hysteria," he said quietly. "Just like you're acting now. All of us agreed it would be better if you weren't told."

"Nanny." She collapsed back in the chair. Nanny was the hardest. She'd trusted Nanny.

"Don't be maudlin, Letty. Nanny's a servant same as the others. They take their orders from me."

She sat where he had left her, staring at the fire. Who had Joan of Arc been able to count on? She watched the logs blazing up. Fear had made her icy. Fear and a sense of shame. She raised her head, looking once more into the mirror that hung on the wall behind Nathaniel's now empty chair. She'd thought they'd respected her—the servants—the members of the household who pressed about her, tapping with subservient fingers on her doorway, answering the peal of her bell. It was an illusion, like all the other illusions she'd seen through. She ran her tongue over her stiff lips, feeling them puckered as from acid fruit. Already she saw the bars on the windows. Where would he have her taken? Stories of wives shut up in attic rooms took on a new reality. She had scoffed at them till now.

He would cage her. She got up and went to her desk, drew paper toward her, and dipped her pen into the inkwell. She supposed herself ready to make up that party list.

Her pen moved. She sketched a bird in flight, gave it talons, a scrap of flesh between the talons. Something that had once been a rabbit. Mountains beneath the bird.

A male bird. Didn't they call them cocks? Cocky in power.

Brett had a heavy cold.

"But I want him to see the Christmas greenery!" Letty told Katie. "In fact, all the children can come downstairs, just before the guests arrive. Have Nanny dress them."

Katie nodded and went back to the nursery to convey the message. Letty turned before the mirror. It was so hard to get one's face to match the party mood. She stared at the sea-foam silk, picked out dully from among the models Miss Puxley had showed her. "You will be ravishing, madame. Not one will be able to equal you."

What did she care if her body were encased in folds, the deep flounce of lace that crossed over her breasts lost among the scatter of roses, blush and cream? That her painted fan had just come over from France and that her skirt was heaped into a train, festooned with crimson ribbons, emerald velvet bows? It was so hard to be joyous.

"Madame should smile," coaxed Nanette. She fussed with a tiny tendril of Letty's hair that had escaped the myriad pins. Tucked it back and fastened it, standing on tiptoe to assure herself that the jade ostrich plumes were secured. "There! You are quite ready."

"Dear Nanette, this is Christmas week, you should have some time off."

"I shall, madame, never fear."

Well, thought Letty, I have achieved the impossible, at least outwardly. She had cast aside her mourning, just how she wasn't sure. She had thrown herself into making lists, ordering food, seeing that the great Turkey carpet in the salon was rolled back. All this she had done

126

with an enthusiasm she hoped would impress Taft, her head held high anytime he looked her way.

Only in the secret dark of her own bed did she relax, her face pressed wet and taut against the pillow as she stifled her sobs.

This reprieve, too, was denied her when Nathaniel joined her. Pressing his stocky form against the mattress, he might decide to pull her to him, indicating she solace him according to his mood. She would comply by clasping him between her hands, or let him rub his organ against her breasts until he spurted. She was a tool to him. A tool whose use was limited. She knew he pleasured himself elsewhere. She tried not to speculate on it. Determined to be the perfect wife. To convince Nat that he should change his mind about having her put away. She had to believe in a future.

There was a tap on the door. It was Katie.

"Nanny sent me to say—" Her eyes moved over her mistress. "Oh, begging your pardon, madam, but I've never seen you more lovely. Sure an' the guests will be terrible impressed."

"Thank you, Katie. What was it Nanny wanted to tell me?"

"She'll be after takin' the little ones down the back stairs now, ma'am. Only we don't think Brett should go."

Two days ago, Katie had carried Brett into the hallway to see the decorations. He'd stared at the greenery, the holly boughs, and the swags of yew tied over the fireplace. Taft had reached up and wound the bell. Its cleverly devised musical box, hidden in its silvery interior, had played "Adeste Fidelis." Brett's attention had been caught. Looking all about, he had finally been able to understand the tinkling tones came from the ornament.

"See, darling—" Letty had held him up. "See the bell?"

"Bah," said Brett.

"No, precious—*bell.*"

"Bah." He had reached for it. Hands sticky. Why did she love him when he was so unattractive? Yet she did. More than any of the others. Was it because he alone needed her? Polly needed her as one needed pretty frocks, a beaded reticule, or a tortoise shell comb for the hair. Brett, having no vanity, needed her concern.

She stared now at Katie. "Why don't you think Brett should come downstairs with the others?"

"He's that poorly, ma'am. Coughing like he is, Nanny thought it'd be best if he was to be kept in one atmosphere."

"Oh dear, I hadn't realized his cold was that bad." She was frightened suddenly. She must go to Brett. "I have to visit him. The others can wait. Has the doctor been called?"

"Beggin' your pardon, ma'am, but wouldn't it be best if we let the little ones see the downstairs? It's close to time for the guests to arrive. I don't imagine we should wait, now should we?"

Katie was tugging at her with her common sense. Letty wanted to slap her. Of course the girl was right. The guests—it had been planned for the children to slip down before the guests came.

"Of course you're right. We'll have to get it over," she said, pushing Katie with her haste to get to Brett. "Tell Nanny I'll meet her downstairs. Not to bring the baby. You stay with him, Katie. Do what you can?" Her eyes pleaded.

Polly spun, holding her dress out like butterfly wings on the unnaturally smooth floor of the salon. *"Wheee!"* she screamed. "I can dance! See, Mama, I can dance!"

Nanny ran forward, her finger to her lips. "Now, now, Miss Polly, no noise, mind. We've only come to see, not to play about."

"But it's for dancing!" Polly ignored her. Feet tripping high as a goat on a steep mountain—caught up in her own fantasy of ball gowns and music playing. "It's so beautiful, Mama—and you are like a queen!"

Amelia stood by and watched it all. Not for her the need to dance, to move her body about in celebration of candlelights and dark green boughs, red ribbons like satin roses crowning festooning yews. She could rejoice in her mind, absorb it all and take it away with her, back to the dreary nursery. Someday she'd have a house like this. She would be the hostess, waiting under the portraits—and in a ball dress that draped her body like Mama's, she'd greet her guests. Yet, even as she tried to cloak her vision with reality, she felt removed from it. Her solemn face grew longer and quieter as she sensed the great crevasse that separated the grown-up world from that of children. Warm gruel for supper, set at the nursery table, while below they waltzed and dined on duckling, pheasant, thinly sliced ham. Would she ever grow up into it?

"Now, children, you've had your look. Up the back stairs with you!" Nanny's voice rounded them up. Just the two of them, for Albert would be coming downstairs for a while. Turned eleven, Albert was becoming a man. Besides, Sam would be there.

For Amelia, Sam was a figure of mystery. Whenever she could, she would watch for him, whether it was on a trip to the schoolroom or passing below—two flights below—in the hall. She would have died had she suspected Sam knew of her gaze. Walking in the twilight world between boyhood and adult climes, he strode with ponderous step. Needing all his energies, Amelia half guessed, to maintain the appearance of more youth than child.

She saw him now, as she had hoped she might, coming down the long staircase. As a guest, it was his privilege to tread the front stairs. She stared up at him, fearing—dreading—he might catch her gaze.

"Good evening, Mrs. Mackenzie."

"Good evening, Sam."

"Mr. Mackenzie invited Father and me for a drink before the guests arrive." He indicated the closed study door.

She bowed her head. "Tell my husband I'll be right down."

He seemed puzzled, then presumed she had some further errand to take her to the upper floors. He nodded quietly and opened the study door.

"Where is your sister?" Letty asked before the boy had disappeared.

"She's with us." He spoke calmly.

Letty received it in her own way. Livvie could go where she, Nathaniel's wife, wasn't invited. It was simple really. An idiot could understand it.

As Sam closed the door the voices and laughter were blended—low tones a background for the spinning ribbon of a girlish treble. "Oh, Uncle Nat, you're such a darling!"

Letty gathered up her skirts and went upstairs.

One look at the child told her that her worst fears were being realized. His eyes were closed, his breath coming in wheezing gasps. Katie hovered like a ministering angel, her kind eyes dark and sad, the flames of her hair extinguished in the shadows of the night nursery. "He's that poorly, ma'am."

"We must fetch the doctor at once!"

"Yes, ma'am."

Nanny joined them. "It would be as well. I've rubbed his little chest—used the mustard plaster—and you can see the steam kettle's going, but it doesn't seem to be doing very much good."

The girls had come to stand in the doorway and stare.

"You two girls, go back in the nursery. Get your sewing or something to keep busy. We've got enough things going on here tonight without you causing trouble."

Letty saw them with eyes that had lost their awareness. Brett was her only concern. Her lovely frock crushed beneath her knees, she knelt beside the crib. Observed the flushed cheeks, the breath that came at such cost. The odor of friar's balsam, part and parcel of the sickroom whenever the steam kettle was called into service, mingled with the sour smell of fever, the indigo sharpness of kerosene from the lamp turned down low behind a screen. Faces took on sinister lines as silhouettes moved across bare walls. Letty laid her hand on the fevered child, moaned to herself.

129

Nanny drew near. Placed her concern around Letty. "Milady, with all due respect, ye've guests coming. Let us take care of the boy. If word could be sent to the doctor—"

Letty looked up with startled eyes. "Guests? Nanny, you can't expect me to go downstairs with Brett like this?"

"Milady," her voice chiding, as if she were speaking to one of the children, "the master'll be looking for you. I don't mean to talk out of turn, but God love ye, Mrs. Mackenzie, there's no way it'd look right, you up here and them that's invited down there."

Nanny's soft, pleading voice got through to Letty. Of course she'd have to go downstairs. She got to her feet awkwardly.

"You're right, Nanny. I'll see that the doctor is summoned at once. But please—please let me know the moment there's any change." She couldn't bring herself to say "worsening."

"Of course, milady. You know you can count on us to do the very best we know how."

Would the best be enough? What had that strange doctor said? "If he should take cold—pneumonia. The best way in the long run. Might seem harsh to you but—"

She sat at her desk in the morning room to pen a note to Henry Porter. As a family friend, he was invited to the party and would be at the house anyway. What she was asking was for Henry to come sooner —at the earliest possible moment.

Then she realized that she didn't want Henry. The words Henry had spoken to Nathaniel about her made her never want to see him again. She felt ill when she remembered what he'd said—that she should be watched, that she might be succumbing to "melancholia." Pen poised over paper, she realized how much she loathed Henry. More, she feared him, his power to bring about what her husband wished. "We can put you away" echoed in her mind.

She wrote: *Dear Dr. Grey. My little son is gravely ill. You assured me I could send for you. Please come just as soon as you can? I realize this is an imposition, considering the hour and the season, but I am beside myself.* She signed it with a pen that bit deep into the paper, *Laetitia Mackenzie.*

As she walked down the stairs, the first guests were on the doorstep. She slid into the salon, looking about for someone to hand her note to. Taft was busy with the arrivals. The maids were bringing in plates of food. Phillips was guarding the steaming punchbowl, ensconced in the middle of the long serving board. To whom could she turn?

It was already too late to go in search of anyone. She took up her position before the fireplace, conscious suddenly that her dress was the same color as the one worn by Sarah Mackenzie in the portrait above her.

Nat came to join her, his glance cold. Yet, by the slight lift of an eyebrow, the flutter of his lids, he conveyed to her that her appearance satisfied him. She seized the opportunity to ask him about the note. "Oh, Nat, Brett's cold is so much worse. He's terrible ill, I'm afraid." She fumbled for the envelope in her purse, "I've written to Dr. Grey, begging for him to come."

Hearing herself babbling on, she handed him the slip of paper. "I'm so afraid for the baby. You do think Dr. Grey will come, don't you?"

Nathaniel took the note, read it briefly, and without a word threw it into the fire.

"Nat!" Her cry was anguished. "Nat, how could you! Our child is desperately ill. We must have a doctor!"

He gripped her elbow. "Madam, we have company. Pray do not make a spectacle of yourself." His fingers bit into her skin, steel teeth that held her in a vise.

Amanda and Matthew Frogge came forward. Amanda's gown, the color of a forgotten pond on a dull day—greenish and without embellishment—did nothing for her sallow skin.

Matthew, muscular and hearty, moved to wring Nathaniel's hand, then leaned forward to place a wet kiss on Letty's cheek, his manner at once familiar and disdainful. Behind Matthew, Amanda quivered, seeming not to know in which hand she should hold her fan, which her reticule. Wan from too frequent childbearing—there was always another Frogge on the way—she clung to her husband as a tender vine reaches for support.

"And how are the children, Letty?" she asked, her eyes moist and bloodshot, for she rubbed at them continuously, hoping thereby to clarify her nearsighted vision.

"My youngest is very ill—" Letty turned wildly, feeling Nathaniel's hold on her arm slackening. She saw out of the corner of her eye the discarded note, blackened and lying in the bottom of the hearth. "I must send for the doctor—"

"Oh my," said Amanda softly, "I do hope it isn't scarlet fever. It's about, you know." She gazed around her as though searching for something. "Children are so susceptible. Yes, indeed they are. But you know that, Letty, as well as I."

Matthew clapped Albert on the back, his hand meaty and large. "When're you going to come to the club again?" Then he recognized Sam. "And here's our champion! Put on a fine show, lad. Liked your style. Albert, you'd do well to copy this boy here."

John Abbott strolled over and put his arm about Albert's shoulders. "The boy did well for what he was bucking," he said quietly. "Never let on he had a fever. Doctors had him in bed for months—just

131

because he was courageous enough to let us talk him into fighting."
He smiled at Albert.

The boy flushed, unaccustomed to such support. "Thank you, sir."

"Don't thank me, son. You deserved it. Sam here agrees with me. Don't you, Sam?"

"Well," said Matthew, backing off. "That puts a different face on it. Nat, you should be proud of your boy."

"Oh," said Nathaniel, his face a mask, "we'll make a man of him yet."

Nat wandered back to Letty. He spoke between clenched teeth. "Your audacity, madam, leaves me speechless. You know very well Henry will be here within the hour. Yet you deliberately try to go over his head and invite some strange doctor to see the boy. What has got into you?"

"Dr. Grey seems to specialize—"

He looked at her pityingly. "Letty, the child has been a hopeless case from the start. Your efforts to run from the truth will make us the laughingstock of Philadelphia. I suppose that pleases you—that people are talking behind our backs, joking about us at the club." He glowered, his dark eyes snapping.

Nathaniel was at his handsomest tonight—dark cutaway, wine velvet waistcoat, a pearl gray ascot speared by a stickpin sporting a single diamond. If Letty had not known what he was like, if she were a young girl again, enamoured and unafraid, she would have been flattered to be near him. But she did know him now. .

His gaze was one of scorn. He turned his back to her, his "host" face open and friendly toward the guests who were arriving in small groups now. The bare floors of the salon echoed back their laughter, their freedom to be lighthearted.

Nat moved with outstretched arms to the guest who most caught his eye. "Livvie, my dear, are you having a good time?"

Her sly glance atop the white neck, her bosom like upturned cups, half-hidden under white silk. "Oh, Uncle Nat, I just adore parties!"

Letty stared at the dark hair caught in a welter of small curls atop the fine head, the sparkling eyes, the step that almost danced—and pitied her. She should have hated her. Young and spoiled, pretty enough to catch Nathaniel's eye. But she was Letty of yesteryear. She could even have been Amanda Frogge. Wifehood, childbearing, had robbed them of their peach bloom, their hopefulness, their little faith in themselves.

Livvie would be more resilient than most. Lacking an adequate mother, she had gained a warm, caring father. That would stand her in good stead, carry her farther than most. But in the end, she too would succumb. It was inevitable.

Arranging a taut smile on her lips, Letty went forward to greet their guests. "You look lovely, dear," screamed Lily Gregg. Lily fortified herself with "elixirs" before she appeared in public, but everyone was expected to act as if she were quite herself.

But then, were any of them being themselves? Panic seized Letty in waves as she watched her company, the women's dresses swishing in the flattering candlelight. Who were they? Peel them, each of them, like an onion bulb, and what would you find? Wrappings about nothing.

She found herself staring up at the face of Sarah Mackenzie. "How would you have acted in my place?" she asked her silently.

There was no reply.

Henry Porter was arriving at the door. Letty shuddered and thrust her shoulders back, reminding herself to smile. Let them watch her. She was of sound mind, stalwart. She clenched her hands about her fan, moving it back and forth with studied effect.

10

They were dancing. The sweet strains of a violin, the tinkling of a piano, the harp with its undercurrent as of water murmuring within hidden caves—and on occasion the mad demands of the fiddler, commanding the younger ones to try to outrun him. It was, after all, in keeping with Christmas, a season of festivity. Except for those who served—and the ill.

Letty watched from a high-backed chair. Her green silk dress swirled about her like falls in the forest. Her fan poised, she gave her greatest attention to appearing attentive. All the while waiting for the summons she was sure would come from Nanny.

Thrice she'd been on the point of excusing herself. Thrice she had her departure denied by the net of a guest's conversation, thrown across her determination, entrapping her. Her resolve weakened in the miring politeness with which she had been reared. "Letty," Emma had said, "one never leaves one's own party, no matter what the excuse." How long must she sit here?

She'd approached Henry on his arrival. "It's Brett!" She'd dispensed with the usual formalities, friendly greetings, "Oh, Henry, would you look at him? I'm so afraid!" She had tried to communicate with her eyes, her tone, the reasonableness of her fear, that it was not based in her instability. The illness was real and grave.

Henry had bowed, letting Taft take his silk cloak. "Excuse me, Letty. Taft tells me Nat wants a word with me in the den."

Her heart had stopped. One foot had stepped forward to follow him, demand entrance, insist she be present for whatever dialogue was going to take place. Then courage had failed her.

Taft had stepped between them. "This way, sir." He had whisked the doctor off, leaving her to face the empty place where Henry had stood.

It had been filled almost at once by ladies with important trivialities on their minds. Did they collect them in cardboard containers, like hats, until such social occasions as this, and then drag them out as being appropriate? Any of these women, spoken with alone, would not have carried on so. Yet placed here, in this house and at this time, they became flowers as artificial as the rose Letty wore on her bosom. Tittering and coy. She supposed they meant to impress one another, since the men were for the most part huddled near the punchbowl discussing politics, financial affairs—secret matters that were fenced off from the ladies, unsuitable topics for such delicate ears.

Henry had emerged with Nathaniel at last. Watchful, over the heads of her twittering guests, she'd moved forward, as resolute now as a ship on a course.

"Nat, is Henry going upstairs? I should like to accompany him."

Nathaniel had patted Henry on the back. "In good time. We'll be sitting down to eat soon. Go later, if you wish."

"Nat!"

He'd looked at her then. The men had exchanged glances, infuriating her in their tacit understanding. She twisted her hands. "Nat, I asked a question."

His nostrils quivered with annoyance. "Taft is about to serve dinner. If you think it is your place, Letty, to be absent when you are expected at the head of the table—"

Taft was indeed on the job. Standing by the dining-room doors.

Henry put his hand on Letty's arm. "Go on in. I'll glance at the boy."

Letty must have held her breath longer than any other human being on earth. Henry was there at last, being shown to his place halfway down the table. Letty tried with all her might to catch his eye. He was being served. Thanking Phillips, tilting his head to catch the comment of the lady seated next to him. Henry was without his wife tonight. Letty might have counted on the help of Edda, but Edda had excused herself from the party. "She's suffering from a cold," was all Henry had said, with the expression of a man freed. Letty wasn't the only one who knew that when Edda stayed at home, Henry's eyes wandered.

Finally, she caught Henry's eye across the ranks of chattering guests. "Oh, Henry," she begged with her eyes, "tell me the worst— no, just tell me."

His answering look said, "Later." Then he turned to Nat, who was sipping from a refilled glass of chablis.

She bit her lip and glanced about her distractedly. There wasn't a way she could make her exit.

Matt Frogge, on her left, patted her hand, his manner intimate. "Did Nat tell you of our new partnership?" His breath, fumey.

"He mentioned something about factories."

"I'd be charmed to give you a tour someday," he said, eying her where her dress plunged. She flushed with annoyance, then could hear Nat warning her, "I don't care if you do dislike him, Letty, he's important to me. Don't say anything to put him off." She tried to smile.

Her attention was far more on Henry. If Brett had gotten worse, wouldn't Nanny have sent for her? She could take comfort in that, surely.

But she was grateful when John Abbott, across from Matt, leaned over and said quietly, "You're worried about your boy, aren't you? Want me to see if I can find out anything?"

"Would you?" Was there ever a finer man? As he slipped from the table she glanced at Matthew. She'd never realized how coarse he was before. He made her feel undressed. She cleared her throat delicately and raised her wineglass to her lips. Sipped without tasting.

It was an eternity before John came back. He took his seat as unobtrusively as possible. From the far end of the table Nat stared, curious. John gave him a pleasant smile, then leaned toward Letty. "The lad's holding his own," he said comfortingly.

"Oh, thank God. Thank you, John. If you knew how much it means—"

"Nonsense, it was nothing," he said.

It was time, at last, for the ladies to leave the gentlemen to their port and their cigars. Letty gave the signal, setting in motion the rustling all over the room that indicated the female guests were following her lead. Even before they were gone, the men were relaxing, leaning back in their chairs, crossing legs and addressing one another over the gaps that the ladies had left. Taft, Phillips, and the extra help engaged for the party moved in to clear away dessert dishes, bring decanters. Nathaniel's best port would begin to make its passage from glass to glass.

Letty led the way into the parlor. The ladies seated themselves, wide skirts of velvet, silk, and tulle cascading over the stiff furniture. Fans lifted to flutter gently, a handkerchief drawn from a satin reticule patted a worrisome nose.

In their midst, a puppy taking her place among the litter, Olivia wriggled. Her dark hair was dressed as became one of her age—curls piled atop her head, one single lock lying against her neck. It accentuated her pearly skin, her extremely good health. Her bared shoulders were thinly disguised by a wisp of gauze. Her waist did not have to strain to meet the demands of fashion. Letty stared at her with frank amazement. Had *she* ever been that young, that vibrant?

Feeling Letty's eyes on her, Olivia said, "Aunt Letty, so sorry to hear your little boy is sick." Her voice had the lilt that told discerning ears she had grown up in Virginia.

"Yes," said Letty, "it is a grave worry." She sighed. When the coffee tray was put before her, she lifted the heavy silver pot. "Mama, are you drinking coffee tonight?"

Emma shook her head. "It would keep me awake till all hours." She sniffed loudly, asking them to share her sense of being denied. Heads nodded politely.

"Amanda, coffee?"

The sallow face responded, "I do hope it isn't scarlet fever, Letty."

"It's unlikely to be that," said Letty. "Brett takes cold easily."

"It is Brett who's ill?" Hitty asked, her blue eyes warm with concern.

Letty nodded, her hands busy with pouring for her guests.

"Olivia," said Emma, her voice cracked and high, like the shattering of pottery in their midst, "did I hear you address my daughter as 'Aunt Letty'?"

"Why, yes." Olivia's look of innocence made her an easy target.

"I thought so," said Emma, nodding. "I was unaware that the Mackenzies and the Abbotts were related? Or perhaps it is through my own family, the Hydes?"

Olivia, undaunted, replied, "It's really quite simple, Mrs. Benedict. It's a courtesy title—at Uncle Nat's request."

" 'Uncle Nat'?" The old lady drew back in mock horror. "Now I know there's something wrong with my hearing. 'Uncle Nat'?"

"I think Uncle Nat's just an old darling." Olivia glanced from one to the other, her eyes wide and sincere. "I feel I want to hug him every time I see him. It must be wonderful to be married to a man like that, Aunt Letty. Aren't you so proud of him you could cry?"

Letty nodded lightly. The girl had hit it exactly. Letty could have wept easily right at that moment. Instead, she had come to the last cup to be poured. She added just a touch of cream, watching it float on the surface of the demitasse, then took a thin coffee spoon and stirred, causing the cream to disappear. Yet it was there—like her relationship to Nat, her concern for Brett, her grief for Warren. She raised her head, summoning all her willpower to disguise her depression beneath cheerfulness.

"I just love to come and stay with the Mackenzies," Olivia was telling the room. "My father and brother and I have been coming here since I was a little girl. It's like a second home." Olivia beamed at Letty. It was impossible to be angry with her—publicly.

Time moved like incoming waves, bearing them after an interminable distance of conversation to the moment when the dining-room doors were flung open. Male laughter emerged—followed by steps in the hall.

"Shall we join the gentlemen?" Released from the prettiness of the parlor where Letty's portrait looked down on them, witness to the ravages of age. Was it fifteen years since she'd sat for it? Had her eyes been that confident, or had the artist wished to convey them so, seeking to flatter? She turned her head away.

Oscar Benedict was emerging from the dining room slowly. His heightened flush and slight tremor indicated he had drunk well of the brandy.

So had Nat. Standing close to John and Livvie, he had put his arm about their young guest's waist. He said something in her ear that amused her.

"Oh, Uncle Nat, I do declare—" What she declared was lost by her leaning forward, whispering in his ear.

Letty gazed at Nathaniel. "Are we ready to give the signal to the musicians?"

He still had his arm about Livvie's waist. "You want to dance, little lady?"

She laid her head on his shoulder, prettily. "I swear—I have the nicest uncle." She pulled away enough to stare him in the eye. "Who would you have me dance with?"

"Who do you pick?"

Letty turned away, disgusted. She had other thoughts on her mind. She must find Henry.

Before she could locate him, Nathaniel approached her. "Madam, we must lead our guests." He offered her his arm extravagantly.

She went into his arms. Thinking, of all the people in the world, he was the one she understood least. They were less than strangers. With strangers, there was the hope of a relationship. With Nat, this had long ago become impossible.

Over his shoulder she caught sight of Norah. The maid, incongruous as a blackbird among multicolored parrots, was trying to catch her attention.

"Nat—" She stiffened in his arms. "Something's wrong."

"Letty, for God's sakes!" His voice was icy, but not loud enough for ears other than her own. "You must finish the dance!"

"It's Norah—she's come for me. Oh Nat, I have to go!"

"Always the child! Have you never a thought for the husband?"

She gazed at him in astonishment.

The dance wound down to its inevitable close. In a daze she went through the last steps, bowed to the musicians. Then almost ran to the edge of the room.

"What is it, Norah? Is Brett worse?"

"No, but no better either. He's sleeping. Nanny said for me to come and tell you. She knew how you were worrying."

So it wasn't a summons. Nat had been right to restrain her. She nodded. "You will come for me if—" Words left unsaid.

"Oh yes, ma'am. Should there be any change at all."

Letty had gone back to her guests and taken her place in the high-backed chair. Listening to the music, listening over it for a call.

It came through Henry.

His pink face appeared out of the haze of cigar smoke. "Letty, Nanny has sent for us."

"Oh!" she said, rising in one movement. "Oh, Henry, I've been trying to speak with you all evening." She kept up with him as he made his way through the thronging guests. It was cool in the hall. Taft was just closing the door. Perhaps Mother had kept her word and had taken Father home early. Had they said good-bye? Letty realized with a start how poorly her attention had been on anything the entire evening.

"Henry, what is your diagnosis?"

"My dear Letty—" He was puffing. The stairs were almost too much for him. He stood on the second-floor landing to get his breath, his face pasty.

"Henry, are you all right?"

He waved away her concern and moved toward the next flight of stairs. She knew she must wait for his comments. Her dread was enormous—spreading out through her chest to suffocate her.

On the third-floor landing the smell of friars balsam reached them. Steam, invisible at this distance from the kettle, wafted toward them, aromatic. Spelling sickness. Murmuring voices came from the night nursery.

Brett's crib was hung with muslin curtains. Dr. Porter walked with measured tread over to the small bed. Nanny and Katie stood on the far side of it.

"He's too quiet, sir—" Nanny spoke softly.

Henry said nothing and bent to examine the child.

Letty came up behind him, her hands crossed about her breasts, as if to shelter them from a blow. Katie glanced from the baby to her mistress' face.

"We done all we could," she said apologetically. "Pore lamb. Nanny's kept his little chest rubbed—we made sure the steam—"

139

Dr. Porter straightened up. "Letty, I'm afraid you must brace yourself." His expression was controlled, unreadable.

She gave a little cry, then ran forward, pushing him aside. She reached into the cot, lifted Brett, and held him to her. He was already cold.

"Why didn't you call me?"

"We did, milady." Nanny faced her. "We thought he was just sleeping—oh mercy, milady, we wouldn't keep a thing like that from you!"

"My baby—my baby!" Her weeping was dry, tearless.

In the next room, Amelia heard her mother come upstairs. Because of Brett's illness, she and Polly had been put to bed, feet facing one another, on the long couch, pillows under their heads. The nursery fire burned bright, but its comfort didn't reach all the way to the end of the room.

Amelia had been lying awake. Unable to sleep, she'd been content to stare at the flames. Hypnotic—they soothed her. She'd liked to have sucked her thumb, but that was unthinkable. Only babies like Polly did that. She placed the back of her hand to her nose, smelling its warm odor. Comforted.

But not quite. Voices from the night nursery. Earlier on, she'd heard Dr. Porter come up the stairs.

"What do you think, doctor?"

"He can't last the night, Nanny."

"Oh, sir! We must call his mother. I made her a promise, just as soon as there was any change—"

A long silence. Amelia sat up, straining to hear, catch the words. At last, out in the corridor, "—send Norah down to tell her not to worry."

"But that's not the truth, sir!" Nanny's voice, shocked.

"Now, Nanny. What can she do if she drags herself up here?"

"I just don't feel right about it, sir. I give her my word."

"What would you say if I told you that Mr. Mackenzie—" The voice dropped. Amelia couldn't catch the sentence that followed.

Nanny's murmur. "If you say so. We won't let on. But I don't feel right about it."

The sound of Dr. Porter's feet going slowly back down the stairs.

Amelia's attention drifted—out onto a raft that rode the ocean of sleep. Gently dropping deeper and deeper into slumber. But voices roused her again.

"Mr. Abbott, you startled me, sir!"

"Mrs. Mackenzie was worried about the child. I said I'd bring word down to her."

"He's sleeping, sir. Cough seems to have subsided, poor little angel. Couldn't seem to get his breath."

"I can tell her he's resting, then?"

"Oh yes, sir. The doctor was here a while ago. Said he'd be up again in a while."

"Ah. Well, I'll tell her. She'll be comforted to hear that."

Amelia clutched Sophie to her as she heard Mr. Abbott go down the stairs. So much comings and goings. It was hard enough to sleep on this narrow couch. But at last she did.

She wasn't sure what woke her. Amelia sat up, aware suddenly of something amiss. She couldn't put her finger on it. Then voices, muffled, the sound of weeping. Gripping Sophie tightly, she crept from the makeshift bed and crept soundlessly to the door. Sophie still held to her, she peeped around the corner, enabling her to see into the night nursery.

Everything was the same—with one difference. Nanny was crying. Seated next to the fire, rocking softly back and forth.

"We should've called her. It wasn't right—I don't care what Mr. Mackenzie's orders were—what the doctor said—it wasn't right. Katie, my heart will never be able to let this go."

"Nanny, what could we do? He said to wait an hour. Norah wasn't to be sent before. Dr. Porter knew there wasn't nothing Mrs. Mackenzie could do. Her place was at that party."

Amelia walked into the room. She rubbed her eyes as if she'd just been roused. "Nanny, I heard voices. They woke me up." Made her tone sound plaintive.

"Lord 'a mercy, Miss Amelia, how you startled me!" Nanny half rose in her chair, wiping her eyes with a corner of her apron.

"Is Brett going to die?"

"Whatever made you think that, lovey? Now you run along to the nursery. I know the sofa's not too comfortable, but soon we'll lift you and Miss Polly back into your own beds again." She stroked Amelia's brown hair. "You can be a good girl for Nanny, can't you?"

"Ye-es." Amelia looked uncertain. "Is Brett asleep? You sure he's not dead? I heard voices—"

"Go on with you. Pop off to bed. Like as not you had a dream. Katie, see she gets tucked up on the couch."

Katie's strong, firm hand tucked her in. "There you are, Miss Amelia." Quiet so as not to wake Miss Polly. "Comfy, are you?" Katie knelt down and, unexpectedly, gave her a kiss.

Once more Amelia lay there, seeking sleep. Restless, she turned about on the couch and woke Polly, who'd been moaning and tossing for minutes anyway.

Polly said, "Want Nanny." She sat up and stared around the unfamiliar nighttime surroundings, her hair clinging to her high domed forehead in damp tendrils.

"Go to sleep, Polly," commanded Amelia.

Polly opened her mouth to scream, but Amelia shushed her hastily. "Shut up and listen!" Her tone was sufficiently stern to discourage Polly from making a noise.

Amelia got off the couch quietly. "I'm going to go see," she said firmly. Sophie under her arm, she made her way on bare, padding feet toward the door. Then, as Letty began her ascent downstairs, Dr. Porter behind her, Amelia ran back to the couch again and pulled the quilt high over her head. Polly, emulating her, did the same. Feeling nameless panic pursuing them, lying there like animals in the underbrush.

Nanny came into the room softly and pulled an old wicker chair up to the fire. "Imagine the doctor'll send for the undertakers—"

Katie said, "Can't very well till the guests have gone."

"There's the back stairs, girl. He'll have it done quietly. He won't want fuss."

With the return of bright sunshine in the morning, Brett was gone. The girls came to gaze at his empty crib, to ask questions of an exhausted Nanny and Katie.

Letty they did not ask. Night had not ended for Letty. Though she would go to the funeral, make the motions of being a wife to Nathaniel and mistress of his household, her eyes would stare. She would sit for hours gazing unseeing at a book open on her lap. Walk in the rain and return, unmindful of the chill to her ungloved hands.

"Grieving," the household said.

Nathaniel was seldom home, and to her remaining three children, Letty was becoming a stranger.

II

In desperation, Letty sought out the Reverend Mr. Evans. Surely he must know what it was all about, how God made His plans? But Mr. Evans had disappointed her. He shook his head and said in that resonant voice, "He works in mysterious ways, Mrs. Mackenzie!"

"Can't you give me some help? I am at a loss to know what to believe anymore, where to turn."

"Ah, the human scene is indeed a trying one. I have thought on all this so many times—each occasion when I'm called upon to bury a child, or a young mother taken in the prime of life."

The dark eyes looked tragic, powerless. It annoyed her to see them thus. He should have had answers for her. Was he not a minister?

"Then you've come to no conclusions?" she asked.

"One or two," he said sadly. "It has become my opinion that we are put here in this veil of tears to learn patience."

"Patience!" She scoffed. "I've lost two sons and you ask me to have patience."

"Not I, Mrs. Mackenzie, a Power far higher than I. I told you, it was merely my thought-out conclusion." He shrugged with an air of hopelessness quite in contrast to the ringing tones, the manner of confidence with which she was accustomed to seeing him harangue the congregation. "I do believe we're put here to learn. Furthermore, the ladies, God bless 'em, are better at applying themselves to the lessons than menfolk are." He gave a sweet smile. "Perhaps that's why the Almighty put you here. To lead us menfolk to better ways."

"Mr. Evans, I assure you my sex knows of no secrets that are not just as available to yours." She stared at him.

143

His eyes met hers, dropped away discomfited. He drummed with his fine fingers on his desk top. The fire in the vicarage parlor's grate crackled.

Olwen, the minister's bustling wife, popped her head inside the door. "Would you like a nice cup of tea?" she asked in a voice that was, if anything, more lilting than Llewellyn's.

"Oh no, thank you." Letty gathered her politeness, her despair, about her like a cloak. "I've already taken up too much time, put you to too much trouble."

"Nonsense," said Llewellyn. He glanced at the clock on the mantel, the dial under the simple wooden peak showing it was not quite half past three. "Stay and have a cup with Olwen. I must leave. I've an appointment over at the church in five minutes. A baptism—" He let his voice trail away.

"The child of a little couple who come to our church regularly," said Olwen pleasantly. "He's coachman to the Frogges, but they're staunch Episcopalians. His mother emigrated from England, so naturally there's no church for them but this one. Such a nice pair—the Frogges give him time off to attend the baptism."

"Ah," said Letty, knowing the Frogges to be infrequent churchgoers.

In the ordinary way, Letty might never have met Olwen Evans, except over discussions of the church bazaar, flowers for the altar, or other matters that staunch supporters of the parish were expected to become concerned with. But tea in the vicarage parlor came about circumstantially.

Letty would have left the vicarage, but she liked Olwen's face; she drew a sense of comfort from her way of speaking. It reminded her of Katie—of friendly firesides and a way to savor life in a large family, one where people laughed at the little things—cared. She heard herself agree to stay to tea.

Olwen brought the tea on a wooden tray. The china pot sat under an enormous knitted cosy, only its spout and ears showing, like a child dressed for snowy weather. Raisin buns were covered with soft butter and strawberry jam runny with syrup.

"It's nice," said Olwen, pouring, "to share a cup. It's the one thing I miss, teatime."

"We have tea almost every afternoon," said Letty slowly. She spoke as someone who had been very ill. Yet her health had never been better. It amazed her that she, who needed so little from life, should be blessed while others about her suffered. The grippe, the dread signs of consumption, scarlet fever—all were among the households she knew, taking their toll. While she, Letty, remained untouched. Surely that was a token.

But of what?

"I really miss home," confessed Olwen. A little woman, she had robin's eyes, brown and bright, and a way of seeming to bustle while she kept her movements quiet, sure. Dark hair, turning gray, like Letty's, pulled into a simple pompadour fastened with steel pins. "Have you ever traveled to the British Isles?" she asked Letty.

"No." She said it heavily. Now that tea was poured, raisin buns passed, she wondered what she was doing here. It was so hard to make decisions to accept an offer or refuse and remove oneself. She stirred the tea, noticing that it was far darker than she usually drank it.

"I think you'll like it better with a little milk in it," said the Welsh woman. "Or at least let me dilute it with hot water. "You see, it's the way we take it back home."

"With milk?" Letty asked. She agreed to try it. The tea at once became more palatable. Milk cut the sharp taste that had seemed to curl the edges of her tongue. Still, it was a drink that would take getting used to.

"It's all so much the same over here," said Olwen, settling back in her chintz covered chair, "yet when you get down to it, it's quite different."

"It is?" said Letty vaguely.

Olwen was talking about a country everyone knew. Almost all the families the Mackenzies were acquainted with came from the British Isles. Many of them traveled there on fairly regular visits. Even their servants were for the most part Scots-Irish or, like Nanny, from England. Letty realized she'd not the remotest idea what this island fastness was like.

"I've never been," she heard herself say. "I suppose you must get homesick." It was like stating, "I suppose you must eat three meals a day."

"You've never been?" Olwen's voice held astonishment at once covered by confusion, an attempt to understand. Here they were, two women sharing tea and little else. Common ground seemed to have been removed. "Oh, you should go," said the minister's wife. "It's terrible to have never been there."

"I suppose it's very lovely."

"Well, now. It depends on what part you're talking about. You see, Llewellyn and I, we come from Wales. North Wales—we have to say it that way, for it's different from South Wales."

"It is?"

"Oh, yes. Oh my, yes. All of Wales is beautiful, except where the mining's spoiled it. Great slag heaps rising up behind tiny villages, cutting up the mountains as if they were cake. It's a living to our people —but a living death too." She spoke bitterly.

"Ah," said Letty. She sipped her tea. What was she doing here with this birdlike woman with all her energy, her enthusiasm for life?

"You've had a hard time, haven't you, love?" said Olwen suddenly, setting aside the manners, the small talk, and leaning forward to peer at Letty.

Letty felt herself drawing back. A need to shield herself—not let anyone inside. "I—it's been a difficult winter."

"Look, love, I know." Olwen picked up the teapot, motioned toward Letty's cup. "You don't drink tea like I do. Hardly touched your first and I'm on to my second. Yet it'll warm you on a cold day like this." She splashed milk into the blue and white willow pattern china, filled it with tea to the brim. "I lost two children myself," she said matter-of-factly.

"You did?" Letty sat up. The fog with which she was surrounded was beginning to lift. "When was this?"

"Oh, just before we made the decision to come over here. We hadn't been married that many years, Llewellyn and I. One baby was took from the diptheria, the other never seemed to have the strength for life he needed." Olwen shook her head.

"But that's like Warren!" said Letty in amazement. That she should find someone else with the same experience was incredible.

"I know." Olwen nodded. "When Llewellyn came back and told me, I said, 'That poor woman, I know what she's going through.' I wanted to come and call, but it's not like it is back home." Her eyes looked mournful, troubled. "I make so many mistakes, me and my rushing in. It's terribly hard for Llewellyn—" She shook her head.

"Oh, but surely—" Letty stopped, knowing what Olwen Evans said was true. A gulf divided them, a gulf of social mores. Left to herself, Letty wouldn't have cared. But she was Laetitia Mackenzie, Nathaniel's wife. He would never put up for a moment with their entertaining either Llewellyn or Olwen Evans. It was one thing to meet them at the church, quite another to invite them to sit at their table.

Olwen read Letty's face. "So you see," she said brightly, "I couldn't have come. But my prayers were answered because you came here instead."

"Yes," said Letty cautiously. Discussion of prayer, in her present frame of mind, made her nervous. Angry. What right did this stranger have to be praying for her?

Olwen went on. "I wanted to tell you that no matter how dark things look, they will get better." She stared at Letty. Her eyes were remarkably kind. "Oh, not for what seems like a long time. I understand that part too."

"Tell me," said Letty, leaning forward. Deciding, while still stiff with anger, defensiveness, to take a chance. "Tell me how long it takes."

"Oh that's hard to predict. It comes and goes, you see. One day you wake up—you say it doesn't hurt so badly. Maybe this will be the day you'll stop remembering, dwelling on it all. It works for a while. Then some little thing brings it all back. You judge yourself as back at the beginning." Olwen shook her head. "I suppose that's why my husband told you to have patience. He did, didn't he?"

When Letty nodded, Olwen went on. "It's the only thing he knows to say, poor soul. I used to tell it to myself so often. Yet what does it really mean? That you're willing to hang on, not allow yourself to feel much of anything because feeling's dangerous."

"How did you know?" asked Letty.

"How do you suppose I know?" Olwen's eyes twinkled. "It's going to get better, my dear. It's the only thing I'm sure of. One day you'll wake up, and it's not the fact that it isn't hurting so badly that startles you. It's that for days now—maybe weeks—you've not remembered any of it at all."

"That happens?" said Letty, wonderingly.

"It happens." Olwen raised a finger in warning. "When it does, you'll know that you're living, that you're in the midst of life—and that will make you feel guilty."

"Guilty? I don't follow you."

Olwen stared at her intently. "It takes a kind of courage to go on after something bad has happened. You feel as if you shouldn't. My sister died when I was fourteen. We both had the measles. I lived, she didn't. It was like I'd been punished because I wasn't taken. Mam—you should've seen my mother's eyes. Dadda too. I knew they loved me, but when they saw me, they missed Meggie. It got to the point I was praying to die."

"But why?" asked Letty.

"It's a terrible responsibility, being handed life. I was so afraid I'd fail, that Meggie could have done it better. It was a very kind lady who taught us Sunday school who opened my eyes." Olwen stared beyond Letty, as if in another scene. " 'Olwen,' she said, and she really scolded me, 'you think because you've been spared, you've got to hide yourself. It's not like that at all, child. It wasn't your decision that kept you alive and took Meggie.' "

Letty's lips parted in astonishment. "I prayed for both my sons, Mrs. Evans. I even told God I'd give Him my life if He would preserve theirs."

"Oh, I did the same, Mrs. Mackenzie. Made bargains with Him—"

"So did I!"

Olwen smiled. "When my children were taken, it was like I'd forgotten what the Sunday school teacher'd told me. One day, seated in the church, after we'd buried the last baby, it came back to me. The woman was dead by then. It was like I could hear her talking with me, putting her hand on my shoulder. 'Olwen,' she said, 'none of us knows what the Good Lord has in mind when He puts us here on earth. Nor do I think we can know. All we can be sure of, there's a purpose. We are His creatures, just like the flowers planted in the garden.' She was a great hand with the flowers, was Mrs. Hughes. Anything would grow for her. But she showed me that the flowers don't know why we plant them where we do. We're the ones have the idea how we want them to be. It's like that with us. God puts us here because He wants us to develop according to some purpose He has in mind. Perhaps it's courage He wants for us. Got some grand plan way down the line that we don't have any idea of. All He asks us to do is to trust. Trust—and go on." She sighed, her eyes gleaming. "Well, it was right after that Llewellyn had the dream—"

"The dream?"

"Oh, he doesn't talk about it very much. But he was shown in a vision he was to be on a big ship. Cross the waters, come to a foreign place to work in a church. He was training for the ministry at the time. He told me he thought he'd be sent to Australia." She smiled.

'It might have been Australia. Quite a few Welsh were going out there—emigrating, you know. Then he met Mr. Davies—"

"I heard Edward was instrumental in persuading your husband to come to St. Stephens."

"Mr. Davies' relatives lived in the same town where Llewellyn and I grew up. You might say Mr. Edward's the hometown boy who went away and made his fortune."

"Pennsylvania coal," said Letty vaguely.

"Struck lucky, he did. Don't ask me how. I haven't much of a head for these things. Llewellyn knows. Anyway, Mr. Davies wouldn't rest until he had my husband committed. Worked it out with the bishop. So you see, the Good Lord knew what He was doing, didn't He?"

"You think it was all planned from the start?" Letty looked puzzled, doubtful.

"Oh, I don't necessarily mean that. I think God gives us the freedom to take our opportunities where He makes them available to us—take them or turn them down. He had me develop courage. That's what I was lacking. Meggie, she was awful brave. I've seen her wade through swift streams, leap from high rocks. Not me. Always been a coward—till that time I was made to see I had to learn to face things, not want to be saved from it all."

"Do you suppose—?" Letty was thoughtful. She stared into the empty cup.

"I don't know for you, my dear. All I know is, it took more strength than I ever knew I had to follow dear Llewellyn here."

"It did?" Letty was astonished. "Here" was home to her, it always had been. It was "there" to the Evanses, coming as they did from an alien land.

"You think it was easy, traveling across the ocean? Leaving home and family behind? Not knowing what we were coming to? No one we knew except Mr. Davies—and him not what you'd call the sort who'd ask us in for a friendly chat."

Letty felt ashamed of herself. "How shortsighted of me." She set down her cup. "You've given me quite a lot to think about, Mrs. Evans."

She felt a stirring in her, the merest lifting of her spirits. A curiosity, prodding her to take the same journey as Olwen, but in reverse. She would see this Wales the minister and his wife came from. She stood up, pulling her coat around her. "You have been far more helpful than you can ever know."

The brown eyes sparkled. "It's been my pleasure. Perhaps sometime you'll come again."

Letty bowed. "I'd like that," she said. And she meant it.

Yet both of them knew it was doubtful whether she would come again. Two strangers had met on a bridge, briefly. They had talked face to face. But they traveled different paths. Each would never embarrass the other, claim an intimacy that had existed over a cup of tea, some raisin buns, and strawberry jam.

Bates was summoned. Letty waved as she got into the carriage. In another time, another place, the two women might have been friends. As it was, they had shared—momentarily.

Olwen Evans closed her door against the damp cold of early March. She was lonely in this place. She imagined Letty Mackenzie must have a great many friends. Such a lady of wealth, importance. Olwen felt surprised at herself that she'd spoken, acted, in such a forward manner. Llewellyn would scold. Yet she'd do it again if she had the chance. Odd, but Mrs. Mackenzie'd seemed more alone than she. That couldn't be possible!

Olwen shook her head.

149

It happened as Olwen Evans had predicted. Letty woke up one morning and knew that it was gone—the sorrow, the weight of grief, the leaden feeling that made it so hard to get out of bed. She lay there holding her breath, wondering if she dared count on it—the freedom.

She rolled over. Nathaniel had already arisen, left without waking her. She thanked God for it. The sight of his face now would be too dangerous. Even the idea of him jolted her back to thoughts of shame.

She turned onto her back again and stared at the ceiling. What was there about her wakening that had been so joyous? Holding very still, she savored it. It was the birds! Chattering outside her window, scolding and swooping with the loud clapping of wings, they announced boldly that spring had come.

It was in the gentle breeze that lifted the heavy draperies. It was in the fresh smell of the air. She stretched herself on the undulating mattress, sensing a strength, a faith in life she'd not had before. Certainly not yesterday, or the very many yesterdays before that. It was good to be alive!

Yet she was fragile, holding herself away from anything that might affect her mood. Guarding herself—crystal that rang with an answering chime if tapped, that reflected every color, every nuance.

By afternoon, she felt she could trust the joy. She went so far as to send Bates over with a message to Emma and Hitty that she would be pleased to see them for tea.

They accepted. Now they were sitting opposite her in linen dresses that defied the wayward breeze. Emma, in dark blue, seemed like a brooding raven, hurt that she hadn't been asked for so long.

"One would think, Letty, that you didn't care. I mean, I am your mother. I like to see something of you." The turtle neck quivered as the old head nodded forth and back, as if on wires.

Hitty remonstrated. "Letty hasn't felt well. Have you, dearest?"

Hitty, in green, looked like an unripe apple. Why did she think she could get away with bright colors? Letty felt well dressed in her tan whipcord. Ecru-colored silk collar and cuffs gave her costume just the right touch. It was something Miss Puxley had sent over last autumn, sure Mrs. Mackenzie would like it. Letty had kept it without even bothering to try it on. She had had Nanette hang it in one of the closets.

"But, madame—"

"Perhaps later—" Letty hadn't known at the time, so soon after the baby's death, that there would be a "later." Today, surprised when Nanette brought it out, she had tried it on, glanced at herself in the mirror, found herself to be handsome.

"Oh, madame—it becomes you!"

"Thank you, Nanette. I believe I'll wear it this afternoon. Even if it is a little elegant for tea on the terrace." What she had wanted to say was "tea with Mother and Hitty," but she refrained from such disloyalty before Nanette. Who knew so much without having to be told.

Letty, pouring now from the silver pot, decided it was time to spring her surprise.

"I have something to tell you," she said, ignoring Hitty's reference to her ill health. "I have decided to accompany Nat to Europe this summer."

She had not misjudged the timing or the information. Hitty flushed, with shock or excitement, it was hard to tell which, and arranged her features into a smile. Emma bit her lower lip and made her face appear longer.

"You might have told me sooner, Letty." Her mother's eyes accused. Bloodshot and liquid as a spaniel's. Mother could make one feel uncomfortable over anything!

Letty parried cheerfully. "I couldn't have let you know sooner. I only decided it myself today. Even Nat doesn't know yet."

"Oh my!" said Hitty, impressed. "He's sure to be pleased."

Emma's voice had turned sharp. "Hitty, you say the most senseless things. By no stretch of the imagination can I see Nathaniel Mackenzie being pleased over anything, unless it would be the news that Letty's entire family had fallen down and broken their necks." She made a grimace at her younger daughter. "Have you quite finished with your inanities?"

Hitty seemed to settle back inside herself, a turtle pulling its feet

151

within its shell. Her face closed. She picked up her teacup and stirred what was left of the beverage.

Emma sniffed loudly, then turned to Letty. "Just why are you going to Europe? It is Europe, isn't it? Or do you mean England?"

"I'm sorry, Mother. I meant to say England. Nat has business there—Bristol certainly, and Southampton and London. I was of a mind to go with him, settle myself in one of the hotels. I'm told the summer's the best time to see the country."

"I envy you, Letty." Emma's voice was harsh. "I always tried to get your father to take me to England—Scotland too. It wasn't the money —we could easily have afforded it." She leaned forward confidentially. "I am perfectly certain he's afraid of the sea."

"Mother, he says he gets seasick," Letty said evenly.

"But he's never been on the ocean. It's his imagination." Emma shook her head vigorously. "I should've taken you girls and done Europe while I was still young. I'd half planned to, the year you were married. If it hadn't been for Nathaniel—my word, Letty, when I think who you might have ended up having for a husband had we made you wait—"

"Mother, please. Let's not go into that again. It was years and years ago." Letty lifted the teapot. "May I pour you a little more?"

Emma wasn't to be put off. "You were the handsome one, Letty. You could have had any of the young men that year—or any other year, for that matter. When I remember how lovely you looked. You are certainly a Hyde, Letty." She glared at Hitty. "The Benedicts don't have the lines."

Why couldn't Mother even try about Hitty? The girl mightn't be a beauty, but she certainly wasn't bad-looking. Some might even describe her as having a pleasant face. Mother didn't even attempt to disguise her feelings.

Emma was on another tack. "I'd go with you even now, Letty—"

"Oh, Mother, I don't think you understand the arduousness of the trip. The voyage alone—"

"Its all right," said Emma testily, "you don't have to go to all that trouble to dissuade me. If for no other reason, the damp climate would raise the merry ned with my rheumatism. By the way, I don't suppose Hitty has told you about the new doctor I've found. It was she recommended him."

"Hitty?" Letty looked at her with mild interest. Noticed the girl had flushed up. Well, that was nothing new. With her fair skin, Hitty colored almost each time anything was said to her. The responsibility of answering could frighten her. "Who is this new doctor?" she asked idly.

"I was afraid to say." Hitty looked upset.

"Afraid? I don't follow you."

"You recall the day the consultant came to see Brett." Hitty wet her lips, paused. "I didn't like to remind you, Letty."

"Go on," said Letty, her voice controlled. "What about Dr. Grey?"

"So you do remember him!" said Emma triumphantly. "Hitty said she thought you mightn't, that his name wouldn't mean anything to you."

Letty spoke coolly. "How silly. Why would I forget?" She knew their caution was out of concern for her feelings. She could acknowledge that. What she could not understand was the way they'd contacted Dr. Grey without so much as a word to her. Why?

She stared over their heads, seeing the garden. How lovely it was this time of year—a crowd of daffodils nodding beneath the birch trees, bonneted ladies gathered outside church. An early flowering fruit tree moved gently in the breeze. At once a confetti of coral and cream petals floated downward, to spatter the brown of the earth, pieces of silk snipped on a dressmaker's floor. She was thinking of England. Would it be so different? She'd read the poems, *Oh to be in England, now that April's here.* Verses their governess had insisted they learn.

"Odd, about poets," she said lightly.

"What about poets?" Hitty's head shot up, her face flushed. Had Letty said something she shouldn't?

Letty yawned, allowing herself to stretch. "It occurred to me, does anyone ever recall which poet wrote what? Even if they remember some line? I mean, it's such a stab in the dark."

"What is?" said Hitty sharply. Strangely, hands folded, white.

"Doing anything for which you'll be remembered." Letty lifted the silver teapot. It was almost empty. She placed it beneath the enormous urn that always took center place on the tray. A dowager, presiding. She turned a spigot, holding it with a napkin, for the thing always got hot. Water flowed slowly into the teapot.

Like my life, she thought. Trickling away while I sit here, talking to Mother and Hitty of inconsequential things. She closed the pot's lid with a snap after remembering to twist the spigot. The napkin she laid aside. It too had been changed by an action. Now it would have to be laundered and ironed, a little bit of its life swirled away down the waters of the washtub as they were dumped into an outside drain. It must be difficult to be a laundress, like Katie's mother. Or a Laetitia Mackenzie, wondering where her youth had gone.

A Hitty Benedict? Letty stared at her sister covertly. Did Hitty mind that she had so little of life? At thirty-four this May, Hitty could hardly be called a girl. Hitty had a warm, sensitive manner—a way of caring, but not deeply. Hitty took life as it came, never rebelling, as Letty would have, at her fate.

Emma broke in on her thoughts. "I've taken a fancy to Dr. Grey. Did you know his given name is Compton?" Emma could pick up a conversation anywhere she wanted it. "And Letty, he's a widower!" She spoke it as if she were presenting a jewel.

"Really?" said Letty politely.

"Mother, please." Hitty's voice was strained, her face averted. She began playing with her pearl gray gloves, examining minutely where she had darned them in meticulous stitchery.

"Well, he *is* a widower, Hitty—and you know you find him attractive!" Emma was cruel. Like a bored tomcat, she relished the chance to tease. "I believe he could be hooked if you'd work at it a little." She raised one startlingly heavy eyebrow. It gave her a mannish appearance; overweighted, somehow, the rest of her wrinkled face.

"Mother—" said Hitty faintly. There was pain in the way she clutched her gloves, raised eyes that implored Letty. "He comes to see Mother. He's been a great help. I'm not even around."

"Well, you should be!" Emma said it as a pronouncement. "He always asks for you." She made a face. "Mercy, Hitty, you've never had any sense around men. It's why you're unmarried today." She adjusted her dark shawl about her shoulders, wriggling into her satisfaction that she was right. Could always be counted upon to be right. It was a strong position, one from which she'd ruled Hitty for years.

Letty spoke up. "Do you like the doctor, Hitty?"

"He seems kind," said Hitty, her face noncommittal.

"She should be around when he visits," said Emma bluntly. "I know he needs a wife. His bride died in childbirth twenty years ago."

"Twenty years ago?" Letty echoed it. "Doesn't that make him a little old for Hitty?"

"Nonsense. A man is a man—at any age!" declared .mma with finality.

Hitty moved the old writing table to where she could see the garden as she wrote. She dipped the nib in the inkwell, pausing momentarily. Then she pulled the gilt-edged journal with its wealth of empty pages toward her and wrote.

'a whole week since Letty and Nathaniel sailed. Though the sea was calm that day, I felt for them, the storms that may lie in their path. England seems such a long way away. I have been over to visit with Mrs. Evans. She gave me tea, hot tea, though it was such a fearfully warm day, being already June, and she's promised to tell me all she knows about Wales. I think I have found a friend at last!

Hitty stared at the words, then went back and underlined the words *at last.* After dipping her pen once more, she continued.

I don't care what Mother says about Mr. and Mrs. Evans not being socially acceptable as friends. I don't think you can go much higher than a minister—after all, he has given his life to God, which if you believe in Him must mean something. Besides, I like them. I feel at my time of life I should have a right to choose who I will see something of—unless of course it should be compromising. I'd like to tell this to Mother—if she'd listen. Maybe, if she carries on about it enough, I will.

I do like Mrs. Evans. She's asked me to call her Olwen. I think that's an exceptionally lovely name. It sounds so foreign. Sometimes she and Mr. Evans speak Welsh in front of me. I'm sure it's just that they forget, not rudeness. Such a melodious speech, almost singing. Olwen says the Welsh would rather sing than eat. Sometimes they are forced to. Wales is a very poor country, and a lot of people go hungry. Working in the mines must be dreadful.'

She gazed over the paper and out the window. The roses in the ornately patterned beds were coming into bloom. She could see old Jaspar, his gnarled hands moving across their stems, checking no doubt for aphids or other pests that could ruin his display. She wished she knew more about gardening. It seemed such a secret art. Like cooking. Who was there to teach her, should she desire to learn? Jaspar would tell her things if she asked. But he would keep his lore, like an untapped source running clear and deep beneath the ground—waters of molten gold. She wanted to know. She would like her own garden in which to try it all out.

Her mother's garden was another matter. So trim, so well cared for, it overwhelmed her. Like Letty's house—a complicated and highly structured endeavor. Hitty felt tired just thinking about it.

Yet here, in the perimeter of her room, she led an almost useless existence. She sighed, placing her now dry pen on the table beside the journal. What was the point of her scribbling, her attempts to convey what she wanted to say?

She'd read one poem to Olwen and had been rewarded by the admiring look in the Welsh woman's eyes.

"You wrote that, Miss Benedict?"

"I asked you to call me Hitty."

"Hitty, then. It's lovely, my dear. You are a real poet. You know that, don't you?"

Did she know it? Seen on a page, her verses always seemed to fall short of what she'd intended them to be. Like a mountain climb, each step an effort—taken with daring, calculated feel. Yet the peaks seemed farther off than ever, more inaccessible.

What did she want? The view from her window gave no answer. Neither did the swooping birds. She envied them. They at least knew what they were about—nest building, gathering food for their young. She even envied the old gardener and the servants whose dust cloths moved like soft moth wings across the Benedicts' fine furniture. Mrs. Prentiss the cook had a menu to follow, Mother's personal maid must press and mend—they were busy-fingered till nightfall.

All of them knew where they were going, what they must be about. Except her. She knew with a sense of utter futility that her life was worth nothing to anyone. Particularly not to herself. She closed her journal with a snap, her breath shallow and rapid. Drowning for want of a raft. She must find a way out of this meaninglessness. Lose herself and thereby find solid ground.

A tap at the door interrupted her.

"Yes, Hooper?"

"Your mother has asked you to come down to her rooms for a moment." Hooper's face was enigmatic, all sense of personal reaction hidden behind a clever mask. Unless her secret was that she had none.

Hitty pushed her chair back from the table. "Very well. I thought Dr. Grey was with Mother?"

"He is, miss. Mrs. Benedict simply asked that you be sent for."

She entered Emma's morning room. The old lady was seated in her favorite chair, one similar to the pair that sat in Letty's sitting room, but it lacked Letty's tasteful elegance. A brooding seat, its high, flanking wings blotchy with cabbage roses, crawling leaves. Lace curtains hung at the windows, filtering the pleasantness of the June sunshine. A littered place with no arrangement that hung together, it lacked orderliness. It suggested movements made with pain, self-discipline excused from frailty—a lazy mind that repeated what others provided. Enthroned in light shawls amid the smell of arnica, Emma was holding court.

"Ah, Hitty, come in. Dr. Grey and I were just speaking about you."

Hitty flushed. She didn't like being talked about. Fresh from her ruminations, she felt vulnerable, unprotected. Certainly in no mood to be asked to defend herself. Emma's barbed tongue was something both her daughters dreaded, each in her own way.

Dr. Grey stood up politely, extended his hand. "Miss Benedict. I haven't seen you for quite some time."

His hand was warm, firm. Like the rest of him, it had a clean feel. That faint odor of ether. She supposed it was always that way with doctors. They must get used to it; like bad breath, they carried it with them unbeknownst, until some kindly soul thought to mention it.

"Dr. Grey." She took the chair he indicated, felt their expectancy of her. About what? She sat, perplexed.

"Now, Hitty," said Emma complacently, "I should think you would be curious to know what we've been discussing."

She was. But, put that way, she drew back. It suggested she was an object to be examined.

Emma went on, not the least put off by Hitty's silence. "Dr. Grey, that is, Compton," she said with a satisfaction that pressed her lips together, moved her rheumatic hands to clutch each other, diamond rings winking in the lace filtered light, "Dr. Grey has asked permission to court you."

Hitty's astonishment was matched only by her consternation. Suddenly Dr. Grey assumed menacing dimensions. While he'd remained a doctor, he represented no threat to her. As a suitor, he became someone she'd never met.

Dr. Grey rose from his chair and approached her. Took her hand in his. "Miss Benedict, Hitty, I know I am not the best of suitors." He stopped, inadvertently catching Emma's eye. "Your mother has explained to me that your natural reticence has caused you to become

157

shy." He smiled suddenly. "I do understand this. That first day we met, at your sister's, I remember having to apologize. I've never been mannerly. My mother died when I was a lad. Then, when I married, my wife was spared me only a short time." He stopped. He had come to a railway station at which he seemed to have a need to descend.

He held her hand, gazed at her with cool eyes that seemed to seek something in her own. "Miss Hitty—" he said, a hesitancy in his manner.

"You were mentioning your wife—"

"Ah, I was." He let Hitty's hand fall, turned back to his chair. He was about to speak when Emma interrupted.

"You mustn't press Dr. Grey for details, Henrietta." She only gave Hitty her full name when she was angry with her. Angrier than usual. "All in good time. Something to talk over while you and he are getting to know each other."

Hitty felt herself flush. Was it all settled? She threw back her head and asked, "Has Papa been consulted?"

Emma moved her hands over the plaid rug she'd taken to placing on her knees—winter and summer. "Of course your father's been asked. Hitty, how could you believe otherwise?"

"I'll have it from his own lips," said Hitty, surprised at her tartness. She was being rude and wondered why.

"You wish to know about my former wife?" said Compton Grey. He smoothed the blond hair that was bleaching to white away from his forehead. His eyes looked unhappy. "She passed away in childbirth about twenty years ago. The boy would have been ready to join me in my practice now, I daresay."

"You never told me it was a son," said Emma companionably.

"He lived long enough to be called after myself."

"Ah. Very fitting."

They are making it all run on without me, thought Hitty irritably. She cleared her throat discreetly. Would they notice? She would insist on speaking with Papa. Only Papa was in downtown Philadelphia, at his club.

"Hitty." Emma's voice was sharp, curling about her daughter like a whip. "Hitty, you are extraordinarily silent. Have you nothing to say?"

Hitty swallowed. "Dr. Grey does me a great honor," she said carefully. Stepping on flat rocks across swirling waters. "I should like to have time to think about it."

As he bowed his assent, Emma exploded. "What is there to think about, Henrietta? A woman your age doesn't get an offer every day of the week. A fine man like Dr. Grey—what is there to hesitate over?"

Hitty's eyelids fluttered—a response to shock waves. She dropped her gaze to her lap and saw her hands as if they belonged to another. Was she really being sought?

Compton Grey leaned toward her. "I merely thought—if we were to get to know each other—?" His manner was courteous. The abruptness that had bothered her the last time seemed toned down. "We might take walks together. The weather is quite fine now." He said it as if they were newly emerged from winter. Had he only just noticed that it was June?

A bird called outside the window. Hollow and haunting, its song wavered up and down. A sadness seemed to settle over the room. Hitty fought against it but found it to be overwhelming. Like the sight of roses just before the frost. She felt weary.

She stood up, letting her dignity lend her courage. "I do thank you for your offer, doctor—"

"Please, let it be Compton."

She bowed. "I would like to take walks with you. We would have an opportunity to explore conversations, mutual interests."

"My intention precisely." He smiled, touched by some sense of inner satisfaction.

In her room once more, Hitty got out her journal.

I have this day received an offer— She stopped. An offer of what? Could one say that this would lead to marriage? If so, would it then lead to happiness? The books she read said so, while warning of the dangers an intemperate life could bring. Drunkenness, the poor wife and children dragged into abject poverty, submission to brutality—the tales were rife. But surely when one contemplated marriage with a man as well thought of as Dr. Grey, such thoughts were irrelevant.

I have received an offer— How well did they know Dr. Grey? He'd asked her to call him Compton. Wasn't that the purpose of courtship, to get to know each other? She sighed. Could one ever really know another human being enough to be able to say with surety that marriage with them would involve little risk?

She approached her father after dinner. "Father, what do you think of my permitting Dr. Grey to court me?"

"Eh—what?"

"Surely Mother has spoken with you."

"Oh, Dr. Grey. Well, little Hitty, someone has come seeking your hand at last." Oscar's smile was entirely uncritical.

"If I should marry him—" Toying with the laced flounces of her dress.

"Yes, m'dear?"

"You would approve?"

"If he was your choice, of course I'd approve."

"Oh, Father—"

"You seem unhappy, my child."

She turned away, not letting him see that her eyes were brimming over with tears. "It's all right."

"Oh, well, I'm reassured. Your mother wants your happiness." He patted her hand. "So do I, sweet child. Can't say I won't miss having you about. Been a long while—" He smiled beautifully. "All your life, right?"

"Right, Father," she said warmly. He couldn't help himself. He really tried. It just wasn't ever quite enough.

Before turning down her lamp's wick for the night, she read what she'd written in her journal, then added:

I think I may marry. But I must marry someone who is very strong. A woman shouldn't be able to destroy her husband. Women have natural strength even while they are supposed to act weak. They should be prepared to lend their energy to their husbands so that it all flows in the same direction. Else it builds the one, depletes the other.

She shook her head. She really didn't know what she was talking about, was merely spattering thoughts on paper. Put that way, they resembled splotches of ink, seeming to create a pattern but in fact not based on anything she knew. She was so lacking in experience! It had been what she'd been bemoaning this afternoon—the sheltered emptiness of her life that left her vulnerable to conjecture, fearfulness. Mother was right. She was lucky to have someone seek her out.

She blew out the candle beside her bed and lay on top of the covers, thinking. She thought of Dr. Grey's clean body, his warm hands —and of marriage. What on earth was it like? There was no one she could ask. No one would tell her those things.

III. TO LIGHT YOU TO BED
April 1887–September 1888

Orange and lemons
Say the bells of St. Clements;
I owe you five farthings
Say the bells of St. Martins;
When will you pay me?
Say the bells of Old Bailey;
When I grow rich
Say the bells of Shoreditch;
When will that be?
Say the bells of Stepney;
I do not know
Say the great bells of Bow.

Here comes a candle
To light you to bed
And here comes a chopper
To chop off your head.

     —*Nursery rhyme*

I

Letty had many times imagined what a sea voyage would be like. She had never envisaged it as quite so awful as its reality. The rolling waters, which tossed them like some plaything upon silk bedsheets, had them absolutely at their mercy. Green waves rose like hills, towering above the tiny ship. The waves disappeared, to reappear beneath them, raising them to a point where gray sky met spume.

The ship's planks creaked and groaned. The passengers' situation grew more perilous as day followed day. Surely this would be the hour in which the protesting fibers of the craft parted company and delivered them to the immeasurable depths? Yet timbers clung together, sailors clambered cheerfully about on feet nimble as a cat's. Nathaniel paid a visit to the bridge and returned, appetite quickened, his long cheeks wet with spray, roseate with pleasure.

It occurred to Letty that men relished danger. If she could have turned the clock back, reversed her decision to cross the ocean, she would have. She might have upbraided Nanette for failing to warn her, but had not the heart. Nanette was confined to her own cabin, too ill to speak with her mistress let alone tend her.

Nathaniel came down and growled at Letty. "Never thought a trip over the sea would be like this, eh? I know you won't take the advice of a seasoned traveler, but if you would get up, act like you aren't allowing it to get the better of you, it'd pay off."

Letty's eyes filled with tears that were warm with self-pity. His stocky body with its muscular resilience had become a sight that repulsed her. She wished only that he'd go away—up to the topmost decks where others of his kind strode about, seeming to thrive on the

163

weather. Why had she come on this trip? She decided she must have been mad. She was willing to take Nat's view of her, that she was feeble of mind, unreliable of judgment. She rolled over in her berth and slept fitfully.

On the last day she managed to respond to the calming of the waters. Perhaps she'd become accustomed to the swell. Unattended by Nanette, who was still too ill to leave her cabin, she managed to bathe herself in a bowl of warm water.

She gritted her teeth. She would show Nat. She planned to appear at dinner that night whether her legs told her she could or no. She selected a dress of sky blue, trimmed with Irish lace—A fitting attire, for they were even now passing the Irish coastline.

Letty braced herself in the dipping cabin, trying to fasten her three-stranded pearl necklace about her neck. She managed the catch at last, then looked one last time in the small mirror that hung on the wall. Her face was that of a stranger, her hair needed washing. The experience revealed to Letty how much she depended on Nanette. Yet Letty would have to engage a temporary lady's maid as soon as she got to London. Nanette had been promised a holiday in France.

"I'll manage," she said aloud. To convince herself. The hollows under her cheekbones, the staring expression of her brown eyes, all told her that the voyage had left its mark. The elegant Letty who had left Philadelphia had been replaced by a worn-out wraith. How had the early settlers managed such crossings? Letty gained a new respect for her forebears.

Upstairs, on the level that held the dining room, she took her place beside her husband at the captain's table. Those who had taken the voyage in their stride sat across from one another as old friends, Nat among them.

He remarked at her appearance, "Well, I have a wife this evening!" He turned to invite others to share his laughter.

She gave most of her energy to toying with food, trying to get her stomach to accept it. She sipped a little wine, feeling it bring color to her cheeks. Weak from lack of food, she knew that drinking wine was dangerous. But her nervous fingers reached for the glass more than once.

She felt the wine lift her. Her body grew light and less wearisome. Her eyes had had trouble focusing all evening. Now the difficulty increased—but now she didn't care.

Hazily, she was aware that Nat took her arm. "—help you to your cabin."

She was doing well now, placing each foot squarely on the stairs. She clung to the railing, feeling as if her hand belonged to somebody else. She glanced up at Nat. "You are still handsome. A little over-

164

weight, but extraordinarily distinguished-looking yet."

"You're drunk, Letty!" he said nastily.

The shock was so great that it brought tears to her eyes. She tried to pull away from him, stumbled, and aided by a particular lurch of the ship, fell. The flooring came up at her. She clung to the rope in panic. Shame—so ashamed. How had she gotten on the floor?

Nat dragged her to her feet. He pulled her a few paces, then held her upright while he opened their cabin door. "Be all right when I come back."

Round and round the ceiling spun, faster and faster. Her head was pounding and her stomach had come up to meet her throat. She groped for the slopbowl, gained it just in time, and vomited up whatever she'd forced herself to swallow at dinner. When she looked about her, gasping and crying, her husband was gone.

She sat up in bed, startled. Nat was there, standing over her. In the dimness of the cabin she could feel him rather than see him. He'd undressed to the waist. His heavy, muscular body smelled of sourness, wine breathed out through the pores. Sweat. They all smelled somewhat, for washing was a task with the limited facilities, the pitching ship. She'd been ashamed to go to the dining room that way, but it was different for a man. Sweat on clothes was a sign of masculinity—given the right circumstances.

He took her wrist in a grip that hurt. "You disgraced me in front of my friends."

"Nat, please, I know I behaved badly, but I've been so sick. I didn't think when I was drinking the wine—"

"Whore!"

"Yes," she whispered. Then, "No! I didn't do anything you could call me that for. I was able to walk from the dining room. When I fell on the stairs, it was because—"

He released her wrist. He was fumbling in the dark—she could barely see his hand tugging at his trousers.

"No!" she cried out. "No, Nat. Not tonight—I'm ill. I beg you to leave me alone—"

In the half-light she made out the source of the sliding sound as he extricated his leather belt from its loops. The metal buckle gleamed dully, answering the odd light that came in at the porthole. Phosphorescence from the sea. The buckle swung.

He tore the covers off her. Was ripping her nightgown, not waiting for her to lift it for him. As she heard the fabric go, she thought irrelevantly of Miss Puxley, saying in her syrupy tones, "Nightwear, Mrs. Mackenzie—so important to choose the best!" Letty wanted to laugh hysterically, scream.

165

Cold air hit her legs, her bared thighs. He was rolling her over, having her face the wall. His short, strong arms had her pinned. She waited, holding her breath, expecting him to slide his flesh over hers.

She was unprepared for the flash of leather as it cut her skin. Again and again and again.

"Nat, for the love of God—" Trying to turn over, to get away, having no place to go to. No space in which to climb—no covers to shield her bruised flesh.

Sour breath, the whistling belt. Pain—all pain.

Somehow she sat herself up, swung off the berth. In the narrow space of the cabin, he caught her, flayed at her, though he couldn't see to direct his movements. She lay on the foul floor, smelling timbers pickled by sea air, never really scrubbed clean.

"—behave like a whore, get it like a whore. You were supposed to have enjoyed it—a whore would've."

He dropped on her like a stone. Naked where she lay, the icy floor against her back, her buttocks injured—she felt sure, bleeding—he came inside her. Battered her, his liquor stench entering her throat as his maleness entered her interior. He took a long time to reach his climax, snorting and puffing with effort. She bore him as she had always borne him. From the first time.

"Raise your goddamned thighs."

Could she? Fortunately, before she had to move, he exploded within her. Lay on her inert, like a sack, pressing her body downward, her spirit far deeper.

He climbed into his berth and was snoring.

She tried to find a towel she could wet to wipe her injuries. She bumped and crashed about, stubbing toes, shivering in the clammy air. Afraid lest she would waken him. He'd been known to come for her again. Not to climax twice—but to toy with the possibility of it, while she enclosed him, his organ assaulting her with movements she would suffer from for days.

She gave up searching for comfort in that dark, narrow cabin. She climbed back into her berth and drew the scratchy blankets around her.

In the morning, light and the ceasing of rolling motion woke her. Outside there was noise, confusion. Footsteps running with quick purpose on overhead decks. She lay there trying to deal with a sense of danger, effortfully considering whether it was real or merely a memory.

She slipped from her bunk, the coarse blanket about her, to peer through the porthole. They were anchored outside a port. England awaited them. Nat's empty berth told her what she already knew. He'd dressed and gone up on deck.

A soft tap on the door found her trembling. "Who is it?"

"It is I, madame." The soft French voice was the first sound she'd had of a friend in all these long days.

Nanette stood in the cabin doorway, ghost pale, her skin taut over her already thin face. "We must get you packed, madame—"

"Yes, I know." Letty said it with the old dignity, then took a step forward and collapsed onto the berth, weeping.

"Madame—" Nanette's face looked troubled. "I'll not leave you to go to France if you aren't well."

"No, no, child. This is a great thing for you, to be able to see your family. I shall manage perfectly well. Perhaps I will find someplace in the country where I can rest."

"Oh, madame, I am worried about you."

"I'm all right—really. Now, Nanette, we must pack!" She must get her attention away. Not let Nanette see the tears—flowing and flowing. Letty, longing to be braver, wished for courage. Prayed.

2

Letty healed in London, at a quiet hotel not too far from Hyde Park. The first day she did not venture out. She took her meals in her room and hid from the world—whatever it was that she feared outside.

The doorman at the Hotel Vandyke took pity on her. "You ought to see the park, ma'am," he suggested to her when she at last appeared, hatted and suitably clad for a July day. "But I'd suggest a 'brolly.' It looks like rain."

She realized that he meant an umbrella, without which one didn't stroll far in London. She went back upstairs to her comfortable hotel room, changed from a cool dimity to a wool. She'd have to buy some additions to her wardrobe if she was to avoid pneumonia. London's temperature of early July was reminiscent of Pennsylvania in March— dampness and all.

She allowed the doorman to hail her a hansom cab and sat back in comfort as the horses' hooves clacked companionably down Brompton Road, turned up Queen's Gate, and after a long but not unpleasant ride, let her off at a large park.

"Could you come back for me?" she asked the cabby.

He pointed with his long whip. "I could. But you shouldn't have any trouble pickin' up another to take you back to the 'otel." Sure enough, he pointed to where a group of cabs waited, horses stamping impatiently or moving from side to side in the traces while Cockney drivers swapped tales.

She took heart at the sight of Hyde Park. It was meant for strolling ladies, for nannies pushing high-wheeled prams, for children in ruffled dresses or sailor suits calling to one another and running pink-cheeked down the paths. There were even iron benches where one might sit without fear of molestation, since so many gently bred women and gray-hatted old men rested there. In the pale sunlight, she felt herself expanding.

She was spared Nathaniel. He had left her at Paddington Station, taking the night train north from Euston. She'd dreaded the parting, not out of any sense of wishing to be with him but because she feared greatly to be alone. Why had she not understood when she planned this trip that so much of her time was going to be on her own? Without even Nanette to tend her, she felt naked. She had no idea she would feel so vulnerable, so in need of support.

Seated in the pleasant park, she understood pleasurably that the venture had been strengthening. As an invalid takes those first tremulous steps. She watched with delight a flock of noisy pigeons drop from the gray skies to clamber over an old man. Evidently it was a tryst. Seated on the bench across from hers, he pulled out a rumpled bag and began to scatter bread crumbs. The noisy birds fought and scolded, landing on his shoulders and shoes.

By the time she was ready to go home, she realized how lonely she was. She envied the nannies walking behind their prams, knowing they had somewhere to go. Even the old man with his bag of crumbs belonged somewhere.

Need drove her to take a step she had been putting off. Once in her hotel room again, she got out the list of addresses Hester Davies had provided. She'd already written a note about Letty to a Daphne Howard.

"A pleasant girl," Hester had said. "If you're going to be in London, Letty, you'll need someone to show you about. I know Daphne would be kind. I've told her when you are coming. Here's her address."

Letty penned a careful note: *I am here in the Hotel Vandyke. Maybe I could call on you?* She sealed the envelope with nervous fingers. What was Daphne Howard like? In her state of uncertainty, Letty imagined a girl who laughed carelessly, who might make fun of Letty's lack of sophistication. Letty almost tore the message up. Instead, she took it to the doorman.

"How would I get this delivered?" she asked.

He received it from her cold fingers. "See to it at once, ma'am. Enjoy the park, did you?"

"Oh yes!" She thanked him with a large smile. Here in London, he was still her only friend.

Whoever Daphne was, she was not uncaring. A warm note, penned in a rounded hand, arrived the next morning:—*lovely if you'd*

169

join us for tea. I'll see if my mother can come too. She's so interested in foreigners. We'll expect you at four o'clock.

Letty was a foreigner! It seemed unreasonable to get upset about it. But the Hydes, the Benedicts, they had all come from England. The Mackenzies traced their ancestry back for hundreds of years. Letty found herself going over it all in her mind.

She dressed with greater care than she might have. Did she wish to appear as a cool and withdrawn alien, or as a casual world traveler? She missed the ministering hands of Nanette. By dint of inquiry, she had found that one of the maids in the hotel was "good with hair." But the girl was clumsy. Letty ended by pulling her tresses down, repinning them herself. She must engage a lady's maid. Perhaps Daphne could help.

Daphne, when met, assured her that she could help. "Indeed, my dear, it is essential that someone who knows about these things be there. Otherwise, I can safely say the agencies that offer prospective maids will simply take advantage of you. They always try to take advantage of Americans."

"Daphne," said her mother in reproof, "I'm sure Mrs. Mackenzie employs servants at home."

"Nothing to do with it," said Daphne evenly. She had rather large teeth; when she smiled, her lips came over them self-consciously. Otherwise her face was long, with high cheekbones that, to Letty, spoke of centuries of English breeding. Mrs. Montacute, on the contrary, was small and round and wrenlike, with a voice chirrupy rather than cool.

How old was Daphne? She had seen a little girl of about five on the stairs. When Letty had arrived, the child was clambering behind a uniformed nanny holding a baby.

The child had waved. "How do you do. I am Crystelle Howard. My mummy is Daphne Howard and my father, Peter, is in the army."

Nanny had grabbed for the small arm, tugged the child upward. "Ever so sorry, ma'am. We just got in from our walk. Little Miss Chatterbox here—"

"It doesn't matter," Letty had murmured as she was led to the drawing room on the second floor. She had a view of tall windows and chintzes as the doors ahead of her opened. The neatly clad maid announced, "Mrs. Mackenzie, ma'am."

Daphne had been sitting on the couch. Letty had thought how young she looked, and then again not as young as the girl she'd imagined writing her note to. Daphne's mother, Mrs. Montacute, was quite swallowed up by the cretonne-covered chair.

"So that's settled," said Daphne abruptly. "I will send a note round to the agency. Can you be here at ten tomorrow?"

"Ten o'clock?" said Letty, playing for time. "You think they can have someone for me to interview that early?"

"Good gracious," said Daphne smoothly, "these women expect to be up and at work by six. I'd say ten would be late for them. It's only you I was thinking of. Did you have something else on?"

"Don't let Daphne push you around," said Mrs. Montacute. Her blackberry eyes twinkled. Mouth serious.

"Now, Mother, I'm only trying to help Mrs. Mackenzie."

"Please call me Letty."

Daphne seemed pleased. "Why, thank you. That is so nice. Look, you must come to dinner soon and meet Peter."

"Your husband?"

"Mmm. He's in the Guards actually. Never knows when he's going to pull duty—at the palace, dining at the mess—that sort of thing."

"Ah," said Letty. "You mean he sees the queen?"

"Of course," said Daphne, her tone dismissing the subject. "Tell me, what are your plans while you're in England? Can you come to the seaside with us? Mother has a cottage at Weymouth. We all pile in there. I'm afraid there wouldn't be room for you and your maid—but you could stay close, couldn't you? Perhaps your husband can come, too."

"My husband? I hardly believe so. He's over here on business."

"Ah," Daphne and her mother said together.

To Letty's relief they didn't ask her what kind of business. Could she have answered? Nat owned ships, this much she knew, and he'd expanded into mining, railroads. Matt Frogge had talked of factories. But as to details, Letty was glad she didn't have to put it into words.

Letty went home in a hansom cab, going over her new commitments in her mind, like purchases made at a large variety store. Wondering what she'd really bought. The idea of a lady's maid filled her with apprehension. Nanette had been with Letty since she'd been a bride.

It was only for a few weeks. Nanette would be back at the end of August—or was it in early September? In a panic Letty realized that that was all of two months! She'd write Nanette tonight. Let her know she'd have to come back sooner. Letty couldn't possibly manage with a stranger for two months.

It was the first time in her life that she had ever been truly alone. It was all so new.

"But I like her!" insisted Letty stubbornly.

There had been only two candidates for the job of lady's maid.

One, a Yorkshire mill girl with roughened hands and a coarse manner, had been ruled out at once.

"We'll have to see what tomorrow will bring," said Daphne in the privacy of her small study. "The Welsh one's quite unsuitable too."

Which had brought forth Letty's cry of protest. She could see that Daphne was right. Gwen Powell was no more suitable than the mill-hand had been. Nevertheless, there was something that drew Letty to the Welsh woman. Her soft voice reminded Letty of a tea before a vicarage fire, with Olwen Evans, back home.

"But I do like her—" she kept declaring, over and over.

"Letty, dear, it's not just liking her that's important. I see that you have a kind heart. Oh my, yes. But, you are looking for someone who's good with hair, who can get your clothes ready for you—do all the things a personal maid is supposed to do. This Gwen Powell is a country girl—quite low class really. You shouldn't be giving her a second thought."

"I can't explain why," said Letty obstinately. "I just liked her." She stirred cream into her tea. "In any case, it'll just be for a few weeks."

"Have it your own way." Daphne's face spoke reams. "But I am frankly worried about you. She isn't at all what you require."

"Nevertheless," said Letty, "I think I shall engage her. Not that I'm not grateful for all your help, your advice. I wouldn't have known what to do without you."

"I was glad to be available," said Daphne, mollified. "If you change your mind, we can always look for someone else."

Later, Letty wondered whether it had been some need to prove to Daphne that she could cope that had led her to make such an appalling choice.

As Daphne had more or less predicted, Gwen was hopeless. Yet, for reasons Letty couldn't possibly fathom, she felt stuck with her. Almost as if she were responsible for Gwen's fate.

3

To see Daphne and Mrs. Montacute at the seaside was to see the English upper class on holiday. Gone was the formality, the trim maid-servant answering the door, the Staffordshire china from which tea was served. No, not gone—it was all there in a sense, but modified.

Letty had settled into her hotel. A solid edifice overlooking the beach. Lapping waters glinted in the morning sunshine, awakening her before the clumsy Gwen appeared to help her mistress dress. Sounds echoed pleasantly as children ventured out before their elders. Dogs barked, ran for a stick along the shaly shoreline.

Weymouth wasn't a particularly good spot for children, Mrs. Montacute explained. "Not enough sand."

"Then why did we always come here as children?" Daphne asked.

"Because your father liked it," was the reply.

"But Father was never with us, Mummy." Sometimes Daphne reverted to calling her mother by the childhood name. Letty could never discover what caused her to do so, unless it was simply that Daphne forgot she was grown. "We could have gone somewhere much nicer. That lovely beach near Swanage, for instance."

"Studland Bay," said Mrs. Montacute. "I agree, it would have been much pleasanter for you and John. But Weymouth was a place your father enjoyed."

"But, Mummy, he never came with us."

"Precisely," said Mrs. Montacute. "Nevertheless, the one time he did come, he knew he liked it."

"Peter and I have often talked of renting a place somewhere else."

"Go ahead," said Mrs. Montacute brightly. "I shall continue to come to Weymouth. I've grown used to it. The place suits me."

They had gathered, as they did every afternoon, in Mrs. Montacute's beach tent at the end of the promenade. There was a whole row of tents, all entirely alike except for what their owners had done with their insides. Constructed of red and white striped sailcloth, they had solid wooden floors and flags flying from the top, flapping in the perpetual wind.

Nanny was encouraged to sit with Crystelle and the baby, a short distance away. While Crystelle moved her small spade about, trying to find what sand she could under the stones, the nurse saw that the baby was comfortable in his carriage.

"Perky's growing," said Daphne contentedly.

"I wish you wouldn't give him that horrid name, darling. It's liable to stick, and then what will he do at Eton?"

"Harrow, Mummy. Peter wants him to go to Harrow. You know how he hated Eton."

"John went to Eton." Mrs. Montacute sighed. "Well, no matter. As long as you have the boy down for one place or the other. I suppose they give an equally good education."

"I wish I could have gone away to school," said Daphne unexpectedly. "I don't understand why boys can go to schools with long traditions just because it's expected. Like John following in Father's footsteps. But when it came to me, there just wasn't any place I could go. I mean, with boys, it's all planned from the moment they're born. Mother, did you ever want to go away to school?" Daphne's clipped voice tugged at Mrs. Montacute.

"Darling, why do you go on about school?"

"Oh, I don't know." Daphne's voice had a hint of anger. "You could've gone with Father on his safaris. But you didn't."

"Daphne, I'm sure this must be very boring for Letty—"

"No, not at all—" Letty sat back, wondering if she were in the way. The conversation had become rather personal.

"You really think I could've gone with your father?"

"Well, couldn't you?"

Mrs. Montacute stared out beyond them. To the sea. "Something you're going to have to learn about men, my pet. You simply can't hang on to their coattails."

Daphne flushed. "Is that what you think I'm trying to do with Peter?"

"In a way, yes. Darling, the man will do what he will do. I know Peter has been fearfully naughty—"

"Mother, you have the most astonishing way of putting things!" Daphne's lower lip shot out. "Peter's behaved abominably, and all you can say is, 'Men will be men.' If a woman acted that way—"

174

"I feel I shouldn't be here," said Letty uncomfortably.

Mrs. Montacute patted her on the arm. "Nonsense. You've become almost one of the family, hasn't she, Daphne?" When the usually self-contained girl nodded unhappily, Mrs. Montacute went on. "It's the army ways, pet. Especially in the Guards. You know how badly they all behave! Peter's young yet. He'll settle down after a while."

"He may settle down sooner than he thinks," said Daphne, her voice tremulous.

"I'm not sure I follow you."

"There's been talk of transferring him to another regiment. I think your little family's going out to India, Mummy."

"India!" Mrs. Montacute swallowed convulsively. She put down the cup she was holding. Then she said in a voice that was almost firm, "I see."

"It's a long way away," said Letty. She felt pushed to say something.

"Yes," said Mrs. Montacute slowly, "it's a very long way." She took a deep breath, as if she'd come to some kind of a conclusion. "So you see, Daphne, you'll have the opportunity to see many things. It will be an experience you'll never forget."

"You never went with Father!" Daphne said accusingly.

"I was never asked, child. I would have given anything to have been invited along. But big-game hunting was a man's toy. Your father wanted me at home. If your husband likes to think of you as keeping the place going while he goes off to war—or to hunt elephant—that's where he wants you. If 'home' is India, he'll expect you to go along."

"Mummy, you make it sound so easy."

"Well, it is rather."

Daphne got up and left them.

Mrs. Montacute blew her nose loudly. Letty looked over at her and saw that she was crying.

"I'm so sorry," Letty said. "I gather this isn't something that is easy for Daphne—or for you."

Again, Mrs. Montacute blew her nose. "My son-in-law is a rotter—a perfect beast. But what can I tell Daphne except that she's got to go with her husband. It's her only choice."

"Couldn't she stay here?"

Daphne's mother shook her head. "It wouldn't be right. A woman's place is with her husband, no matter what sort of man he turns out to be. She has to stick by him. Anyway, I know my daughter. She'd only get into difficulties by herself."

"Yes, of course." Letty paused. "I know so little about India. Is it dangerous?"

"Oh, no. Heat, disease, the heathenish ways bother some people.

175

It's an uncomfortable country. And so far from home." Mrs. Montacute got out of her chair. "Well, I suppose we might as well begin packing the tea things, eh? The weather's been so nice until now. You don't know how fortunate that is. Some summer holidays, we've sat inside and had nothing to do but write letters and work on our embroidery."

Letty sensed that she had contracted some of Mrs. Montacute's gloom, Daphne's desperation. Like a case of the grippe passed from one to another. Her spirits lifted when, on entering her hotel, she found letters awaiting her. From home! That word had come to have a new meaning for her.

4

Letty opened her letters with eager fingers. She felt warmed by the thought that she was not forgotten, yet strangely angered that life at home should go on without her. Changing a landscape so familiar to her.

Emma wrote: *We are consenting to Hitty's engagement, not just because we like Compton Grey, but because we feel it is most probably her last chance to get a husband. On acquaintance, Dr. Grey seems both charming and reliable. We are delaying plans for the wedding until your return, Letty. It is too much of a family matter to be decided hastily. Hitty is behaving rather typically. All girlish blushes and very moody.* The last sentence was heavily underlined in Emma's spidery hand.

There was more—pages of it. Letty sat there—the writing paper in her hands—staring beyond it all to the open sea. Her gaze took in the waves as they moved in slow succession to break up on the beach, suck the pebbles downward, then ripple forward again.

Hitty to be married! Letty had never thought it would be. Yet the idea brought her discomfort; she'd prided herself on being the only married Benedict girl. Mother had made that distinction, made it quite clear. It was agreed that "poor Hitty" would be the solitary spinster, dumpy and undesirable, trailing about picking up Mother's gloves, her lorgnette left on the table in the parlor.

They had all allowed it. Now it would be changing. In the half-light of self-centeredness, only partially acknowledged, Letty wondered how Hitty's marriage would affect her? Was it possible that she and Hitty might become close? Letty thought about Compton Grey and wondered why he wished to marry Hitty.

177

Letty had met the man only once, yet she felt a claim on him. She remembered with a sad bitterness his urging her to call him, to ask his help. She saw once more the note she'd written him, curling black in the hearth's ashes. Nathaniel's cold anger. Did Dr. Grey in some way threaten his alliance with Henry Porter? Had Letty, at the back of her mind, looked on Dr. Grey as a rescuer?

She sat, staring out the window. A small boy and his dog, walking along the moving edges of the tide, caught her eyes but not her thoughts. She watched the dog hesitate to go after a stick tossed in the waves by the boy. Was Hitty sure of this marriage? Did she really know what she was doing, or was this a last desperate grab for security? Avoidance of a spinster's loneliness? And Mama and Papa, where did they come into it? Why had it all come to a head while she, Letty, was out of the country?

Letty returned to the letter. More about Hitty, about Compton Grey. *He isn't exactly what we might have hoped for her. I don't have to remind you that a physician is not socially acceptable in most quarters. But then I think most of our friends will be kind. In any case, Hitty has never been one to enthrall a dinner table, and quite honestly I don't believe she expects to be too active at soirées or teas after she is married. I just hope she'll have the good sense to see she's too old to start a family. I'll mention adoption to them as an obvious solution.*

There was more family news in a second letter.

I forgot to tell you, Letty, that Cousin Frances is expecting to hear from you. I wrote her the moment I knew you'd be in England. Her note just this morning arrived—the mails must be finding calmer seas than I fear you had. I am enclosing her address. Please get in touch with her at once. Old ladies do so wait for the coming of news. As you know, Frances and I have never met, so you will be our go-between. Imagine, she and I have corresponded for forty-one years. A long time. Your visit will make up for all the ones she and I never had. She lives outside Salisbury, and I'm sure you'll find it quite easy to get to. England is so small.

Well, it solved the problem of what to do with the weeks between staying here at Weymouth and meeting Nathaniel at Southampton.

"Where is Salisbury?" Letty asked Daphne and Mrs. Montacute. As if to prove the old lady's words, the weather had turned nasty. The women were taking tea in the summer cottage.

"You are going to Salisbury?" asked Mrs. Montacute. She was seated at a table in the window, evidently to catch the full benefit of the gray light that was wavering in on a broken cloud pattern. She held a piece of a jigsaw puzzle in her hand, poised over the partially finished picture.

"Mother—that silly puzzle. You must have done it at least forty times. Can't we get you some different ones?"

"Of course you can, darling. But I only work them when I'm at the seaside. So I forget in between. They all seem new."

"Is Salisbury hard to get to?" Letty began again.

"You have to take the train," said Mrs. Montacute, trying for another puzzle piece. "It will take you all of one morning to get there. Or an afternoon."

"It's really not far," said Daphne. "Maybe forty or fifty miles." She wrinkled her aristocratic nose. "I'm so bad at distances.

"Would you know anywhere I could stay?"

"The Rose and Crown," said Daphne.

"The White Hart," said Mrs. Montacute.

"Then you do know Salisbury?"

"Oh, everybody knows Salisbury. The way they know Bath—or Bristol." Daphne bit her lip, searching for the exact color silk with which to rethread her needle.

"You're not to tell her another word until she gives us the reason why she's going there," said Mrs. Montacute. She looked up with an impish grin.

"I had a letter from my mother yesterday," said Letty. "She wants me to visit her cousin."

"Your mother has a cousin living in Salisbury?" Mrs. Montacute put down the piece of puzzle. "How extraordinary!"

Letty blushed. "Not really. Both my parents' family origins are here in this country."

Mrs. Montacute went on. "So many emigrants. I know one should never be surprised. I met a woman last year who had cousins in Australia. Now there's a country I'd never admit having relatives from!"

"Why not?" asked Letty innocently.

"Oh, my dear!" Mrs. Montacute's brown eyes took on a wounded look. "Convict ships. Have you forgotten your history? Australia was founded by people too bad to be kept in the British Isles."

"Mother," said Daphne impatiently, "you could be hanged for stealing a sheep in those days. Some of those people were quite innocent."

"Nevertheless, they were found guilty," said Mrs. Montacute stubbornly. "I had an uncle—Uncle Eustace—called to the bar. The British system of justice is the finest in the world, you know. But enough of this. Letty, tell us about your mother's cousin."

"There's not much to tell," said Letty slowly. "Neither my mother nor I has ever met her. She and mother have corresponded for years, though. Her address gives the name of the village and then 'near Salisbury.'"

"You will just have to rent a coach," said Mrs. Montacute with an air of finality.

179

When Letty and Gwen arrived at the tiny hotel in Salisbury, the doorman proved to be an invaluable ally, very much as the man had at the Hotel Vandyke.

"No problem, milady." His speech was slow and resembled a growl in the throat. His smile reassured her that it was merely the native way of saying things. "When was it you were after going to Stoneyford?"

"I'm waiting for a reply from my cousin now. I rather think I might be needing the carriage tomorrow."

"Ah," he said, rubbing his dry hands together. "Not that it matters so much. No matter at all. The vehicle only works for the undertaker. Generally, it don't have many calls on its use."

"You mean, I'm to travel to Stoneyford in a hearse?"

"It's the most comfortable way," he said reprovingly. "There's not a great deal of call for travel between villages in these parts. Folks have their own carts—carriages if they be gentry. But the undertaker converts it, see. The middle section can either drop right down, for the coffin, or be set up to make two nice seats. You and your maid'll ride very nice."

"Oh, I see," said Letty feebly. What else was she to do? At first it had seemed so easy. Now, once again, she sensed mountains closing around her.

The streets of Salisbury were crowded; it seemed to be market day. Women, heavy busted, milled about. In the shopfronts, narrow windows were crisscrossed with leaded panes. Letty stared through a single diamond until a woman glanced up, her expression seeming to say, "Either come in and make your purchase or else move on." Letty felt an intruder. She lowered her eyes and quickened her step. But to where? She was merely strolling, passing time until Cousin Frances invited her.

She made her way back across the green, an open space that protected the cathedral. She would have liked to have sat awhile, but the only seat was occupied by two nannies, talking, their knitting needles going as fast as their tongues, the perambulators of their charges parked close enough to be rocked with a foot. Letty decided her best choice was to enter the cathedral.

It was like going into a stone forest. The immense height left her with a craning neck and a slight dizziness. Ignoring the pews, which she had initially sought for her aching feet's sake, she found herself impelled forward. Down the forested avenue, stone columns rose into slender trunks that met—if the neck could twist back that far—at some central point so lofty it lacked only clouds and birds.

She decided to buy a guidebook before leaving the cathedral.

Feeling the need to move reverentially, embarrassed by her footsteps echoing on the stone, she approached the wooden desk by the great doors. An old man with watery eyes offered her a choice of two books.

"I'll take both," she whispered. Her voice was snatched from her, transformed into a rustle to lodge somewhere high up in the rarefied air. Caught no doubt on a pillar.

"That'll be sixpence," he murmured. Hollow, like the floor itself, the ceiling, she supposed, for a crypt.

She fumbled in her reticule. "Thank you," she muttered, mostly nodding. Attempting a smile.

He stared, then, as if reassurred, gave her a nod back.

She dropped a sovereign in the poor box. As it clinked against the other coins, she thought she saw the old man's eyes glint. She could hear the Reverend Mr. Evans quoting, "the poor are always with us."

But who are the poor? Not just the poor of today, shambling and distorted in their clothes of twisted bone, coarse skin; but the poor of all the other years who must have come to this place. Prayed for what heaven? Gone on to what fate? Or stayed here, caged within their rotting flesh while choirs sang inspiring hymns and a man in a bishop's robes harangued from the stone pulpit she'd admired minutes before.

The sunlight struck her face as she walked through the great entryway. It was warm outside. Fresh smelling from a sudden shower that Salisbury had undergone while she was encased in the cathedral. Her step on the path quickened.

The church clock struck five. She'd missed tea. To an American, that was no disaster. Even if they did have tea at home.

The vehicle seemed to smell of death. Try as she might, Letty couldn't get the idea out of her mind. She half considered telling Gwen about it. But the woman looked as if she had all she could deal with just riding in this heat. It was one of those sultry days in an English August. Not as hot as Philadelphia, but coming on them unprepared, through the showers and heavy clouds. The sun gazed on them, fierce and relentless. Poor Gwen was suffering. Her pale skin was glistening.

"Gwen?"

"Yes, ma'am?"

"Is the countryside like this in Wales?"

"Oh no, ma'am. Most of the time it's steep, see. Mountainsides with little streams running down them. What I'd give to have their coolness now."

How Gwen smelled! Not for the first time, Letty wondered how her maids at home kept from letting their body odors oppress. For surely one couldn't work and not sweat. Perhaps because the rooms at home were larger, the ceilings higher, permitting freedom and personal space.

And Gwen crowded her. A thousand times, Letty had regretted engaging the woman. She was barely a companion. With her sighs and her clacking knitting needles—and the colors the stupid fool took to using! Who would wear stockings of red and green?

Letty sighed. How many weeks till she would have Nanette back? It was too warm to be bothered counting. Just let it be soon.

The driver slowed his horse. "Thar, milady, over against the hillside—" He pointed with his whip. His voice, rumbling and soft in the accent she was coming to recognize as West Country, went on, "Thar's the village, see. Over 'crosst the bridge is the house. Can you see, milady?"

Letty peered. She tried to concentrate on what he was saying. She saw a handsome edifice, rising out of a group of trees. Somehow she had not thought Cousin Frances' house would be so large. Almost as imposing as Nathaniel Mackenzie's. She experienced a feeling of surprise.

"Thank you, driver." She didn't know what else to say. She mopped her brow discreetly. The horse, flicked at by the whip, stirred into movement again. Letty could hear the scrape of the wagon's brakes as they fought to keep the wheels from taking flight down the steep hill. Why had Mother sent her here? Flushing uncomfortably, Letty restrained her anger.

The mare seemed to take heart at the sight of the village. They drove smartly between the cottages, worried an old dog who lay in the sun before the bow-windowed store. It got up and glanced at them with glazed eyes, apparently debating whether it was worth the effort to bark.

Houses, like gnomes with coolie hats, peeped over the top of brick walls. Hollyhocks stood straight and tall by their front doors, entryways open like the mouths of children caught yawning. A woman in a bonnet looked up from her weeding. The coachman waved, and she called back. Her eyes, suspicious, followed their progress.

The bridge was walled by stone. It caught the sound of the carriage and made an echo out of it. Frightening a group of feasting ducks, who registered their protest with flapping wings.

The driver brought the mare to a halt. He got down from his seat and undid the chain on the gate. A large sign read: *Trespassers will be prosecuted.* The sight of it made Letty uncomfortable. She felt for Cousin Frances' note in her handbag, seeking reassurance. Odd to feel that the notice applied to her.

They drove up a long lane enclosed by trees. The sun came through in triangular glints, butterflies of light that kept to the highest branches. Below it was damp, mossy, the road deeply rutted. Graveled in places, suggestive of better care in another era. Suddenly they came to a round driveway, neatly kept and free of weeds. The house was staring at them; tall windows that saw all and revealed nothing. Letty noticed that they were shuttered or curtained. The realization depressed her.

It was not an architectural marvel. Someone must have had the idea to add on a wing here, a room there. Yet it had an aspect of dignity. Perhaps it was its age? Or the apple pink of the bricks, covered in part with creeper. Six round steps led up to the front door. The carriage came to a halt before them.

Letty knew she was expected to get out, but found herself hesitating. She must alight from the coach, climb the steps, and ring the bell.

"Did you want me to come in with you, ma'am?" asked Gwen.

"I think it might be best if you wait here." Letty tried to make her voice sound firm but kind. She pulled herself out of her seat, and with the driver to assist her, reached the pebbled ground.

An old man she'd not noticed before stood at the graveled driveway's edge, leaning on a crudely formed rake. "Afternoon," he said politely.

"Good afternoon," she heard herself reply. A raising of the spirits, as if he'd welcomed her. She gave him a diffident smile.

He replied with a nod and went back to his raking.

She raised her hand and rapped on the door. The brass knocker needed polish. After what seemed like a long time, she heard noises from behind the entrance. A moment of panic. Was she expected? She could still go back down the stone steps. Write Mother some excuse.

The door opened. She tried to smile but felt her face stiff and afraid.

"Cousin Frances?"

Surely this was not Cousin Frances!

The small person before her made no answer but opened the door a little wider, as slowly as she had answered it. Her hand a kind of a claw on the blistering surface. The doorkeeper was hunched—not noticeably so, but her shoulders and chest swallowed her so that one wondered what had become of her neck. Her eyes had gone too. In their place were slits in swollen flesh. From behind them, the seeing organs glittered, taking in Letty.

Letty tried again. "I'm expected. Mrs. Hyde has asked me to tea."

"You'd better step inside," said the creature. She moved slowly, the solid body sliding to the side. An impression of starched white apron, mobcap tied untidily under the elongated chin, carpet slippers.

"Cassie!" called a voice, peremptory and high. "Cassie, are you being naughty again? I told you to let Mrs. Mackenzie in!"

Letty peered down the hallway. She could just make out the figure of a woman leaning on a cane.

"I do apologize." This time the tones were modulated, well bred. "It is Letty, isn't it? Dear girl, come in, come in."

Letty drew in a deep breath. It was going to be all right after all. "Cousin Frances?"

"Oh, child—" They met in mid-hall. An old arm was thrown about Letty's shoulders, Letty stooping so she could be reached. Afraid to hug this frail creature, yet enfolded in a love she wasn't used to.

Cousin Frances regarded her. "My word, you are tall, Letty! We Hydes don't run to stature. I suppose I'd always imagined— Dear me.

Well, come on in." She wheeled about, handling the cane skillfully. "Don't take any notice of Cassie. She's been very wicked today."

"Yes," said Letty, striving to understand. "Oh, Cousin Frances, I have my maid in the carriage. My maid and then there's the driver. Is there someplace they could wait?"

Cousin Frances wheeled again. "Cassie!" Her whole tone changed. Voice sharp and decisive. "Go out to the coach and make them drive round to the back. You give them tea, mind?"

Cassie stared at her mistress. Her hair, smooth as a poppy pod under the cap, was completely white. Not so much as a nod in response. She gathered herself together, as one might a handkerchief one intends to use, and walked with cautious feet through the doorway, down the round steps.

"Come into the parlor, Letty. We shall have some tea presently. But first—" She entered the room behind her.

Letty received a shock. Turning to her Cousin Frances, instead she saw Mother there. Tall, peremptory, leaning on a cane. A sense of height that had nothing to do with measurement in inches, for Frances Hyde was a short woman. Even the profile, as Cousin Frances turned, was Emma.

It was extraordinary! Letty saw herself following her cousin as if in a dream. It was easier when they reached the lighted parlor, a room cluttered to overflowing with Cousin Frances' life.

A grand piano took up an entire corner. Draped with a silk shawl with long, twisting tassels, it stated that it was little used. A skinny vase of dried cattails sat on top and, unaccountably, a pair of long white leather gloves. Suggesting they'd been left there from some party long ago. A lamp was lit on the table, though it was full daylight outside.

"Letty, dear, if you would take that particular chair. Then I can see you from where I sit." Cousin Frances had lowered herself with obvious pain into a cup of a seat. Its fraying and threadbare chintz didn't match the cushions placed there to support her back. Like Emma, she had made some inner insistence on keeping upright, propped and held into ramrod stiffness. Like Emma, her neck muscles had developed a tremor so that Cousin Frances was perpetually nodding. A veined and blotched hand, devoid of Emma's diamonds, rested atop the ebony cane.

"Now you shall tell me all."

Letty perched on the edge of her chair. In this dingy room she felt out of place while still prompted by that odd sensation of familiarity. Like two entirely disparate objects or impressions, it was hard to equate them. She struggled with it all, the room that edged ever closer, the odor of age, the pathetic eagerness with which Cousin Frances was inviting her to share. What could she share?

"Mother sent greeting—love." The word echoed in the room, seeking someplace to alight.

The old lady before her sighed. "Never met. Extraordinary. All these years, corresponding. If we met somewhere in town, we'd pass as two strangers. I'd given up— I'd always dreamed—" The wrinkled face began to crumple, freshets appeared behind the tired eyes.

"Mother would've given anything to be here now." Letty knew she lied. In all the years, she'd heard Emma mention Cousin Frances only a few times. Then, negligently, as if the Englishwoman were a fool for writing. Here in this room, Letty understood. Oh, not Mother. She'd never understand Mother, not as long as she lived. But it was possible that Emma really valued the friendship, covered it up as she covered so many of her real feelings.

The old lady got up very deliberately, making no attempt to wipe the moisture from her eyes. She managed to stand erect, refusing Letty's offers at help with a small wave of the hand, and stalked to her desk.

"I was looking for her last letter. But no matter. It's the others I want you to see." She drew them from a cavernous pigeonhole. The letters were bound with blue ribbon soiled from countless tying and retying. "See, I've kept them all!" She showed other stacks, still stuffed in their compartments. Tied, as the bundle in her hand.

"It must be well over forty years—" Cousin Frances' tone was reminiscent. "Before your mother and father were married. You were thirty-nine last October, correct?"

"Yes," said Letty, startled at this stranger's knowledge.

"And such a terrible time you've had. Losing two babies within months of one another." The old head quivered. Mother's heavy brows, in the surprisingly delicate face, drew together in a frown.

"But you've other children living. Albert, Amelia, and Polly, they can be a comfort to you. And they are well, I trust?" Cousin Frances was peering at her. The bundle of letters lay, like clothes done up for a bazaar, cradled in her lap.

"Yes. At least when I last heard. Except Albert—"

"I know. Emma wrote me. He has to take care not to overexert himself. The lamb." Cousin Frances twisted in her chair. "You see, I had only Clemmy. That is her portrait over there."

In the dimness Letty made out an oval frame. The painting of a child.

"Isn't she an angel? Poor pet. She would have been thirty-four this year if God had spared her."

Letty made a small noise in her throat. Clemmy would have been as old as Hitty. But, like a picture in an ancient story book, Clemmy had no connection with life today. Except, apparently, for Cousin Frances.

"Is she like your Polly? Emma writes that Polly has fair hair."

The door was pushed open. The odd maidservant seemed to stumble in on them, bowed beneath an enormous tray.

"There you are, Cassie. I had almost given up on tea."

"Where do you want it?" mumbled the woman.

"Now, Cassie." Cousin Frances' voice had become patient, molded by the need to explain something very simple to one who was yet simpler. "You know you have to put the tray down, then you can set up the table."

Letty left them to it and walked over to the portrait. As she'd been bidden. She stared at Clemmy. What could one tell from such a face? That it had been loved, to have hung here on this wall for so long? True, the child was blond, eyes like pale violets, lips parted.

"Do you see any family resemblance?" Cousin Frances asked.

Letty felt panic suddenly. What was she supposed to see? She leaned forward toward the painting, groping for time. "Perhaps to Polly—the same coloring."

It was enough. "Ah, I thought so." Cousin Frances sighed. "She was so young when God took her. I'd tried and tried to bear a living child. When we had Clemmy, I thought the world had been given into my arms."

"I'm so sorry."

Cousin Frances moved in her chair, her lower lip twitching, her hands passing over the cups and saucers on the tea tray. "It all happened a long time ago. I suppose it's a sign of getting old—to live so much in the past."

A series of bells fell on their ears like rain. In a running pattern that the room received passively, used to such etching.

Cousin Frances appeared not to have heard. "—so many memories," she was saying.

"But how lovely!" Letty had stopped in her tracks, trying to trace the sound. To be sure, there was the clock—an enormous thing, it stood as if it intended to keep an eye on them all.

Cousin Frances raised her head. She stared first at Letty, then at the clock. "Oh, you mean King Charles. Yes, he's part of the past too."

"Does it have a history?"

"Oh, my dear—" The old lady dismissed the question with a gesture. "We are quite sure he must have. But it's lost, you see."

"Lost?" Letty felt a sense of affront. It was carelessness that had failed to safeguard such a secret.

"I know, I agree with you. It's a real pity. Like so many of the

187

things in this house. When I go, who will know anything about them?" She looked about her, troubled.

Letty's eye had caught another detail of the clock. She bent over, the better to read the carved writing, then said out loud, "King Charles —1651." A man's head, bearded and staring, surrounded by leaves. "What on earth? I don't understand."

"Oh, but surely, dear. Charles in the oak tree? At least you must recall the story of his father?"

"Um," said Letty. She began to wend her way back to the tea table, hiding her confusion in movement.

"Parliament put him on trial. Cut his head off. This poor boy"— Cousin Frances indicated the clock—"was fleeing for his life. The Roundheads rode right beneath the tree where he was hiding."

"But the son escaped?"

"Of course, dear. Otherwise the clock wouldn't be carved that way, would it?"

Cassie came back laden with another, smaller tray. The jam, in a dish curled like a fig leaf; two rather soiled napkins. She stood over them, the tray tipping dangerously.

"Thank you, Cassie. Have you given our two visitors in the kitchen tea?"

"It's what you told me to do," Cassie grumbled, closing the door behind her somewhat noisily.

"She's getting old, just like I am," said her mistress. She lifted the teapot. "She's been with me so long, I've lost track of time. She's all I've got really. That's important, isn't it?" Her old eyes looked quizzical, as if asking reassurance from Letty. "I mean, I know I spoil her, but without any family left—"

"I think it's important for you to do what you want," said Letty. She knew her voice to be hollow, polite. How could she tell this woman what to do? She'd just met her.

Cousin Frances touched her cheek with an expression of dismay. "Dear me, how careless of me. I almost forgot."

"Something I can help you with?"

"No, no. I'll manage." She crossed the room and stopped before a long, narrow closet. She took a small key from a chain about her neck, unlocked the cabinet, and drew forth a pretty bowl with a china bow on its top.

Returned to her seat, Cousin Frances got her breath. Then said in a whisper, "As you see, I'm forced to keep certain things locked."

"Yes." Again Letty was cautious, restrained.

"If I don't—" The long lips, so equine over the yellowed teeth, moved into an expression of disapproval. "Well, she steals it. Imagine having to safeguard the sugar! But she'll take it. She has a passion for sweet things." She drew in a deep breath. "Now, Letty, while we have our tea, I want to explain."

"Explain?"

"How I've left everything. Oh, Mr. Comstock, my attorney, knows. A most reliable man. It's all drawn up. The heirlooms go to you in America. Now don't look surprised. You're the only Hydes left. There's not a lot; you can divide things anyway you want."

"You mean, like the clock—?"

"The clock, the bed I sleep in, the clothes closet. A linen press that we'll see after tea. You must understand. Hydes have used these things for generations. Been born here, laid out here. Now don't look sad. My time is coming, and I almost welcome it." She sighed. "It's been thirty lonely years since my Richard left me."

"Thirty years you've been a widow?"

Cousin Frances leaned over, touched Letty on the arm. "There are worse ways to spend a life. I've kept busy—tending to little things in the village—friends in Salisbury—though they've all gone now. Yes, its almost here." She sat back. "You'll feel like that too, my child, when the time comes. One gets tired."

They had finished the meal. Suddenly Cousin Frances stood up. "I know you have to get back to town soon. But first come and see the bedroom."

It was a command, not an invitation. Letty rose and followed her.

Cousin Frances occupied only two rooms of the house; the others were closed. "Except for the kitchen area," she said. "Cassie has her own domain. I never intrude. Haven't, in fact, for years."

The erect figure, so like Emma Benedict's, led Letty into a doorway down the corridor. "This is mine," she said calmly. "I wouldn't dream of subjecting you to this tour, were it not for the furniture. I think you should have your chance to think."

The room was bright. The tall windows were shuttered only at their tops; their lower halves let in filtered light. On the opposite side of Hyde Manor from the parlor, they viewed crowding trees. The effect was of being in a forest.

Cousin Frances had turned away. Now she gave a cry, causing Letty to whirl hurriedly.

"That naughty girl. Oh, why does she have to do this sort of thing?" Cousin Frances had gone over to a narrow bureau. With a frail hand, she was struggling to push closed one of the upper drawers.

"Please, let me help."

"It's all right." The slight chest was heaving. "Letty, dear, there's a vial on my dressing table—"

"Ah. Here it is."

189

The old lady, leaning against her bureau, removed the bottle's stopper awkwardly. She put the open container to her nostrils, one at a time and deliberately. Sniffed lightly.

"That's better. I shouldn't let her upset me. It's silly."

"Cassie?"

"Yes. She's getting a little peculiar." This last said almost soundlessly. "Worse today than I've seen her."

"What does she do?"

"Such odd things—I'm almost embarrassed to talk of it. She likes to go through my jewelry. Her mind wanders." Cousin Frances made a gesture with her hand, tracing a circular movement. "She—it could almost be amusing—she fancies she's me."

"You're serious?"

"Oh, I've spoken to Mr. Comstock about it. My attorney, you know? He suggested I get rid of her. The voice dropped even further. "But I couldn't send her to the asylum. She's been with me for years."

"She may be dangerous."

"Where is the risk? Two old women, living out their last years. If she killed me, it would only hasten my good friend Death along. No, Letty, my conscience would never let me rest if I had that poor soul committed. In any case, she'd have nothing to gain materially. Except for these heirlooms—the contents of my desk—it's all to go to her."

"You're remarkably generous."

"Not really. She's devoted the best years of her life to my husband and myself. We often talk of the old days. There I go, sentimental again." She touched Letty on the wrist, soft as a cat's paw. "I expect your mother tends to it too. Weakness of the elderly. You must forgive me."

The eyes were Emma's. Letty tried to smile.

"Now listen, dear. When the furniture's to go overseas, the price that's gotten for the house will pay for shipping it. Everything over that will take care of Cassie."

Letty heard herself asking, "What will happen to Cassie?"

"It's all arranged. Such a nice woman in the village. I've known the family all my life. They will take the poor thing. And Cassie knows of it. She's been told over and over that Florrie will care for her." She shook her head. "Though sometimes I wonder how much she understands."

Letty glanced around the room. "Are you sure you're all right with her—here, alone?"

"Now don't you go worrying." The old lady began her slow tread across the room. "And promise you won't tell Emma. I can't have her worrying, not over that distance. Why it takes weeks just to get a letter."

Cousin Frances wanted Letty to see the Hyde furniture. "It's solid oak. No nails, only pegs. You've got to understand, Hydes have been born in that bed for centuries. Brides have placed their trousseaus in that chest over there. It's got to stay in the family, even if it does have to cross the ocean."

"Yes," said Letty, surreptitiously glancing at the watch that hung from the gold chain about her neck. It was nearly five. "Cousin Frances, I don't feel I should detain my driver much longer."

"Oh mercy, so inconsiderate of me—running on while you were needing to be gone." She stared at Letty. Her eyes were kinder than Mother's. Were Mother's kind at all? "I hope so much for one more visit. How long are you planning to stay?"

Letty found herself promising to return. After all, Cousin Frances was her sole reason for being in Salisbury.

"What time should I ask the driver to bring me out?"

The old eyes crinkled. "You really will come? You are so very generous—you might be doing other, more entertaining things. Letty, do you look like your mother? I have imagined all this time that you must."

"Some say I do. More than Hitty."

Cousin Frances took Letty's arm. They walked back to the parlor where Letty had left her reticule, her light wrap. "You are a dear, sweet child, and you've made your old relative very happy." She paused in the parlor doorway. Raised her voice to a shrill pitch. "Cassie? I wonder if she can hear me. She so often pretends—"

The maid appeared in the darkness. Her white apron and cap like a ghost in the tenebrosity of the passageway. The eyes, buried in their slits, unreadable.

"Oh, there you are! I didn't know if you'd be within earshot. Mrs. Mackenzie is ready to leave. If you'd tell the driver—"

"Very good, ma'am." Did Letty imagine the insolence, its suggestion hidden under the surly attitude, the slowness with which the woman moved?

"You will come tomorrow?" Cousin Frances asked.

"I promise. You didn't say what time."

"Anytime at all. I'm just here—waiting."

Letty held on to the veined hands. "I want you to know I never understood what it was like to have an English family—till today."

Cousin Frances fought back the tears that threatened to spill on to her velvet cheeks. She brushed at them ineffectually, her eyes very bright. "We'll talk more tomorrow. It'll be lovely. Now don't keep your carriage waiting."

The last thing Letty saw as the vehicle swung about to leave the graveled circle was Cousin Frances waving. Her old body held erect,

191

one hand on her cane, the other making slow gestures.

The old man was still raking the pebbles. As the carriage passed, he paused, smiling ever so slightly. Touched his cap.

"I didn't care for that maid at all," said Gwen in her thick Welsh voice. "Daft, that's what she is. He felt it too." She indicated the driver.

"My cousin says she's getting very old—" Letty was quiet all the way back to town.

6

Letty decided not to take Gwen back with her to Hyde Manor. "You take the afternoon off. I am sure you can find something you'd enjoy doing. The shops are quite nice. And you could have tea."

Gwen responded by giving a bob. "If you're sure you won't want me, milady? I mean, going all that long way?" When Letty shook her head Gwen said, "At least it won't be so hot today. Could even be a nice ride."

The vehicle that did double duty as a hearse wasn't needed by its owner, and Letty was again able to engage it for the afternoon. Without Gwen, she found the drive almost pleasant, though there was a storm brewing. Piles of clouds, heaped like cream that had gathered stain from raspberry juice, rested atop the hills. The air seemed heavy and laden.

The first sign of a difference was the gate. It was hanging free, blowing to and fro in the wind.

The driver shrugged. "Should I close it behind us, do you suppose?"

"Maybe we should," said Letty. "It must have been left that way because we were expected."

The old man wasn't at his post. His rake was. Leaning against the holly bush. A pile of pebbles pushed into a dirty heap. Signs he'd been there a short time before.

The coach pulled up before the stone steps. How hollowed they were in their centers. Little things she hadn't noticed yesterday. Like the two front windows that had been bricked up. Right in the middle of the row.

Letty recalled Mrs. Montacute's story. "It was the Window Tax, dear. One of the Georges, I think, had this bright notion to impose a tax on the number of windows you had. So half the mansions today have their eliminated windows. Rather silly, isn't it? I mean, they could have been restored, but we don't always get around to things. Not like you efficient Americans."

Letty had brought a few small gifts for Cousin Frances. She clutched her brown paper package under one arm as she allowed the driver to help her down from the carriage. The wind had increased in violence. It was whipping the trees, whirling the dead remnants of summer about.

Letty felt herself jump when the door suddenly opened. "Cassie?"

The woman stood aside. Wordless. Letty stepped inside, glad for the shelter.

Cassie moved forward and waved her arm at the vehicle. There was something expressive in her movement, something not seen in the dormouse of yesterday. "Round to the back!" she shouted, trying to make her voice heard over the wind.

"Your mistress is expecting me," Letty said.

"Yes. She wants you to come in, sit yourself down. I've made a fire in the hearth."

Cassie had. Not a very brave one, to be sure, but a little sign of warmth in the overpowering cold. A cup of tea would be welcome! Where was Cousin Frances?

"Where is my cousin?" asked Letty. Hearing her voice sound harsh, hard.

"In the village," said Cassie. She'd set the tray on a stool as before. Now she drew out the tea table. "She wants you to start. I've made scones. There's jam and cream."

There was, indeed. Cups, plates for two.

"What is my cousin doing in the village?"

"She's gone to see an old friend. It's a person who's coming to take my place when I'm gone. Help run things."

"You are leaving?"

"Very shortly now. Will that be all?"

"No. No, it isn't all. Cassie, sit down for a moment. I want to ask you some questions."

"There's your driver's tea to get," said Cassie, almost rudely. "I can't stay long."

"Where are you going when you leave here?"

Cassie snorted. "Anywhere where I'll not be treated like dirt— taken for granted."

Letty flushed. "Surely, Cassie—"

194

"Oh, the likes of you don't know!" said the maid. She hugged her round body, giving herself comfort. "You'd better pour that tea. Else it'll chill," she commented.

"I can't understand my cousin's absence," said Letty insistently. "She specifically said she'd be here all afternoon."

"Something come up, you see. Around the business of my leaving."

"Wasn't it rather sudden?"

"You might say. I'm going now." Cassie stood up. "She'll be here in a minute, I daresay."

"Walking in this storm? I hardly think that's likely. Now that I think of it, if you were to tell my coachman where to go, we could send for her."

Cassie had pulled herself to her full height. Her eyes were steady beneath the deep folds of skin. "That wouldn't be at all advisable."

"Why shouldn't we send the coach for her?"

"Because—" said Cassie. Then stopped. Stared, her face still and unreadable. The deepset eyes unblinking. "She'd prefer not to be fetched. She has a ride. The gardener took her."

The old man. The downed tools. But he seemed to have just left. Letty took a deep breath. "Very well, Cassie. You go and get the driver his tea."

"That's another thing—"

"I beg your pardon?"

"You're to stop calling me Cassie."

"But?" Letty was dumbfounded. Not so much by the demand as by the way it was stated. A command.

"I'm to be called Mary. After all, it's my name."

"All right, Mary." Letty spoke through stiff lips. "I haven't any idea what this is about, but as soon as the storm's over, please have my driver bring the carriage round."

"Yes, ma'am."

"And another thing—"

"What?" Voice surly. Hands clutched like twisted weeds across the white apron.

In her primmest voice, Letty said, "I am sorry to say this, but I find your manner deplorable. I have good reason to know my cousin has been more than generous to you."

She might have saved her breath. The strange woman had gone. Like smoke that had seemed menacing when it first puffed up, then dissipated on the air.

Letty poured the dark tea into the fragile cup. She took a taste, then set the cup down. Whatever the maid had used to make the concoction, it was most unpleasant. Something stale drawn from the

195

back of a closet. The drink was more than unpalatable—it had a bitter flavor that hung on the tongue. She pushed the cup aside, got up from her chair, and walked over to the fireplace.

An enormous mirror hung over it. Gilt-framed, it reflected the entire room. Letty saw her face, hollowed and pale, stare back at her. She suffered suddenly what she'd read the French call a *frisson*. At home someone would have said, "Footsteps over my grave." She stepped sideways, peering through the one unshuttered window.

The storm was moving on, selecting some other poor hamlet for its onslaughts. Letty sighed and put out her fingers to touch the glass with their tips. How cold it had grown in a few minutes. Where was Cousin Frances? Should she take the carriage and go seeking her? Or should she simply leave and return tomorrow?

She saw that the old man had returned to his raking and went out to ask when he would be driving off to fetch his mistress.

"Eh?" He cupped his hand to his ear. He seemed to be stone deaf.

Letty felt foolish standing there, trying to make him understand. Cassie—or Mary—shouted from the house's doorway. Something about a parcel? Letty saw the brown paper package she'd brought to Cousin Frances.

"I thought you'd left this." Cassie-Mary held out the bundle. "Your coat too. I've got it in the hall."

"Thank you," said Letty coldly. She wanted to lift her skirts to avoid their touching the maid. As if she were something dirty in the road. The woman oozed an odor—indefinable but sinister.

"I see you didn't drink much tea," said the sulky voice.

"Thank you, no." Letty had an overpowering urge to run.

"If you'd finished it, I'd have read the leaves for you."

"I never deal with fortunetellers," said Letty, putting on her cloak.

"Never mind. That's why they call me Cassie—for Cassandra. She could see things. I see for you. You have bars around you. Strong bars."

"You're out of your mind!"

"I knew you'd say that. But I see the bars the moment I laid eyes on you. Not a prison—" The whining voice paused. "What on earth could it be?" She shook her head.

"I demand you let me by!"

"It's a cage. They're going to put you in a cage. I'd fight if I was you. Now that you know, see."

Letty pushed past her, walked with slipping feet down the wet steps. She got into the carriage, her breath coming fast. "Driver—back to town. As quickly as possible."

"Yes, ma'am." The crack of his whip. The carriage being wheeled about on the soaking gravel. As they entered the lane, water was dripping from the arching trees in a steady monotone.

Letty was trembling violently. In her hands she was clutching something. To her surprise it was the brown paper package. She didn't even remember picking it up. She felt oddly faint. Weary to exhaustion.

Letty tossed and turned all night. Gwen had been no help. When Letty had shared with her the fears, the vague imaginings, the sense something was amiss, the Welsh woman had said, "Sounds terribly fishy to me."

For some reason, Letty had desired to deny it. "I'm sure I've exaggerated what happened. I'm sure she really was in the village."

"Then why didn't you wait for her to come home?" The almost black eyes had stared back at Letty.

"I did run off. You're right."

"Could've been for the best," Gwen had said. "What was in that tea she fed you?"

"I didn't drink the tea—" But she had at least tasted it. The memory was on her tongue. Bitter? Acid? An evasive taste that defied accurate description.

"After supper, I'll write Cousin Frances a note and have it sent straight away in the morning. Surely the same man can be persuaded to carry it. The hall porter will help me out."

Why hadn't she waited? *Dear Cousin Frances,* she had written. *I was so sorry to miss you this afternoon. Your maid said you were in the village.* She sealed the envelope and gave it to the night porter—a young man, with a face like a hatchet blade. Then she returned to her room and spent a restless night, worry chasing sleep.

She awoke in the clammy room—the air that tried to penetrate the closed windows had the smell of the river on it. She opened her eyes, heard the cathedral clock strike four. She saw herself running out of Cousin Frances' house—slipping and sliding on the wet stone steps. Asking the old man, "Are you going back into the village to fetch her?"

She tried to sleep. A dream, clear as fear, showed her a long, skinny hand with blue veins standing out on it, skin soft as fish's flesh, long dead. The hand pointed, its fingers beckoning. Letty wanted to call out, had no breath to do so. When she tried to obey the hand, she found she couldn't move.

She was in a cage!

The cage was only as real as the dream, but it encased her, imprisoning her long after the hours of night were passed.

Breakfast was cold. The scrambled eggs tough, the kidneys of leather, and the toast a sour twist that left blackened crumbs on the plate. The tea resembled iodine. Nothing was right. She was impatient —upset and nervous. At the root of it all, a voice in her head kept asking, "Why did you leave without finding out where she was? You didn't even try to go to the village."

After the meal, she thought a walk would do her good. "You needn't come, Gwen. Stay and straighten up here. There's that hem to be mended—if you think you can manage it?" Gwen's prowess with a needle hadn't lived up to her boasts.

"If you think you'll be all right, milady?"

"Of course." Letty spoke bravely. Her spirits dragged, however, like feathers in the mud. Would she be all right? It was a question that teased at her as she descended the inn's shallow stairs.

A man was standing at the desk talking to the day porter. Though his back was to her, she heard him mention her name. Her skin prickled.

"Tell Mrs. Mackenzie I tried to deliver it but couldn't get near the place. The police were all about. Very bad thing. Ever such a lot of talk."

Letty's heart beat with an insistent thud. She made herself approach the desk. "Was there something I should know?"

The man at the desk was the hearse driver. At her approach, both men looked startled.

"It's about the note, milady." The hall porter cleared his throat, leaned forward confidentially. "Hudson here took it to the place, milady."

Hudson. The first time she'd heard his name. "Did you deliver the letter, Hudson?"

"That's what I come about." Hudson had removed his cap at her approach and now scratched his thick, unruly head of hair. "I couldn't deliver it to the person. I mean, not in person, if you get my meaning. I mean the person what was to have the note—"

"My cousin? What about her?"

The hall porter leaned forward. "He hasn't the information, milady. Do you, Hudson?"

"Well—" The driver looked disconcerted, then seemed to catch some message from the porter. "Not exactly, I don't."

"Where is my note now?"

"The police have it. They took it off me the moment I came to the gate. I never got as far as the house, milady. A great hearse was blocking the driveway and then the police have all their vehicles."

She heard only one word: *hearse.*

She would have questioned him further, but a broad-shouldered policeman entered the inn and was peering about in a doubtful manner.

"Can I help you?" The desk porter's manner was deferential.

"Yes, I believe you can. Do you have a Mrs. Mackenzie staying here?"

Whatever the law wanted of her, Letty knew she would have to come forward. She placed a stiff smile on her face and said, "I'm Mrs. Mackenzie. What is your business with me?"

The policeman took a notepad from one of his bulky pockets, along with the stub of a pencil. "I'm afraid I have to ask you some questions."

Letty's knees were shaking. The odd thing was that she was outwardly calm.

His voice sounded a long way away. "You are Mrs. Laetitia Mackenzie?"

"I am." Her hand found the desk's edge, clutched it for support.

"Did you have a cousin—? I'm afraid this is going to be painful for you. Would you like to sit down?"

The floor was coming up toward her. "I think I ought to have a chair. And some water."

When they had been fetched, she said, "It's about my cousin Frances Hyde, isn't it?"

"I'm afraid so." He consulted the notebook. "She was found to be deceased this morning—at approximately ten minutes past seven."

Letty sighed deeply. "May I ask who found her."

He consulted his notebook. "A maid by the name of Mary Ewen." Spelled it out loud.

"Yes," she reassured him. "That's Ewen. You didn't tell me how my cousin died."

"Well, that's the point, madam. I'm afraid I've got to ask you to accompany me to the station."

"But why? Oh, are you going to ask me to identify her?"

He shook his head. "No, madam—it's for questioning. If you'll just step down there with me. It's quite close. We can walk it in five minutes or less."

"You wish to question *me*?"

He saw her perplexity. Shuffled his feet. "I know this must be very distressing to you, madam. It's on account of the circumstances of the death, you see. In the ordinary way we'd not be conducting an inquiry."

"For heaven's sakes, man, what is going on here?"

He looked at the floor, evidently at a loss as to what to say. At last, "We've reason to suspect foul play."

"You mean, somebody murdered her?"

"That's what we'd like to know."

"Sit down, Mrs. Mackenzie."

She took the proffered chair. Everything was unreal—The man seated at the other side of the desk, the fact that she was here at all. She folded her gloved hands, waiting.

The inspector leaned forward. In a voice that was oatmeal ordinary he said, "We didn't bring you here to alarm you, Mrs. Mackenzie. We certainly appreciate your coming."

He glanced at the young policeman, who was now seated on a tall stool, his lanky legs wound about it. "We want every word, Simpkins." The inspector spoke low, firmly.

"Very good sir." Pen poised.

"Now, Mrs. Mackenzie, we'd like a simple statement from you. Just tell us in your own words when was the last time you saw your cousin alive."

She had absolutely nothing to hide. It was the way they'd brought her down here, were planning to put it in writing. A growing sense that she shouldn't be doing this, that a lawyer should be present to look out for her.

For perhaps the first time in her life, she longed for Nat. She licked her dry lips. "I suppose I have to talk to you?"

He was at once considerate. "If you mean, can we force you to give information, naturally I have to say that we can't. Not at this time anyway." He cleared his throat as if he were getting over a cold. "At a later date, we might have the means to detain you. You see, we aren't sure we have a case yet."

"You are talking in riddles. What do you mean by 'a case'? I don't like any of this," she said stubbornly.

"You don't like it!" said the inspector. "How do you think I feel? A murder may have been committed here. I've only one suspect, a maid, and she's so daft she's already confessed to it. Which makes it damnably unlikely she had anything to do with it." He scratched his head irritably.

Letty spoke in an icy tone. "First you inform me that my cousin may have been murdered. Then you state that the maid's no suspect because she's too crazy to have done it." She pulled her cloak about her, attempting a haughtiness she didn't feel. "Before we go one step further, I'd like to talk with my late cousin's attorney. I know she had one. She mentioned him by name the last time I saw her."

"Then you did see her!" He sat forward, pointing the paper opener at her.

"Of course. I came here, to Salisbury, expressly to see her. But I saw her only once—" She stopped, alerted by a look of satisfaction in his eyes.

"Did you get that, Simpkins?"

The boy, engaged in frantic scratching, barely nodded.

The inspector fastened her with his gaze. "You may see an attorney if you wish. I think it is only fair to warn you, the maid said she had an accomplice. The maid implicated you, madam."

She gasped. The sound was audible as a gunshot in the room. "Me! But this is outrageous. How can you possibly believe anything that poor creature said? You stated yourself that she's demented!" The office was closing in around her.

The inspector weighed the paper opener in his hand, then threw it down on the table. "At what time were you out there on your second visit?"

She was silent, staring at him, horror gripping her. "I demand to see an attorney. I will answer no more of your questions."

The inspector rose from his chair. "Very well. Who would you like us to contact?"

"I stated it before. My cousin had someone handling her affairs. Surely you must know his name? I mean, he would have been notified?"

The inspector turned his back on her. With folded arms, he appeared to be gazing out of the window. "You're an American, is that true?"

"Are you going to call the lawyer?"

His eyes were unreadable. No, on second thought, he seemed to be weighing something. He made a clucking sound in his throat. "Simpkins, keep an eye on our visitor here while I go look into something."

He was gone. She allowed herself to lean back in the chair, seeking strength. She wanted to ask for a glass of water, but she wouldn't give them the satisfaction. Surely they'd realize their mistake and let her go with an apology? She was terrified.

A clock on the wall ticked. It seemed an eternity before the inspector returned. He deliberately didn't look at Letty until he'd seated himself behind his desk once more, shuffled some papers lying there.

"I'm afraid we're going to have to ask you to wait," he said.

Fear flushed her cheeks. Her breathing came shallow and quick.

An air of unreality—this wasn't happening, it couldn't be.

"Now mind, we're not arresting you. It's just a precaution. You see, if the maid hadn't implicated you—"

She drew inside herself. "If you aren't going to let me go, what are you going to do with me? Put me in prison?"

He spread his hands. "It's not an arrest, Mrs. Mackenzie. Merely a detention. There's another room you can wait in."

She rose, gathering her cloak about her. She was shivering violently, and not just from the cold.

The new room was almost a cell, but without bars. There was a table, and two chairs.

"You can make yourself comfortable here," said the inspector.

"The lawyer? Are you fetching the lawyer?" she heard herself plead.

"Wasn't that what you wanted?" he asked, surprisingly civil.

"Why, yes."

"Very well then." He closed the door.

She sat on one of the none too clean chairs. She wanted to bow her head in her hands and weep. Instead, she kept her body erect. Eyes dry.

A prisoner! What had that dreadful maid said yesterday? "I see bars around you."

She was trapped. She could be here for hours! The iron self-control began to bend.

She might have broken down completely had not the door opened. A genial gentleman, pink-cheeked and portly, stood there, filling the entrance with his bulk.

"My dear Mrs. Mackenzie. My apologies for the way you've been treated." A warm hand placed in hers. "I'm Lucien Comstock. You were quite right to call me. This is all a dreadful mistake."

Letty was seated in Mr. Comstock's office. He'd brought her there from the police station and had his clerk make her a cup of tea. A fire burning in the ash-laden grate warmed her. Somehow, she managed to stop her shaking. She tended to regard the lawyer as a minor saint —or savior—delivering her from the inspector.

"I'm afraid he was just trying something on for size," he said in his reassuring way. "I gather you foiled him, Mrs. Mackenzie." Something of admiration in his glance.

"I did?" Now that it was over, she no longer had to disguise her lack of courage.

"Good gracious, yes. Stopped him dead in his tracks." He rubbed his hands with every mark of satisfaction in his gesture. "Marvelous to see it. Standing up to the law. They'll push anyone around if they feel they can get away with it. Especially, if you'll forgive me for saying so, a woman. A lady like yourself, traveling quietly without her husband—"

She experienced a sense of concern at the way he said it. But she was so grateful, she let it pass. "You are telling me they had no business holding me?"

He shook his head. "I know Inspector Horton of old. Not that he intends to misuse his authority. It's a play he makes when he doesn't have an ironclad case. Hopes you'll slip up, give him some information he needs to close things out."

"Ah," she said, seeing. "Then I was actually free to leave? I mean, I'm still free to go?"

At that his face changed. "Well, after the autopsy."

"There is to be an autopsy?"

"Pretty well has to be, the circumstances being what they are."

"Please," she said, pleading in her voice, "won't you tell me how my poor cousin died? I keep asking, and everybody seems bound to secrecy." She moved uncomfortably in her chair.

"You see, that's the whole point. No one can tell you because, until the investigation, no one knows."

She was astounded. "The word 'murder' was used. The maid—Mr. Comstock, have you ever actually met that maid?"

"Ah," he said knowingly, "Mary Ewen, otherwise known as Cassie. Yes, she and I have met on more than one occasion. She's the best guess if you ask me."

He got up, stood before the fire, warming his backside. For August, it was a remarkably chilly day. "It all takes time," he said genially. "Now, some things I need to know."

"Yes?" Her nervousness, which had begun to abate, surged up again.

"You are staying at our inn. Comfortable there?"

"Yes, quite," she replied in a tight voice.

"You plan to remain long?"

"I had simply come to see my cousin. My husband is in France. When his business is completed, he will rejoin me. We have passage booked for the second week in September. Why do you ask?"

"Oh, it's nothing to be distressed about, Mrs. Mackenzie. Your husband could be reached, I gather, if it became necessary?"

Instantly she was fully afraid again, more fearful than she'd been at the police station. At the thought of Nathaniel—yet had she not longed for his presence, his support, hours before? That had been the outcome of weakness, of a knowledge she was helpless. Now that she was free, it was crucial all this be kept from Nathaniel.

"Why do you speak of sending for my husband? No, don't put me off with excuses—" She heard her voice, demanding, high almost to hysteria. Face hot with panic.

"Dear lady, I'm not trying to." Then, when her expression wouldn't let him retreat, "Perhaps I am. I know how unpleasant all this is for you. It's why I'm going to make a few suggestions. If you will hear me out?"

She sighed. "Very well. I suppose I have no choice."

"Until the autopsy has been performed, the case cannot be closed. Perhaps it's not occurred to you, but your relative may have died of natural causes."

"Natural causes?" Her head shot up. No one had even suggested such.

He was nodding. "She had a bad heart, she was under a doctor's

205

care. All that will come to light. I am only asking you to have patience. There is no real reason to expect foul play."

She said nothing.

"Go back to the inn, get some rest, do a little sightseeing. Have you visited our cathedral?"

She nodded.

"Have you been out to see Stonehenge?"

"How long am I to be thus detained?" she interrupted.

"Only a few days."

She decided to take his advice and see Stonehenge.

It turned out to be a magnificent prescription. So incredible a sight. She gazed at the stone plinths, some of them erect, others prone. How had they gotten there? This strange country. So full of places that raised questions. The stones, the edifices, even the fortifications dug by long-stilled hands, had always been there. Centuries. Why should anyone ask?

Like the sun and the rain, they were part of the landscape, older than legend, enshrouded in mystery. She wanted to put down her impressions on paper.

She had herself driven back to the inn and went to her suitcases to find the paints and the inks she'd stowed. She wanted to paint. To make the penned lines, the washes of color, go her way.

The next day, she tried to capture the stones. She sat in a pool of sun, meted out by the stinginess of the English climate. How to record roughness—lichen—the odd sense of solemnity?

Gwen was walking over the rough stubble of the field in which the stones "grew." Sprung like toadstools from what early, spawning belief? The driver had left them there—to come back in two hours. It was part of Gwen's crossness, being left. Letty knew it was fear.

Now the driver was returning. The *clop-clop* of his mare's hooves could be heard sharp and clear on the isolated road. Few vehicles came up here on the windy downs. Local people kept away.

"Milady, the carriage is back."

"I know." She wanted to finish the painting. It was all done except for the highlights, the dark shadows that would make it stand out. Even as she worked the view changed, cheating her of a chance to record with any veracity. Clouds swept low over the sky.

She could feel Gwen's irritation. It interfered with her concentration. Drat the woman. How did she manage to make her sulkiness so pervasive? Letty finally packed her paints. Pad under her arm, the small case of brushes and colors in her hand, she climbed into the carriage.

Gwen followed, inducing her lumbering body to gain the carriage's height. Letty could smell her sweat. Somehow the woman was more than usually upsetting today.

Letty glanced critically at her painting, lifting the cover with which she was keeping it clean. Amateurish. Well, what did she expect? It was just a hobby. There'd never been any idea she could be a real artist, even had she dared to aspire. It was foolish to feel so blocked in what she wanted to do. She should be content to play about with the paints the way Hitty did with bits of verse. To want more not only was silly but was asking for problems.

Mother's feelings on the subject echoed. "Letty, it's unladylike to become too involved. It's all right to dabble. No one thinks there's anything odd about that. Can be quite charming—little sketches to show one's guests. But girls who are brought up correctly, Letty, have more sense than to get involved with painting."

Letty had taken the advice in her stride. Had Hitty? Leaning back in the jolting carriage, Letty closed her eyes, remembering. Hitty hadn't always been so retiring, so secretive.

Looking back, Letty asked herself how much Emma's decision to dismiss Miss Sprules had been due to Hitty? A scene she believed she'd forgotten concerning the governess floated into Letty's thoughts.

Hitty, in striped pinafore and black stockings, bounding up to Mother on one of Emma's rare visits to the schoolroom. "Oh, Mama, I've written another poem, and Miss Sprules says, when I grow up, I could think about becoming a writer!"

Letty standing, listening. Watching. Didn't Hitty know one didn't say things like that to Mama? Hitty was such a little idiot.

"Henrietta, I thought I'd explained my views?"

"Don't you even want to hear my poem?"

"Henrietta, I don't like having things read to me that aren't nice. The last poem you wrote was wretchedly distasteful."

"But Miss Sprules says to write about what one feels."

That statement had sealed the governess' fate.

207

9

As Letty walked into the inn's vestibule, she saw a familiar figure sitting there. Shock waves traveled through her.

"Nat—what a surprise! I never expected to see you here in Salisbury."

He took her by the arm, his grip telling her what she already knew from other small signs. He was beside himself with anger.

"Nat, what in the world—?"

He let her lead him up to her room. Motioned for her to open the heavy oak door. Once in the room, he secured the door.

"Now," he said, drawing a rolled-up newspaper from under his arm, "you shall explain this to me. Read, Letty. See what your stupidity has gotten me into."

Her eyes covered the words rapidly. The tabloid, for it was surely that sort of newspaper, said in the boldest of lettering, *American Woman Implicated in Murder.*

She gasped. "Oh, Nat, it's not true!"

"Read!" He thrust it at her.

She scanned the horrid details. *Wealthy recluse's body discovered in her mansion by maid. Mrs. Frances Hyde, who seldom appeared in her neighboring Salisbury, was found Thursday morning to be dead in her bedroom. Sources alleged she had died of asphyxiation. A female cousin, Mrs. Laetitia Mackenzie, wife of the prominent Philadelphian Nathaniel Mackenzie, was asserted to have been visiting with her relative hours before the death was discovered. . . .*

Letty couldn't bear to finish it. She let it drop on the table by her side.

He began to pace. "I was coming to fetch you. My business was finished sooner than I thought it would be. I was in Paddington Station when I came on this rag! I don't know why I even stopped to read it."

"It was the word 'American,' " she said in a hollow voice.

"Of course, of course." He was testy. Swung about to glare at her. Just at that moment there was a knock on the door.

From the other side of the door, the porter's voice said, "Madam, are you there?"

Letty asked softly, "Shall I answer it?"

Nathaniel shrugged. Glancing backward at his stubbornly set face, she went to the door.

"Madam, a note came."

"Thank you." She took it, turned back to Nat. "It's a note."

"Well, go on! Open it! It must be for you."

She slit the envelope with her fingers and cut herself—a hairline wound that bled in one bright bead. The same color as the sealing wax on the back of the envelope. She sucked on her finger, wondering at the amount of injury she felt from such a tiny place. All she was experiencing seemed to have been poured into the cut. Defenselessness, anger. The smarting.

"It's from Mr. Comstock."

"Who?" The question was pointed. Indignation at her lack of explanation. Nathaniel's face loomed over her, his hand out to seize the letter.

She forestalled him by putting it into his hand. "He'd like to see me right away. He didn't know you were here, Nat, or else he'd have included you."

"Letty, who in the hell is he?"

Her mind was like the porridge they served for breakfast, stodgy and stirred into a lumpish mess. The note! What did it mean? Once she'd longed for Nat to be here. Now he was, and she could look to him to know what was for the best. But could she?

"Letty!" His voice snapped her back to reality. "Answer me! Who, in God's name, is this Comstock?"

"The lawyer who's looking after Cousin Frances' estate. He's sort of representing me too."

"You mean, you've engaged an attorney? Gone ahead without a word to me?"

"Nat, I—"

It was useless. He'd already taken her arm again and was propelling her out the door.

Mr. Comstock clasped her hands between his. "I have news, excellent news."

"Mr. Comstock, this is my husband. He arrived this afternoon from London."

209

"Ah! Delighted. We just got the autopsy report." He blurted it out. His eyes seemed to bulge slightly. Pleased?

"Yes?" said Letty.

"It was heart failure. Death due to natural causes. The coroner is perfectly satisfied. She died the morning of your second visit."

"Oh, mercy me," said Letty softly. She began to cry without movement, tears simply welling out of her eyes, falling with a splash on her coat.

"That leaves most of my questions unanswered," Nat said bluntly. All I've been informed so far is that you are the attorney in charge of defending my wife."

"Sir, won't you have a chair? I think there are matters that need to be cleared up."

"Thank you. I prefer to stand. I've sat two hours or more in that disgraceful train."

Mr. Comstock made a noise in his throat. Letty sensed he was trying to take the measure of her husband. His astonishment—for indeed he thought he had brought them good news—was making his task harder. He fussed with papers on his desk.

"I cannot rightly be said to have defended your wife, since she was never accused of anything."

"Oh, no!" Nathaniel had brought the newspaper along. He flung it now on Mr. Comstock's desk. "What about this?"

Mr. Comstock adjusted his spectacles. "Dear me," he said on scanning the headline. "But of course it is one of those appalling gossipy publications. Unfortunately they get wind of everything. One wonders just how, eh?" He looked up at Nathaniel. Blinked, as if the light hurt his eyes.

"That's what you're going to tell me!" thundered Nat.

The tight feeling in Letty's stomach had come back. Like a fist formed from her innards. It was difficult to breathe. Why had Nat decided to join her in Salisbury? And why had he chosen the very day when everything might have been cleared up? He need never have known. Except—of course he would have known. Mr. Comstock was sure to present a bill. An account which, while it was fully earned, fully legitimate, she hadn't a penny in the world to pay. Nat always settled everything. Staying alone in England these few short weeks had been the first time in her entire life he'd entrusted her with money. Even then, she'd kept the careful records he insisted on.

She lifted her eyes and looked about the room. Really, she'd managed very well, even in the face of fear. Now, when it was almost all over and things had been settled, would she fall back into her old ways again? She behaved as if Nat could shrivel her, menace her very life. Sitting there quaking, was she the same woman who had insisted to Inspector Horton that she have an attorney? Who had evoked a look of admiration, even words of praise, from Mr. Comstock?

How quickly it all went away. She got out a handkerchief from her reticule. Tears of relief for herself—or weeping for Cousin Frances? Nat was right. She wasn't clearheaded. Always drifting from one matter to the next. In a daze, she heard bits of their conversation.

"—get to the bottom of this filth in the paper—"

"—fully appreciate your reaction. Assure you, no control over what the press gets hold of, other than to make sure they do not bring libel laws down about their ears."

"Any chance of suing them?"

"Let me see."

It went on and on. She shut her ears and thought of poor Cousin Frances. She must be buried now, in the village churchyard, alongside her ancestors. Letty's ancestors!

She broke into their discussion. "The funeral! When is it to be held?"

They stared at her as one. Then the lawyer, clearing his throat, said haltingly, "Tomorrow I believe. At two o'clock."

"Nat, we must go. We may be her only relatives."

His face was nasty. "Letty, may I remind you that we have a ship to board. It will take us half a day just to get to Southampton."

"Then maybe you'll have to go without me, Nat." She was defying him. "I intend to go to my cousin's last rites. I met her only once, but she's still my family." Her nostrils flared. She could feel her cheeks burning.

She'd made him furious. His cold eyes glittered in the dour face. Finally he said, "Letty, if there is to be an ugly scene, the least you could do would be to spare this gentleman. As far as I can see, he has shown you only kindness."

If he wanted to shame her, he was succeeding. She wouldn't show it, however. "I mean no embarrassment. I merely wish to state that I want to be present at Cousin Frances' burial."

Unexpectedly, Mr. Comstock came to her aid. "She almost has to remain here tomorrow, Mr. Mackenzie. By the terms of my late client's will, there are certain questions that have to be settled."

The heirlooms! They were to be hers now. Hers and Mother's and Hitty's.

"You want me to say about the furniture?" she said in a rush. "Could we visit the house, after the funeral?"

"My plan, exactly," said Mr. Comstock. "I had thought, if you were going to extend your stay, we might defer the decisions till another day. But in view of the urgency?" He stopped, folded his hands with a wounded air. "You never mentioned to me, you know, the imminence of your sailing date?"

"But you see, I myself didn't know—"

Nathaniel said in crisp tones, "My business terminated sooner than anticipated. I changed the reservations.

"Ah." The tone indicated Mr. Comstock was appeased.

IO

Nathaniel insisted on accompanying her to the funeral. His silence, his disdain, conveyed everything he wished to say. She did her best to ignore it, shut him out. It wasn't easy. The stocky figure, dignified in his disgust, stood by her side in the tiny church. Although the pews behind them were crowded with villagers, they alone occupied the front row. Without the Mackenzies there, Frances Hyde would have been buried unacknowledged by family—unless you counted the silent witnesses in the graveyard.

It wasn't until halfway through the service that Letty thought of Cassie-Mary. What had become of the maid? After the village mourners dispersed to their separate cottages, Letty must have a chance to inquire.

Mr. Comstock unlocked the front door of Hyde Manor with a key that someone—perhaps the police—had taken the trouble to label. As the four of them—for the young clerk from the office had emerged from Mr. Comstock's coach—entered, the odor of a shut-up house came at them. Stale and musty. A faint trace of something sweet. Nasty.

"Nat, we need to go through the things Mr. Comstock has listed." She was by now burning to ask about Cassie-Mary, but prudently didn't wish to do so in Nathaniel's presence. She must make a chance, somehow.

"If you have business to do," he said unpleasantly, "then get on with it. However, I'm warning you, Letty, try to fill our house with these relics and you'll have me to answer to."

She was left with her mouth open. Up until now, she'd never

thought—yet of course she would have to have his permission.

"Nat, Mother and Hitty also are mentioned in the will. The estate will take care of the shipping costs."

He shrugged. "I've had my say. Go and choose for your mother and your sister." He sat himself gloomily down in one of the parlor chairs. "This place is like a charnel house. Can't we at least get more light in here?"

The clerk had been directed to open one set of shutters. Impatiently now, the attorney motioned to him that he was to open them all.

They went into Cousin Frances' bedroom—Mr. Comstock confidently, the clerk deferentially, Letty anticipating a reprimand.

Cousin Frances was there—in the way the dressing-table silver had been arranged, in the clothes hanging in her armoire. Mr. Comstock opened the giant oak wardrobe, peered inside, and sniffed delicately. Lavender, brittle and almost dusty, camphor against the moths, musk from some perfume Cousin Frances had worn years ago.

Now, Letty realized, was her chance to ask about Cassie. She swung on Mr. Comstock. "What happened to the maid?"

Mr. Comstock stopped in mid-stride, tapped his fingers against one another. "Very unfortunate. Especially when she was provided for. So many aren't. Face the workhouse."

"What do you mean?"

"She took her own life, dear lady."

"What!"

"As I said, very sad. Most regrettable."

She turned on the lawyer. "We did this!" she accused him.

"I beg your pardon?" Affronted.

"You and I—we are responsible. We knew her mind was affected. The estate was left to her in bulk. You could have taken better care of her, just as I could have inquired, seen how she was."

Mr. Comstock pulled himself to his full height. Said in a huff, "No one was more shocked than I when I was informed this morning that the poor unfortunate had hanged herself."

"Did she leave any kind of a message?" asked Letty.

"Matter of fact, yes." Mr. Comstock drew a slim piece of paper from his pocket. "Won't tell you much," he said, handing it over.

But it did. Letty read: *I died before. You found me in my bedroom.*

"You see, it makes absolutely no sense," the lawyer said.

"I agree," said Letty, handing it back. She wouldn't share what she knew. She heard Cousin Frances saying, "You see, she believes she's me." In Cassie-Mary's twisted mind, she couldn't survive her mistress. One and the same, they must depart this life together. The suicide was merely a way of bringing clarity to what others hadn't understood.

Cassie-Mary had died when Frances Hyde's heart stopped.

Letty turned away and looked out the window. It was closed today, but the forest was still out there. Soon, unless new owners took healthy steps to chop it back, it would encroach, take over the mansion and the garden. A generation or two and no one would be able to read the name of Frances Hyde on her tombstone.

"Shall we begin to work through the list?" said Mr. Comstock. She nodded.

When they reached the parlor, she said, "If there are any packages of letters in the desk, I'd like to have them."

Mr. Comstock opened it up. "Lot of written material here. Looks like it could be some kind of diary."

"You're crazy!" said Nathaniel, who had come up behind her. His breath was heavy with alcohol. He had been drinking deeply from the silver flask he always carried.

"And the portrait of Clemmy?" Letty said firmly.

"The child's head? Over there on that wall?"

"Yes. I'd like to have it. I believe she would have wanted that."

"Make a note of it," said Mr. Comstock to the clerk. His only comment. Somehow, Letty wanted him to agree with her. She asked insistently, "Did you ever meet Clemmy?"

"No. I knew there was a child, of course. She survived about six years."

"Such a tragedy. My cousin spoke to me about it the day we had tea."

"For heaven's sake, get on with it, Letty," grumbled Nathaniel.

"It is getting late," said Mr. Comstock.

To confirm his statement, the clock struck. Filling the dusty room with melody first, it pronounced in solemn tones that the hour was four.

"Great Scot, what was that?" muttered Nathaniel.

"Probably the finest of the heirlooms." Mr. Comstock's voice was oily. "Tradition says it was given to the family by King Charles II. May not be true. But it's a fine specimen of its kind."

"Worth something on the market?" Nathaniel's values were aroused.

Letty stood by, stiff with anger. Suddenly, she knew she wanted the clock for herself. More than she had ever wanted anything.

"Oh, I'm sure it would reach a goodly price."

"My wife can take it," said Nathaniel magnanimously.

She stared at him. No words passed her lips. In this moment, she despised him. "Do you know where it will stand? Or are you planning to sell it?" she asked at last.

"We'll keep it for a while. It can go in the hallway."

"There was a stipulation," said Mr. Comstock slowly. "Mrs. Hyde particularly wanted these items to remain in the family. To be passed from generation to generation." He licked his lips.

"Of course," said Nathaniel impatiently. "We do have children, Mr. Comstock. We also make up wills, legal documents where we come from." The sarcasm was embarrassing.

"It was my duty to point out the intention of the deceased, sir."

"And you've done that quite adequately. Now tell me, are we finished with all this claptrap?"

Indeed, they were finished.

"What will become of the house?" asked Letty of the lawyer as he was locking the front door.

"Now that Mary Ewen has gone, it will be sold. The proceeds will be donated to an orphanage Mrs. Hyde had an interest in."

"Where is this orphanage?" Letty asked.

"In Manchester."

"Where's that?"

"Good heavens, Letty. In the North of England. You can look it up on a map when we get back to the inn." Nathaniel had had enough.

They drove away from Hyde Manor for the last time. The setting sun was turning the windows to gold. They flashed their message across the valley. Letty took one last look as they gained the hill on the opposite side.

Had she dreamed it all? Would the furniture, the clock, the picture of Clemmy really arrive in Philadelphia? If they did, she told herself, then she would believe it had been no dream.

Gwen had left Letty a note: *Ever so sorry yore husband believes I told on you to the papers. I didn't but best I leave now before more words pass. Look after yoreself, madam. Your respectful servant G. Powell.*

She handed it to Nat. "How could you treat her so? You'd no proof she said a word! I know for a fact she didn't." Trembling.

"What you know 'for a fact,' Letty, could be written on the back of a postage stamp."

"You're insufferable! What have I done to cause you to treat me with such disdain?"

"What have you done? Letty, is your memory so short? This whole business—headlines in the newspapers—"

"One newspaper. A very discredited one at that."

"You ask me how I can fail to respect you? It's your judgment, madam. Your judgment's lacking. How could you employ a woman like Gwen Powell to start with?"

He looked at her with the scorn she knew he held for her. Contemptuous. She wanted to reach out to him, beg him to comfort her.

Not only was she alone, she was overwhelmed. Gwen had irritated her, often driven her to distraction, but in some way Letty hadn't grasped till now, she'd been a bulwark. Against isolation. Gwen was now a memory, lingering as smoke in the air.

In two days Nanette should rejoin them. For two days Letty could comb her own hair, pack her own clothes—somehow manage. Of course she could.

Nathaniel left her. "Going down to see if I can find a drink—"

She wandered about the beamed bedroom. Its low ceiling oppressive, telling of danger? She paced.

In her wanderings, she came across the painting of Stonehenge. Had she really been hopeful that day? To cast aside the trappings of living long enough to give thought to such irrelevancies as the line of shadow on stone. What freedom! Now she was entrapped once more in Nat's lowering presence, his muscular body would be beside hers at night.

She sighed. The sojourn in England was almost over. Would she look back and wonder, not that it had ever been, but how it had been?

That she, Letty, so used to living in the same house, could move to hotels, to guest bedrooms, even to the solitude of a walk in a park thousands of miles away from her own garden. That she could accomplish this and survive.

What must she do with the survival? What had she learned? The self-confidence, frail as gossamer, should it be stowed away in a steamer trunk, carted up to the attic on her return? Or should she get it out and try it on, as a dress purchased in a strange shop? In the raw light of Philadelphia, with its atmosphere of established customs, would it still fit?

She feared not. Hours in Nathaniel's company had given her a glimmer of that. Self-confidence, the space to pursue her own interests, they had no place in a marriage. It was no wonder she felt sad. Today they had buried more than Cousin Frances. Something newborn and tenuous also had been entombed. Like the other granite markers, it wouldn't be long before its inscription would be obliterated.

A sigh was not appropriate. It just wasn't enough. But then, an inner voice scolded, wasn't she just feeling sorry for herself? She felt ashamed.

IV. LAVENDER BLUE

April–September 1887

Lavender blue, and Rosemary green,
When I am king, you shall be queen;
Call up my maids at four of the clock,
Some to the wheel, and some to the rock;
Some to make cake, and some to shell corn,
And you and I will keep the bed warm.

—*from Forgotten Children's Books,* 1969

I

The girls didn't see Letty at first. She had caught them as if in a painting.

Amelia's serious face, in profile, talking to her dolls. A row of them, lined up against the wall, their legs splayed out from under flannel frocks, rag faces regarding their mentor with wide-mouthed smiles. Amelia was scolding them.

Polly, seated by Nanny, holding the remains of a plush rabbit in her small lap, the much-loved toy worn from days of clutching, nights of clinging.

"Nanny, he wants to go for a walk."

"But the weather's poor, love."

It was—for April. The sun had teased them, enticing them to cast away fur muffs, heavy wraps, while all the while holding chill winds in abeyance until their cautions were set aside. Then gray skies threatened, and daffodil spikes were whipped by snow flurries.

Letty gazed at her daughters. Polly still had the rounded lines of a baby. Not so Amelia. In the time her mother had been away in England, the girl had changed. The winter had speeded up the process. In another week, Amelia would be ten.

Such a solemn child. Independent too. Letty had once heard the maids talking about Amelia.

"Funny little thing—wants her own way. You heard her go on at her dolls? Wonder what she'll be like when she has children of her own?" The snapping of a sheet stretched across a mattress. "Strict. Anyone can tell that. Not like Miss Polly. Miss Polly likes to laugh."

Did that mean Amelia didn't?

Letty became aware, not for the first time, how little she knew of her children. They were separated from her by a barrier of maids, tutors, nurses. Children grew so fast.

Feeling her mother's eyes on her, Polly looked up. "Mama—it's Mama!"

A loving child. One to be picked up and cuddled, hugged like the plush rabbit. Polly made it so easy. She asked almost nothing except to be reassured momentarily. Praised.

She needed this now. It was the horse still. Would Polly never grow out of it? Back and forth on its wooden stand, its wide eyes gazing about the nursery, its nostrils splayed with the effort of galloping over imaginary fields.

"See me, Mama! See me?"

"Yes, darling."

Nanny had pushed her darning aside. In preparation, in case she had to rise.

Letty gestured with her hand. "No, Nanny, it's all right. Go on with what you're doing."

"Very good, milady. It's so nice to see you again." The hands moved across the mending. "Miss Polly, that's a lot of noise. Miss Amelia, aren't you going to greet your mama?"

Amelia turned her small, shapely head. The gray eyes looked at Letty with a glance that was cool, self-contained. "How are you, Mama?"

"Well, thank you, darling. How are your dolls?"

"They trouble me." Amelia sighed, lifting her narrow shoulders. "It's that naughty Sophie again. And Agnes has soiled her hands. They don't seem to pay me mind. I've whipped them and whipped them."

"Whipped your dolls?" The word had a harsh sound.

"Oh, I must cane each of them three times a day. But it's no use. See how they smile at me, Mama?" Amelia's lips pressed together in disapproval. When did Amelia laugh?

"Dearest, do you do anything besides whip your dolls?"

Nanny spoke up. "Oh, she's finished two samplers, milady. You ought to show them to your mother, Miss Amelia. They're all ready for framing, ma'am."

"How lovely. Of course I want to see them."

"I can't abide sewing." Amelia's voice was level now.

"But you do such a nice job, darling."

"No I don't. Nanny unpicks all the uneven stitches and does them over for me after I've gone to bed. I've seen her."

"Oh, Miss Amelia! Why would you want to go and tell your mother a story like that?" Hurt in Nanny's voice.

222

"Why shouldn't I, when it's true? It's the only way my samplers become fit to frame. I hate them."

"But, dearest," Letty tried, "it's something a woman has to do. Learning to sew is part of growing up. You want to be a wife someday, with your own house to run, don't you?"

"If I have my own house, I shall have somebody in to do the sewing. You do!" she challenged Letty.

Letty felt at a loss. Why did this child challenge her? It was true, the seamstress came in once or twice a year. Stayed for a month at a time, making up maids' uniforms, hemming sheets. In between visits, the maids and Nanny kept the mending down.

"Nevertheless," Letty said evenly, "it's important for a lady who runs her own home to know about needlework. In fact, she should be informed about everything she asks others to do for her."

Amelia gave her mother a hard stare. The look said, "I don't believe you. It's not that way at all."

Letty chose to ignore it. Unthinkable she could become embroiled in an argument with her own child! "Speaking of sewing," she said, diverting the subject smoothly, "I have a surprise for you."

"A surprise?" Polly's blue eyes looked alert, excited. "I love a surprise. Is it a party?"

"Sort of," said Letty, to whom the anticipation of a wedding was more work than pleasure. Mother had finally given the nod to the day on which Hitty and Compton could plan to be married. The first day of September. A fall wedding, the clothes must echo the choice.

"Mrs. Crocker's coming soon to make up bridesmaid dresses for you two."

"Oh, my!" said Nanny heartily. "Are my little girls going to be asked to be in the wedding?"

"What wedding?" Amelia had whirled about, her eyes intent and curious.

"Your Aunt Hitty's wedding."

"Oh, that." Amelia showed her disappointment. "I knew about that already. It was the other wedding I wanted to know about."

"What wedding, darling?"

Amelia twisted around, her hands behind her back, her arms stiff. Something furtive about her attitude. "I'm not sure."

"She's just a little mixed up, ma'am, that's all," said Nanny. "Go get your samplers, Miss Amelia. Let your mother see what you've been busy with."

"No!" said Letty, staying it all, her voice sharp. "I want to know what she's talking about, Nanny?"

"Nothing, milady—nothing at all." Nanny's face was red. She

223

picked up her darning and squinted at it as if her life depended on the next stitch.

"She doesn't want me to tell you what I overheard the maids saying!" Amelia's voice flared. "It was Papa's wedding, Mama."

"Your father's!" Said with astonishment. "Oh, you must be joking!"

"No I'm not. Nanny knows because I asked her about it."

Nanny flustered. "It was something shouldn't have been discussed in the first place. Certainly not before the child."

"Amelia, Papa is not going to marry. I don't see how you could make such a mistake."

"He will if you die. They said you probably will if you have another baby. They even said who Papa would marry."

Letty's own hands flew to her throat. "Nanny has been saying such things? They had no right. No one has that kind of right!" She wouldn't acknowledge the thickening in her throat.

Amelia had the information readily available. "They said Papa will marry Sam's sister. They talked about how he danced with her at Christmas as if they were sweethearts. Mama, what does it mean to be 'sweethearts'?"

Letty's voice came as a moan in her throat. "Whatever *they* said, don't listen to any more of it."

Nanny's rebuke came down like a blade. "That's enough, Miss Amelia. Another word out of you and you'll go to your room. Oh, milady," on a quick, trembling breath, "I'd have given anything in the world for you not to have heard this." Face heavy with grief.

Letty gathered herself together. "It's all right, Nanny. It is nothing that bothers me. I'm extremely strong. I shall live for years and years."

"Just a nasty bit of gossip. I don't know what gets into maids, I'm sure." Nanny's hands reflected the shaking in Letty's limbs.

"Then you aren't going to die, Mama?" Amelia's question came into the heat like cool drops on an iron. Sizzling before them. "If I am to have a stepmother, I would prefer it to be someone more like Aunt Hitty. I regard Olivia as terribly silly. Will she be coming to Aunt Hitty's wedding, Mama?"

"How should I know? I suppose so. Your father and Mr. Abbott have always been the best of friends." Letty wanted to scream. Livvie was a minx. Even as she thought it, Letty knew her wishes in the matter would be unimportant. Nat invited whomever he wished to the house. He made all decisions of this nature—who would be their friends, their guests.

She took herself in hand. "Now, we were discussing bridemaids' dresses," she said smoothly. "Your Aunt Hitty is to have a fall wed-

224

ding. That means we are going to have colors that go with the season. Yellow, dark red, lavender."

"May I choose my own color, Mama?"

"Why, Amelia, that may be a little difficult. It all has to go together, you see. A very nice Miss Puxley is helping us plan it."

"She's the one who makes *your* clothes, isn't she, Mama?"

"Well, Amelia, she doesn't exactly 'make' them. She has the models sent over from Paris and I choose. I suppose you could say she takes the orders for them. She has a large number of girls working for her."

"Ugh," said Amelia violently. "I'm glad I'll always be rich. I wouldn't want to have to sew for Miss Puxley."

Letty's lips pressed together. "I think we should always show appreciation for what we have. But that is no excuse for your not learning to make your stitches, Amelia."

"Can I wear yellow?" asked Polly, moving the rocking horse under her again.

"Mama," said Amelia concisely, "I'll wear lavender. I not only prefer it, it is the one color I think of as my own. Will you ask Mrs. Crocker to choose it for me?"

"Why would you suppose it to be up to Mrs. Crocker to decide, Amelia? I thought I explained to you, darling, the wedding is being planned as a whole. Miss Puxley—"

"I still want lavender," said Amelia.

Letty felt herself flush with annoyance. "I can give you no assurances you'll be wearing lavender. It might turn out to be yellow—or dark red."

"Then I shan't be in the wedding." Amelia had lifted a doll so that its cotton body touched her cheek. She seemed to be inhaling its odor.

Nanny bridled. "That's no way to talk! You'll do as you're told, Miss Amelia."

"If I'm not allowed to wear lavender, I shall get sick and die."

"Don't be such a baby!" said Nanny hotly. "You apologize to your mother right now. You hear me, Miss Amelia?"

"I'm very sorry, Mama. But I mean every word of it."

"Amelia, come here." Letty beckoned to the girl. "Darling, it's important to learn to give in."

"Why?" The gray eyes were level. Challenging.

Letty wanted to look away. The child was so like Nathaniel. In looks, no. Albert had the profile, the stocky body. But Amelia was her father in personality.

"All girls have to learn obedience, Amelia. Part of life is giving in. When you have a husband—" She stopped, listening to what she was saying. Well, it was all true, wasn't it? When had she ever been allowed her own way? As a girl, it had been Mother who'd made the rules. Married, it was Nathaniel.

"I shan't marry," said Amelia bluntly. She laid her cheek against the rag doll again. "I shall have all the things you have, Mama, but I won't marry. I think it's awful to have to please a husband. To give him babies and that sort of thing."

"Amelia, you're very young—you don't know what you're saying!"

"I'm not really. This is the month when I'll be ten. Only yesterday Nanny said I was getting to be a big girl. She said there were certain things I should be told, and you were the one to talk to me."

The walls were beginning to close in on Letty. She got out of her chair. "After your birthday I think a talk would be appropriate. If Nanny will be so good as to remind me?"

"Of course I will, milady." Nanny's voice was soothing. Her eyes shot lightning at Amelia. "A naughty miss I know is giving herself airs and graces. Busy as you are, milady, it's shameful her talking like that. I don't know what's come over her to be sure."

"It's all right, Nanny. But I do have to go. So many details to see to with this wedding coming up. Even though it's several months away—"

Did Nanny see that it was an excuse? Letty surely could have stayed a few minutes longer. It was something about the way the talk had gone—the questions Amelia had asked. Nanny herself was to blame, telling the girl to ask her mother to explain. Surely Nanny could explain? But that was one thing Nanny could not do. Well, not easily.

Nanny was loving, skilled in the art of child rearing. And as surely as her sisters she spilled her blood on a mysterious monthly schedule. Yet Nanny was a virgin. Was it fair to leave the explanations of womanhood to one who was like an unopened door? Letty's head ached as she left the nursery, made her way down the stairs.

What had Mother done about this matter? Reaching her morning room, Letty tried to remember.

Emma had done little. She said quite a lot, but it all meant nothing. "You will have to prepare yourself—bleeding will start soon."

"Bleeding, Mama? What sort of bleeding?"

"Letty, why do you always want me to be so specific? It's a delicate subject as it is."

"You mean, I will bleed?"

"Yes, Letty. Every woman does."

"But bleeding means injury—"

"Not in this case, Letty. Oh, you will see when the time comes. There are little linen napkins you must wear. When they are soiled, they can be washed and—"

"Where will I bleed, Mama?"

"Letty, I'm not going to tell you anymore. It's too embarrassing."

There had to be only one place. It was "down there"—the mysterious point where the legs joined, where hairs had oddly begun to sprout. The body in general was not to be talked about. But "down there" didn't even exist.

So many years ago, she'd almost forgotten the first, awful shock. It had been waiting for her, in a task she dreaded. Telling Amelia.

How did one prepare a young girl? There was of course no way to explain womanhood. Womanhood wasn't to be understood. Merely endured. Was that what she must teach Amelia?

2

Hitty and Letty were talking in the parlor. The heat was insufferable. A cooling fruit drink stood in a glass pitcher on a table between them, small chips of ice floating like crystals, miraculously weightless on a bed of mint leaves.

"So you are almost ready," said Letty. She placed the tumbler to her cheek, feeling its chill. Held it there, savoring its temporary comfort. August sunshine, like a ravening lion, clawed at the tall windows, attempting to gain the room with its long, slanting claws. Heat shimmered just beyond the heavy draperies. How long was it going to go on this way, the temperatures mounting every day? In late summer they should be seeing some signs of relief.

"I suppose I'm as ready as I'll ever be," said Hitty. She seemed to compose her face. "What did you feel like before your wedding?"

"Oh my," said Letty, purposefully vague. So many things she'd rather not remember. Why was it when occasions like this came up, people were forever opening memory albums? Playing the game of "Do you recall"? She set her glass down, wiped her fingers on her handkerchief. Odd how moisture always transferred to the outside of a container when it held something cold. Was that the way it was with feelings? They seemed enclosed, safely locked away, only to seep through the impenetrable as insidiously as this beading on the tumbler.

Hitty was watching her closely. Too closely.

Letty felt uncomfortable under the scrutiny. "You've had your final fitting?" she asked.

"Yes. The dress has already arrived. Just a few more of my going-away clothes to be delivered. So strange to see them hanging in the closet."

"How so?" said Letty cautiously. "I mean, you're pleased with them, aren't you? I thought Miss Puxley did an excellent job."

"Yes." Hitty picked up her glass, sipped thoughtfully. "It's just—I look at them and they aren't me."

"Not yet. But they will be."

"I suppose so." Face a little frightened. "When you moved into this house, it was new, wasn't it?"

"Nathaniel had it built, if you remember. When we married, it wasn't quite ready. Nat was furious. We had to take rooms in a furnished house. It felt like being a boarder. Nat used to come here twice a day to watch the progress. Then, when we could take possession, the house was such a mess. I was already expecting Albert."

Hitty lowered her eyes. Her sister knew it was from embarrassment. With a sense of merriment, she wondered how Hitty—staid and spinsterly Hitty—was going to manage all of it. The commingling of man and woman. Would Hitty be girlish? Would she show fear? Letty wanted to giggle hysterically.

That was what Hitty wanted to talk about, but Letty wouldn't give her the satisfaction. Hitty would have to find out the way they all did. By experiencing it. Bitterly. Oh God, it was bitter!

All of a sudden Letty felt guilty. She should talk of it. She should help Hitty prepare herself for what lay ahead. Compton Grey, for all his kindness, what would he be like on the wedding night? Letty jerked her thoughts backward, like panting dogs on a leash. She'd no business to pry, even mentally, into her sister's business. She felt a slow flush creep over her cheeks and picked up her fan.

"Mercy, it's warm. Even the fruit ade doesn't help. How do you stay so cool, Hitty?"

"It's really quite pleasant in here. You look warm, Letty. I hope you're not catching a fever?"

"Good gracious," said Letty, dismissing the idea rapidly. She knew what summer agues were like, striking with chills and aching when the heat was greatest. Some said they had to do with the smells that came from the river when the waters became low, brackish. So many tales, explanations. Yet everyone knew that fevers, like winter colds, came and went. Mysteriously. Probably no one would ever trace their origin. Like so many troubles, they were a part of life.

Letty was puzzled about the inner heat, though. It had become noticeable this summer. As if the room had grown unaccountably warm. Yet others didn't feel it. That was what alerted her. She found herself moving the air about her with her fan, unable to do more than endure the burning sweeping upward and over her like a tide. Inexorable. Breaking finally, in small beading on her forehead, under her armpits, between her breasts. The inner furnace expelling its buildup through runnels of moisture. Dabbing surreptitiously, or bearing it all —the prickling beneath her dress, the streams of salt fluid that ran into her eyes. Her most intimate clothing was often soaked through at the end of several hours. It was worrying. Mystifying. She'd wondered a time or two if this could be what Mother had hinted of. What Mother herself had suffered from when Letty was an unmarried girl.

"It's something that happens to a woman. Change of life, they call it. You'll know when it happens. I can't tell you what causes it. Only it's most embarrassing. Like so many other things women have to put up with. Now, don't ask me about it, Letty. It's just—well, you have to get through it, that's all."

Like the monthly freshet. Like the iron hand of cramps that went with it. Like bearing children. Like being a woman. Yet Nat, when disposed to be conversational, which he was in the early days of their marriage, had hinted that men too had problems.

What were they? The need to shave, to decide whether or not to grow a beard or a moustache? Things could go wrong for them later, too. Mother had mentioned Father had to get up in the night many, many times. Occasionally he dribbled from his privates. Had Mother said that? Or had Letty imagined it? Heard it at some gossipy tea party?

The heat was subsiding, thank the Lord. Letty removed a handkerchief from her cuff, feigning nonchalance. She wiped her brow with a gesture that said she was almost unaware of what she was doing. "I seem to feel the warmth more this summer."

Hitty hadn't noticed. Letty was grateful. She was safe for now from questions, prying. Sometime she'd have to ask someone who knew about change of life. But who? Surely it wasn't a doctor's province? Or was it? She could hardly imagine asking Henry Porter. Perhaps some older woman? Not Mother! Mother not only wouldn't have answers, but she could still frighten, even when one was prepared to disbelieve her, to hold her off with a light laugh, an air of amusement. Mother always managed to terrify.

"Don't let Mother scare you about marriage," Letty said to Hitty unexpectedly. She must have hit home, for her sister looked up, her eyes wary, startled.

"You really mean that?"

"I most certainly do. What's she been saying?"

Hitty toyed with her glass. It was almost empty. "Might I have a little more? It's delicious."

Letty refilled it. "I'm afraid the ice is mostly melted."

"It doesn't matter. What did Mother say to you when you were to be married?"

"Let's hear what she's been telling you."

Hitty blushed. She was quiet for a long minute, examining the inside of her refilled glass. Finally she got it out. "She said she supposed Compton would be gentle. Because he was a medical man." Hitty's face started to crumple. "Oh Letty, what did she mean? I mean, I'm getting married, not going to a doctor for a diagnosis. It sounds so peculiar. Frightening."

"Mother's a gem!" said Letty heavily. "She really is."

"Then you think she's just being her usual self? What I'm asking—" Hitty stopped. Scarlet with confusion. Embarrassment.

"Don't worry about it," said Letty soothingly. She was going to give Hitty this much. But no more. Compton could be different from Nat, couldn't he? What would it be like to have someone different from Nat? Someone who did all those things men had to do, with tenderness? Even with love? She jerked on her thoughts again. There she was, invading Hitty's territory.

Hitty was blowing her nose to cover the mortification. "You really think I shouldn't?"

"You and Dr. Grey, do you talk when you are together?"

"Oh yes. That is to say—" Hitty was startled once more. "What do you mean 'talk'? We exchange ideas. He's very intelligent. When he talks about things I don't know about, he often leaves me behind."

"What does he talk about?" Letty was curious. It also got Hitty off the subject of wedding nights.

"His work mostly. In fact, that's all he likes to discuss. I suppose that's natural." Her face held a question.

"Men generally get wrapped up in what they are doing. I'm afraid that's something you'll have to get used to. But at least he's willing to share. Do you find medicine interesting?"

"I don't know." Hitty's nose wrinkled. "Do you think it's awfully silly to want to talk about books? I mean about poems you've read or—"

"Not at all. Just don't try to bring it up at the breakfast table. It's generally safe to say that if you let the man lead the conversation, determine the subject under discussion, you'll keep him happy."

"Yes," said Hitty thoughtfully. "That's what Mother's told me. But of course she must have said the same thing to you."

"Yes," said Letty heavily. "Now tell me more about what you and Dr. Grey find in common."

"Nothing," said Hitty simply.

231

"Oh, but surely—dearest, you are going to marry him."

"I know," said Hitty. "Mother says when we are together all the time, there will be things to discuss."

"Do you love him?"

"I'm not sure." Hitty began to cry softly, without in the least disturbing the calmness of the atmosphere in the room. But tears, slow and painful, welled out of her eyes, running in glistening streaks down her round face.

Letty tried not to feel cross. "Hitty, if you don't marry him, there's the wedding to cancel. I'm not even sure if it could be, at the last minute like this."

"Oh," said Hitty, "I intend to marry him. It's all right. I weighed it all, you see. Thought about it for hours. I really don't believe love enters into it. Not at my time of life."

"Are you sure you don't love him?" asked Letty.

"I don't know. I—well, I'm trying to. I really am." The face earnest, pathetically strained.

"Yes, I am sure you are." Letty tried to sound comforting.

"I don't think we'll be together that much."

"What on earth do you mean?"

"Ah, I don't expect anybody's told you. He plans to buy a piece of property in Vermont. He's making it into a Home for Distressed Women."

"Distressed women? What on earth? Hitty, I'm afraid you've lost me."

"I know. It does take some explaining. You see, Compton feels women—gentlefolk of course, women who can pay—need a special place where they can receive attention."

"Ah." It sounded lovely—being paid attention. But Letty didn't even know what she meant. It was just a longing to be looked after and have the troubles smoothed away. No, it'd never be that sort of attention.

"Compton feels there's a need for this sort of thing," Hitty continued.

"Why does he have to establish this place in Vermont? Do the Vermont women need special care?"

Hitty laughed. "Far from it. I gather they're much more independent than we are. Milking, working on farms, that sort of thing. Compton's terribly impressed with them. He used to stay there with relatives. Then these cousins of his went West, and the woman who bought their house is a widow. Her husband was killed a year ago. Compton thinks she'll sell. If she won't, there are other properties."

"If Compton goes there, why can't you go with him?"

Hitty looked down at her hands. "He wouldn't want that. He says some of his patients might be disturbed."

"Disturbed?" Letty felt cold suddenly.

"Oh, not all of them. Compton says a lot of women lose their minds when they get to a certain age. He refers to it as *melancholia.* He says women are more prone to this sort of thing. In fact, we'd be amazed how many times it happens."

Another of those mysterious heat waves was beginning. Letty could sense it deep within her, like a tension building. She wanted to scream. Instead, she reached for her tepid glass of fruit drink. She must be extremely careful, set a guard on her tongue.

Hitty was still explaining. "In many really prominent families, women are said to be ill, but they've really gone off their heads."

"You mean, they've become crazy?"

Hitty's eyes looked troubled. "Compton doesn't like me to use that word. He says the ladies he's had for patients are badly frightened when it's described that way. Many times, a sedative is all that's needed. Something like laudanum."

"You sound very knowledgeable."

"Do I? It's from picking up things Compton lets drop. As I was saying, the ones that aren't awfully bad wouldn't trust him if they thought he was calling them crazy."

"The ladies who are his patients—does he help them?" Letty asked.

"I suppose he does. He's got a very good reputation. You knew that when Henry Porter brought him here."

"I thought Compton was interested mainly in children?"

"He was. Don't you remember? He explained how he'd found out a mother's feelings can actually affect her child. Even before birth!"

"But why Vermont? You never finished that part of the story."

"The fresh air and good country food. Compton says it'll do wonders for nervous disorders," Hitty explained.

"Does Compton have the money to purchase property, build, up there?"

Hitty looked puzzled. "I suppose so. Compton doesn't encourage me to speak about money. He's very strict about that. Is Nathaniel like that, Letty?"

"Yes." Letty sighed. "I haven't the slightest idea how much money we have. He thoroughly controls the purse strings."

"I suppose," said Hitty thoughtfully, "that because Mother's the way she's always been with Father, it comes as something of a shock. You know, the way she sort of tells him what to do."

Letty's smile was sad. She wasn't sure why. Whether it was for

233

Father or for the other marriages. Like hers and Nathaniel's. Like Hitty's would be. "You get used to it. After all, dear, when have we ever had a penny of our own?"

Hitty agreed. "I really must be going. Oh, Letty, you won't tell anybody what I said—?"

"Of course not. I won't speak of it to a soul." Surprising herself, Letty leaned forward. "Take care, dear. I'm glad we had this talk."

Hitty looked flustered. "It was nice. We've never actually spoken like this before. Do you realize?"

"We'll have to again," said Letty.

It was like with Olwen.

Yet different from Olwen. Letty couldn't remember being so careful with Olwen. It had been all right to let her guard down a little— the way one spoke to strangers on a ship. Knowing one would never have to face them at a later time. They could be entrusted with secrets.

Hitty was reachable. Mother, for instance, could get things out of her. This Compton might go to Nathaniel. Letty licked dry lips.

Hitty rose, gathering her things. "I suppose the carriage can be brought round."

They stood on the steps. Suddenly Letty thought of England— Cousin Frances. Irrelevantly, she wondered what had become of the old man with the rake. Was he still keeping the stones tidy? It was almost a year since she'd attended the funeral. How time sped when one was getting older. She sighed, feeling herself past her prime. It was true then. She knew it beyond a shadow of a doubt. She was in her change of life.

She waved good-bye to Hitty as the carriage wheeled about. Taft was hovering, waiting to close the front door.

"It's still so hot," she said to him, feeling the need to fill the gap between them with some inanity.

"Yes, madam." His look accused her of staying him in the midst of whatever mission he was upon. Taft was always going somewhere.

"You can tell Phillips to clear the parlor."

"Yes, madam." Did she imagine his surliness, his disdain?

She gained her morning room. Where was Compton getting the money? She knew her father was settling an endowment on Hitty, as he'd done on herself. Nat had it "invested" and became irritated when she asked him about it.

Was Compton using Hitty's endowment to buy the property? She'd gone cold suddenly. A widower, out of the blue, seeking Hitty's hand. It had an ugly explanation—marrying her for her money.

She was being foolish. That sort of thing almost always went on in wealthy families. The romantic idea of marriage was mostly a fairy tale. After all, Compton was in a sense rescuing Hitty. Plain, dumpy, rather silly Hitty. It was a contract. Hitty's transformation into wife-hood, Compton's to property in Vermont. So why was Letty trembling? Why did she have that small feather of fear tickling her mind? Hitty would be all right.

Letty wanted to cry. She sat at her desk and pulled blank paper toward her—the old, familiar lines growing under her pencil. A cage.

Letty pushed her drawing away. Cassie-Mary. Could she really see the future? Oh, dear Lord, she'd got to forget.

3

Letty was reading her letters. A ship had come in, bringing a letter from Mrs. Montacute and another from Daphne Howard, forwarded by Mrs. Montacute. It was the second letter, written from India, that spoke to Letty.

This awful country. Oh, I know I shouldn't complain, but it is so horrible. Your little girl becomes sick in the morning, and by sundown you have buried her. As if she'd never been. Letty, I remember that you too suffered the loss of children. I feel I have to write to someone who'll understand. Mother lost a baby by miscarriage between Jack and me, but, Letty, my Crystelle wasn't a baby. She would have been eight in November. She's gone, Letty. Some dreadful disease nobody knows the name of, even though the M.O. (that's what they call the army doctor) came and honestly did his best. He was crying when we lost her. I wasn't supposed to see, but he brushed tears away. He had to tell me about the rules— burying bodies by sundown. It's because of the heat—they even have to go into special graves because the jackals dig them up. Indians generally burn their dead. But I couldn't bear that. Not my little girl. Do you remember how sweet she was?

Letty saw again the child on the staircase. "I am Crystelle Howard," she had said. As polite and nice as you please. Golden-haired and eager for life.

Letty sat there staring at the page. She slit open Mrs. Montacute's letter with slow fingers.

The poor child, I feel for her so. Perhaps there's something you could say in the charming way you have, dear Letty. She recalled you'd lost a baby. I've sent her a cable that I'll come out to India to be with her. But, funny old stick that I am, I'm not going to be much use. The doctors say I've developed a bad heart. So it's rest for me and taking care. I don't want her to know, so do not mention

236

it, please? I mean it. Jack—that's my eldest—is furious with me for thinking of going out there. But when it's your child? After all, what better use could I be than to give Daphne some comfort?'

Katie was at the door. "Begging your pardon, ma'am, but it's Miss Amelia." Katie twisted her apron in her hands. "A fearful carry-on, and Nanny sent me down. We honestly don't know what to do with her."

Letty turned in her chair. "What on earth can be the matter? Two grown, healthy women cannot manage a child?" She'd felt the dreaded heat begin as she spoke. Her heart was pounding.

"It's her bridesmaid's frock, ma'am. She claims she won't wear it."

"You're not serious?"

"I'm afraid so, ma'am. She keeps saying she told you and Mrs. Crocker over and over. She's that determined, ma'am. Nanny and me are at a loss to know what to say to her."

"All right, Katie. You can bring her downstairs to me."

The young maid's face showed relief. Responsibility had been removed from her. Letty, on the other hand, felt overburdened.

She turned back to the letters. She picked up Daphne's, feeling the horror. The little girl lost as by stealth, a thief coming to rob them in the night. Leaving the mark that would remove the living, glowing child from their midst.

All the investment that bringing a baby into the world meant. As if it weren't enough to be tempted by the years of safety, the survival of childhood diseases, into daring to believe the child might attain girlhood. Then snatched.

Why was life so cruel? Letty recalled Daphne's plea to her mother, blurted out one seaside afternoon. "I don't want to go to India. I have this awful feeling—"

How many feelings did people have that were ignored? Cassie-Mary? There it was again. Letty felt an impulse to scrunch up the letters in her hands, push away their news, their plea that she write back with understanding. God knows, she had enough of that.

Letty read the rest of Mrs. Montacute's letter. It was at the bottom of the last page.

Letty, I blame myself so terribly. What I told you about Peter's wild ways was all true. Yet, did I have a right to force my daughter to stay with him? She wanted to remain behind, you know. Oh, the heart grieves, Letty. Don't ever be sure you know what's best. I've been pig-headed. Well, at the least I can try to make it up to Daphne. But to Crystelle? I keep asking, why did God take her?

Letty could hear the quiet well-bred voice as the written words jumped from the page. See the hand tense on the pen. The small blotch where a tear had fallen, hastily wiped away, but not before it had swirled the ink about. Letty sighed deeply, staring away from the missives, out beyond the window.

A single bird alighted on her windowsill. It looked about and flew off again. Strange how life went on, no matter what happened. Indeed as if it had never happened. The momentous things—the heartaches. Warren, Brett. Now Hitty was to be married. Changes, always changes.

A tap on the door. Why wouldn't they leave her alone today? "What is it?" she asked impatiently.

"You said to bring Miss Amelia down, ma'am." Katie ushered before her an enraged Amelia, the girl's solemn face suffused with fury.

"Thank you, Katie. You may leave us alone for a few minutes."

"Yes, madam." The door closed discreetly.

"Now Amelia, what on earth is this about?" Letty, already disturbed to the point of wanting to stride about the room, to cry out, gazed at her daughter without patience. "I hear you are causing a hardship."

Amelia appeared to ignore the words. "Mama, it is not to be borne! It is intolerable."

"What on earth are you talking about?"

"The dress you are going to make me wear to the wedding. I distinctly said I wouldn't wear yellow."

Letty's lips pressed together in annoyance. "You are making all this fuss over a dress?" She stood up, to match her mood. She was surprised to see Amelia so tall. Had that many years passed by since she'd given birth to her?

"You make it sound like a small thing, Mama. It is very large to me. I insist you hear me out!"

"You insist?" Letty stepped backward. "Amelia, you astonish me. That you should have the effrontery to speak this way. What has gotten into you?"

It was disconcerting to see how much in control of the situation the child appeared. "I've told you I will not wear yellow. I asked that my frock be lavender. I can't abide yellow."

"You will wear what you are told!" Letty heard her voice sharp.

"Then, Mama, I must warn you that I will not appear at the wedding. Or, if I must appear, I'll sit at the back with the servants. I refuse to wear a yellow dress. It is the sort of color one of the Maloney family would wear and—"

"That's enough!" Letty shouted it. "Stop it at once. You will wear what has been planned for you. You will do as you are told!" Her hands were trembling, her eyes bright with tears of rage. Shaking as from an inner volcano.

"Mama, I am warning you—" The eyes that faced Letty were unmoved, defiant. I will do something to make you regret—"

Letty hadn't heard her. Afterward, she was to remember the full contents of the conversation. But now she knew only one thing. Amelia's cause was frivolous.

238

Letty whirled about, gathered to her breast the letters that had come from such a distance away. "These," she screamed at her daughter, gulping to get enough breath. "These letters are about terrible things. Awful, terrible things. A little girl I knew, a lovely child, got sick one morning and was dead by nighttime. In India. You don't know the people and you don't know the place. You don't know anything! You just think you do!"

"Mama—"

"No, don't say a word. You've already said enough. I'm sending you back upstairs. I expect you to appear in the wedding as Aunt Hitty's bridesmaid. I expect you to wear the dress. Above all, I expect you to do as you are told. Without another word—do you hear me?"

Amelia stared at Letty. Slowly her face tightened into obstinate lines. Mouth firm and determined, eyes level and proud. Without another word, she turned, opened the door, and closed it quietly behind her.

Letty stood rooted to the spot. Now that it was over, she felt stunned. Ashamed of herself. Why had she allowed herself to indulge in this outburst?

No, she wasn't sorry after all. Someone had to speak out. To say what was important and what wasn't. To quibble over a dress when a child had died in India—she felt better all of a sudden. As if by lashing out at Amelia she'd played some small part in setting it straight, all the injustices, the sufferings.

What could a ten-year-old know of these?

Hitty was writing in her journal. She'd just penned the date: August 28, 1887.

It was a full day. Letty said the furniture was coming but it wasn't until I had word from Nathaniel that it was actually at the docks that I knew some of it was to be mine. Really mine.

I told Compton we were going to have to have it delivered to the house. It still seems like his house, even though in three days I'll be married and mistress of it. I think that's the part that is so hard to grasp. That it's really happening. I have to confess that I'm scared. But I suppose when it's actually taken place, it'll be different.

Hitty dipped her pen again, paused for a moment, then continued writing.

The furniture is lovely. Lovely isn't the best word. How do you describe something so old yet so solid? A four-poster bed, an enormous oak chest that seems to have been designed for clothes to hang in, another for linens with strange raised carvings on its top. Several chairs with rush bottoms. A footstool of much later vintage and a table with sides to fold down. Rather like Mama's tea table, except it's extremely old.

I thought to arrive at the house before the wagon got there. To my distress, not only had it beaten me, but Compton was there too. I was astonished. He'd never expressed any desire to be present when the furniture was unloaded. To be honest, it made me feel reprimanded. As if by being there he was saying to me, "It's my house until we're married. After that you can do what you like with it."

I'll confess it because no one will ever see this journal—at least I trust they won't. Maybe it will have to be locked in the linen chest after all. To be sure of

240

privacy. Anyway, to my confession. I do feel as if I were coming into that place a stranger. Let me try to put it into words.

There are three servants, all of them black. That's confusing in the first place since I've never been around black people. A lot of Mama and Papa's acquaintances have them. They are supposed to make excellent coachmen. And laundresses. It should not bother me, but it does. They seem so different. I try not to stare. Tildie, the cook-housekeeper, was with Compton's first wife. She came up from Georgia when "Missie" and Compton were married. Tildie's the one has me the most worried.

I mean, I can't help it that I'm taking Missie's place. It's been twenty years since she died in childbirth. All that time, Tildie's never had anyone else in the house, giving her orders, taking an interest in the kitchen, the housekeeping. I feel like an intruder.

There's two other servants. Joseph, who's married to Tildie, and Jakes, who's a much younger man. Joseph was kind to me this afternoon. He asked me if I wanted a cold drink. When she heard him, Tildie stood there frowning. Joseph went and drew it for me himself. Jakes drives Compton about in the carriage. Joseph's hair is white and Tildie's very fat. I wish she liked me. When I asked Compton about her, he smiled and said he could scarcely remember a time when Tildie wasn't there. In front of me, he told Tildie to be sure and give me a lot of help. I was embarrassed. She just stared and said "Yassuh" in that soft voice of hers. But she didn't smile at me or make me feel welcome.

I'm not welcome. That's the God's truth.

I wish I wasn't getting married. Now, I've said it. It's too late to back out, with the wedding three days away and all the guests invited. To say nothing of that beautiful furniture sitting in the upstairs bedroom of Compton's house. Will I ever be able to say "my house"?

Will I ever feel comfortable about being married? Compton shook his head over the furniture. Somehow, I don't think it had occurred to him till he saw the four-poster that he was going to have to give up his single bed. Odd, when I've worried about it over and over, every night for months. Tried to imagine what it would be like, lying beside him. Even if he is a doctor.

Compton has given me the most beautiful pin. He took it out of his bureau drawer when we were getting the furniture settled. (Of course Tildie was there and so was Jakes, so it was quite respectable.) It's an emerald with pearls all round it, in the shape of a flower. He said it had belonged to his mother and he wanted me to have it.

I wonder if she wore it. I mean Missie. The way Tildie stared, I am almost certain it was hers first. Well, it would be natural, wouldn't it? To have given it to her. Then when she died, he probably just put it away.

I'm at the end of the page, and besides, I have to get changed for dinner. I wish I were braver—about marriage, the trip to Vermont, everything. I keep wanting to cry. So cowardly.

She stared beyond the simple table, out toward the garden. Wondered, could she have flowerbeds of her own? It would be something to keep her busy. She could come over here and ask old Jaspar for advice. She closed her eyes. One tear, like an oval pearl, dropped from her eyelids and splashed on the cover of the journal.

5

Letty stirred sugar into her tea, bit delicately into her toast.

What was that commotion? Was she imagining the sound of feet running? Noises in the back hall? The baize-covered swinging doors between pantry and dining room successfully muffled most kitchen noises. And when she and Nat were silent you could almost hear the tick of the clock in the hall. Her cousin's clock. Miraculously running, thanks to the tender ministrations of an able Swiss clockmaker.

There was a disturbance! She was sure of it now.

Taft entered, his ordinarily composed face concerned. "Begging your pardon, sir—madam. Nanny wishes to see you on a matter of some urgency."

"Nanny?" Letty's thoughts became a whirlwind, dead calm at the center, spinning wild terrors at its periphery. "Is there something wrong with the children?"

Nathaniel put down his paper, annoyed. "Couldn't she wait? We're in the middle of breakfast!"

Nanny appeared in the doorway. "Oh, milady, you know I wouldn't be bothering you at this hour. And this the day Miss Hitty's to be married. I understand what it is to disturb you, the long hours you've got ahead and all."

"It's all right, Nanny," Letty tried to reassure her. "Just explain what the problem is."

"Well," said Nanny, suddenly struck dumb. She fiddled with her apron, smoothing it and glancing about the room. Her terror rose chiefly from her employer.

Nathaniel looked over the top of glasses acquired recently for reading. "Come, Nanny. Is one of the children ill?"

Nanny became even more flustered. "I hardly know how to tell you, sir. It's Miss Amelia, sir."

"Amelia?" This time it was Letty. "An accident?"

"No, at least not to the child."

"For heaven's sakes, Nanny! Spare us the guessing games." Nathaniel was sputtering. "What has Amelia done?"

"She's cut up her dress, sir."

"She's what!" Nathaniel was half out of his seat, his chair pushed back, a look of incredulity on his face. "You mean she's taken a scissors to one of her garments?"

"Not just any dress—her bridesmaid's frock, sir." Nanny was trembling so badly she looked as if she might fall.

Letty glanced at her plate. The buttered toast was cooling. She had a feeling all of this had happened before. But that was ridiculous.

Nathaniel's voice broke into her thoughts, like a door banging in the wind from a sudden storm. "Good God, woman, have you nothing to say? What do you make of this? Absolutely incredible!" He slammed his fist down on the folded newspaper.

"Nat, I'm afraid it may be my fault—"

"Nanny, send Amelia down to me at once!" Nat exploded. "This moment, do you hear?"

"Begging your pardon sir, but the child's been carrying on for three or four days—ever since the dresses arrived. She said she wouldn't wear the frock made for her on account of its color."

"It's color?" Nat's eyebrows were as high in his head as they would go.

Letty broke in. "I knew about it days ago, Nat. The child came to me and said she refused to wear yellow—"

"She refused? You sit there with a perfectly straight face and tell me that you allowed your daughter to refuse to do as she was told?" Disdain, spreading like a damp spot.

"Indeed, Nat, I did not. I informed her in the clearest terms that she would wear the frock as planned. I was very firm with her, I assure you."

He stared down the length of the table, drummed his fingers. "Out-and-out disobedience, eh? Well, Nanny, I want to see her. At once, you hear me?"

"Yes sir. I'll fetch her, sir."

There was silence between them when Nanny left. Thick and sticky—like treacle. The air was hard to breathe. What would he do to her, this obstinate, stupid daughter who wouldn't accept rules? Surely she must be all Mackenzie? No Benedict would act this defiant. Except, perhaps, Mother.

"You sent for me, Papa?"

He'd replaced his spectacles on the end of his nose, took his time about acknowledging her. At last he looked up. "Tell me about the dress, Amelia," he began, almost pleasantly.

"I told Mama I wouldn't wear it, Papa."

"You *told* your mother? I want to make sure I heard you correctly. You *told* your mother?"

"Yes, Papa. Quite clearly."

"And what did your mother say?"

"Mama said I had to wear it. She wouldn't listen to me, Papa. So I warned her." A glance at Letty then, the gray eyes not as calm as usual. Shooting darts.

"You *warned* your mother?" Nathaniel's brows came together. The long face seemed to lengthen. "Just how did you do this?"

"I told her I'd do something. If she made me."

"Ah." Nathaniel sat back. "I see. Or I think I see. In fact, you threatened your mother?"

A silence. Then Amelia said, "It could be seen that way. I am determined not to wear yellow, Papa."

"Now you are threatening me?"

Letty could barely breathe. Nat was being goaded. Perhaps Amelia was too naive to perceive it? But it was like a bull being prodded in the face with an umbrella. A child's umbrella.

"I've already done what I meant to do, Papa. The dress is in ribbons."

"We've been informed of that." Nathaniel rose, pushed his chair back under the table. "Follow me, Amelia."

He stared briefly at Letty before leaving the room. His expression said, "You stay out of this. You've had your opportunity. Now it's my turn."

Out into the corridor. Across the hall and into Nat's den. The sound of the heavy door closing. The clock they'd none of them had time to get used to yet chiming the half hour.

Nothing could be heard from the study. This house was too well built, with timbers selected by Nathaniel himself. Double-thick walls, doors solid, floors formed so tightly they creaked only in the dampest weather. What was going on in there? Letty caught up her napkin, crumpled it in her hand.

"A fresh pot of tea, ma'am?" For once, Taft's eyes were conciliatory. Almost kind. Yet one glance at his back, the set of his shoulders —he wanted an excuse to come into the room again. How difficult servants were!

245

"Thank you, Taft. No more tea." She moved the disheveled piece of linen from one place on the tablecloth to another. "I must be getting upstairs. So much to do."

"Very good, madam. Will there be anything else?"

She wanted to scream at him to leave her alone. "Nothing else. I know you servants want to get on so you can be free to go to the wedding." She'd risen. "You can clear the dining room in five minutes if my husband hasn't come out by then."

"Very good, madam." At last he left, the baize door swinging behind him.

She couldn't go upstairs. She walked to the window behind Nat's chair. The curtains had to remain open for breakfast. Afterward, when Nat had gone to the office, they could be closed. Keeping out summer's intensity.

The noise of a door opening startled her, though she'd been straining for it. Amelia pushed it before her in a strange way. Her face was very white, set.

"Mama, I am to be in the wedding. I will wear the dress of my choice." She said it in a dead tone.

Nathaniel's hulk filled the doorway. He nodded at the girl. "You can go upstairs. We have made our bargain. I'll expect you to abide by it."

Amelia nodded. She was holding her hands in a cupped manner. They might have held water from a brook. A shadow, she slipped past Letty.

Letty reached out to grab her. "You'll not leave till you tell me. I demand to know." But she missed the shoulder that had moved past her. A cat, sliding away into the shadows.

"Let her go, Letty. Her bargain is with me."

"What about my problem with her? The children's dresses are my affair. I have helped plan this wedding—I am the one who has made the decisions. You're not going to shut me out."

"Letty! Come into the study. Close the door."

She pulled it to behind her, felt its knob slippery. She glanced down, discovered her hands to be stained. "Nat, this looks like blood!"

"Amelia must have left it there when she opened it." He took a clean pocket handkerchief out, wiped it assiduously.

"Nat, what did you do to the child?"

"She knew what it was about." He folded the handkerchief. "The girl received her whipping."

"Bloodied hands, Nat?"

He lifted his head proudly. "She had her choice. A lesser punishment and she would have worn a dress of your choice. A greater—and her own selection. She chose to pick her own garment. Are you satisfied?"

"No! You had no right to strike this bargain with her without asking me. Nat, you've put me in an intolerable position with Amelia. Never again can I tell her to do something without running the risk she'll go behind my back. Arrange to defy me—through you. Have you any idea what you've done?"

His eyes narrowed. He leaned forward, his manner quietly menacing. He seemed to fill the room. "What I have done? Who was it that mismanaged the affair in the first place? Who proved herself so pathetic, so ineffectual, that a ten-year-old daughter would go ahead and thumb her nose in her mother's face? Not I, Letty. Not I." He shook his finger under her nose.

"You're not being fair, Nat." She felt faint. Her head was pounding unmercifully.

"All right, Letty. I've had enough. If you elect to waste the morning in hysterics, it's none of my business. But I happen to remember that we're attending a wedding not many hours from now. Before you go, you are to give Nanny orders."

"What orders?"

"Amelia may wear what she wishes." He bowed his head. "The girl has earned the right."

Letty made a sound in her throat. Something between astonishment and rage. "Impossible. What shall I tell Mother?"

"Not my concern." A light in his eyes now. "Your daughter has courage, Letty. She has her wits about her, strength, willpower." The drooping lips tightened, suggesting the twist of a smile. "At any rate, she dresses how she pleases. Now you may go, Letty. Be sure to instruct the nursery staff."

At the door she turned and looked at him. "How badly did you injure her hands?"

He shrugged. "She'll probably wish to wear gloves."

"She could get blood poisoning."

His lips curled. "Letty, you are so dramatic, you could have gone on the stage. It might have afforded you more scope than marriage to me."

Through the open door she could see Taft, hovering. How much had he heard? She felt dull inside. Wordless, she began to mount the stairs.

Nanny said, "You got a talking to, I'm sure. What's the matter with your hands?"

"They just need washing."

247

"Well, you know where the china jug and basin are."

"*Pitcher,* Nanny. In America we call it pitcher."

"None of your sauce, Miss Amelia. Your mother knew I was English when I was engaged. If she wishes to make a complaint, it's none of your business. Hurry up with that washing. We've got to get you and Miss Polly dressed."

Amelia came back. Her hands were shining, wet.

"Well, miss, didn't you take time to dry them?"

"I didn't want to get blood on the towel, Nanny."

"Blood? Whatever are you talking about? Here, let me see those hands." Grabbing at them.

But they were pulled away from her. Still in that odd, cupped way. Dripping. Little rivulets ran out of the enclosure of the palms as if they were bowls beneath a fountain, spilling over.

"Well, I never!" said Nanny, stepping back. "Oh my, you did get a whipping. They used to take the switch to us like that when I was in school. Don't recall so much messing up, though."

"My father and I made a bargain, Nanny. I'm to wear whatever I please."

"Nonsense!" said Nanny quickly. The caning had made Miss Amelia fanciful. "Katie, are you there? You go downstairs right away."

"Nanny, there's blood in the water in the washbasin. I went to empty it and— Oh, Miss Amelia, look at your hands!" Katie stood stock-still.

"We'll have plenty of time to talk about it later, Katie," Nanny broke in. "Now I want you to go downstairs—"

Amelia's voice was crisp. "I know what you want to ask Mama, Nanny. But it's from Papa that I have the permission. When I took my whipping, I won my choice."

Nanny came close to the girl. She put one arm about her narrow shoulders; with the other, she felt the high, smooth forehead. "There, there, lovey. Nanny understands. She does have to make sure, you see, dear. It would be awful to get Nanny into trouble."

Katie had gone. The palms were horrible. The flesh was pulpy, and if there hadn't been so much blood, the skin would have looked like snow after it had been rutted by carriage traffic. Long lines that bubbled up with dark insistency.

"I don't know how we're going to get this stopped," Nanny clucked. "You must be in terrible pain, child."

Betsy came up the back staircase, puffing slightly. It was a long climb when you took it without a break. She found Nanny in the washroom. "I've been sent up with a message for you."

"Oh? I hope it's about the frocks. I just dispatched Katie."

Besty leaned against the door. "This one"—she jerked her head toward Amelia—"got her own way." She clicked her tongue against her teeth disapprovingly. "The mistress says she can wear what she wants to the wedding." Betsy shook her head at Nanny. "It make any sense to you? I thought the dresses were all made up special."

Amelia lifted her head in challenge. "You see! I told you. I'm going to wear the gray cambric."

"Gray for a wedding!" Nanny's voice pealed like a church bell. "You can't do that. It's supposed to be a happy occasion. What'll your Aunt Hitty think?"

"It doesn't matter what she thinks," said Amelia. "Next to lavender, I like gray best."

"What's she done to her hands, Nanny?"

"A bad girl got punished, Betsy."

Betsy snorted. "You best have them hands done up. It'd be a shame to mark up anybody else's dress. Miss Polly's, for instance. She still going to wear that real pretty green?"

"Far as I know," said Nanny. "Far as I know. But the way things are going this morning, anything could happen."

"I told you over and over, but you wouldn't believe me," said Amelia, setting her chin obstinately.

"Oh, you told me all right," said Nanny. "I just wish I could see your papa's face when you appear in that cambric. Except, knowing your papa, he won't care. Likely won't even notice. But your mama will, Miss Hitty will, and Mrs. Benedict—oh my!"

6

"Letty, we'd about given you up!"

Emma's eyes reproved her daughter as Letty was shown into Hitty's room. They were all there. Hitty, radiant and fragile in white. Not a true white, for Miss Puxley had hinted that old ivory would be more fitting in view of Hitty's age. Now Hitty was encased in it, draped about with the traditions that made bridal occasions at once so solid and so fragile.

Emma was presiding, as befitted her rank and her position, from a stiff-backed chair that her black-laced body did not deign to touch. Her ebony cane with its gold handle was her sole support. Hooper was there too. She had been with them for so long that Letty couldn't remember a time when Hooper wasn't. And Parkes, Emma's lady's maid, grown ancient with her mistress, her hair gray as a steel hairpin, her mouth puckered as she knelt to arrange the draping of Hitty's dress.

Hitty was as pale as her garments, as solemn as her robes. The blue eyes seemed to have been washed, their innocence put away behind a glass wall.

Letty put her hands over her sister's. "I'm sorry I'm late. Something came up to detain me."

"Its all right," said Hitty.

Letty could see that it wasn't. Nothing was right. It was nervousness. Letty recalled the same feelings many years and five children ago. The way the women crowded around her, suffocating her in their solicitude, their unspoken sympathy for what she must suffer in initiation. When it was over, she would be one of them.

250

"Well, anyway, you are here at last!" said Emma, as if it were an edict on something. Perhaps the wedding could now go ahead.

Chaplain, the underbutler, came to the door. "There's a visitor below, madam," he said quietly.

Emma rounded about in her chair. "At this hour? Who would take such a time to pay a call? Surely all our friends know—"

"It's a Mrs. Evans, madam." Chaplain's eyes were reproachful. It wasn't his fault he had to report such news.

"We know no Mrs. Evans," said Emma indignantly.

Hitty stepped forward. "I asked her to come. I particularly wanted her to be here. Please, Chaplain, show Mrs. Evans up." Hitty's pale face had flushed. "So lovely—so good of her to come."

"Hitty!" Emma's voice rapped out, harsh, dictatorial. "I must say I am amazed. This is a very private time. One when only your family has a right to be present." She hunched her shoulders in a gesture that indicated acute resentment.

"Oh, Mother, don't be silly. You've met Olwen. Letty knows her too."

Emma's mouth was twitching. Her hands clenched and unclenched. "You can't mean that vulgar minister's wife?"

"Hush, Mother!" said Hitty sharply. Her concern was to shelter Olwen from Emma's cruelty. "You remember her?" she said to Letty.

Letty rearranged her silken stole. It had fallen back off her shoulders. She coughed lightly. Wedding day or no, Hitty was alone in this unwise invitation.

Hitty went to the door. Her eyes searched the stairway. "Olwen, dearest! I wasn't sure you'd come."

"Oh, I wouldn't let you down for the world," said the singsong Welsh voice. "I waited till the last on purpose. Had a sense I might be intruding."

Hitty reached out to enfold her, the ivory-clad arms going about the woman, pulling her into the room. "Intrude? I asked you—remember?"

Olwen was an unknown quantity. Seeing Hitty hug her, Letty had a slight sense of revulsion. Such close contact with someone who lived by a set of rules different from their own. Why, Olwen even made her own tea. Sewed her own curtains. She probably wasn't above pressing Mr. Evans' trousers, sponging fruit stains off his coats.

Emma huffed and puffed. "I don't know if you realize it, Mrs. Evans. This is a family gathering. Completely private."

"Oh," said Olwen, flustered. "I was afraid of as much. It was why I said to Llewellyn this morning, I don't much relish butting in. Supposing they take offense? I mean, everyone has their customs, mind. When Mr. Evans and I were married—"

251

"It's all right, dear," Hitty interrupted with unexpected firmness. "I invited you, and you are my friend. Now, let me see, can we find you a chair?"

Hooper delivered the chair.

Olwen sat cautiously, then looked at Hitty's dress. "Why, you're the loveliest thing I've ever seen. My word, Hitty, I see so many brides, playing the organ for Llewellyn like I do, at the smaller functions. There's been none I've laid eyes on as sweet as you, my dear."

Olwen rambled on. "Are you nervous, Hitty? I remember when I was waiting to go to the church—I was wed in a very small village, you see—"

Letty tugged gently at her collar. She could feel the wretched inner heat beginning. Nausea filled her throat. This room was stuffy, utterly airless. She felt she might die. What would they do if she did? She repressed a desire to laugh hysterically.

Emma's sharp eyes had picked up her daughter's disturbance. "Letty, are you having a hot flash?"

"I'm all right."

"Letty, I believe you are having one. You never told me you were in the change of life."

"Mother, I'm all right."

Emma extracted her lorgnette from her reticule. "Letty, if you are having signs, it's as well to take care of yourself."

"Care, Mother? What sort of care?"

At once Emma was testy. "Oh, I don't know. Don't try to pin me down. You always do that, Letty. Besides, now isn't the time to talk about it. This is supposed to be a happy time."

"It's the stories one hears—isn't that right, Mrs. Benedict?" Olwen tried to fill the awkwardness. "I mean, a woman never knows what to believe. It's like that with so many things. People can hardly wait to fill a young girl's mind—terrify her. Yet, when you come down to it, all these events are quite natural."

"I agree, Mrs. Evans," said Emma distinctly. "But just because they're natural doesn't make them a suitable subject for conversation." She turned smoothly to Parkes. "How is that hem coming along? I can't see how Miss Puxley could have sent it out loose like that. She's generally very particular."

Hitty flushed. "Mama, my shoe's toe caught in it. It wasn't Miss Puxley's fault."

Emma fanned herself impatiently. "I really don't care what the reasons are for the hem being down. The fact is, it was down and has needed repair."

It was finished at last. Letty placed the small, beaded cap on her sister's head. She was all of a sudden Juliet. Then, when the disguising veil was draped over it, she was no longer just an aging girl. Nor was she "a bride." She was The Bride.

We are all beautiful, thought Letty. For one moment in our lives we are beautiful, and there is no one who would deny it. Lost in a welter of matronliness, swollen bellies, and overheated cheeks, it is evanescent. But for these few hours it exists. Cannot be taken away, ever. Is this why women cry at weddings? A butterfly's life lasts six weeks. A bride's, but a few hours.

"Now," said Letty, "you are ready." She gazed at her sister. Overcome by the emotion of the occasion, she placed her hands, one on either side of Hitty's cheeks. Eyes met eyes. Letty read the excitement in Hitty's. The fear.

"Oh my," said Hitty, her shaking becoming noticeable. "I—I hope I'm not going to faint."

"Stuff and nonsense!" said Emma, rising with the help of the ebony cane, to her full height. "Henrietta Hyde Benedict, pull yourself together. You will not disgrace this family." Emma raised her cane in a brief gesture. "Get on with it. Attach the train. I won't leave till she's completely finished." She seemed to have shrunk suddenly.

Parkes came to Letty's aid. The train was weighty. Ivory satin, like the dress, it had to go underneath the veil. It should have been fastened first.

"It's done!" said Letty, stepping back.

With Letty's help, Hitty maneuvered about until she was facing the full-length mirror. "Is that me?" she asked, amazed.

"Of course, dear." Letty placed her hands on Hitty's shoulders, giving them a slight squeeze. "Olwen's right. You look lovely."

"I'm afraid." Hitty spoke softly.

Olwen said, "You'll be right as rain. Just keep your chin up, lovey."

"She's right," added Letty.

It was time to go to the church.

They had left in a flurry of horses' hooves and wheeling coaches. Dust flying, stones crunching. Hitty stood there in the hall of her childhood, watching.

Watching with Oscar. Into the space left by the speeding conveyances, Andrew had moved, bringing the Benedict carriage smartly up to the front door. Oscar raised his hand in signal. He'd taken out his watch. Now he murmured to Cox, the head butler. "Tell Andrew we can't leave yet. It's too soon. Mrs. Benedict said a full ten minutes."

Cox moved slowly. Age had stiffened his bones. Hitty felt a moment of panic. She was leaving a household that was past its prime. Why hadn't she seen this before? The household had seemed to tower, a forest around her. Now they were like bent giants, reaching down toward her with gnarled fingers, their resilience brittled. What strength they had was mostly illusory, best left untested.

How long would they last? Cox, Chaplain, Hooper, Parkes—even old Jaspar? Especially old Jaspar. The familiar figures who knew her as "Miss Hitty" would never settle for "Mrs. Grey." Would they be here when she came back? Back from wherever it was Compton was taking her? She glanced sideways at her father. Oscar was staring at his gold watch, his lips moving soundlessly. Repeating to himself Emma's instructions. Lest he forget. As he often did lately.

"Oscar, you can't keep something in your head five minutes."

"That's not true, my dear."

"You forgot we were having guests for dinner!"

"I'll try to do better in the future."

"It's very tiresome, Oscar."

"I know, my dear. Don't rub it in, eh?"

Hitty moved her body around. The long train had been left rolled up behind her feet in such a way that those assisting her to get into the carriage could lift it easily. Turning on the spot was difficult. She sensed she might tear something.

"Father?"

"Yes, m'dear?"

His eyes gazed at her. Such a very sensitive person. She knew that from the liquid sweetness of his eyes. Eyes almost on the verge of crying. Yet they never did. Papa would just look at one. Not say much.

What did she want of him? The longing in her was so great that it filled her throat, making her feel she must take her breath through cotton batting. An ache that began at her midriff and was working its way up so that it encased her breasts, her shoulders. What did the pain ask? She put out her hand to him.

"Only five minutes to go," he said pleasantly. Not a tall man, he might once have been muscular. Now he was rounded, his gray beard trimmed to a neat point below his chin. A paunch shook when he laughed, usually at himself.

"Yes, m'dear? Something you wanted to ask me?"

Now that she had her opportunity, she couldn't. Habit had thrown bars around her. "I think," she said softly, clutching the pearl-handled wedding fan more firmly, "I would like to know you better."

"Oh, my dear—" His eyes clouded and he looked away. Staring out from the shadows of the house to the bright lake of light the driveway made.

"I feel, Papa, that we've lived in the same house all these years, yet we've never known each other. As people."

He patted her hand. "I always felt you to be the best of daughters."

"When I come home again—" She stopped, bit her lip. "I mean, when I get back from the trip to Vermont, may I come and see you?"

He squeezed her hand. The hand that already wore Compton's sapphire ring. Like the pin, it had belonged to his mother.

"We will be happy to see you anytime, Hitty," he said.

It wasn't what she wanted to hear. Not phrased like that. But it was the only way he could say it—and she could receive it.

"I've always loved you," she said carefully.

He let her hand drop. "Devoted to you, m'dear."

The horses were growing restive. Well trained, there was nevertheless a limit to what they'd endure. Andrew let them take a turn around the driveway.

Oscar returned to his watch. "Well, you could say it was time." His head with its fluffy white sideburns raised. A smile of achievement on his lips. "Your mother said ten minutes."

Suddenly she wanted to run up the stairs, slam her bedroom door, and refuse to come out. Stop time in its tracks. Defy inevitability.

"So, shall we go, m'dear?"

"I'm going to need some help with this train." Bending away so that he couldn't see her face. Yet he'd not read it anyway. If she did as she was prompted to, he'd merely come to the bedroom door and call out, "We mustn't keep your mother waiting."

Was that what she wanted from him? Some sign of strength— some evidence he could stand up to her mother? Not let her push him around. Like a barrow full of rags, the way she'd seen them on the side streets of Philadelphia—the rag-and-bone men. Collectors. Father was a collection of trite phrases, traditions observed, customs respected. He toadied to Mother. She saw that now, with anger. Yet surely there must be a real person underneath?

"When we come back, I want you to come over and see me, Papa. By yourself. We'll sit by the fire and drink tea. I want to have a chance to talk to you." She said it firmly, but it was still a question. Would he come? Could they really talk?

"Be nice, m'dear." He patted her shoulder while Cox and Hooper helped to lift the train. "Comforts me, you would want to have me over. Not many places to go anymore—just the club."

The pity of it! Oh, getting old was cruel. Crueler by far for him, who'd never been able to dare enough self-exposure to gain him friends. Loyal, caring friends.

They managed to get into the carriage. It was an ordeal with the awkwardness of the bridal trappings. Another, smaller coach, hired for the occasion, waited to take Cox and Hooper. The house would be entrusted now to temporary help. The striped tent on the lawn, the piled-up sandwiches and the urns of lemonade, all waited for the triumphal moment when the newlyweds would return. Orchestra seated with violins poised. Maids in white aprons, streamered caps, ready to take wraps, to direct and serve.

She was on her way to a wedding. Hers. She was sure, as she sat in the coach, that she'd found herself in somebody else's body.

Oscar, beside her, glanced at the smiling sky through the windows. "Well, it's turned out a remarkably fine day," he said cheerfully. "Suppose you'll find the same weather up in Vermont?"

"I wonder," she said politely. A tumbril. It lacked only the crowd shouting, "Death—death to the *aristos*—"

It could very well be raining in Vermont. In fact, pouring. It was such a long way away.

She restrained a sigh. The church was coming into sight.

7

As a nightmare that develops by stages, so the first hours of her marriage. The train trip from Philadelphia to New York should have been a relief. It was not. Seated against the hard-backed benches covered with shiny leather that gave no purchase against the train's jolting, Hitty tried to fight the weariness.

Compton, more adaptable than she, slept. His mouth fell open and he snored slightly. His arms folded over his chest, he looked at once undignified and human. A stranger to her, for she'd seen him only as a god, from the height of his superiority. She stared at him. At first covertly. Then, as his sleep deepened and his breathing became guttural, she regarded him openly. Aware that others in the compartment found him less interesting than she.

He was, of course, a stranger. If she'd had any doubt about it, she was sure now. She didn't know, for instance, that he was given to dozing with his mouth open. That he could relax in situations where she was all tenseness. That when he sat thus, he not only sagged but his belly was paunchy, like Father's.

He awoke as if prompted, just as the train was pulling into the station, and smiled at her. "I must have dozed—"

"Yes. Do you feel more rested?" She disguised her disdain that she had discovered him to be so human. What else would she find out?

The hotel where they were to spend the night had their room waiting for them. A bellboy in buttoned splendor, his pillbox cap making him look like a monkey, set their suitcases down. Compton drew forth coins and placed them in the lad's palm.

Hitty was frightened. It wasn't just the weariness from the journey, else why would she be shaking? She'd heard tales of the wedding night.

257

Tales that hinted of much yet told practically nothing. Now she was cold with anticipation.

"You're chilled. I'll see if I can encourage the fire." Compton fussed with it, obviously not sure what he was doing. "Well, we'll be in bed soon. I don't suppose it matters."

She felt sick. She looked about the accommodations they'd been given. Elegant with red velvet, black tasseled. She avoided looking at the double bed. Set in the center of the room, it dominated. She fought panic.

"My dearest." Compton took her in his arms. "You are trembling. Is it just the cold?"

"Perhaps I'm a little tired. And unsure." She added the last because she had to give voice to it.

"Unsure? Surely not of our marriage? Isn't it a little soon for that?" His smile teased.

"No, no. Of course not our marriage," she lied. "It's that I don't know what you expect of me."

He held her at arm's length, met her eyes with his. "My darling, you aren't supposed to know. I mean, I married you in the full knowledge that you were a virgin."

"Yes." Trembling violently.

He pulled her to him, "It's the man's job to know. The woman— the wife—merely has to please him. Now you will see, my love, that it's all going to be very simple. You've worried yourself half to death for nothing. Here, you must let me help you out of your clothes."

He was going to violate her! Some interior, native sense of self-preservation came to the fore. She tried to pull away. But it was no good. She was married to him, and the deed had to be done—whatever it was.

"My love—"

Was she his love? A startling question. She felt he was merely going through the motions of love. She sat there, frozen, while he played with the fingers of her hand. The two rings he'd given her, one the sapphire, the other the gold band placed there this afternoon, seemed to act as a focus. Temporarily.

He spoke softly. "Hitty, we are both weary—"

"Yes." Hopefulness, like a spatter of rain, suggesting a shower.

"Yet I have waited so long for this, my love."

She said nothing. The lifting of spirits was over.

"It will not be so bad for you after the first time."

"What do I have to do?"

"I told you. Nothing. It is up to me."

"I heard what you said. Now tell me, how am I to act so that I shall —how did you phrase it—'please you'?"

"Yes." He nodded, rising to tower over her. "You need to know that." He fingered the lapel of her coat. "These have to come off. In those suitcases are your nightgowns?"

"You wish me to get ready for bed?"

"We cannot be close in street wear."

"If you are too nervous, Hitty, I can give you something to calm you."

She stared at him. Not yet in his nightshirt, he was all male in the cotton underwear, which was entirely of one piece. A long slit at the front showed her how it might work if he wished to relieve himself. Likewise, an opening at the back. She glanced away, ashamed of her curiosity.

"You probably aren't used to how men dress."

"No," she said feebly. With enormous difficulty she had gotten into her own nightwear. Wriggling and contorting, so as not to let him see any part of her nakedness.

Now she was seeing his. It was unavoidable. The lump that had been growing from behind the forward slit suddenly thrust itself out, a stubby rod. Not unaided, for he'd pulled aside the cotton. As if the thing needed air. Space for further extension.

How large would it get? She was fascinated, in spite of her fear, her sense of imminent threat. She tried her best not to stare.

"Do I take it you are ready for bed, Hitty?"

"Almost." She looked about her wildly, searching out an excuse. Finding none. "I have to brush my hair," she said.

"Come, let us take out the pins together."

"No, no, I can manage—"

But he was already at the task. She set out her box to hold the pins. He plucked, with his clean, neat fingers. She had a memory, as haunting as a melody, of a time when she'd wondered what it would be like to be married to him. Him and his hands. Flesh warm and scrubbed. Now she was finding out.

He placed each pin, as if it had a separate, special identity, in the box lid. Her hair came tumbling down. She reached for her silver-backed brush, its homeyness comforting her.

He stayed her hand. "Let me do it, sweetheart."

She hadn't had anyone brush her locks since Nanny had been replaced by Miss Sprules. Self-consciously, she waited for him to pull the bristles through. He did so unsurely, annoyingly. Getting caught in a tangle. Tugging at it.

"I need practice," he said. He set the brush down and used his fingers for a comb. "It's very thick. You are a healthy woman, Hitty."

She had the feeling she was a patient. She wanted to ask him to stop it—to scream it at him. She knew her nerves were frayed by the day's ordeal. Would this farce never end?

He placed his hands on her shoulders, from behind. Then slipped them lower until he was touching her breasts. "Firm—for your age," he pronounced. "It also shows you've not had children. Breast feeding tends to break down the contours, causing them to sag prematurely. You are fortunate you've not had that experience."

She opened her mouth to say something. Thought better of it. What did he know of her desire to have children? The clinging feel of an infant in her arms. A child running up to her, calling out "Mama!" He couldn't possibly know this.

His hands had cupped her breasts now. She felt their touch as upsetting. The violation—was it beginning?

He blew out one of the lamps. "It's time to go to bed."

Said so naturally. As though he were locking the house for the night, as though they had been married for years. This was an illusion. The bed stood there, velvet covered and menacing. He turned down the covers.

"Just lie down," he said, pointing to the center of the bed. He began to remove the cotton undergarment, lifting it carefully over the extrusion. Somehow it had shrunk a little. Or was it her imagination?

She got into bed feeling dreadfully foolish. A desire to run—to get out of this room as quickly as she could. Away from this man and whatever it was he was going to do to her.

"Sure you wouldn't like something to calm your nerves, Hitty?"

"Do you think it would help?" Playing for time.

Stark naked now, he strutted across to where he'd had the bellboy place his doctor's bag, opened it, and searched around inside. At last, he produced a vial. "There should be drinking water somewhere."

The thing he carried before him really had shrunk. It was half of its former self. She was amazed to see how much body hair he had. His chest was a pasture of golden curls, touched with snow. Above his legs, too, it was furry. Like herself. She'd sometimes touched herself down there. The hair was different from whatever grew on the head. Short and wiry. It would snap back into place when straightened.

She drank the medicine dutifully. Had she not sworn to obey? But to obey implicitly, one must trust. Did she trust—fully?

She was becoming a little dizzy. It was hot in the room, a fact she hadn't noticed earlier. Perhaps she was feeling more comfortable now that she was in her nightgown? The soft flannel had been selected for Vermont's chill nights; in New York she'd prefer the cotton batiste. But she'd pulled the heavier gown out of her overnight case.

"You're certainly looking after me," she told him.

260

He didn't answer. He had lain down beside her, the weight of his body making the mattress sag. Up on one elbow, with his free hand, he lifted the bottom of her nightgown.

She gasped at once. Stiffened.

"Just do as I say and only move when I tell you to. I promise you it will be easier after the first time."

The stubby extension had grown again. He'd lifted her clothing up to her breasts. They smiled at the ceiling, exposed and pale. Her heart began to pound unmercifully.

"Now, open your legs to me." He showed her what he meant by parting her thighs.

Stiff, apprehensive, she lay there, feeling him climb on top of her, suffocate her with his weight.

The thing began to probe. With his fingers he aided, exploring the soft, secret sides of her privacy. Once she'd touched herself down there and was alarmed at the sensation. She had it now, briefly. What he was doing to her was the forbidden—making it into the bidden. Confusion took her and mingled with the pain. For he'd become a battering ram, demanding access to her inner fortress.

She almost cried out for what it did to her. The flame searing her with a bright tongue. But at the instant when she would have given way to sound, he cursed.

"Goddamned virgins—always the same problem."

Then, when she absolutely knew she could bear it no longer, he began to jerk convulsively. His thrusts brought him even deeper into her cavity. They were locked now, she enclosing him with all her being. He had explored her and she no longer had secrets left. Sanctity gone. This must be the violation always hinted of.

He pulled out and said abruptly, "You will need to wash yourself."

She lay there, stunned. Too surprised by the whole proceeding to move. She watched him walk, naked and a little tired, to the washstand. It was out of sight, in the dressing area the suite provided. She heard water splash in a bowl. He came back, a towel in his hands.

"If you stand up, it will be easier. Besides, lying down like that runs the risk of your becoming with child."

She heard him dully, from a long way off. His words did not mean much. She was conscious of a stickiness between her legs, as though she had begun her monthly flowing. If that was the case, she was going to die with embarrassment. Wearily, she supposed Compton must know about such things. But to understand them intimately was something else.

Fervently, she wished to retain modesty in her marriage. But after what had just happened, modesty was hardly the right word.

Slipping and sliding it came. Down her legs as she stood up. A colorless egg white—reminding her of frog spawn collected from streams with Miss Sprules. And a staining. What was this? She had been right then. Her flowing had begun.

Compton handed her the damp cloth. "Don't let the blood frighten you. We had to break the hymen."

"The what?"

"You were a virgin. There's a small amount of skin—"

She wasn't paying attention. He could go on with his Latin words. She had blood, real blood, and the pain was bright. She'd been torn.

"If you put a second towel between your legs, it'll protect the sheets."

She nodded, did as he suggested, and lay down in bed. The presence of the rough linen, staunching her, was comforting. A sudden thought caused her to sit back up. "What'll the maid think when she finds the towel?"

She heard him laugh goodhumoredly. "They expect it with a honeymoon. It's taken into consideration with the price of the room."

"Oh." She was conscious of a lethargy. Her limbs were heavy. Drifting. Out on a small boat, a long way from shore. A giant wave hit the side of the craft. It was Compton, getting into bed. The mattress lurched.

"Good night, Hitty."

"Good night." So this was marriage?

"I told you, it will get easier."

She didn't answer him. It was pleasanter to sleep than to reply.

8

They were driving down a long tunnel of trees. The *clop-clop* of the mare's hooves lulled. A sleepy afternoon, and out of the heat of the early September sun, it was pleasant.

They'd broken out into the clear. Up on a hillside, they could see way down into the valley below. The small houses, built like toys for children. Bride white, steep roofed, each with similarities and Yankee individuality. Porches for rocking on. Decently dressed old women sitting there in shawls, usually staring at them. But today they were with Honor Proctor. And so there were smiles, the wave of an arm. But suspicious looks behind it.

"They want to know who you are," Honor explained. "We live such close-knit lives, to us everyone's a stranger."

The buggy stopped as the road divided. Honor, her competent hands reining in the mare, pointed with her long whip, "It's a nice town, Dr. Grey. You can see the inn from here if you look real good."

They all stared. Of course one couldn't miss the inn, any more than one could miss the railway station with its harsh red roof, the steepled church, humbling in its simplicity.

"But then," went on Honor, "I forget. You and Dr. Turner made a visit out here when you was up for a visit. Right?"

"Yes," he agreed. "But I wanted Mrs. Grey to see it. The view from here's impressive." Compton turned about in his seat. "Don't you think so, Hitty?"

"Oh yes." She gave him what he wanted. Her reassurance. They'd been parted by stiffness since this morning. Her tone said she wouldn't

263

spread their quarrel in public. He could count on that. She saw him look relieved.

"If one could buy the property on this side of the road, why you could look out on that view every morning."

"Yes," said Honor, giving the mare a signal with the reins, "but what would you want with two houses? I mean, isn't the Grey Homestead the one you're interested in?"

"You haven't understood," he said, his tone deferential. "The Grey Homestead is for a clinic."

"It's a marvelous plan," said Hitty, sitting forward. Surprised at herself. But she realized she'd felt left out. She wanted this woman's friendship.

"I thought," Honor went on, "as how you and Dr. Turner—well, he's Ted to me because we were in the Dame School together. Anyway, I thought as how he was taking you into the office. Like a partner."

"I was aware you were friends from a long time ago."

His voice was rumbling now. Pleasant. Hitty sat back, prepared to shut it out. She'd come to know him the last few days. Had it been a week since her marriage? They'd had supper with Ted Turner. If it hadn't been for his wife—what was her name now?—Caroline, that was it. Caroline Turner. Extraordinary, because she wasn't a Caroline at all. Nor was she a Jane or a Betty. Perhaps a Ruth, faithful in her marriage vows.

Hitty's voice broke into a silence at the front of the buggy. "Did you also go to school with Mrs. Turner?"

"No," said Honor easily. She had a comfortable voice, like the gray serge jackets she wore, the old leather boots, done up in tight bows, the leather thongs tugged, Hitty suspected, till firm. "But I've known Caroline as long as anybody else. She come over from Paget— that's the other side of the mountains. Ted brought her back one time —injured she was. It was after he took up doctoring. You recall, Dr. Grey, him getting his license in Philadelphia?"

"We were students together." Compton took off his hat and scratched behind his ear. A small insect must have bitten him. "I believe I know the story about Caroline maybe better than you do."

"Haven't a doubt you do, being as you two've been close all these years. All I'm aware of, she was abused. Said to be the reason he took her into his home. Not long after that he married her. But she could never bear children."

"How sad!" said Hitty. Meaningfully.

Honor went on. "'Twas told her father took advantage of her, if you get my meaning."

"Yes," said Compton noncommittally.

"Bruised something awful when she first came to Tunbridge. But there I go, running on when you was telling me something."

"You wanted to know about the clinic."

"Course I did. How did we get on to Ted's wife?"

"I believe it was Mrs. Grey who brought her up."

"Ah. Now go on about this plan you have, doctor. It does sound unusual, if I may make so bold."

Hitty sat back and let her body move with the jolting. Would it be like this to ride a camel over the desert? She was in a desert—a desert of despair. Well, that wasn't quite true. She was having new experiences. Some of them marvelous. Like talking with the old lady on her porch that morning. After the fight—no, the disagreement—with Compton, she'd taken herself off, away from the inn. She was furious at what he'd said.

"You will allow me to plan our intimacy, Hitty. It would be unfortunate were you to conceive."

"Not have a child? You can't be serious, Compton!"

"Never more serious about anything in my life. It would be nothing short of ridiculous for you and me, at our time of life, to start a family."

"I want a baby very much."

"Hitty, you are well advanced into your thirties."

"But I want a child—lots of children. I want—" For the first time, she had opened her legs to him voluntarily.

He'd rolled over, off the bed. Refused her. "If you wish to please me, my love, we can resort to other ways."

Suspiciously. "What other ways? You showed me this way."

"Hitty, you've so much to learn. There are many variations on how the act of love can be performed. We don't know your cycle yet. The days when you aren't well."

Sullenly. "I know the dates. It was just before we were married."

He reached for his clothes. "We don't dare go by that. As it is, we've taken risk. Travel, to say nothing of trauma, can change the way the body reacts."

"What trauma?" She was stubborn. Amazed at herself for speaking up to him.

"Now, my dear, we don't have to spell it out, do we? Anytime a woman who is a virgin—"

"All right."

"If you still wish so much to please me, there is a method we might try. I have known it to work sometimes." He had his underwear on. But the slot gaped. He was growing inside for her. Not really for her. For want of her. Strictly, for himself.

"Hitty, cup me with your hands. Here, let me show you." Grabbing her wrists. "Now while you are holding me, you must press your lips down—so."

She'd been angered enough to feel she was choking on what he'd asked her to do. On his refusal of himself, except to present what he had for her in one way. Riskless.

Afterward, she'd walked to the edge of the town. Stopped by the last house on the road. She'd stared at some blue flowers, graceful and dignified as swans, bell sprayed, down a long green stem. Oval leaves, some of them with veining lines, coming to points, as if presenting the crown with a pedestal.

"Lovely," she said out loud. "I wonder what they're called?"

"Hosta lilies," said a dry voice. Withered and snapped off in sound. But comforting, as the creaking of a rocking chair.

She looked about. Beyond the level of the ground was the usual porch, painted gray. Likewise a slatted seat, the kind hung by chains from a strong beam. On it, an old lady, her white hair wispy and light catching as a halo. Her face seamed. A smile.

"Hosta lilies. They grow excellently up here. Pretty, aren't they?"

"Oh yes!" agreed Hitty. "In fact, they're beautiful."

"You just visiting?" the old lady asked.

"Yes," said Hitty and then, in a rush of confidentiality, "I'm on my honeymoon."

"Honeymoon? My, my. That's downright nice." She almost seemed to be smacking her lips. "Where are you and your new husband from?"

"Philadelphia. We may settle here," said Hitty informatively. Of course it was stretching the truth. She didn't care.

"Buy a house, will you?"

"No. My husband used to visit up here as a boy. He wants to acquire some property and establish a hospital."

"A hospital," said the old one conversationally. "That'd be right nice. I mean, when the townspeople come up sick, there's pretty much nowheres for them to go except the Sisters of Mercy's place near Rutland. Be handy, having somewhere close."

"It's not going to be an ordinary hospital," said Hitty. "It's to be a clinic where women can come."

"What sort of women?" Why was she letting this old hag cross-question her? Was it because she seemed to represent the town? A hope that the community of Tunbridge would rise up, forbid the establishment of this place? Yet she didn't even fully understand what Compton had in mind.

"Women who have things the matter with them," she said. Her tone was purposefully vague. She knew she'd gone too far. What would Compton say when he found out? As assuredly he would.

"What sort of 'things'?" the comfortable voice demanded. "I mean, if it's sick women, then it could be babies, or not having babies, or stopping having them and having other troubles. Swelling up for no cause, female complaints. Myself, I been fortunate—so have all my daughters. But it's not typical. You going to have advice for that sort of thing?"

Hitty truly didn't know. "I expect so." She tried to sound bright, confident.

The old woman settled herself in the seat. It swung lightly, blown as much by the breeze as pushed by the frail body. "Folks'll come out to see what he's going to make of a thing like that," she said chattily. "Be a lot of women crowding into the dispensary, same as they do to talk to Dr. Turner."

"My husband knows Dr. Turner."

"Well, why didn't you say so? That's different. Dr. Turner, he's been in practice a long time. Grew up right here in Tunbridge."

Hitty said, "I don't know him very well. My husband, Dr. Grey, went to medical school with Dr. Turner. We had dinner with the Turners two nights ago."

"Ah. That wife of his can't cook too well. Come to think of it, isn't much of anything she does well. Except fill bottles. She keeps all his bottles readied, the ones given out in the dispensary. You can't have sick folks and not have tonics now, can you? I expect you'll be doing that sort of work yourself now you're married to a doctor."

"Perhaps," said Hitty. "I must be going back."

"You staying at the inn?" Without waiting for an answer, she added, "It's a nice way to visit. No beds to make, meals to set on the table. You know which house you're going to purchase?"

"We're visiting one this afternoon. It's south of town, on the ridge."

"Wouldn't be the old Grey Farm?" The old head nodded. "You say your husband's last name is Grey? Was it his people—took up and went out West?"

"His cousins."

"Then the Peabodys bought it. A nice bargain on both sides. But he went and slid off the roof, broke his neck. Property's come to have a bad name. You sure that's where you want to invest?"

"It's really my husband's decision."

"Who's buggy you taking? Honor Proctor driving you?"

Hitty nodded. A sense she was escaping. Yet she'd enjoyed the talk at first.

Hitty's thoughts jolted to a stop. Honor had reined the mare. "Well, there it is!"

"It's a nice house," said Compton quietly. "When Ted first brought me out here, I could remember so distinctly the way it had been to visit as a boy. It seemed almost shocking, Aunt Martha not being there on the porch. She was the closest thing I could recall to having a mother."

"You must have been up here quite a few times as a boy, then?" Honor said it easily.

"Only twice. My father felt it was too far to send me." He took off his hat, fingered the insect bite again, tenderly. "It didn't make sense. He was away all the time. I was a very lonely child, Mrs. Proctor."

Abigail Peabody was on the porch. As they alighted from the buggy, she waved. A small boy clung to her apron as if it were a rope, connecting him with life. He was tousled-headed and very blond. A sun child with reddened cheeks and a peppering of freckles. Wary eyes.

"Been looking for you," said Abigail. "Wanted you to see the property afore it gets dark."

"Well, we're here," said Honor cheerfully. "Had to finish a batch of loaves. Couldn't trust that idiot Louis to take them out, and Hiram's pushed building the new wing."

"He about done?"

"No," said Honor as they walked across the grass. A goat, tethered on a long rope, must be the reason for its sparseness. "Aims to complete the outside. Then when winter gets here, he and his brother can work out of the cold. Finish the rest of it."

Compton had reached the porch first. "Nice to see you again, Mrs. Peabody."

"Nice to see you, doctor. You said you'd be back, remember?"

Honor recalled Hitty. "Oh, I plumb forgot. You haven't met Mrs. Grey, have you, Gail?"

Abigail said, "You wasn't up here last time your husband visited?"

"They just got married, Gail." Honor said it boastfully. "Come to spend their honeymoon at our inn. All the way to Tunbridge."

"Fancy that," said Abigail. Hitty sensed she wished to move them on. "Might as well see the barns—the property."

"All right with me," Compton reassured her.

The barns, like the house, were painted red. In need of some

269

repair, they gaped sunshine. It penetrated the inner blackness in shafts, stirring up motes. A chicken scratched near the doorway, finding something edible and sweet beneath the piled-up sawdust. As they walked into the first barn, something scuttled away.

"I know the rats been at the grain," said Abigail. "Tom—that's my older boy—takes after them, but they keep coming back. It's reasons like this make me know I'd do better to sell. You can have it any time you want, Dr. Grey."

"I need to review the property before making a decision," he said. He kept talking, asking questions that indicated he'd remembered details. The plan he and Ted had—it had already gone so much further than Hitty had supposed. She'd been allowed to see it as tenuous. Now she was discovering the project had limbs. A hand, projecting from leaves on first sight, had led to a body. Alive and growing, tumescent as Compton's privacy. It was, after all, his scheme.

Yes, she saw it now. Not just a plan. A well-thought-out plot to get her here, commit her to this project so that she couldn't say later, "What is this about? You didn't tell me."

Honor joined her. "It'll be nice when he gets it the way he sees it laid out."

"Yes," said Hitty, folding her arms across her breasts.

"You want to walk over to that field?"

"Why not?" said Hitty.

They had to step high, lift their skirts because of the tallness of the grass. As Hitty's foot came down, there was a slithering. Something fled their approach.

"Mercy!" Hitty had given a low scream. The back of her neck prickled.

"Won't hurt you none. Lot of snakes hereabouts. Said to be rattlers on the hills the other side of town. But myself, I think it's a story. Lived here all my life and never seen hide nor hair of a rattler."

They'd reached the beginning of the field. A wide barrier formed of tree stumps, gnarled and twisted into a gray tangle, ended the meadowland where they were standing.

"It makes a good fence," said Honor, "except for the likes of him." She pointed. Far away, where the field before them sloped green and lush, stood a bull. "It takes a lot to stop a bull," she said quietly.

"Are we in danger here?" Hitty's heart had begun to lurch.

"He's tethered—or should be. Jeremiah Jones rents this land from Gail. She depends on the rents, the way things are for her. But she doesn't like the bull that close to the house. He's tied, but what if her little boy should decide to go exploring? It's a worry."

Compton and Abigail had come up.

"All this is part of the property?" He surveyed it with his eyes.

"Oh, it goes farther than this. Acreage beyond the end there."

They moved down as a group. Honor seemed to be tireless. Hitty knew she'd been up since dawn, baking, attending to the clamoring tasks of the inn—though they were the only guests. But she strode out, her legs strong and carefree under the long skirts.

Hitty turned her ankle and almost fell. Compton's hand went out, steadying her under the elbow.

"Thank you," she said, almost surprised. They seemed so very separated today. Was it just today? Seven days of marriage and each of them different.

They were at the gate.

"We can skirt the field from here," said Abigail. She unhitched the loop that wired the gate shut.

It took them nearer to the bull. Hitty could feel it aware of them, of the commotion they made as they bent the grasses, moved the air with their conversation. She could feel the odors about it strong and stenchy as they got closer. Or was she imagining it?

"Hitty, there's a fence between us and the animal." Compton's voice reproved her. Showing up her fears before them all. Before Abigail, who managed to live alone, a widow. Before Honor, who baked bread as the dawn was slanting its light over the town.

They stood before the brute. It regarded them, suspiciously and primitively. Its close-curled hair was molded to its skull. Hitty had seen Greek gods cut out of marble that had such pates. Touting their maleness. It tossed its head, brought its mean eyes back to keep a sharp watch on them.

"It has to be tied up that way," said Compton, his voice like a museum guide, "because of all animals, dairy bulls are among the most dangerous in the world."

"You wanted me to see him," Hitty said.

"Brought up in the city, you've never had the chance to get this close. I just thought it would be interesting."

"You seen enough of the property, Dr. Grey?" Abigail's voice was noncommittal. "We don't often come this way when the bull's out."

"It's a wonderful piece of land!" he said, rubbing his hands enthusiastically. "I'll make you an offer on it just as soon as we get back to town. Dr. Turner's attorney's going to draw it up."

"Ah," she said, as if she had been the one to pay.

They walked back to the house in silence. Behind them, the bull kept lowing. Once, Hitty glanced about and saw it pawing the earth.

A young man, his growth elongating his features into thin lines, came off the porch shyly. Abigail Peabody's older son.

"Hello, Tom," said Honor. "This is Dr. and Mrs. Grey."

He nodded. His eyes were polite, evasive.

271

"We can go on in, see the house, and get some cold water to drink," said Abigail politely. "One thing this place can boast of—we got our own well. The sweetest water of anybody along the ridge."

"Water," said Compton. "That's a point I grasped at once. You can't have a lot of people occupying the same building and not have adequate water supplies."

"Sounds like you're planning something real ambitious, Dr. Grey," said Honor pleasantly.

"Well now," his own voice reflected her amiability, "that depends. It has the possibility of becoming quite an enterprise. It's why I want to make sure enough land goes with the place."

"Oh?" Hitty was roused. "I thought it was just the property immediately surrounding the farm you had in mind?"

"My dear," his voice was unctious, "I'm not buying for just now. Over our evening meal, I'll try to explain it to you."

Would he? She followed them into the house. What was this place going to become? She felt fear brush her.

At dinner, Compton toyed with his explanation much the way some people do with food. Yet Compton was in high appetite and had ordered wine.

They were alone in the dining room. It stretched around them, discreet and shadowed. September was late for travelers this far north.

"You wonder how Honor and Hiram can make a go of this place," said Hitty conversationally. She had to keep the press of the room's silence away from them. Their table was an island.

"It's our good fortune," said Compton carelessly. "It will be somewhere for relatives of patients to stay." He thrust a forkful of ham into his mouth.

"Tell me," Hitty said, drawing out the words, "how many patients you expect to keep out there?"

"I don't like the way you phrase that!" he snapped. "We are not planning on 'keeping' anybody. They'll be coming to us for treatment."

"Sorry," she said, her eyes lowered. Yet she guessed he was lying. She'd already seen too much. Yet how did she know? A nice farmhouse, surrounded by pleasant meadows. Was her own thinking becoming a little strange?

"You said you'd try to explain it to me this evening, Compton." Her glance challenged him.

"I said that, yes. It's as well not to speak of plans while others can overhear. I hope you haven't mentioned this purchase to anyone?"

"Just an old woman I met while walking."

"You allowed yourself to get into conversation with a perfect stranger?"

"She spoke to me first. I admired her flowers. Compton, I think I might like to live up here. It's a friendly town."

"Out of the question."

"Why? You're going to be up here so much of the time."

Annoyed. "You're meddling now, Hitty. I warned you before we left Philadelphia, we might have to spend some time apart."

"But why?"

His tone was acid. "For one thing, it snows up here—far more heavily than anything you've ever dreamed of. They are pioneers up here. Used to battling the elements. You, with your upbringing, your sensitive ways, wouldn't last five minutes in a Vermont winter."

"I still don't understand you," she said. But she did; he was hiding something. She was sure of it now.

"I can't help it whether you understand me or not. You are spending the winter close to your parents. I have to have someone to keep an eye on you while I'm away."

"Am I so likely to get into trouble?"

"I don't know," he said unhappily. "I thought I married a sweet, loving girl. Instead, I find you to be almost a stranger."

"Because I wish you to give me a child?" She was amazed at herself. But his handling of her, his abrupt denial of her wishes, had given her boldness.

"Hitty!" Pained. "Have a care. We appear to be alone, but walls have ears."

"You want me to be ashamed that I hope to become with child?"

He'd picked up his fork. "Watch yourself, Hitty. I might consider divorcing you." He tried but failed to keep his voice light.

She was shocked. "On our honeymoon?"

"Oh, nothing like that. But you are provoking me in a way I'm not accustomed to."

"I'm sorry," she said. Ashamed. His tone had brought out the mother in her. She saw him as wounded. What had gotten into her?

"If you are truly sorry," he said softly, "you will show me you mean it by becoming the gentle girl I married. All this fuss because I wish to protect you from the exigencies of childbirth. I should have thought you would have seen it as an indication of my love for you."

"Yes," she said, contrite. "I think we both have to have patience —to give our being together time."

He dropped a veil over his eyes. "Dearest, trust me. I do know. After all, not only am I a doctor, but I am also a man. In addition, I'm

273

years older than you are. Do you realize, I will be fifty-three next birthday?"

She bowed her head, gazing at her plate. Only women aged. Men weathered, given help. If they didn't, it had to be the fault of some female. Who hadn't loved them enough.

She resolved to try better. After all, he had at least rescued her from spinsterhood.

10

She would never have Papa over for tea . . . to sit by the fire and talk . . . without anyone around, including Mother. Especially Mother.

Had he known, when they stood on the doorstep, waiting for the carriage to take them to the wedding, that they would never meet again? Mother's news, telegraphed to the railroad station in Tunbridge, brought by messenger to the inn, had said little: *Father taken ill. Suggest you curtail your trip.* Nothing to warn that it might be serious. Serious as death.

Mother had met them in the hallway. Too late then to break the news gently. The coffin, draped in purple silk, had occupied almost the whole space of the vestibule. Not that Father had been a large man. There just wasn't room for anything else.

Mother, standing like a black leaf blown in on a winter storm, her hands placed one on top of another as if they'd been stacked there. Too heavy for movement.

"Well, Hitty, it's a sad homecoming." She trembled suddenly, keeling sideways, a ship that suffers an unexpected wave. Compton and Hitty grabbed at her.

"Mother, sit down. Come into the parlor."

They got her to her chair, settled her. Hitty knew Hooper would be hovering. Mother's tea would be warming.

"Hooper?"

"She's been doing well, Miss Hitty. The staff's relieved you're home, though. Miss Letty's been over two or three times every day."

Emma's wavering voice. "Hitty, where are you?"

"I'm here, Mother. Hooper, if we could all have some tea?"

275

"Very good, Miss Hitty."

It was unreal. Him in there! Hitty glanced at the box, the regal purple, the great gold cross embroidered down its length. It didn't become him. Such a modest man, always deferring to Mother. Usually dressed in a smile, not wanting to upset.

Emma wanted them to hear it all. "—so when he didn't ring for his shaving water, Cox went up to see. It was then we found out—we knew—oh, Hitty, could you find me my smelling salts?"

Compton took something out of his bag. He held it under her nose and she breathed deeply, her color coming back while they waited.

"You are a dear boy, Compton. Hitty's lucky to have found you." The tears now. "It hits you suddenly. I'm going to be alone the rest of my life. Completely alone."

It was the moment for them to step in. Say she could make her home with them. Not that she'd ever have considered it. It wouldn't have been right, giving up the Benedict mansion for two rooms and a chimney seat under the roof of her younger daughter. Things just didn't happen that way.

Mother would always live in her own style. She was wrapped in it. Frail as she might appear today, she was made of steel. She needed a certain degree of worship; without it, she became naked. Hooper, Cox, and the others would serve her on their knees if need be.

Oh, she'd complain. Of the aloneness, of being neglected and left to fend for herself. No one to talk to. But as to moving to a smaller house or sharing with others—it would be out of the question.

II

It was February. The cold rain spit across the frozen ground in swathes cut by the relentless wind. Each tree had its own coating of ice, sliding like some evil kind of sap down its dark length. Roads were rutted and encouraged horses' hooves to slip. The *clip-clop* of the bay's gait resonated in the steel world. Jakes, perched atop the carriage, huddled in the great coat Compton had bought him just last Christmas.

The carriage halted outside the rectory. Hitty couldn't imagine how Olwen managed to keep so cheerful in that great tomb of a rectory. The manse was set in a huddle of trees that eternally convinced the sun it was fruitless to try and bring warmth, light to their midst.

Hitty rapped the brass knocker.

Almost at once, Olwen came. In an old gray sweater, her hands in mittens, she gave a cry of pleasure.

"Now, isn't this nice! You've come for tea, haven't you? And me in my old dress. But come in anyway."

The fire was burning in the grate. "But I can't seem to get it to make much impression on the chill!" said Olwen cheerfully. "Great barn of a room. Oh, I know I should sound grateful—we get the living for free. But you won't tell anyone, will you?"

Hitty and Olwen's friendship had sprouted up like unsown flowers dropped by some wayward bird. Unwatered by convention, almost suffocated by the weeds of Emma's discontent and Letty and Nathaniel's pointed comments, it had flourished. Hitty and Olwen had much in common. Both responded to life warmly, not persuaded their feelings should be snuffed out. Yet each existed in a world where to

277

respond, except in a mannerly fashion, was to draw criticism.

"How are you?" Olwen asked as she stirred up the fire's embers, added another log.

"Oh, I'm well." Hitty's voice was guarded. They knew each other, but the trust had to be unrolled each time. Reassured by the formalities of tea and scones.

"Do you know, I believe I've begun chilblains," said Olwen conversationally.

"We used to suffer from them as children. A very old maid Mother had told her we should eat chalk."

"Well, I never!" Olwen's face was open with wonder. "It was what we did in Wales. For expectant mothers too. Lose a tooth for every child, they'd say. If you could find it, chalk was the answer. Why didn't I remember that?" She extended her mittened hands. "They itch something fearful. Chalk—where do you suppose I could get some?"

"Does your husband know any schoolteachers?"

"Of course, that's the answer. I'll mention it to him when I take him his tea." By custom, Llewellyn always took his cup in his study. Olwen sensed her visits disturbed him. An impulsive, emotional man from the pulpit, he could be quiet, self-contained when he took off his minister's robes.

"Do you mind if I ask you to come into the kitchen with me?" Olwen's look was apologetic. "It's Ruby's day off and I told Aggie I could manage. She's getting so old, poor soul. Needs to be off her feet between lunch and dinner."

Hitty said quickly, "Of course I'll come with you."

The kitchen was black as an oven. It smelled of soapy water and spices, warming the shadowed air. Olwen filled a kettle at the pump by the sink. Its spout was an inquisitive nose, curved to smell out gossip. The walls here, hung with brass pans and tea towels waiting to dry, crowded in on their conversation.

"I almost never go into my own kitchen," Hitty said reflectively.

"Don't you, dear? Why's that?"

Hitty thought about it. "It's got to be on account of Tildie, the housekeeper."

Olwen cocked her head to one side. "Are you letting her frighten you, do you suppose?"

"She was very devoted to Compton's first wife." Hitty stared at Olwen, asking her to accept that as an answer. "And she's been with Compton all this time. She knows how he likes things."

"Ah," said Olwen wisely, "she's got you convinced she knows best? Old retainers like that think they can take over after a while. Does she go to him, sometimes, behind your back?"

"How did you know?" It was such a relief to be able to talk about it.

"And I suppose he laps it up?"

"He'll be gone soon," said Hitty irrelevantly. She longed to disclose to Olwen some of her unhappiness with Compton. Would that be going too far? She could see Mother's face, scolding. But it had to be done or Hitty would burst.

"Do you mind giving me a hand, dear? If you'd take the cake plate and the scones, I'll bring the tea tray. I'll come back when the kettle's boiled."

They followed the icy corridor back to where a prudent Olwen had closed the sitting-room door. She dragged the gateleg table toward the fire.

"We'll have it as close as we can. Oh, I am glad you stopped in today. I was feeling in need of cheering up."

"You?" Hitty stared at Olwen in astonishment. "You always seem so contented."

"Ah," said Olwen and shook her head. "Not true. But then, don't we all get down at times? I know, even Llewellyn—he misses being able to walk up the mountain." She stared at the hearth, seeing things Hitty couldn't share. "You'll never know what it is to miss a hillside. Bracken, knee deep in mist of a morning."

"My," said Hitty. She was being polite. Momentarily, she had lost Olwen, as she always did when Olwen talked about Wales.

"I've often meant to ask you," Olwen said suddenly. "Do you think, from what I've told you of Wales, it could be like Vermont?"

Hitty turned cold. "Why do you ask?" Stiffly.

"Oh, it was just an impression I got. Llewellyn and I have a holiday coming every year. Well, you know that, don't you, being a church member? Anyhow, I thought that some year it would be lovely if we could take it in a place that reminded us of Wales. But what I really want, someday, is to go home."

"For good?" Hitty's voice was strangled. Her tone revealed nothing of her sense of loss.

"Well," said Olwen, "Llewellyn will have to retire someday. We aren't getting any younger. I admit, it's a dreadful trip back."

"Silly of me," said Hitty. "I just thought that everyone who came to America to settle would stay."

"To settle, yes." Olwen raised her finger, as though instructing a child. "But we came over for a job, love. That's all it ever was—a living in the church."

"You make it sound as if this parish were a mission."

"Oh, no!" Olwen was shocked. "Normally, we wouldn't be in this

279

parish at all if it hadn't been for Mr. Davies wheedling and getting his way. He brought us over hoping we'd think of it with permanency. But neither Llewellyn nor I could die in America. It's a wonderful country —please don't get me wrong. It's just so far away from everything."

Hitty looked down. "I never realized. I always thought you were happy."

"I am happy. Almost all the time. It's just that I get homesick. *'Cymru fo am byth'*—'Wales forever' they play on the harp. It's true. It's in you."

Hitty felt rootless. Odd, in her own country, to have no sense of strong identity. No need to cling to any memory, any part of the land. Her envy of Olwen clutched at her throat. Why had she come here anyway? She recalled, as if it were a different person, herself making arrangements to have Jakes bring her here. It took some doing because, as a rule, he was at Compton's beck and call.

Olwen set the teapot down. Arrayed in its knit cosy, it had joined them like a third person.

"You don't mind if I just pour Llewellyn a cup, do you?" Olwen dropped milk into one of the blue china cups, stirred two teaspoons of brown sugar till they dissolved, and placed a cake on a plate. "If I didn't take it to him, he'd just work straight through till dinner," she said informatively. "He's translating the New Testament into Welsh, you know. Not that it hasn't been done before, mind, but he feels the need for a different version."

Hitty could feel the pride in her voice. Another source of envy. Had Hitty ever been proud of Compton?

"We were talking about your housekeeper," said Olwen when she came back. "You mustn't let her scare you. After all, you are her employer. She has to take orders from you."

"I wish I could have started out with someone of my own choosing," said Hitty.

"It's hard, dear," said Olwen comfortingly. "Is she old enough to be retired?"

"I don't know," said Hitty uneasily. How old was Tildie? Hitty could feel the depression settling over her. She'd been so excited when she'd set out today. Where had it gone?

"Isn't that how you like your tea?" said Olwen, handing her a cup. "Now we can sit back, have a good old gossip. The way I go on, though, I never let you get a word in edgewise." She lifted the heavy pot, poured her own tea. "So, how've you been, lovey? You look paler than I'm used to seeing you. It's this wicked winter."

"I wanted to talk about something rather special," said Hitty, all in one breath. She owed it to the papers she carried in her reticule.

But Olwen had taken herself away, while remaining present in person. The old gray cardigan person who wore broken-down shoes and made tea in the kitchen. But a small warning flag had been raised. Hitty asked herself, did she still dare to share with Olwen?

"I brought something to ask you to read," Hitty said, feeling her cheeks grow hot.

"How lovely!" said Olwen, putting down her cup. "Something you found in a book? I know how you read. I admire it so."

"No," said Hitty, flustered, "it's something I wrote myself. Three poems."

"Poetry?" asked Olwen, her eyes shining. She clapped her hands unself-consciously, "Oh, you must let Llewellyn read them."

"No!" said Hitty quickly. Horror had spun a white web around her. "You must promise me not to show them to him."

"I should think anyone who has a talent would be proud to share it." Olwen seemed puzzled.

"Yes, I know. But no one's ever read what I've written since I was a very young girl."

"That doesn't mean you don't have a gift, my dear."

"I don't think I do," said Hitty. Her eyes were betraying her. She could feel them begging, "Please say that I do." But who was Olwen to judge? She hadn't even been sure she could let Olwen see. Months she'd pondered on it, as their friendship grew. Then the plan broke into her mind. It had been like coming upon a fresh-laid egg half hidden by straw.

She would send some of her poems to a publication! The idea terrified her while she felt its rightness. Others, far less able than she, had verses printed in the ladies' magazines that littered the boudoirs of the genteel reading public. Hitty knew how long she worked to select just the right word. Surely she had a chance?

She handed the folded papers to the Welshwoman. "Promise me you won't read them till I've gone?"

"Not if you don't want me to."

"I'd like you to be alone when you look at them."

"We-ell. Oh, Llewellyn would be so interested."

"No," said Hitty firmly. She was trembling. "You must keep them for your eyes alone. Or I can't leave them."

"As you say," said Olwen. "A poet! Just think. Oh, dearie, it's wonderful. I'm so proud of you."

Hitty regarded Olwen through half-shut eyes. Such effusion. She wasn't the right person to judge. Instinctively, Hitty knew that she'd chosen the wrong critic. Olwen, far from understanding the verses, might be offended by them. It was too late now.

The sound of horses' hooves was almost welcome.

"My, is that Jakes already? How the time has flown, Olwen."

281

"You were a dear to visit me. You'll come again soon?"

To fetch the poetry. Nothing would keep her away.

Inside the seclusion of the carriage Hitty gave herself up to despair. Why had she decided to show the poems to Olwen? She'd only laugh—or wonder what sort of person she had for a friend.

Impulsively, Hitty pushed aside the cover that made it possible to talk to Jakes. "Jakes, do we have time to stop at my sister's house? Dr. Grey is dining out tonight—?"

"Yassum. I isn't to fetch him till way late. You got time, Miss Hitty." Both male servants addressed her that way, in contrast to Tildie. From her, it was always "Mizz Grey."

What had possessed her to make this decision? As Taft opened the imposing door, Hitty asked the question of herself.

"Is your mistress in?"

"I shall have to see, Mrs. Grey."

Hitty waited in the parlor. Unfastening her wraps, for the house held comfort. Lamps were lighted. The tantalizing odor of roasting chicken had managed to defy the baize doors. She would like to have been staying for dinner—if it were only her sister. Hitty loathed Nathaniel almost as heartily as, she suspected, he hated her. A mutual avoidance had gone on for years.

Taft reappeared. "She would like to have you attend her in the morning room, madam."

Letty, seated at her desk, swiveled, waving. She had a letter in her hand. "Oh, I've such news. A dear friend of mine I met in England went to see her daughter in India. But her heart got queer and she had to return. Oh, do sit down, Hitty. Where are my manners? Do you want a glass of sherry?"

"Thank you. That would be nice."

Letty got up, a waltzing movement, describing joy. She tugged at the bell pull. "She met a friend on board ship. Well, they weren't friends to begin with, but when you're all cooped up together." She stared at Hitty. "But I keep forgetting, you've never been to sea."

"No," said Hitty, removing her gloves, warming her fingers at the fire.

"Oh, Betsy, we'll want some sherry. Have Phillips bring us a tray."

"Very good, ma'am." The door closed softly.

"Mrs. Montacute—my friend—writes that this woman she met had just finished a journey to India. She saw the pyramids too. Incredible to think a lone woman could do such things. Don't you agree?"

"Oh yes," said Hitty, meeting her sister's eyes. Agreement held between them like a sheet that needs straightening, folding. All out of their ken. Yet Letty had traveled alone. Hitty felt inferior. She let her eyes fall away.

"This woman—the one who does all this adventuring—is coming to America soon. Mrs. Montacute asked me to invite her to stay. Isn't that interesting?"

"Well, I suppose—"

Phillips knocked discreetly at the door. He set down the tray and poured two glasses.

Letty was rereading the letter. "It couldn't be as interesting to you as to me."

"I suppose not." The sherry tasted sharp. Glowed the throat as it went down.

"She's not only some sort of a writer, she does her own illustrations too. I think that's terribly interesting. Don't you see, maybe she can give me some help." Letty pointed to the row of sketches that, lately, she'd been displaying about her private rooms.

Hitty glanced at them. "It would be nice for you. Did you say this friend is a writer?"

"Oh, she's a published authoress. She writes under a penname, but Mrs. Montacute doesn't say what it is. I wonder if I should give her a party?"

"I don't know," said Hitty. Her heart was beating hard. A published authoress! What did one have to do to achieve that elevated height?

"Anyway, she's visiting friends in Boston at the end of May and will be here in June." Letty sat down and sipped her sherry. "I'm sorry to seem so elated. The letter just came. By the way, I'm glad to see you, dear. Was something wrong that you stopped by?"

"No," said Hitty hastily.

Letty laughed. A girlish laugh that Hitty hadn't heard for years. Even their deep mourning for poor Papa couldn't dim her merriment. "The thing that is so amazing is that this famous authoress wants to visit here. She specifically asked Mrs. Montacute to write."

"What's her name?" asked Hitty.

"Fiona Macleod. That's her real name, of course. June will be just right. We can have a party. Hitty, you will be here too, won't you?"

"I expect so," she said flatly. She didn't want to think of June. It was too far away.

"The reason I ask is that Nat said Compton was planning to spend most of the summer in Vermont. Won't you be with him?"

"No," said Hitty, keeping her voice colorless.

"Dear—?" Letty's attention was caught for the first time. "But surely, if Compton is to be up there? Isn't he building some sort of place?"

"Yes," said Hitty. Her hands tightened on her gloves. "They have to get most of the outside work done during the summer. The cold comes so fast up there."

"I imagine." Slowly, deep in thought. "Hitty, why aren't you going to Vermont with your husband?"

"Because he doesn't want me to," was the reply. Said so simply, it was a pronouncement, without manifest emotion.

"Oh, you can't be serious. Hitty, aren't you teasing me just a little?" Letty's eyes were quizzical.

"I am perfectly serious, Letty. I am to remain here in Philadelphia."

Letty was alarmed now. Her brown eyes held a flickering light. "Is your marriage in trouble, dearest?" Softly.

"I really don't know," said Hitty. "There are so many things I haven't the answer to."

Letty interrupted her. "That's true for most wives. If you asked me what Nat did with his evenings, most of the time I couldn't tell you. Is that what you had in mind? It's part of marriage, not to always know." She was being the elder sister now.

"Oh, that." Yes, you're right, and I don't ask, ever. In fact, I've ceased wondering. Compton and I are married, but he still very much leads his own life." She too could be superior. It was this vying that had kept them apart. All Hitty's life.

"Then what is it you're questioning?"

"I'm not sure. Something about Vermont. Well, I really must be going." She rose. "I'm so glad about your friend. The woman authoress."

"You might like to meet her too." Letty was trying to appease her now.

"Thank you," said Hitty. "I will look forward to it." Polite, withdrawn. Gathering on her coat.

"You were a writer too, once—"

"A long time ago. Too long even to remember. I'm surprised it came to your mind."

"Still, Hitty, you might like to meet a real writer."

"Yes. Yes indeed."

In the darkness of her carriage, Hitty wept.

V. THE NARROWING
February–August 1888

> When lovely woman stoops to folly
> And finds too late that men betray,
> What charm can soothe her melancholy?
> What art can wash her tears away?
>
> The only art her guilt to cover,
> To hide her shame from ev'ry eye,
> To give repentance to her lover,
> And wring his bosom is—to die.
>
> "Woman,"
> —Oliver Goldsmith

I

It was St. Valentine's day. Compton brought Hitty a card. "Open it,'" he said, smiling at her.

She was seated by the fire. Dinner was past, and fresh logs had been piled on the glowing coals.

What did he want? For it was certain he wanted something. She lifted the envelope's flap, breaking in two the dark wax that sealed it, snapping apart the impress of Compton's signet ring.

The card was flouncy, with paper lace and rosebuds fashioned of tiny cushions of velvet, artfully shaped, glued. The verse read:

> *My heart beats only for you*
> *You should know I am true.*

She stared at it. It was a mockery. She pulled back her lips into a smile. "That is dear of you, Compton." She pulled her mending box toward her. His dark socks were on the top. She loathed to touch them, sensing the sweat and sourness that had been washed out of them as if they were still there.

"You are going to sew?"

"I had thought—do you object?"

"Only, we might go to bed."

She couldn't mistake his meaning. She said evenly, "If you will turn down the lamps, Compton, I will go upstairs and prepare myself."

"Are you in your safe time?" His question was always the same.

This time she sighed audibly. "We can get the card out, Compton."

She hated him. But if he could give her a child, not all of it would be wasted—the effort, the pretense.

She undressed neatly, folding her clothes and laying them over the chair that was hers. His stood on the opposite side of the room—the same side he slept on. Their bed "parted" as cleanly as their lives.

"You are ready?" He came into the room and closed the door behind him like a jailer. He sat on the edge of the bed and removed his laced boots. His socks—another hole. She noted it dispassionately. At least she could darn with stitches that formed a completely even weave.

"Don't wear that pair again," she said.

"What? Oh, you mean the hole. It'll be good for another day."

"No it won't. It'll just make the hole bigger. If you had to mend them, you'd understand."

He'd shrugged. "Go get out your calendar. I want to add up where you are in your cycle. You've been keeping it up?"

"Of course." She said it idly.

He mistrusted her. Took the piece of paper to the lamp, examined it. "Today is the fourteenth. You haven't marked all the crosses, Hitty."

"I marked the first one. It's the only one that counts."

"It's not done with the care I expect of you. All the days should be crossed off, not just the first one. How can we tell if there's a variation in your cycle?"

She was so tired of it. She was a frog, laid out on the dissecting board, pinned and trussed, each part of her marked, flagged, and labeled. She heard herself say, "Does it matter? I mean, does it really matter?"

"Well," he said at last, after what seemed like a long time, "it looks as if you are safe. We'll go ahead with it."

She placed herself across the bed. The way he liked her. Her head supported by the rearranged pillows, her thighs bared and hanging over the edge.

Naked, he came at her. Waving his staff, which was fully engorged. He rubbed it across the softness of her stomach and through the bramble of her pubic hair.

"Now, you may caress me."

She noticed at this point that he liked to keep his eyes shut. Standing, swaying gently, giving himself up to who knew what ecstasy. It was hard for her to imagine what he experienced.

She fondled and touched him with her lips. What if she should bite it off? It was a terror she fought almost each time, as in his arrogance he stood over her. Would her teeth be strong enough to cut clean through?

Tonight he chose entrance. Her thighs curving like white arches over the bed, her opening waiting for him, she braced herself. He went in thoughtfully, his eyes lidded into slits, allowing him to see her yet maintain that interior experience. He battered at her until she thought she could stand no more. Then he muttered in impatience, "The pillows—we have to raise your hips."

He pulled out, his organ moist and beginning to go limp. "God-damn—hurry with the pillows."

She pulled one across the bed and tried to raise herself on to it. He watched, annoyance spreading over the operation like a cloud. "Why are you so clumsy?"

For not the first time, she wondered with whom he was comparing her. Whoever she was, was perfect. Artful in her movements, ravishing in her kisses, playing him into a mood where his joy could erupt—a white fountain gushing forth from his central being. Calling him a king.

He pushed into her again, tearing the delicacy of her flesh with his urgency to be brought upward—enticed into release. She could hear his litany beginning—a volley of curses so low that she'd had to hear them many times to comprehend them. They took peculiar shapes in the atmosphere of the bedroom—grinning gargoyle faces that wanted to rip her apart.

Falling on her at last. The slow convulsions. Quiet now. Close like that, she could smell him. Pipe tobacco breath, whiskey.

Parting then—as if they'd shaken hands. He said, his back to her as he bent to the washstand, "I'll be gone by the first of March."

She got up painfully. His effusion was between her legs. Sticky, cloying her tidy hairs, leaving snail traces down her legs. She reached for a towel. He'd allow only one basin in the room and made her wait to use it. His ritual took preeminence. Why shouldn't it? His assumption of his right to direct the play had always been unquestioning.

"Are you going by train?"

"Hardly know how else. You'll need Jakes here. I'll leave you the carriage."

"Thank you," she said politely.

He moved away, drying himself with a soft towel. She poured the sudsy water into the slop basin, taking care not to let it splash the floor boards. Undirected movements infuriated him. She'd known before she met his office nurse exactly what she'd be like. Thin, with a face like a hatchet. Clever hands. Quick, intelligent movements.

"Who will run your office while you're away?"

"I'm taking in a partner. A younger man. Name's Paul Schwartz-kopf."

"How much younger is he?"

"Why do you ask?" Voice sharp with suspicion.

"Just wondered." She sponged her traumatized tissues.

289

"Hitty, for heaven's sake!" He lay down on the bed, his silk robe around him lightly. Not altogether concealing his paunchy torso, his collapsed masculinity. "Stay out of my practice," he said wearily. His voice chided her.

She opened the bedroom door. Taking a candle, her hand curved about it to protect it from drafts, she made her way down the corridor to the small room where she kept her sewing. Her writing was locked away in a small desk. She had her own desk at last. It was one of the things she was grateful to marriage for.

She pulled paper toward her. Above the desk her bird regarded her with puzzled complaint. No matter how often she came here at night, the bird never seemed able to forgive her. Its feathers ruffled, it glanced down at her with one beady eye. Wire-thin feet clutched the roughened perch.

The outpouring of words into her journal took the edge off her pain: *He's leaving the end of this month. He told me tonight he'd taken on a new partner. Am resolved to stop being concerned about things that are none of my business. I long for spring. Somehow, to be able to get outside, dig in the moist earth—*

She paused, thinking, mentally seeing the calendar. Not the one Compton had drawn up and so assiduously checked, but the one she kept in the hidden drawer of her desk. The one that truly told the record of her body's activities.

Not that she needed it. She knew, as surely as if she'd been able to see into the future, she would have a child. That child would be carried to full term, would be born whole and perfect. It was written on her determination, enscribed on her optimism. Carved on her faith in prayer answered.

If God gave her a child, her marriage could become bearable. If not, if her arms remained empty, she dared not think of the years ahead. Only Compton to cherish. She had to give birth to something. She was too fertile to tolerate the idea of simply withering away.

2

She asked Dr. Schwarzkopf to come to see her. She sent him a note: *If you would have time to oblige me—?*

Jakes came back with his answer. "He said to expect him this afternoon. Just as quick as he can git heah after office hours, Mizz Hittie, ma'am."

Alone in the parlor, Hitty stared out at the trees that were in full leaf, the peony buds beginning to form. She touched her breasts secretly. Could she, after all, have fancied she was with child? Now that the doctor was coming, she felt cold, stiff with anticipation he would dash her hopes. Through the child, she would live. She pressed her hands against her breasts, feeling their tenderness—their ache. As she sensed heaviness capturing her body, so she felt lightness, freeing her spirit.

She walked with a new step.

Dr. Paul Schwarzkopf came into the parlor. As soon as she saw him she wondered where she had felt this way about a man before? A sense of shame hung around the memory. It was all she could pick up as she stared at the young doctor. Something she'd written about a man. That he seemed from another world. Michael! Idris Michael Hughes, the curate who had come from across the sea to assist Llewellyn. How clearly it came into focus. For ages now, she'd been able to look at the curate in church and not see him. Rowena's husband. The girl would arrive this summer. It had been a foolish maiden's dream. Hitty was still angry at herself. She believed she had tucked it all away, as one sets aside a dress that is unbecoming.

Staring at Dr. Paul, she knew that all this time she'd lived a lie. Once, when Compton had entered her, she'd imagined it was Michael. Clarity speared her thoughts, denying her flight from the truth. The reason was simple. Dr. Paul roused the same wonder in her she'd felt the first time she saw Michael. So beautiful!

"Mrs. Grey? I came as soon as I could. What is the trouble?"

His eyes were dark brown. Lighter than Michael's, but liquid and sweet with feeling. What would it be like to have him hold her in his arms?

"I am sorry to trouble you. With my husband away—"

"Of course. I assured Dr. Grey I would take over all his patients."

It perched there between them, a bird momentarily stayed in flight. A patient. She was not Compton's patient—she was his wife.

"I think I have to be somebody's patient," she said with a smile.

"You are ill?" His look was first caring, second appraisal.

"Not ill. I want you to tell me whether or not I am with child."

"I see." His lips pressed together. "What makes you suspect you might be?"

"First, I want you to promise me something." She pressed her palms together, a little girl saying her catechism. "It's to be a surprise for Dr. Grey. I don't want him informed. I want to tell him myself—when he comes back."

"I see," he said, but she could tell he didn't. He was puzzled—and too intelligent to be fooled by a story.

"Let's see whether you're going to have a baby or not," he said, avoiding her request. "Tell me your symptoms."

"I've missed twice."

"That doesn't always mean anything. You could be upset, having Dr. Grey away."

"There are other signs."

"Tell me."

She shared them with him. The first human being to hear them. She watched conviction begin to come into his face.

"You want a child very much, don't you?"

"Oh yes." She clasped her hands before her. Holding her hopes between them.

"You look healthy enough. May I ask how old you are?"

She told him.

"You won't be the first woman to give birth at thirty-six," he said matter-of-factly. "I take it this is your first?"

"Dr. Grey and I were only married last fall."

"You really must want this child," he said.

"Oh yes!" She gulped for air, feeling the room close about her. "Very much—more than anything else in the world."

292

"A lucky baby," he said, and he smiled. Seeing deep into her.

"Are you married?" She knew the question sounded odd.

"Why, no." He said it casually but her heart leaped. Could he see?

"Would you care for a glass of wine?" she said. "I could ring for it to be brought."

"Thank you, no. I have some other calls to make." He stated it softly. Nevertheless, she felt refused. She blushed, high and panting, wishing him already gone. Willing him to stay. What was the matter with her?

He was giving her his diagnosis. "—safely say you are carrying a child. Of course time will confirm everything. But all signs point to it. You are to be congratulated, Mrs. Grey."

"Thank you." She had done it. She had defied Compton. "Do you have news of my husband?"

"Probably as much as you do."

"He writes infrequently. I suppose him to be very busy."

"Quite so," he said, irritatingly vague. Yet the eyes were kind. He was counting on his fingers. The day when she had last "sickened." "Looks like your baby will be coming in time for Thanksgiving," he said lightly. "A reason to celebrate, eh?"

"Yes," she said, forcing it. The full impact of Compton's anger was closing her throat.

"You aren't worried about carrying the child?" he asked, perceptive. Seeing into people. Or did he just have a vision into her?

"No, no," she said quickly. "I've known for a long time I could bear a child easily. It was merely the getting of it that took patience."

"Ah," he said, nodding. He was looking about for his coat, which he'd removed when he came into the room. Refusing Joseph's offer to take it. He was his own man. Wrong—his own person.

The coat had black velvet lapels. Against the smooth cloth they gave it distinction. Reflecting the dark eyes, the glossy hair that touched the top of his collar.

"It's coolish for late May," she said conversationally, watching him do up the buttons.

He stepped to the window. "You have a pleasant garden."

"Thank you. I plan to enlarge it this summer. I shall be able to work out there for a little while, won't I?"

"Do you like flowers?" he asked abruptly.

"Why, yes." He'd taken her by surprise.

"Then I think it would do you good to be out there. Your body will tell you when you are overdoing."

"That's what I thought."

"I would guess you enjoy roses," he said, again unexpectedly. "I have a small house and a maid who scolds me. In the back I have one

293

of those very old gardens. Planted by some colonist. The roses tell me they were brought from England."

"The roses 'tell you'?" She gathered her face into a frown, but she was laughing.

"They talk to me. You don't have to believe it. I'm thought mad by many."

"I think it's delightful!" she said warmly. "You must have brick paths too—and box hedges."

"Yes. I have all that."

"You make me realize how much I've still to learn. I'm going over to my mother's, to talk to the gardener. He's one of those who can make anything grow."

He put out his hand, she realized, to shake her own. "Now call on me anytime you have symptoms that don't feel right. Otherwise, nothing to do but take care of yourself. Engage a good midwife—" He stopped. "But Compton will know what to do."

"Yes," she said uncertainly.

When he had gone, taking the sunshine with him, she stood where he had stood and gazed at the garden. This one was too big. She wanted to be enclosed, held by the encircling arms of tall walls and established shrubbery. But her child could play in a larger garden. It was only for now that she needed this comfort.

She rang the bell for Joseph.

"Have either you or Jakes done any carpentry?" she asked him.

"Buildin' somethin'? What you got in mind, Mizz Hitty?"

"See there?" She pointed. "I would love a summer house. Do you think you could build me one?"

His old eyes were noncommittal. "Haven't never tried somethin' like that. Not since I was a boy. Jakes, he might know more."

"If we put our heads together—?"

His face said he couldn't refuse her. "What will Dr. Compton say when he git back, missus?"

"Perhaps we can have it finished before he has a chance to stop us."

He thought that was remarkably funny. He rubbed his hands together. "It ain't that easy—but we can surely have a try if'n we puts our minds to it. Mebbe, if I think it over, I kin find some other colored man wants work. Someone who knows carpentry." He grinned. "Yassum, we git it done, one way or another."

3

Letty was nervous. The carriage had gone to the train to meet Fiona Macleod. She would be here any minute. In this house—a real author.

Letty glanced at herself in the mirror. Every hair was in place. The ruffles of her green dress cascaded in casual grace, falling away from her neck to cross her bosom. An emerald pin nestled among them. She touched her cheek with an inquiring hand. Would this woman writer be very elegant?

Her eyes went from the mirror to the portrait of herself, done at eighteen. She had aged. Hard to tell exactly how it showed. Perhaps in the lines of her chin? The look in her eyes was no longer appealing. Crows' feet had formed at the corners. In another, they would have been laugh lines. In her, they were from frowns. Yes, and of course there were wrinkles.

An old woman. At the thought a wave of heat hit her, confirming it. She was well into the dreaded change of life. No longer could she deny it to anyone. Would she survive? Mother had said, "It's a time when women go queer in the head." A dark forest to be crossed without lamp or guide.

Were women that delicate? It was thought so, Letty knew, by most physicians. She sighed. So long had she dreaded getting to forty, she wanted to scream out loud she was willing to get it over. But please, let her know the worst.

The face in the mirror was sour—disillusioned. Unforgiving that nothing had come of her expectations except disappointment. She almost smiled as she thought of the naive creature she'd once been. Wanting to marry Nathaniel had been part of it. Not seeing through

295

Emma's persuasiveness—that it was a marriage designed to bring the Benedicts glory.

Letty had been a pawn. A silly one at that.

The sound of the carriage wheels broke into her reverie. She smoothed the front of her dress and turned herself away from the mirror, patting each wing of her hair flat against her temples. Hands trembling.

Fiona came tumbling into the front hall. An apparition farther removed from what Letty had imagined she could not be. Letty had to recollect herself from standing there, staring.

"You've got to be Letty! Oh, my dear, I'm so delighted to meet you. Such a fantastic trip—I love your trains. But in this heat—as you see, I'm not dressed for it—it was the same in India. I wilted. Always wear the wrong togs."

Somehow she was in the parlor. Was there some mistake? Had Bates fetched the wrong person off the train? But no, there could be no mistake. The woman was English. Furthermore, she knew Letty's name—knew where she was supposed to be—and out of her mouth rolled the most marvelous flow of language.

"Is it always so hot in America? Of course it is! The stupendous people in Boston—you know I was visiting there? Of course you do, I wrote you from Boylston Street—such colorful names—I might have been back in England again—well, the Prentisses warned me, 'Its always suffocating in July.' But a sea breeze, when you can catch it. They drove me out to a remarkable town on Cape Cod. Have you ever visited Cape Cod?"

Letty shook her head, afraid to try to stem the flood. Words, information, swirled about her until she almost feared she'd drown. At least it gave her a chance to study the woman. And to think she'd worried about her own appearance!

It was hard to judge Fiona's age. Skin of leather, wrinkled as favorite boots. Tanned as no lady allowed her flesh to become. She wore a bonnet, pushed onto her hair. Whatever coiffure she'd started out with from Boston was reduced to ropes, hanging from beneath the straw headgear. When she moved, she risked a shower of hairpins, steely and cheap as a servant's. Her costume—if that was what one might call it—was sewn from linen. Heavy and unshamed by dye, it clung to her form as it wished. All wrinkles when she stood up.

"I look a mess! What you must think of me! Mama scolds me for my appearance, but I have to confess, Letty, I've got to the point where I simply don't care. I mean, when you work at it and work at it, and come out looking like the same ragbag—well, wouldn't you give up?" A wide smile on the leaf-brown face. Freckles outlining the bridge of a snub nose. Eyes calm one moment, roguish the next.

"I expect you'd like to freshen up."

"Know what I'd really like? A good strong cup of tea! Do you drink tea here?"

"Of course. Every afternoon—except when it's too hot. Perhaps you'd rather a cool fruit drink?"

"No, my dear." The head, freed now from its bonnet, shook. "One thing about the English. If it's cold, they want tea to warm them. If it's a heat wave, they ask for it to make them sweat. You should see them drink it in India. Very 'pukkah sahib.'"

"Pukkah—?"

"Oh, you'll have to forgive me. When I pick up new words, I dote on using them. *Pukkah*—proper, you know, starched. And a *sahib*—well, that's supposed to mean someone like a squire or a sir. In India, it's anyone who isn't native." She shook her head in disapproval. "Oh, my dear, don't get me started on the British in India. It needs to go in a book, but I'm afraid I wouldn't find any publisher except an Indian one." She laughed loudly, slapping her thighs. "You should just hear the things the poor white memsahibs get away with. *Memsahibs* are sahibs' wives. Not that they don't have their troubles—but, my God, the airs and graces."

Letty was lost. She rang for the tea.

"Personally, I found the Indians themselves fascinating! I got myself into a lot of trouble just for saying it. Can you imagine—just for making a statement that Indians were far more interesting to talk to than Europeans!" She stared at Letty. "I know I'm supposed to know better, but sometimes I don't. The colonel's wife actually took me aside, lectured me. 'We have to remember, dear Fiona, that out here, we represent the Empire.' As if I didn't know. It's in everything they do. Suffocating, my dear Letty. That's why I am so sure that going out West will be refreshing."

"You're traveling to the West?" Letty stood there as if frozen. "Why would you want to go out there?" Too late, she remembered this was the woman who'd seen the pyramids.

"It draws me." She said it as if it had a sensual meaning for her.

The door opened gently. Taft, answering the bell.

"Could we have tea served? Oh, and Taft, ask Cook to make it a little stronger than usual. You'd like it that way, wouldn't you, Fiona?"

"Please. Except I'll be spoiling it for you, won't I?" Distress, the face of a naughty child caught in the jampot.

"A little stronger, Taft. And a pitcher of cream?"

He looked disapproving. "Very good, madam. Did you wish cakes served?"

"Yes, of course." Then with irritation, "Why do you ask? They were on Cook's order this morning. She was to bake cupcakes."

"Just to be sure, madam."

It wasn't that. She knew from his expression—he was telling her that he didn't welcome her guest. She was not Taft's idea of a lady visitor. How dare he!

Her eyes blazed at him. "We'd like the tea right away. Miss Macleod has had a long journey."

"And I'm shockingly hungry!" said Fiona. Shattering the attempt to shame him with icy dignity.

Letty bit her lip, feeling betrayed.

Fiona was to be here for two weeks. Till her ship sailed.

"I thought you said you were going out West." Letty reminded her.

"Oh, but by sea, my dear. The ocean route is much more fun. I'll come back overland. Then I'll have seen it all."

"I have heard one can go as far as Panama and cross that way. Then catch another vessel up the Pacific Coast."

Fiona crossed her feet in front of her. "I'll do that if I have to. But my intention's to go around the Horn."

Letty was startled. "Do you have any idea how dangerous that voyage is? How few ships succeed in getting all the way around? My husband's in shipping—we've heard the stories. Oh, Fiona, I think you'd be wise to at least think it through carefully."

"My mind's made up. The whole thing's planned." She sat back, her dress pulling up to ankle height. She began scrabbling about in a great carryall of a bag embroidered with bilious green flowers, scarlet dragons, and mustard butterflies.

"Do you like this? I got it in the bazaar in Bombay. I was told I'd paid too much for it, but the man selling it looked as if he'd never had a decent meal in his life. I mean, how can you ignore those people?" Out of the bag's maw came a folded handkerchief, its edges marked with grime.

"I must apologize for doing this—" She began dabbing at the perspiration at her temples, the cotton square in her hand becoming damp. "I suppose I ought to buy some new clothes."

"If you'd like," Letty's voice was silvery, melodious, "we could go on a shopping expedition while you're here." Already she pictured herself ushering Fiona into Miss Puxley's. No, that would never do. Suddenly Letty knew what she dreaded most. Nathaniel's meeting Fiona.

There wasn't a thing she could do about it. No amount of manipulatory tactics could keep the two apart. Fiona was to stay two weeks, and Nathaniel, as master of the house, would be within its walls from time to time. She noted with irritation that her hand was trembling. Was she really that afraid of Nathaniel? Futile fury possessed her. She tried to concentrate on what Fiona was saying.

"The Indians are wonderful with children—European children. No English child is ever that reassured, played with, comforted. It's a rude shock, I can tell you, when they get old enough to be sent home."

"Why would the children be sent home? I assume you mean to England?"

Fiona shrugged. "Sorry. Yes 'home' is always the Old Country. Tradition has it, the little devils must be protected from the evil effects of India. Boarding school for the boys, you know. At six, they're packed off. The girls get pushed on to aunts, grandmothers. Locked away in some Victorian castle while Mama and Papa go on enduring India, getting paler and thinner and more and more spoiled."

"Spoiled?"

"Nothing like having the power to push another race around. Pretty soon you begin to understand you're superior. More intelligent, that sort of thing. Oh, they adjust badly, the retired majors and colonels, when they finally come home to roost in England. Spend the rest of their lives talking about the good old days—and the fool Indians." She puckered her face in thought. "I wonder what I'll find in California? I'm determined to see if I can make friends with some of the redskins."

Letty shuddered. "They are still dangerous, you know. My brother-in-law had some cousins who went West by wagon train. A marauding party wiped out the lot of them. I think you ought to be careful."

"You see, that's the trouble when it's a territory matter. If one could just meet them on their own ground—as visitors. Well, like I'm meeting you."

Letty stared, not sure whether to take it as a compliment or an insult. Evidently it was expressed as neither.

Fiona was gazing into space. "I suppose I should have been a missionary. Only trouble, I'm not much on all that God business. Oh, of course I'm a believer. Mama and I have always attended church. Have the minister over to lunch, that sort of thing. But as to going out and converting—" Again the puzzlement. "I mean, why should we convert? Is it actually any of our business? I detest meddlers. I say, these cakes are delicious. Would your cook mind if I went out to the kitchen and told her so?"

"Actually, I don't know." What an odd request. "I can tell her when she comes for the orders tomorrow."

"Would you, love? But I should like to meet her. She must be very talented. Mother and I don't have much of a hand at getting cakes light."

299

"You cook?" asked Letty faintly. Perhaps it was just a pastime? Some of Letty's friends did cook on occasion.

"Of course we cook. I'm afraid we don't have a marvelous house like you have, Letty dear. You see, Papa was a professor, and when he died we just had to manage as best we could. Of course we'd started being careful quite a bit before. He knew he was going to have to retire, on account of his ill health. We moved away from Oxford and took a cottage in the country."

"Whereabouts?" asked Letty.

"That's right. You've been to England. We moved to Berkshire. It's all downs and rolling chalk land. We managed to get the house for very little. When I'm home, I help Mother with the garden. We grow things we can bottle for the winter—salt away. And jam of course. Plenty of jam." She licked frosting off her fingers before wiping them on a napkin. "I do make a rather fine strawberry conserve, if I say so myself. I should have brought you some."

"It's a long way to bring preserves," said Letty in a voice that was meant to console. But she was staring at the licked fingers. What would Nathaniel say?

"Perhaps you'd like to freshen up now?"

"A splendid idea!" Fiona could have no knowledge of why Letty wished her elsewhere—to give her an opportunity to prepare Nat for Fiona.

Yet no preparation would be adequate. She saw it flatly.

"Now what shall we do today?" asked Fiona. Her energy seemed boundless. She'd just come back from taking herself around the garden. "A marvelous place you have here. If you don't mind, I'm going to take my notes out under the trees and write."

"Please do. Do whatever you wish," said Letty, trying not to sound relieved. Fiona's delight in everything was wearing. One never knew where one would find her—in the linen room, chatting with Norah—in the safe, watching Taft select pieces of silver to be polished. She'd even found the wine cellar.

"How did you get down there?"

"Taft showed me. He explained to me how he's the only one to have the key."

"Nathaniel has one," said Letty calmly.

"Oh, your husband," said Fiona unself-consciously. "Yes, I'd imagine he'd have one." She wrinkled her nose suddenly.

"I'm sorry Nat was rude this morning. You see, he doesn't like to talk at breakfast."

"Yes I know." Fiona was little-girl contrite. But the corners of her mouth twitched. "I'm afraid I'm going to give him a bad two weeks."

"It's all right," said Letty in a strained way. "He'll get over it." But would he? She wasn't so sure.

"I'm being wicked. If you notice, I have trouble worshipping men. It's got something to do with the way I was brought up. Don't get me wrong. I adored my father. But it was just because I loved him so— and we had a very special relationship—I can't see men from a dis tance."

"What distance?"

"Oh, the pedestal view. I'm down here and men are up there." She'd walked over to the morning-room window, stared out. "I had a chance to marry, you know."

"Really?" Letty was glancing through the lists she'd made for the day. Cook she'd already seen. There were Betsy and Norah to give orders to. And flowers to be picked, to take to Hitty this afternoon.

"I suppose, to look at me, you'd never believe a man would want me." Fiona's voice was odd. Strident? "But I wasn't always such a rough diamond. Mama's really done her best with me."

"Dear, you don't have to tell me all this."

The Englishwoman turned, a forced smile on her round face. "He was an old friend of my father's. I want to tell you. Don't ask me why. Normally, I don't breathe a word of it to a soul. Mother and I mention it sometimes. That's the extent of it."

"I don't need to know."

"Yes, you do. I'm not quite sure why, yet. Something about the way your husband takes advantage of you. No, don't tell me that's not so because I've seen. He has you bamboozled."

Letty set the lists aside. Would this woman never cease to astonish her? What right did she have to criticize someone's marriage?

Fiona was ahead of her. "If he valued you—if he treated you like the person you are—I wouldn't object. Oh, I know I'm just an on-looker. But let me tell you about me. Draw your own conclusions."

Letty shrugged. Helplessness sat on her shoulders like a shawl. Who could expect her to protest from a position of powerlessness? Disloyalty was another matter. But Fiona had whipped it out of the meadows of disloyalty and turned it into her own tale.

"He and Father did research together. Botanists. I worked with them, preparing specimens, assembling collections, collating findings. Hard work, but I enjoyed it. When Father died"—her voice stopped momentarily—"I couldn't get back to the work for a while. There wasn't any point. Gerald"—she lingered on the name, as if it were hard to say—"Gerald brought in most of the specimens."

"What happened?"

"The workroom was away from the cottage. Gerald drove down one day—Oxford's not that far away. He was my father's age, Letty." She stared, her face solemn. "He asked me to go with him to the laboratory. It was a natural thing. We'd been a team—Gerald, Father, and me. But I'd not been there since the week Father died. Gerald took my hand and said I had to face it. He was like an uncle—kind, under-standing.

"Once there, he started talking about Mother's and my life. It seems there was no money left. Father had put everything in Gerald's hands. He trusted him. The same as I did—the bastard!" The word spat out bitterly, like an insect flown into the mouth.

Letty was shocked. She'd never heard such a word before—from a lady.

"Of course it wasn't true about the money. He was lying. I found that out afterward, when I went to our solicitor. Gerald had intended to keep me in the dark, make me feel I'd nowhere to go. Mother too, of course.

"He said he assumed we'd marry. I must have looked as if I thought he'd taken leave of his senses. He went on about how he had promised Father he'd support Mother and me.

" 'Why don't you marry Mother?' I asked. I was about eighteen then. 'Why didn't you mention marrying me to Father?' I wanted to know.

" 'Your father wanted you all to himself,' he answered.

"When I informed him I wasn't for sale, he didn't seem to hear me."

"You mean he forced himself on you?" Letty said.

"No. Not then. He kept coming back. Made Mother think I'd agreed to marry him. I never found this out till later. He'd told it as if it were private—nothing to be discussed between Mother and me. Mother's very sweet, believing.

"One afternoon, he knew Mother had gone down to the village. He came out to the workroom and took me by surprise. That's the time he forced me."

"What did you do?" Letty's eyes were wide and staring.

"I screamed. I'm strong too. But he was a big man—over six feet and kept his health up. I suppose he thought I was just one more item to add to his collection." She met Letty's gaze. Her lower lip was trembling. "No one within miles to hear—"

"How awful for you."

"There wasn't much I could do. I threatened to have the law on him, but he was ahead of me there. He'd already told it around that I was enticing, that I'd had my eye on him long before Father died. That, because of his money and our penuriousness, I looked toward a settled future. No one would believe me if I said anything to the law. I'd just damage my reputation, spoil my chances of ever marrying anyone else. It took me a long time to get past hating him." Fiona's eyes were hard, steel bright.

"It's horrible!" said Letty. "You mean there was nothing you could do?"

"His word against mine. When I told him to clear off, I found out he'd stolen more than my virginity. He'd been taking away Father's papers—a few here, a few there. I didn't miss them until too late."

"Were you able to get your father's work back?"

"I tried. Went to see a few old friends. They persuaded me that for Father's memory, I shouldn't press suit. Same thing again. Who would believe me? I began to see it their way. Besides, I didn't have the money to go to court."

"What happened to this dreadful man?"

"Oh, he went to Africa and got eaten by some tribesmen. Served him right, I'd say." But her eyes were wistful. "It's funny, Letty. He abused me so shockingly—yet when I look back, after all this time, the thing I feel strongest is a sense of loss.

"I loved him like I did my Father. In a way it was a double loss. Both of them going out of my life at once. I'd always felt I could rely on him. When he changed, something inside me didn't want to accept it. Kept seeing him the way he'd been. My sitting on his knee as a child. His bringing me humbugs." She made a face. "Years of trust gone. I'll never look up to a man again as long as I live."

Letty nodded. "I can see why you'd feel that way. What did your mother say?"

"Mama? Good gracious, I couldn't tell her. When Gerald didn't come around anymore, she was able to accept it about his stealing Father's papers. We packed up every one of the specimens and sent them to a museum. Then we sold the house and moved to Devon. Our village is close by the sea. Mother has a woman to look after her when I'm traveling. I've a room with a view of the sea to come back to. You've no idea how nice that is, for writing."

"It sounds lovely," said Letty. "But why do you do so much traveling?"

"It's part of my assignment. My editor likes the world from the 'woman's viewpoint.' One of those mushy magazines. But there are ideas in travel for serious writing." She pushed her hair away from her face. With one of her sudden changes of mood she said, "Why, Letty, do you paint?"

"What?" Letty was startled.

"The pictures—I've been in here before but didn't notice them. That's like me. See nothing unless it's under my nose. That's Stonehenge, isn't it?"

"Yes," said Letty. Her defenses curled around her, like armor on a pill bug.

"You know, you've captured something. But then you do know that, don't you?"

"No," said Letty truthfully. "I never gave it much thought."

Fiona was rushing about the room excitedly. "And these are your children? This has to be Amelia, with that straight nose and that solemn look. This one of Polly is remarkable! And your Albert—he keeps pretty much to himself, doesn't he?"

Letty nodded.

"If I sat, would you do a painting of me?" asked Fiona shyly.

All at once, Letty saw how easy it would be. The battered face, the kindliness, the hair that needed a good comb. The personality of Fiona, expressed in her dishevelment, her uncaring. Contrasted by her ability to love, to enfold and cherish.

"I'd love to try," she told Fiona.

"Oh, good," said her guest. "Now tell me, what are we supposed to do this afternoon? You hinted it was to be a busy day."

"Neither Mother nor Hitty would forgive me if we didn't come for tea. They want to meet you as soon as possible." She didn't say she'd boasted of her famous author friend.

"This is your family, I gather?"

"Yes. Just the four of us. My sister's having a baby and it's beginning to show, so she can't go out in public."

"Ah," said Fiona. Understanding. "Well, what should I wear? Perhaps I should press something up?"

"We can have Nanette do it," said Letty gently.

"You mean she'd iron something for me? Oh, what a delight. But awful for her on such a hot day. Now let me see, what on earth can I put on? Everything's too heavy for this climate."

"We must go shopping tomorrow," said Letty. Happily. After all, the world was a pleasant place to exist in.

.

They were seated in the parlor. As Hitty poured the tea, she said, "How do you like Philadelphia, Miss Macleod?"

"Well, I haven't had much chance to see the sights," said the Englishwoman.

Her voice was crisp and pleasantly modulated, but her mode of dress seemed disorganized. And her hair didn't become her. A woman who climbed through bushes, thought Hitty. Thinking of it as the first line in a poem. What could possibly rhyme with bushes?

Letty spoke up. "Fiona's sailing around the Horn."

Hitty noted the pride in Letty's voice. Her eyes had a kind of a glow in them today. Mildly, Hitty wondered about it. Was she proud to be entertaining somebody famous?

"Isn't that a fearfully dangerous thing to do?" asked Emma.

Her turtle neck fell away loose, swinging like skin about a cow's full udders. Hitty had seen them that way in Vermont. Vermont! She automatically turned her mind aside. She refused to think about Compton's returning. What would he say when he saw her? A dress with the fullness arranged at the front. She felt like the subject of an Italian painting—or had it been Dutch? A woman—it must have been meant to be the Virgin Mary—standing, her dress gathered before her, its drapes falling away out of her hands. Eyes downcast and humble, listening to the words of an angel.

There was no angel here. Only Fiona. The English accent jarred on Hitty's ears. Involuntarily, she sighed. Audibly.

Emma's quick ears, tuned to what she really listened for, said, "Hitty, are you still sick in the mornings?"

"No, Mother. I am mostly over that."

Fiona smiled cheerfully. "We tuck childbearing away," she said boldly. "Yet among some of the primitive tribes I've visited, it's reason for pride. The women walk down between the mud huts—their bellies full and their breasts uncovered. You just know how wonderful they feel about the coming baby."

"I feel like that." Hitty said it quietly. Something about the way Fiona mentioned it enraged her. "But delicacy dictates one keep oneself from public view. Have you ever borne a child, Miss Macleod?" She knew the question was outrageous.

"No," said Fiona. Did she say it sadly? But then, as if Hitty hadn't spoken at all, "It's what you are illustrating. Society demands we hide away the whole process. What is it that forces us to assent to this stupid modesty, as though being expectant were something to be denied?" She looked at Hitty as if she were talking to a friend.

"Ridiculous!" sputtered Emma, coming to Hitty's rescue. "I don't know how you were reared, Miss Macleod, but in our country, we try to preserve the ways of gentility."

"That's my point," Fiona went on unperturbed. Almost as if an argument delighted her. "We call it 'gentility.' Why? What is so desirable about denial? What is so dreadful about the act of reproduction?"

"Fiona is a botanist by training," said Letty hastily. "She looks at things very scientifically."

"Mercy!" said Emma. "I'm thankful you explained it, Letty. Else I would have been tempted to think of it as vulgarity."

"You're delightful!" said Fiona. She stared at the old lady, who began to blush, slowly.

"I've never been called 'delightful' before," said Emma.

"You should have been! Because you say exactly what is on your mind and don't mince words. You're like me, and I'd wager that when you were very young, you were always getting into trouble."

"I've never been in trouble." The old lady's cheeks were trembling. Yet it was just the sort of banter she adored.

"Well, you've developed a reputation for outspokenness, haven't you?" Fiona prodded.

"Now Mother," said Letty. "You have to admit that's right."

"Nonsense," snapped the old lady. Terribly pleased. She sipped the hot brown tea with pleasure. "So, Hitty, your husband is to return soon," she said.

Hitty slumped in her chair and said, "Sometime before the end of July, I believe."

"That's not what he writes me," said Emma. "He thought it would be by the middle of this week."

"Compton wrote you?"

307

"Why ever not? I am his mother-in-law." Emma's eyes were calm, unblinking. "Silly girl. Wouldn't he be the best one to reassure me it was safe for you to have a child?"

Hitty heard the words coming from very far away. She put her hand out to the chair arm to steady herself. Someone, in a clipped English voice, said, "Watch it—she's going to faint."

Ammonia, acrid and suffocating. Hitty gasped. She tried to sit up, all strength having run out of her body into invisible pools on the floor. Voices ebbing and flowing.

"Now, a touch of tea," the voice commanded. "Lots of sugar in it for strength. There, you'll be right as rain in a few minutes."

But she couldn't be all right ever again. Compton was on his way home. And he knew about the baby.

Yet she didn't have to tell him herself. Weak with realization of her deliverance, she gazed out at the faces in the room. Looming large and pink with concern.

Letty said, "Are you going to be all right?"

"I think so." She touched herself gingerly. As if she'd fallen. But she hadn't. She'd stayed right there in her chair.

Letty said sharply, "You had told Compton about the baby, hadn't you?"

"No. I was planning to, when he came back." She deliberately didn't say 'home.'

Emma spat it out. "Just as I suspected. I knew you were going to have this child behind his back. You don't treat your husband right at all, Hitty."

"Mother!" Letty reproved automatically.

"You know what he'll think," said Emma, a note of triumph in her voice, "he'll think it's not his child. What month is it now?"

"I—I believe I'm in the fourth month."

"Surely you know for certain?"

"Dr. Paul said—" She stopped. Too late to withdraw the words.

Emma's eyes, hooded, watched her. "And who is this Dr. Paul, Hitty?" Hands folded deliberately in her lap, "Does your husband know you are being attended by another physician?"

Hitty's eyelids fluttered. "Paul Schwarzkopf is Compton's new partner, Mother."

"I suppose it wasn't convenient for you to summon Henry Porter? The doctor who's been attending our family for years. What's this new doctor like, Hitty? I must say, you've been keeping him to yourself. I wonder why Compton didn't suggest he attend me while he was away in Vermont." The whine, which could become the twang of an arrow, on a phrase.

Hitty tried to pull the parts of herself inward, the way she'd learned to do as a child. Then, with an attempt at courage, she touched the teapot. "Would someone like their tea freshened?"

"I would," said Fiona, warmly.

They hedged Mother away by talking of Fiona's travels, her writing.

"What's it like to be a published writer?" asked Hitty.

"Can't say as it changes one much," replied Fiona.

"Oh, but surely—!" Hitty heard herself insist.

Emma sliced in. "Hitty used to imagine she could write."

"Oh?" said Fiona. "What did you write? I mean, do you still?"

Hitty blushed. "I just scribble."

"The most awful poems!" said Emma. "I used to find them hidden all over the house when she was a girl. I told her she'd have to stop it. It was making me so nervous. Where she got some of her ideas from—"

"Have you ever submitted anything for publication?"

Hitty weighed whether to answer. She stared at Fiona, licking her lips. "A poem or two."

"Did you receive any answers?"

Hitty shook her head. "Nothing. It's as if they never got them." Her eyes were hot with wanting to weep.

Fiona put her hand out and touched Hitty's. "It's hard," she said sympathetically. "So very hard. How long ago did you send the poems in?"

"Several months ago. In February or early March."

"Ah," said Fiona. "Sometimes they are slow to answer. I'd keep trying. Send to several publications. Not just one or two."

"How did you get published?" Hitty finally had the courage to ask it. The question she'd wanted to know ever since Letty had said her guest was a writer.

"A friend of my father's was an editor and he took an interest in my work," said Fiona. "Maybe I could come back here sometime while I'm still in town. We could talk. I'd like to see some of your work. Before we leave today, why not give me something to read?" Her brown eyes twinkled, encouraged.

Emma snorted. "Hitty, I think it's too bad of you, taking up Miss Macleod's time. You shouldn't take advantage of her kindness."

"But she's not, Mrs. Benedict," said Fiona crisply. "If you remember, I offered. I truly am interested. If I weren't, I would not have asked. So don't blame your daughter."

"There are several short stories," said Hitty softly. "I need to look them over. They weren't written in final form, I'm afraid—" She was terrified. A real writer seeing her work. Could she risk the judgment?

But if she didn't, she'd never know. "I'll get them," she said.

"It's wonderful of you," said Fiona, "to trust me with your work. I consider it an honor."

Funny woman. As Hitty climbed the stairs to the desk where so many of her treasures were stored, she thought about Fiona Macleod. She was truly kind. Maybe she'd misjudged her? Or had Hitty merely been jealous of the woman's success?

Once Letty decided to discard her former ideas of how Fiona should be entertained, it was easy. Tea at Hitty's had been Letty's only concession to convention. Fiona was inappropriate to the eyes of Philadelphia society.

That didn't mean she wasn't precious—of greater value daily. Letty learned to take her easel out under the trees where, beside Fiona, she sketched. Fiona, of course, sketched too. In an entirely different style, drawing broad strokes on her paper after paling it out in tones the background suggested. Blues, greens, and dull brown. Superimposed on this, lines that lent form. Shadows, pulled across a foreground. A tree boldly emphasized by giving dark strength to its trunk. Catching the gaze of a window with a gash of white. Trapping the eye. Transforming color and paper into reality by suggesting dimension.

Letty worked diligently. Beside Fiona, she could put her thoughts, her energy into what she was doing. She approached painting differently. Fiona had learned, with speed holding a timepiece over her, to get down an impression. Letty saw the whole picture. Saw it as she wanted to portray it. Spent effort trying to approximate that picture.

"Oh, Fiona, it's so hard. How do you get it so right without even working at it?"

"Practice. An ugly word, I know. But the more you do it, the easier it gets. Effortless. That's when you can begin to refine." She tapped her paper. "I will work from these sketches when I get home."

Home. Letty heard the word and wondered at its echo. That would break the sense of loneliness, abandonment.

It was silly. She'd known Fiona only a little over a week. Letty knew

311

more about the days she had left than the ones that had passed. These last three were so precious.

Letty had never had a friend. It made her excited and at the same time nervous. That she could say something to somebody and know her question would be taken seriously—her statements valued, instead of being brushed aside. All her life she'd been brushed aside.

She had been so alone until Fiona. When Fiona's ship sailed, the loneliness would all be back. And this time it would be worse because she would understand it.

Frantic, she'd even thought of going with Fiona. Booking passage on the ship. But Mrs. Laetitia Mackenzie of Mackenzie House in Philadelphia had no money. Absolutely none. She'd toyed with the idea of sending Phillips to pawn her jewelry, but she couldn't put him in the position of being apprehended—reported to Nathaniel as a thief. Nat, if she enraged him enough, might allow her to leave. It would be ugly, the scene, but it might be engineered.

Then why didn't she go? Truth, naked and clean, faced her. She was afraid. Fearful of erupting from the role she had played for so many years. Fearful, too, of the waters through which the tiny ship would have to plow. Unequipped with Fiona's courage, Letty thought of the trip with heart pounding, hands clenched to an imaginary deck-rail.

Fiona was coming down the stairs. She was dressed to go out.

"How did you know what I had planned?" Letty asked her.

Fiona seemed disturbed. "Did you have something planned?"

"Of course. It's almost your last day, and I thought we'd drive into the country with our sketch pads and—"

"Oh dear. You see, I've promised your sister." She touched her bag. "I have her writing. I must return it. She's remarkably talented."

"You read it?" said Letty, uneasily.

"Of course. The short stories need revision, but they hold the attention. Definitely good. I thought if we could spend the afternoon —You don't need to come along. In fact, it might be better if I visited without you. That way, we could get down to the stories. With only a little help, she could be pointed in the right direction." Perceptive now. "Oh dear, I've disappointed you, haven't I? There I go again, doing the wrong thing."

"No," said Letty quickly. "It's all right. You go see Hitty. When was all this arranged?"

"Oh, just yesterday. Hitty sent a note to remind me. I hadn't given her as much as a word to go on. We writers are such a sensitive lot." Shaking her head. "It was thoughtless. You and I, we got busy—so many delightful afternoons." Touching Letty on the arm. "Letty, can you forgive me?"

"Don't hurry yourself," said Letty with suppressed anger. "I shall be spending the afternoon with Mother."

"Your mother? Now, that is nice. She'll like that."

Letty watched Fiona drive away. Hitty had sent the carriage for her. Black Jakes with his shining skin at the reins, taking Fiona away from her. She hated him. Yes, Mother would be delighted. A neglected monarch, Emma waited every afternoon for the courtiers who seldom came. Nevertheless, she got herself all dressed up. She had Parkes arrange her thinning strands of hair in a pompadour, deck the wrinkled neck with jewelry, ropy and luminescent. Emma wore all her jewels at the same time.

Seated opposite her mother in the shaded parlor that crushed them with its velvets and its ferns, Letty saw the gem-laden bosom, watched the encrusted fingers toy with an embroidered lace handkerchief.

"So you decided to visit me, Letty." Emma's voice was sharp with reprooof. "Where is that hideous English friend of yours?"

"Mother, she's a writer."

"Well! I'd like to know what sort of people would read her books." Eying Letty closely. "She hasn't left yet, has she? Seeing you're so crazy about her, I wonder you've let her out of your sight."

Letty stared at her mother, then looked away. "She's visiting Hitty today."

"Hah!" Emma pounced. "With Hitty, eh? I suppose she's going to persuade that poor imbecile that she's a writer too." She shook her head. "Letty, we've always known Hitty was fanciful."

"Yes, Mother."

"So this woman who's staying with you—what does she think?"

"About what, Mother?"

"Letty, you seem nervous this afternoon. Is there something the matter?"

"No, Mother." The hands clenching. Neck muscles stiff, aching. A headache on its way.

"Well, stop fidgeting then. Letty, if there's something wrong, you've got to tell me. It's for the best."

"Mother, it's nothing." How many times had she been drawn to confide in Mother and then regretted it bitterly? What was it about Mother? She invited trust—begged for it. Then did something with the knowledge, the secrets put in her hands. They came back to their owner, twisted—subtly damaged.

"What *does* Miss Macleod think of Hitty's work?" her mother asked.

"She mentioned it showed talent."

"Bosh! Oh, this will only put ideas in a head already full of stupid

313

idiocies. Letty, do you think Hitty is having an affair?"

"Mother, how could you even imply such a thing? It's dreadful."

"Now, Letty." The old eyes were cunning. "Listen to me. Your brother-in-law, whom I would trust with my life, has been away for months. Why do you suppose?"

"Is it any of our business, Mother?" Wearily.

"Why, yes. It's definitely our affair. Hitty is your sister, my child. The fact she is going to have an infant and didn't want her husband to know of it all points to one thing. Hitty is suffering from guilt."

"I don't see that at all."

"When you get to be as old as I am, Letty, you will be willing to think the worst of people rather than the best. You've always been a dreamer. Like letting that Macleod woman into your home. Sight unseen. She's leaving soon, isn't she?"

"The day after tomorrow." Heavily. "Mother, do you think we could have something cool to drink?"

"We can, if you just get up and ring the bell. But Letty, it's not hot in here. It's rather a cool day for early June."

Hooper answered the bell. "You rang, madam?"

"Mrs. Mackenzie is feeling the heat. If she could have something refreshing to drink?"

"Nothing for yourself, madam?"

"A glass of water." The dried-up skin must reject liquids now. An opinion, not long in coming. "Letty, I am concerned about you."

"Now, Mother—"

"I know what you are going through. I've seen so many women go through it. In our own family. There was Aunt Carrie Hyde. She went insane. Then there was Cousin Althea Crump. She had to be restrained. A maid in attendance for the rest of her life—but she functioned. Great Aunt Hitty—the one your sister was named for—she took her life." All uttered with satisfaction.

"Mother, I don't want to hear about it." The tears pressing. She would swallow them back. "I only ask that you leave me alone."

"Letty! You are my daughter. My eldest daughter. Whatever concerns you concerns me. I am going to tell you that at this time, I am very, very worried."

Hooper entered, her face set into careful lines. She offered a tray to Letty. One tall glass, stuffed with mint leaves, chips of ice, and two strawberries. Very little fluid. Letty's mouth watered, parched as the side of a house in a dry wind.

"Hooper knows all about the change of life. Tell her, Hooper."

"I don't quite follow you, madam."

"Nonsense, Hooper. Tell her how you suffered."

In a monotone. "I used to have very bad nights. Dreams I was

314

drowning. Madam was kind. She took me to Dr. Porter in her own carriage. Had me take a tonic. It got me through. I was lucky, they said. Very lucky. So many women, madam, don't come out of it. The less fortunate end up in the asylums. Ladies of madam's acquaintance can have help."

Letty spoke in a cracked voice. "Help with what?"

"Dr. Porter explained it to me. It's the energies that would be used for childbearing, madam. They've nowhere to go. It's the way a woman's body goes once it has no more babies to nourish. The ability to give birth, it turns back on itself, into fevers. They rise up until they reach the brain. Once there, they've got no place to go. A woman starts to feel their effects—storms raging inside her brain. It's quite real, Miss Letty." Eyes solemn.

"Heat? Did you say heat—fevers?"

"You're most probably too young to have experienced it yet, Miss Letty."

"Like an inner heat?"

"Exactly. Then it breaks—oh, sometimes you think it never will, but it does. Soaking your arms and your body—begging your pardon for being so outspoken, madam."

She stared at Letty. A faithful old retainer, enjoying her brief moment of glory. "If you ever feel the signs coming on, you go to a doctor, Miss Letty. He'll help you."

"That will be all, Hooper," Emma said. "You've been most helpful."

"Yes, madam." Glancing at Letty. "You make sure you see a doctor, Mrs. Mackenzie. Good gracious, I recall the day you were born. How times flies—" Fingering the tray, unaccustomed emotion. "It's important to let them take care of you at certain times."

"Thank you, Hooper." Emma's voice was kind but firm. "We will ring if we need anything else."

"Oh, yes." Hooper moved quickly from the room.

"Now, Letty!" Emma's voice crackled like beginning thunder. "Surely it is obvious you must see Compton."

"Why Compton?"

"Oh, my dear child, Henry Porter is an excellent doctor in the ordinary way. But Compton Grey has made a study of women's problems. He understands things." Her voice dropped, softness creeping over the stern features. "So many men don't. They regard it as simply hysteria—nonsense. Change of life is real. It can be dangerous—even fatal if a woman takes a notion to kill herself. Promise me you'll see Compton. I've already spoken to him about it."

"What? You had no right!"

"Of course I had a right. The way you've been acting. Nathaniel

315

came to me about a week ago. It was after that dreadful woman arrived. Asked me if I believed you to be ill. I promised him I'd speak to our family doctor. Didn't tell him it would be Compton."

"Mother—" Letty said it hopelessly. She was hedged in. "None of you had any right."

"My own daughter behaving peculiarly enough to have her husband complain about her—"

"Nat always complains."

Emma's eyes were shrewd. "You mean he has before? What is the matter with you, Letty? I thought I taught you girls a man has to be managed. Deceive him with what you are doing if necessary. But never arouse his suspicions. Oh, you are as big an idiot as your sister."

Letty began to gather her things together. "Mother, I must be leaving—" Haste in her movements. She had to get out—to get away —before she learned more. Before she found out what else they'd been deciding for her benefit.

From the picture next to the mantel, her father's painted eyes stared back at her. Funny, she'd never seen before how small his portrait was beside Mother's. In life, he'd been unable to stand up to Emma. In death, he asked forgiveness. Letty felt sadness overwhelm her. So choking, so filled with aching need for an adequate father, she scarcely heard Emma's words.

"Compton only married your sister because he couldn't have you. I've known it all along. He never had to tell me. The way his face lights up when he asks for you. 'Your handsome daughter,' he always says. I've wondered that Hitty hasn't guessed it. Except that she's so stupid."

"What you are telling me makes it all the more important I *not* consult Dr. Grey."

"Oh, Letty, how stuffy. If I were in your place, I'd have an affair with him. After all, that hideous man you're married to can hardly suffice. You need a man who's understanding. Compton told me himself that lack of sexual activity can precipitate all these symptoms you're having." A wave of the hand. "If he were my doctor and if I were his age—I'd make no bones about it. The man fascinates me."

"Mother, did you ever betray Father? Deceive him?"

The old eyes danced. "Now that would be telling! But I'm advising you, Letty, while you're still young. Don't be too prudish."

All the way home, Letty dealt with shock. Passing over her like waves. Awakening her body—her mind—to new possibilities. It was monstrous! She must stop this at once. Put her mind onto other matters.

Nathaniel going to Mother? That terrified her. Not that she could believe everything Mother said. If that were so, could she believe her about Compton? Mother liked to create situations. They pushed back the blankets of boredom that deadened her life. With Father gone, she had little else to do but sit about and sniff out scandal. Create it? At least that way, she'd have front-row seats at the play.

What was there for a woman? A nice woman, reared gently? Of course she was supposed to have no needs "that way." And it was true. Letty was quite sure she never had. Not with Nat. Then why did the idea Compton might be in love with her move her so?

7

It was the day before Fiona would sail. They were having lunch in the dining room, a traditional Sunday lunch that Fiona was managing to eat with relish.

"Roast beef and potatoes—it makes me think I'm at home!" She smacked her lips.

Letty watched Nathaniel wince. He grunted and looked for a newspaper to hide behind. It wasn't breakfast. He would have to put up with them. At least, she knew he was thinking, it's the witch's last day.

With her mouth full, Fiona asked Nathaniel, "Why do you say the trip around the Horn is so dangerous?"

"Grave of ships," he said with gusto. "You're determined to go, I gather?"

"Oh yes. You see, if I survive, I shall have such a story to write."

"And if you don't?" He'd laid his knife and fork down, neatly, across his plate.

"That's between me and my Maker, isn't it? At least it's none of your concern." She regarded him, her eyebrows like two arches on a Roman bridge—thick and unyielding.

"Matter of fact, you're wrong there." Nathaniel had been baiting a trap. He placed his fingertips together, making a steeple over his hardly touched food. "Because, my dear lady, if you are lost at sea, people in this town will say I neglected my duty."

"Gracious!" Fiona filled her mouth with a forkful. Stared at him intently. "Your fault? Oh, come now."

"Miss Macleod, this is a shipping family. We have been deeply involved with boats and cargo ever since this city has been a port.

318

That's a long time, by American standards. Now, you don't think my friends are going to let me off the hook easily for not warning you of the hazards of this voyage?" He glared at her.

Letty understood. Fiona irritated him. Everything she said and did —her manners, her habit of contradicting him whenever he gave an opinion—drove him frantic. Since her arrival, he'd been looking for some reason to take her to task.

"My last article, which will be published soon after I sail, tells how my host and hostess tried to dissuade me. Says it all very plainly." She took a sip of wine. "Delightful Bordeaux. Wine makes a meal, I always think."

"The article must be stopped!" Nathaniel was furious.

"You're not serious?" Fiona put her fork down. "Stop what I've written? Sir, I may be a guest in your house, but I'll take you to court if you plan any such action."

"Did you name names?"

She appeared puzzled. Not flustered, just concerned. "Why of course I did. Hospitality such as yours."

He was uncomforted. Purple. He banged the table. "What did you say about us? I demand to know—what did you say?"

"Why, I've got a copy of the article among my things. You can read it after lunch if you like. It's highly complimentary." She glanced at him. "What did you suspect? Is there something you're trying to hide?"

He was about to explode. His reaction stopped, as if one might stay time. A commotion in the outer hall? "What the devil!" said Nathaniel, switching his fury. His terrible tension was pulsing the ropy veins in his temples, clenching and unclenching his hands.

Taft appeared in the doorway. Something about his appearance made him look in disarray, yet there wasn't a hair out of place. "A person, sir. A person demanding entrance—"

"Stop talking in riddles, man! Out with it."

"Yes, sir. Indeed, I tried to stop him. As a matter of fact, there are two of them, but only one is insisting on coming in. Very obnoxious behavior."

"Well, what does this person want?"

Taft ran his palms over his hair. "Demands to speak with an E. M. Hardcastle, says there is someone staying here of that name."

"Why, it's me they are looking for." Fiona had risen. "My editor must have sent word. Taft, do you have any notion if these people are from the press?"

The butler shook his head.

"The press! You have given the press reason to seek out my home —invade my privacy?" Nathaniel was apoplectic.

319

Fiona had full command of the situation. "Yes, it must be, or they wouldn't have used my penname. If you will excuse me, I will go out and see what it's all about."

Nathaniel pointed at her. "Not in my hallway—they don't cross the entry, mind."

"Nat, it's not fair!" Letty exclaimed.

"Have you gone out of your mind, Letty? Did this impudent female ever ask my permission for any of this? Our name connected with scandal. Outrageous!" His hands were white on the back of his chair.

"She's a writer, Nat. They probably want to ask her about her travel accounts. Couldn't we at least let her talk to them in the parlor? She shouldn't have to speak to them outside."

He shook his head, struggling with frustration. Then he shrugged. She knew, unexpectedly, she'd won. She walked past him carefully.

A young man was standing on the steps, notebook in hand. "—told you'd be a man!" Another, older individual was hovering on the gravel, beyond the entryway.

Fiona seemed unperturbed. "Well, I'm not. I cannot see what that has to do with my ability as a writer."

The young man on the steps looked insolent. "You want me to tell you?"

"I can see little is to be gained by this conversation." The precise English voice. "If there was something specific you wanted to know—otherwise, I'm going back to finish my lunch."

"Wait a minute," said the older one. "What ship're you sailing on? What's your reason for going?"

"If you're as all-knowing as you seem to think you are, you'll find that out, won't you!" Fiona turned around, her head held high. "Please close the door, Taft."

"Mercy!" said Letty, profoundly shocked.

"You see, you have to show them." Fiona's eyes gleamed wickedly. "Shame them. Have no dealings with them. It makes them think twice."

"Does it always work?"

"Unfortunately, no. That's why I protect myself with a penname. E. M. Hardcastle tells nothing about my sex, though it suggests I am male. Both men and women can accept me because they don't have to grapple with the uncomfortable fact that I am a woman. It makes everything easier."

"I see," said Letty. Who saw nothing. She'd always thought of ladies as being bowed into rooms by butlers—doors held open. Gracious treatment was what women merited. Upper-class women, at least. For common women, it would be foreseeable they would be handled less tenderly.

They had returned to the table, their meal cooling.

"Perhaps some hot gravy, Taft?"

"Certainly, madam."

Nathaniel had finished eating. His plate was scraped clean. "Well, I was right, wasn't I?"

"Yes," said Fiona lightly, "you were perfectly correct. I had hoped that this time I would find an exception. But, as usual, they were quite vulgar. I must say, it was wonderful to have the strong arm of Taft behind me."

Nathaniel placed his hands in his lap, satisfaction pulling down the corners of his drooping mouth. "What you get for meddling where a woman has no business," he said sardonically.

Fiona picked up her fork, pushed a cold roast potato over the shining surface of her plate. "One day," she said slowly, "women will penetrate the world of men. They will hold jobs hitherto considered the sacrosanct province of the male. It will come about with difficulty but, once achieved, it will be taken for granted."

"You're mad!" said Nathaniel softly. His lips twitched in amusement. "A crazy old woman—that's what. You deserve to go to the bottom of the ocean and have your bones make food for the fish. At least then you'd serve some purpose." His eyes moved over her lumpish body, her crumpled skirt, her hair that refused to stay pinned.

Letty spoke up. "Nat, your rudeness to a guest in our house overwhelms me."

"No, no, Letty. He should be able to say what he thinks." Fiona gave a small laugh, a sound that was laden with tears. She had set down her fork and was touching her cheek with a wandering hand. "I have given him reason to be disgusted with me."

Nathaniel growled, slumped back in his chair, watching under scowling brows. His amusement was veiled now. Still alive behind his eyes—lurking.

"At least she has the wit to know how she has baited me, Letty. That's more intelligence than I give to you. Both of you acted without either common sense or restraint going out there—giving those men an excuse to say what they wished!" His eyes blazed.

"No," said Fiona evenly, still toying with her fork, "that was just a small incident—an excuse for you to call your wife and me names. Your feelings about me go much deeper. I challenge some of your fondest ideas."

"What nonsense." He pushed his chair back. "I'm tired of waiting for you two to finish your meal. I'm going into my study."

"You aren't able to answer me, are you?" Fiona was like a small dog, growling and standing her ground.

"Miss Macleod, I have already said all I am going to say." He glowered. Amusement washed away. "The subject isn't worthy of pursuit."

"Hah!" she proclaimed. "You do not wish to get into it because you are at a loss for words. You have no well-thought-out ideas on why women should be treated differently from men. You simply assume it should be so. That it was decreed by nature and will always remain thus."

"And so it will!" He pointed a finger under her nose, shaking it with such violence Letty feared he would have a stroke. "You, Miss Macleod, are a monster—an insult to your sex. You go against all laws of man and God—by defying what is right, what is proper, what is—"

"Nat!" Letty had risen from her chair, gone over to him with quick footsteps. His broad, muscular shoulders were quivering in volcanic tremors, his skin suffused, his breath coming in gulps.

"Letty, don't interrupt me!"

"I must!" she said, surprised at herself. "Nat, you must calm yourself—it's not good for you. Come into your study and lie down. Taft, help me."

They got him into the small room across the hall from the dining area.

"Taft, fetch a blanket. And send Bates for the doctor!"

"I don't need a doctor, Letty." He pressed his chest. "It's only indigestion. Just get rid of that woman."

Letty said in a whisper, "I can't ask her to leave until tomorrow. She sails at noon."

He groaned, taking the soda mint she was handing him from the package. "Just keep her out of my sight. You understand?"

On her own decision, Letty sent Bates for Compton Grey. It was a Sunday. She would surely find him at home.

8

Compton and Hitty had finished lunch. They were in the parlor, sitting on opposite sides of the room. The door to the terrace was open. Through it, it was possible to see the partially constructed summer house.

"You assume those niggers know what they're doing?" Compton's voice was nasty. She was surprised to hear him use the term. She'd seen him treat his servants with gentleness, respect.

"They found another colored man to help them. Silas—"

"Hitty, you think I don't know that? You can't keep everything from me, you know."

"Please, Compton, do we have to go into that again?"

"I suppose you are innocent enough to assume I will believe the child is mine?"

"Compton!" Shock waves passing through her body. Had she heard him right?

"I am informed Dr. Schwartzkopf visited here in my absense."

"He agreed to make a house call."

"That what you describe it as?"

"Compton, I wanted professional advice—to confirm I was carrying a child."

His hand came down, flat on the table beside him, causing china and picture frames to clatter. "Then why didn't you call in Henry Porter?"

She licked her dry lips. "Because I thought—foolishly—that you would wish me to see your own partner." Had that been the reason? For the life of her, she couldn't remember why she'd decided against

Henry. Her memory seemed blocked from her.

"You found Dr. Schwarzkopf attractive, I am told."

She had never said such a thing. Who would have twisted her words, making something out of nothing. Mother! It had to be Mother! "You've been talking to my mother," she said unhappily.

"Interesting you should say that—and in just that way." He cleared his throat, twirled the stem of the brandy glass he had picked from the table beside him. When he'd struck the flat surface, the liqueur had slopped. Stains of it marked its sides, seeping back slowly to the main body of the drink, like tidal tongues. He tasted it, savoring the fine flavor.

He was trapping her in something, some hideous lie—and for what? What purpose did it serve him? She knew him well enough by now to understand that he didn't do anything casually. Even her marriage had had its reasons. Nothing to do with love. Compton was incapable of love.

Perhaps she was too—for him. Her hand lingered over her belly, reassuring her that the baby was still there, that the rounding was no illusion.

There were sounds in the hallway. Someone was arriving?

Joseph stood at the door, apologetic. "It's Mr. Mackenzie's coachman, doctor, suh. Mizz Mackenzie, she says the massa been takin' ill. Wants you to come on over, suh."

Compton rose. Startled. "I saw him just yesterday. Had a little indigestion." He turned to Hitty. "No knowing when I'll be back."

When she heard him drive away in the Mackenzie carriage, she left the parlor eagerly and climbed the stairs, a little more slowly than she would have done a month or so ago. She sought her own room.

Hitty read what she had written following Fiona's visit: *She told me I have talent. It has encouraged me so. But then she became serious and said writing is hard work. As if I did not know! She told me there were no guarantees one would ever be recognized. That the odds against being published are impossibly high—especially for a woman. It's why she writes under a penname that implies her to be a man. But she has stories published that are strictly for women, in women's publications. She says that's often luck. Editors believe that women choose to read syrupy material. Fiona feels women enjoy stories that are true to life. But they don't always have the freedom to know that because they read what's available, what they are supposed to read.*

Anyway, her message from one writer to another—yes, she really said that—is to always be true to what's in you. It's much more important in the long run than the recognition would be.

I have so many things I'd like to write about. It's putting them into some sort of form that would be interesting. I mean, a short story can't be just an excuse to expound on deep thoughts.

As Hitty sat there she felt a stirring within her. Involuntary, as separate from herself as a bird on the sill. Yet inside her. Startled, she put a hand to her rounded form. Beneath her palm she felt it again. A movement!

Her child was moving. She sat as though in prayer. Humbled by the knowledge that she was the chalice for this life. She carried life. Until now, the baby had never been quite real. Now it was more real than she could ever have imagined.

She had to tell someone. She left her desk and ran down the staircase into the kitchen.

"Tildie—oh, Tildie."

"Some'pin wrong, Mizz Grey?" Tildie reached for the edge of her cotton apron, to wipe her fingers.

"No, something is very right. I felt life, Tildie. The baby moved!"

The black face seemed not to comprehend for a moment. Then she smiled. "That's right nice, Mizz Grey. Now you know fo' sure you're gonna have a baby."

"Yes," said Hitty, feeling suddenly foolish.

"You mind if I go on with the dishes now, Mizz Grey?" Tildie asked. "Water's coolin'. Won't cut the grease."

Hitty went back to her desk and picked up the pen again: *I felt life. For the first time! I was so joyous I wanted to share it with somebody. It was a mistake. A dreadful mistake. I should have kept it to myself—and my journal. Why is having a baby such a lonely thing? I never knew it till now. Perhaps it's because nobody wants me to have it but me. Compton has said awful things, made horrible accusations. Mother is disgusted—Letty doesn't really care. Though her eyes say I will learn about disappointment. Her tragedies are shadows I try to avoid. Why should my baby be a Warren or a Brett? Anyway, they all have this message for me, whether spoken or not. I was foolish to think of a family.*

It was like her poems. Not really very good, though brought forth in labor. Conceived quietly, as her child. She closed her eyes, shutting away Compton's part in the business.

Tomorrow Fiona was leaving. Going away from them. Would she ever come back? Not quite understanding why, Hitty wept.

9

Compton examined Nathaniel. A clean, careful job of probing and prodding. Letty watched him, admiring the way the neat hands knew where to point, where to touch. Compton smelled warm. An odor like blankets brought in from airing in the sun. His clothes were like himself—beautifully cared for, newly pressed, and without the sharp tang of sweat. No day-old stains ignored on his white shirt front.

"I think we can safely say it was indigestion, Nathaniel. But, as I warned you yesterday, there are things you're going to have to avoid."

"Like what?" said Letty, a serious wife.

"Oh," said Compton hesitantly, "you and I will talk. I am going to give him something to slow him down. He should sleep most of the afternoon."

Nat growled from under the blanket. "It's that woman, Compton —that friend of Letty's. Damn fool writer. Brought the reporters here, smelling her out as if she were a bitch in heat."

Letty winced at the vulgarity. For the unfairness of what he'd said. "She didn't do it deliberately, Nat."

Compton put a hand over hers, warning her. His touch said, "Withdraw from this. Talk to me in private."

"Keep that witch away from me."

"Nat, I've already given you my word. You can have your supper on a tray—in here."

He had pulled the blanket up to his ears. She almost expected to see his thumb in his mouth.

In the parlor, she closed the door behind herself and Compton. Her look questioned him. "How serious?"

"It may have been a warning. Hard to tell in these cases. At any rate, your job is to keep him from getting upset."

She sighed. "Compton, do you realize how difficult that's going to be? I have absolutely no control over Nat. He comes and goes as he sees fit."

"Letty, word has been coming to me—"

Something in his tone? The kindliness was there, yet with an underlying warning. "What word?" she said.

"Now, don't look like that. I don't wish to upset you further. It's just that I want to help. Not only as a physician but as a brother-in-law. More than that. As a friend, Letty, a friend to you and Nat."

"What do you suggest you can do for us?" she asked, her face proud. She placed dignity over her like a shawl.

"It's not Nat I'm worried about," he said evenly. "It's you, Letty."

"Why me?" Was that the underlying current she'd felt?

"I don't feel this is the time or place to talk about it. Yet it needs discussion. Would you come to my office tomorrow? Let me explain some things to you—important matters I need to share with you."

Tomorrow was like a leaden weight hanging over her. She would never get around it. "I'm not sure I can come tomorrow. I have to see my friend off."

"The writer?" His face had closed.

"Yes. Miss Macleod sails tomorrow. The vessel is due to leave at noon."

"I'd like you to come to my office afterward. In the afternoon. You could be the last patient if you like. That way, we could talk without having to watch the clock." His lips were parted. Sensuous?

"If you say so." It was her own voice but it came from a long way off.

He had risen. "Now remember, I'm expecting you. I will leave word with my nurse. Just mention who you are."

"I will be there," she promised.

He laid a warm, firm hand over hers. "Good, Letty. I'll be expecting you."

Fiona was standing in the hallway.

"Fiona, this is my brother-in-law, Dr. Grey. Compton, this is Miss Macleod."

Compton said, "You must be the authoress." He made the word sound obscene. Then without giving her time to go on, he added, "You've met my wife."

"Yes. I spent two very pleasant afternoons with her."

"I know," he said. "She's talked of it. Claims you thought she ought to go on with her writing."

"Indeed, yes!" Said warmly, enthusiastically.

"She's having a baby, you know."

"She told me. But when she has time, I hope she'll go on with her work."

"Her work is being a wife and mother. But then, you're leaving tomorrow?"

"Yes. That's right."

Fiona's creased face was flushed. She straightened her back, then looked at Letty. "I will be upstairs packing, dear. If you need me."

"Yes, of course. I have to see how Nathaniel is. Dr. Grey was on his way out."

At the door Compton said, "Remember, Letty, I will expect you tomorrow."

She nodded. Watched him get into the carriage. Bates had been waiting, to take him home. Home, she thought, to Hitty. She went upstairs to find Fiona.

Fiona's whole mien was thoughtful. "Dr. Grey, Letty, he reminded me rather strongly of someone."

"Ah."

"It was that friend of my father's—the one who 'forced' me." Fiona bit her lip, her eyes sad. "I find I always have trouble with that kind of man. It shows my prejudice."

"What kind of man? I don't understand you. You talk in riddles." Letty felt anger, harsh and grating. It wasn't fair of Fiona to compare Compton with her father's friend. There couldn't possibly be any resemblance.

"Perhaps it's best we don't discuss it. I see I've upset you."

Letty glanced about her guest room. "I see you are all ready to leave?"

"Yes, almost." Fiona sighed. "Oh dear, and this was going to be such a special day. First I've annoyed your husband— By the way, how is he?" There was genuine concern in her voice.

"He's sleeping. Compton administered a draft of something. He's supposed to rest. Which reminds me, do you mind if we have dinner in my morning room?"

"No, of course not. Oh, I see. I'm not to irritate your husband. Isn't that it?"

Letty looked down. "It's not that at all."

"Yes it is. Well, I promise I'll behave. I could even stay at a hotel in the city if you'd prefer?"

"Of course not. Now you're the one being silly. Compton just said Nat's to have rest. I thought trays would be quieter. Nat may sleep anyway, then eat later at his club."

"Letty, you don't deceive me one bit. I've been a fearful nuisance." Fiona sighed. "Well, I'll be on the high seas tomorrow. That should be a relief to all of you."

"Please." Letty begged it. But she knew her eyes betrayed her. It would be a relief. Why did Fiona upset people so? Hitty hadn't liked her at first. Mother detested her. All the men, with the exception of the Reverend Mr. Evans, a fellow countryman, couldn't stand her. In some way Fiona threatened them. With her baggy clothing, her scarred boots, her seeming refusal to pay attention to female frippery. They didn't know what to do with her.

"If you're finished packing," Letty said, "I could order some tea for us." An attempt to make up. After all, tomorrow she would sip her tea alone. She regretted spoiling these last moments with Fiona. "Come on down when you want to. I'll send for a tray. Cook was going to attempt your scone recipe."

"Oh then, by all means," said Fiona.

Perhaps Fiona would drown on the voyage. Or meet a sea captain who would devastate her? But no. Fiona would go on being Fiona— sketching views, making notes, wearing her disreputable clothes.

Letty went down the hall to her morning room. The sun had come out from behind a cloud. Perhaps, later, she and Fiona would walk in the garden. Admire the last of the roses.

10

The ship was so small!

"To go around the Horn! All the way to California!" Letty kept saying it while she followed Fiona down to her cabin. Apparently there were very few passengers.

"There will only be three others besides myself. I booked the passage while still in England. It's a *British* steamship line. They mainly deal in cargo," said Fiona pleasantly.

Letty was staring at the cabin, far smaller than the one she'd shared with Nat across the Atlantic. And heaven knows, that was confining. As she took it all in, a bent-shouldered woman with a face the color of skim milk entered. In her arms she carried a fractious child.

"Is this where we sleep?" the woman asked in a dragging voice.

"It's one of the two passenger cabins," said Fiona brightly.

"There, Timmy, we're going to share a bedroom with this nice lady, I'll be bound." She sat down, releasing the tow-headed youngster to her lap.

Fiona smiled and got on her knees to meet the child at eye level. "I can see we're going to get on famously!" The boy grinned shyly.

"My husband's a missionary," said the woman as if it hurt her to talk. She seemed so tired.

"Are you sailing all the way to California?"

The woman nodded.

"I think it's time I left the ship." Letty felt unexpected panic. As though, should she tarry one moment longer, they would set sail without warning. Trapped, she'd have to stay on this boat, be tossed about by seas and wind all the way to its destination—wherever that

330

might be. Possibly at the bottom of the ocean.

"Must you go so soon?" Fiona's brown eyes pulled at her. One capable hand touched Letty's arm. "Yes, I can see you must. All this is making you nervous. I'll come up on deck." She bent to the child. "Be back before long—right?"

Letty's heart tugged. Why was Fiona like that? It was similar to the way she'd insisted on saying good-bye to the servants. None of them expected it. It just wasn't done. Letty felt embarrassed for Fiona.

Taft hadn't approved. "Good-bye, Miss Macleod." The set face. Taft knew how to rebuke without uttering a word.

None of it had bothered Fiona.

Letty walked up the creaking stairway. Feeling the familiar, pricking surface of the rope against her hand.

"Now," said Fiona, when they were on deck, "you keep on with that painting and drawing, mind?"

"Yes," said Letty, her thoughts elsewhere.

"And," Fiona went on, "I wrote Hitty a little note. I knew you'd see she got it. She wanted to come to see me off, but in her condition—well, there you are, anyway." She placed the note in Letty's palm.

A sailor moved past, intent on his work. Were they making ready to sail? Letty looked about wildly for the gangway. It was still in place. But a puff of black smoke disgorged itself from the tall, narrow stack, urging her to disembark.

"Good-bye, Fiona dear."

"Oh, Letty, take care of yourself." Sudden worry in Fiona's voice.

"Me? I'm staying here. It's you who are setting off on a journey."

"I know." Fiona's voice was low with some struggle. "But I can take care of myself."

"I can too," said Letty.

Fiona released her from a hugging embrace. "I wish I felt sure of that. Oh my, here I am fretting like an old mother hen." She gave Letty a gentle shove. "Go on with you now. Get off the ship before you have a nervous spasm." She laughed, a gnome quality to the tanned face, the puckish frown.

Letty forced herself to concentrate on the gangway. It was a swaying chute that stretched over the maw of the waters. If she looked down at anything, anything except the slats of wood, she knew she'd get sick to her stomach. She stepped slowly, deliberately, her heart pounding a fierce accompaniment, until at last she was on land again.

Only then did she permit herself to turn about and wave at Fiona.

The ship slid away at last. Slowly at first, while Fiona and the missionary family, who'd appeared suddenly on deck, called unintelligible messages to friends below.

Fiona's face was indistinguishable now. Was that her waving?

Letty watched, her arm sore. Then she waved again. Did Fiona see her? Did she know? Feeling she was letting her friend down, she allowed her arm to drop to her side.

Letty pushed her way through the crowd on the dock to reach her carriage. Her relief at seeing Bates was enormous.

"Where to, madam?"

"Home, I think. Cook was going to keep lunch."

She ate alone—cold chicken left over from last night, creamed peas fresh from the garden, potatoes swimming in butter. She toyed with the food. She ate some strawberries, tasting their sweetness and wishing, poignantly, that she were sharing them with Fiona.

She rang for Taft. "Please see that the children have some berries too."

"Very good, madam. Bates asks, do you need the carriage this afternoon, madam? You said you'd let him know."

She glanced away. Would she keep her appointment with Compton? "Tell Bates I won't be needing him."

"Very good, madam."

She pushed her chair back and left the dining room. In the parlor it was still and fragrant as a bouquet of flowers. Her own portrait smiled down at her. How long ago had it been since she had stood in this spot waiting to meet the famous lady authoress coming from Boston?

She glanced at herself in the mirror. The face that looked back was still handsome. The wings of hair at her temples were dark brown and smooth. Here and there a hint of gray.

She smiled as she recalled her shock when she'd first seen Fiona. Well, it was one of those odd friendships—brief and intense—for they'd talked of many intimate matters. She drew in her breath sharply and turned away from the great gold-framed mirror. She was ready to go upstairs.

In her morning room, against the wall under the window, Fiona had left a painting. Letty recognized it at once. It was the one she'd sat for, which Fiona would never let her see. There it was. Letty, as Fiona saw her.

But I'm not that pretty, Letty thought. She's made me look clever somehow. Odd, because intelligent women usually have no looks. Did she see me that way or was she trying to flatter me?

A note was pinned to the picture: *Letty, dear. This is my surprise. It's the way I picture you. You have so much to give—an inner light. I'll treasure your friendship always. Fiona.*

Letty stared at the portrait. *An inner light.* No one had ever seen anything like that in Letty.

She began to cry, soundlessly at first. Then sighing, audible sobs. Weeping away the sorrow, the sense of blanketing loss. For what?

A voice from the past, kindly and caring. Not Fiona's—much further back than that. "You have real talent. If only I weren't being sent away." Miss Sprules. Letty had never seen her again. The poke bonnet, the shawled shoulders, firm and narrow—Miss Sprules had been a tall woman—the tightly booted feet, descending the staircase, away from the schoolroom.

Letty and Hitty close momentarily, perhaps for the only time in their lives. Clutching at each other.

"Letty, she's not coming back, is she? I mean, ever?"

"No, Hitty. No, she isn't. Mama has dismissed her."

"But she said she'd write! She will, won't she?"

"If she said she will, she will. Miss Sprules always keeps her word."

They'd shared their notes when they came. Then the notes stopped coming. No word at Easter. Nothing for Hitty's birthday in early June.

Mama, coming into the schoolroom, looking like a messenger. "I heard today from Miss Sprules' employers."

"Miss Sprules! You heard! How is she?" Chorusing.

Emma clutching her handkerchief. "I hope you aren't going to be unpleasant about this. Miss Sprules—well, she died. In a hospital."

"Oh no!" It was a protest that had echoed in their heads. Like a bell that clanged too loudly.

Emma no comfort. There never had been any in the stiff body, the wire-like arms. "I asked you not to make a fuss—"

Letty cutting through her mother's protests. "How did she die? How did Miss Sprules die?"

Emma pursing her lips. "Something growing inside her. Nasty. Spinsters are prone to these things."

She'd left them speechless and white. Not able to comfort each other. Miss Sprules—severe and prim—but loving.

Weeping now, Letty felt it all over again. What was wrong with her, dredging up the past? She sat down in one of the two lemon silk chairs and found herself trembling, her face flushed with more than crying. The dreaded heat again, surging like furnace flames, was consuming her from the inside out. She tugged at the fabric of her dress. It surely couldn't be all herself? It was the room! It was growing so hot! Late June, slipping into July. Nobody should be asked to stand such temperatures.

The tide of warmth broke. Like a lava flow, pouring black and glowing down the mountain of her body. Consuming her, first with its fury, then with the rivers of perspiration that soaked her clothing. She felt dizzy. The room shifted slightly, as if some hand had reached up to move it. Her body was melting. She put her hand to her face, feeling the pounding of her heart through her whole being.

Downstairs, the great English clock chimed three.

Compton! She'd keep the appointment with Compton. She hadn't sent word to tell him she'd not be there. In a panic, she rose from her chair and rang her bell.

Norah was staring at her.

"Please tell Bates I shall need him after all."

"Very good, madam. When should I tell him for?"

"At once. He must bring the carriage around at once. Summon Nanette too—I need her."

Letty turned away. She must hurry, she must hurry. Compton could help her. He must be her friend. Know what was wrong with her, cure her if necessary. But of what?

II

Compton came toward her, hand outstretched. "Ah, Letty. I was afraid you'd changed your mind." He indicated a chair.

"Oh no," she lied. "I had decided to see you." She looked around the office furtively. Light, mahogany furniture. A seascape on the wall —all blue and aquamarine. Behind his desk, an oil painting of a forest —muted, as if hushed with bird calls.

"Nice," she said approvingly. "Your office. It has great appeal."

"I'm glad," he responded, lighting his pipe. "I have mostly female patients, you see."

The flame Compton applied to his pipe flared as he puffed the tobacco into a glow. The light pushed shadows away from his face, making it seem kindly. Lines she hadn't noticed before—of aging— about his mouth. The inexorable mark of time. Did he feel it as she felt it?

"So," he said slowly, "how do you feel today?"

"Why today?" She said it edgily, on guard for no real reason.

"Your friend has gone, I presume."

"Yes," she said quietly.

"Nathaniel was here today."

"Yes, he told me this morning he would see you. How did you find him?"

"He's all right." Then, as if needing courage, "Letty, it wasn't a casual reason I had for asking you to stop by."

"What are you trying to tell me, Compton?" Her eyes challenged him.

"Letty, may I speak plainly?"

335

"Of course." It was what she'd been waiting for.

"I regard you as an almost perfect woman."

"What?" The statement was so unexpected. She'd thought he was going to tell her about her time of life. About—about anything but how he felt about her.

He repeated himself carefully. "Almost perfect. As near perfection as any woman I've seen."

"You can't be serious?" She felt her face flush, but it was from something strange and rare.

"I have never been more serious about anything in my life." He watched her, his mouth tightening on the pipe. His eyes held secrets.

"Compton, I came here to ask you to help me." Conscious of rebuking him, showing him their roles.

"How can I help you? Anything, Letty. Anyway at all."

He was smiling at her, and she felt terribly alone. "Compton, I came here to ask you— I have these symptoms—"

"Nonsense, my dear." He put his pipe down and placed his hands flat on the table between them. "You are healthy as a horse, Letty. I have observed you over a considerable time. Adored you from afar." Then, as she started back, alarmed, "You are a magnificent woman!"

She gasped. "I didn't come here to hear you say things like this. You are married to my sister—"

"I should have been married to you."

She was quiet. There was nothing to say. She would leave soon. Never come to this place again. To her chagrin, she began to cry.

"I didn't mean to upset you. I'm afraid I spoke too hastily. I've been dreaming of this for so long."

"I must go now."

He looked up. "No, you can't. Not until you tell me why you came. There was something you wanted me to do for you."

"I started to explain it to you. I came because I have these symptoms."

"What symptoms?" For the first time, he seemed to have heard her. He looked annoyed. "You aren't ill! Your skin is like peach bloom —your eyes are healthy—your appearance—"

"Compton, I am said to be in the change of life."

He stared at her. His expression heavy, unbelieving. At last he said, "If you need a physician, I can recommend an excellent one. My partner—"

"Yes," she said, "I think that would be best. Do you suppose he would see me?"

His face was vague, his attention unconnected with what she was saying. "I don't understand you," he said slowly. "I believed you cared—"

"Of course I am fond of you as a brother-in-law."

"Not that way!" He said it with hardness. Ice in his eyes.

There was a tap at the door. It was the nurse who guarded the outer office. "I'm going now, doctor. Unless there was something else?" Her gaze wandered to Letty.

"Thank you, Miss Soames. Mrs. Mackenzie and I can manage quite well, I believe."

"Very good, doctor. I'll see you in the morning."

Letty wished she were the nurse. So poised and self-sufficient. Leaving.

He spoke at last. "There hasn't been much between you and Nathaniel for a long time, has there?"

"I hardly think—"

"I'm making it my business. You see, I want you. What's more, I think these 'symptoms,' as you call them, are connected with your body." Just as any woman, you need to be loved. By a man."

"Thank you," she said crisply, polite as a china shepherdess, "for taking the time to see me. If you will submit your bill, I feel sure Nat will pay it."

"I am being rebuked."

"Yes," she said. She had risen. "I came to you for help, and all I receive are advances. From my own sister's husband!" Her nostrils flared with indignation.

"So. You are going to wait to dry up. Like an old woman. Isn't that what you have in mind? Surely you cannot imagine that Nat deserves your loyalty?"

"Leave Nat out of this."

"Letty, he sleeps with a new woman every night."

"I don't want to hear about it." Cheeks flaming.

He had risen again. He came around from behind the desk—to place himself within reach. "Are you going to deny yourself—and my love—forever?"

Letty stared at him. What was he like with Hitty? Had he wooed her in the same way? It was appealing to toy with the idea that she could believe his flattery. She represented a need to conquer—even within the forbidden limits of family. Yes, he was handsome, and he was a man. But he wasn't what she needed.

He stepped back a pace. "I thought I knew you," he said. "You were a woman set apart. Now I see I was mistaken. I owe you an apology. I made a mistake in offering you my love. I thought you had courage. I should have known, with a mother like Emma Benedict and a sister like Hitty." Sneering in his tone.

"I can see myself out," she said with dignity.

"Nonsense. At least you can let me do that for you."

He moved past her to open the door. When he was alongside her, he wedged her in between the desk and the wall. Pressing her against himself.

"No, please."

"Yes!" He clasped her. Not violently, not in any sense she could have used as an excuse.

She wanted to scream for someone to save her. Conscious that the nurse was gone, that the building was probably empty, that it was late in the afternoon and they could dally here undetected. She had instructed Bates to wait on Nathaniel, certain that she could get a hansom to take her home. Why hadn't she told Bates to wait?

She felt his lips on her cheek, her neck. His nearness was powerful. Her only contact with a man had been with Nathaniel. Demanding, boastful, approaching her as if she were an object. She was a person. She knew that now with poignancy. She wanted to melt into him and forget herself. Yet that was wrong.

He was suffocating her will. His body smell was all she could breathe, his touch all she could feel. Buoyant—responsive—letting his mouth play on hers. Her breasts moving against his coat, her thighs whispering that she open herself.

Violently, she pulled herself away. "No! This is wrong. This is terribly wrong."

It was. More especially, it was what he had done to her inner self. Awakened a lithe animal that lived within her—still all these years. A female cat with smooth flanks and panting mouth, that wished to entice the male. She was no better than a whore!

She straightened her coat, not meeting his eyes. She was at fault. Had he not said that he had watched her for a long time? Something she carried, like a dormant disease, had alerted him. She was vile. Not sick, she was disreputable—unworthy of her sex. Was this why Nathaniel had always been so scornful with her?

Compton took her wrists, imprisoning her. Ah, but really it was she who had captured him. Poor man, he had no idea. She was able to meet his eyes now.

"You liked it," he insisted. "For a moment, you wanted me to hold you."

"I know," she said. "I behaved disgracefully. Now, please let me go. Call a cab."

He held on to her wrists. "Disgraceful? Letty, you've got it all wrong. We could be together this way—here and now. There would be no harm. I am a doctor. It would be for your own good."

She stared at him. "I try to behave like a lady—I always have."

He laughed, dropping her wrists and tugging her to him. "You live the way you've been taught. It doesn't mean to say that's the only

338

way. My God, Letty, don't you want to experience anything at all before it's too late?"

She quivered. Passive in his embrace. "Please, I beg you to let me go. For both our sakes."

He pushed her away. "Why did you come here?"

"It doesn't matter."

"I think you came so that this could happen."

"No!" She thrust her indignation at him like a lance. "I came because I imagined you could help me. I know now I was wrong. Utterly wrong."

His face became impassive. "You will return to me," he said smoothly. "I have made sense to you. Think it over, Letty. We could even go away together—I know a place that would be beautiful this time of year."

"And what about my sister?"

His nostrils distended. "She has gotten herself with child. I am almost positive the infant is not mine. She has made a cuckold of me."

She gazed at him with horror. He'd gone mad. Hitty might be a lot of things, but unfaithful she was not. Like Letty, she was incapable of it. She bit her lip. Incapable? How near had she come to taking just that step—minutes before?

"You have proof of this?" she asked.

"What makes you think I need it?" His gaze was heavy. She read pain in it and wanted to comfort him, to say the right words.

He read her willingness. Came to her. She was the one to hold him now.

It was another woman he led from around the desk. She watched him, as in a dream, help her out of her coat. She knew that her dress was damp from her own torrents, that a river flowed between her breasts, and that the odor of lavender with which her clothes were permeated must be mingled with another scent. Herself.

Another woman in her body tugged at his clothing. His shirt became unbuttoned. His chest was different from Nat's. The hairs were lighter in color, silken and soft. She laid her cheek against them. "I can hear your heart beating." This other woman, who was behaving so extraordinarily, laughed.

He bent his face and kissed her full on the mouth. With one hand undoing the rest of his clothing so that it slipped to the floor. Leaving him bared to her, showing her his need.

He lifted this woman she had become and placed her on the couch. "I adore you," he said. He stepped backward slowly, not removing his eyes from her body. Behind his back and with sure dexterity, he turned the key in the door.

He was at her side instantly. Cupping her breasts, stroking her thighs with his fine hands. "Don't be afraid." His voice warm.

He tipped her chin so that he could reach her lips. His tongue parted them, swift and inquiring as an asp's head. It seemed to impart venom to her, compelling her to give up resistance. Again her thighs waited for him—this time with impatience.

But he wouldn't release her yet. His hands spoke to her body, calling forth a wisdom she had not known she'd had. The cat within her purred, flowing in milky abandon, into contours that were not her own. The last of her clothing was gently teased from her flesh, she wasn't quite sure how. Each time her breathing sharpened, he would soothe her. "This is what you need—why you are starved—I have known since I first set eyes on you. I will make you over—you will be more splendid than you have ever been."

"Yes," she heard herself murmur. Odd, the voice came from her throat? Her lips? Surely, not from her mind?

He parted her then. Not entering yet. Placing her as he wanted her, hips raised so that she was split for him—a ripe grape that spills itself, tender and juicy. Astonished at herself, that she had become lubricated for him. Without Nanette to apply the ointment.

He could not hurt her. He slipped in so easily, it was as though she were designed for him—for that hardness which she craved, which sought out her inner depths. She received him, waiting for him to thrust deeper, to penetrate her utterly, while her legs closed about his waist and she moaned with pleasure.

With pleasure.

She shivered violently and at the same time he filled her. She laughed and began to weep at the same time. Tears of amazement flowing down her face.

"My love," he said, looking down at her. "You see—I was what you needed."

"Yes," she said softly. "You are right."

He pulled himself out tenderly. "Not every male understands women as I do. I think you have found me to be a specialist."

She had gone cold then. Saw herself through her own eyes lying naked and exposed on his silken couch. Pillows at her back, beneath her thighs. Having given way to him, permitted this disgusting display of looseness to occur. She was damned forever. She and how many other women? He was a "specialist."

She grabbed for her clothes, pulling them over her in a futile attempt to hide her wantonness, her hideous betrayal of what she had been—a pure woman, a wife faithful to her husband.

"How many women have you seduced?" she asked levelly, her voice frigid.

"Letty, Letty. That is unfair of you. It is you I adore. I am no virgin," he confessed. "But then, you yourself are married."

"Yes." She lowered her eyes.

"Do you really feel Nat deserves your loyalty—your denial of your own needs? I know something about Nat. He's a cold bastard. Sadistic —utterly unfeeling. I wonder how you've stood him so long."

He was stroking her. Everything he said was what she needed to hear. That she was loved, that she was safe with him. She trembled for him, pressed her flesh against his and invited him to explore her again.

This time he entered her more quickly. Thrusting deep, with the movements she wanted to take and make her own. Enclosing his flesh so that he was all hers. She would never allow him to leave. She shuddered and broke suddenly into a spasm that was so violent it terrified her. From a long way away, she heard him laughing. As if he'd achieved a victory.

She clung to him, digging into his shoulders with her nails. "Am I dying?"

"No, no," he whispered. "It's all right. You will be well now. I have restored your youth."

Uncomprehending, she felt him begin to move in her again. Once more the spasm. This time slower, like a stone thrown in water— ripples spreading to touch the farthest shores of herself. She was at peace.

After they had moved apart, she asked him, "What was that you said? What happened to me?"

He kissed her lightly on the lips. "The next time we are together this way, I will explain. For today, you have had enough."

"Yes," she said, a small child who is being instructed. The next time? She shook her head. "Today was—was unplanned. I hadn't meant—"

"Do we have to go into all that again? Look." His fingers had found her nipple. They played over it, inducing it to press against the fabric. "I have a place to meet that is better than this." I will write the address on a piece of paper. When you've memorized it, it would be as well to tear it up."

"But how shall I come to see you? Bates would wonder."

He kissed her on the end of her nose. "You will have him bring you to the office. Then the nurse can summon a hansom."

"The nurse, she will know?"

He smiled soothingly. "We have to trust someone. She has been with me a long time. Believe me, you can rely on her."

"When do you want me to come to this place?"

"Tomorrow," he said, as if it had been settled a long time ago.

341

She put the piece of paper in her reticule after reading it briefly. "125 Cedar Street." An easy address to remember. It was already engraved on her heart. "What time?"

"The same time as today. I will be there instead of here."

When he put her into a hired carriage, she heard him tell the coachman her address in the same daze she'd heard everything. He was polite and discreet out there in the street. His eyes alone signaled.

She leaned back against the soiled seats. She felt sleepy. Only her blood was awake, pulsing wildly.

12

She despised herself—as she did every time. And he made her wait an eternity before he came to the door. Why did he take so long? Did he wish to humiliate her?

It couldn't be. There he was, standing in the doorway, pulling her in, toward himself. Behind her, the hired carriage was moving away.

She was within the house. Safe. But today it wasn't quite like that. She had something to tell him. Something about herself that could only disgust. She even smelled her odor as he helped her out of her light coat. August! How hot it was! Was it really just a month since they had started to be together this way? She bowed her head, her mouth full of saliva. Wanting him. Knowing that in her condition she could not have him. Weak with being denied.

"My love—something is wrong?" He had taken her hand. "You are cold? Are you ill?"

She smiled. "It is my time of the month."

He didn't move, but she could feel that he had stiffened. Some kind of excitement. "I am glad you didn't stay away."

"Are you? But we can't—?"

He led her into the small parlor. The first time she had seen it, it had been a shock. Now she was used to it. She stared at the couch. Pink and lascivious, it beckoned, its velvety covering enhancing the shell shape. Pearly pillows tossed in a heap. The carpet was all red. It flowed to the edges of the room like blood. Met scarlet curtains, damask and heavy as musk.

She had seen the upstairs. It, too, was dewy with longing. One bed, made up solely with counterpane. Cushioned—an oyster shell.

They used it sometimes, reveling in its mothering womb. It enclosed them, as she delighted to enfold him, holding him to her in an embrace that claimed eternity.

He led her to the couch. She paused there, fearful that by sitting on it she would leave a stain from herself. From that portion that dirtied her—made her untouchable. She wanted to cry for the shame of it—for the denial of pleasure. She swallowed convulsively.

"I'm afraid I may soil the silk."

"Then kneel," he said unexpectedly. With laughter. He was happy! She could see it now—wildly happy.

She obeyed him at once, kneeling on the blood-red rug. A courtier, obeisant before her monarch.

He had it out. Fully clad, he had his maleness out. His trousers slid like a sheath to the floor. He beckoned her to come nearer. "You can at least kiss me."

She bent forward, cupping her hands. Taking its full, soft butting end to her lips.

He sighed. "Go on—don't stop."

She did as she was told, his tension communicating itself to her through his moaning, the way in which he was so hard, so erect. "More —more." She stroked him with her hands, her fingers moving through the short, golden hairs from which his glory sprang.

Suddenly, he thrust himself deep between her lips. She was shocked and appalled at what he was trying to get her to do. To hold him in her mouth! She tried to move away from him.

"No!" he said. "Don't move. You can still have the same pleasure, even though it might seem strange."

She stared at him. Uncomprehending. She had never heard of such. She was confused—frightened even.

He bent down, lifted her chin, and placed his mouth over hers. It was reassuring in its familiarity. She tried to push aside her own excitement. Not today—not for her.

"Why should you reject me?" he murmured. "We are both beautiful people. All clean—all our parts. Even the most secret."

"No." She shook her head, speaking as his lips sought her, moving under them. "No, I am ashamed of my body when it is like this."

"So what if you are?" he whispered. "Come. You shall show me how you feel about me."

"I worship you."

"No." He shook his head, "I think not. Otherwise you would have allowed me to place myself inside you as I asked. Instead you pushed me away. You must feel I am only lovable if I approach you in the customary way."

344

She gazed back, wide-eyed with shame. "What should I do? Should I kneel for you?"

He nodded. "But first, what have I done to be deprived the sight of your breasts?"

She undressed partially, keeping her lower self hidden. Then she sank to her knees, as he had bidden. At once he came to her, asking her to place his engorgement between her rounded orbs. It seemed to afford him some excitement. He was panting slightly.

"Now—now, kiss me—like before."

She thought it would never end. Her body stiff and held at an awkward angle—nearly choking—while he went wild with what he was experiencing. An inner, secret lusting that she couldn't share. Intimate as they were being, she was shut out.

Used. It was the first time she'd felt it so. It astonished her. So different from what she'd known before. He was a stranger, towering over her.

At last he was finished. "I have filled you with my potency," he said. "It is the same."

It wasn't. Perhaps it never would be.

She dressed silently, quickly. He had gone to wipe himself. He was always so clean. She had liked that about him. Yet always before she had enjoyed the odor of what they had brought about. She fancied it remained on her clothes. She would change when she got home, not allow Nanette to attend her. She would press her underwear to her nostrils, inhaling it, taking him in as she had before. Her own odor, different, mingled with his starch smell. Sweet and damp fresh. Rolling from her to be trapped by an eager hand. Once she had tasted it— warm, viable.

Now she knew its savor more fully. It would never leave her. She could close her eyes and be a hundred miles away. It would remain on her tongue, entwine itself about her teeth, close the back of her throat. Choking.

He pulled at her arm, demanding she look at him. "It was the same!" he protested.

She didn't answer. Swallowed convulsively. Was it just what they had done? Or was it something else?

He pushed his mouth over hers. "You're funny today. I suppose it's because it's your time of the month. It makes the female irritable."

"Female?" She pulled away. Stared at him, flushed with anger.

"Well, you are female." He leaned over, flicked at one of her nipples. "Aren't you?"

Her fury made her hot. She took a step back, glaring at him. "You are never to treat me that way again."

"What? You liked it. You like pleasing me. You said so yourself."

"Not that way."

He grew white suddenly, his mouth small, like a tightened purse. He raised his hand as if he were going to strike her. "Don't ever refuse me, Letty. I can ruin you."

"What?" She wasn't sure she'd heard what he said. She stared at him, seeing a stranger.

"I said, don't refuse me what I ask. I can force you to do whatever I want."

"You're serious, aren't you?"

"Perfectly. You came here of your own free will. My nurse will testify that it's not the first time you've sought me out."

"You seduced me," she said icily, fear claiming her.

"Ah, Letty," he chided her. "You came to me for help. Remember?"

She was silent.

"And I gave it to you. Have I not given you of myself every time you've asked? Have I not made you strong again? Look at yourself in the mirror." He led her over to it. "A young woman! Alive and beautiful. Have I not nourished you, Letty?"

Tears of rage sprang from her eyes. He was so arrogant! Why had she never seen it until today? She wanted to kill him.

"Enjoy your youth, Letty. It must end sometime."

"I despise you. Let me go. I am leaving, at once."

"No," he said. "You want me. You will return and return until I am sick of you. For that will happen. I cannot give myself too long to any woman. Once they bore me, it's over."

She hit him—striking aimlessly, futilely. Just wanting to vent her rage, her humiliation.

He pushed her to the floor, the blood-red floor. "I don't find you uninteresting when you are this way, Letty. In fact, you stimulate me." He tore her linen paddings aside. Her white thighs were exposed, as they had been bared so many times for him—but willingly.

It hurt her. She pained deeply, as when in labor, feeling him in the small of her back. His maleness was an infant, clamoring to be brought to birth, as all mankind are born, ripping apart the womb that has housed them. She waited for the stone to drop, the clock to strike, that the vibrations might ripple their way from her center until they reached her extremities, gaining her farther shores with light running fingers.

She waited. Waited for the moment—the death spasm—that would free her.

He pulled out. Bloodied and defiant, he lay over her, laughing. "You need me. But you can't have me. I am going to punish you."

"Please—" Hating herself, she begged him. She was walking along a high wire from which she would fall if—

"Beg me!" He was tremulous with triumph.

"Please?"

"That's better. Now don't ever try to defy me, you hear?"

She nodded. Waited.

He delivered himself into her. The rock fell. She exploded over herself—covering him while he accepted her humiliation.

"Now, you are not to visit here unless I send for you."

Numbly she heard him. She'd forget him. Slice him out of her life with the knife blade of her resolution. No longer would she permit this degradation. She had only to stay away. It would be as easy as that.

"But when I send for you, you are to come?"

Had she imagined the slight query replacing the note of command? She didn't answer him.

He grabbed her chin, looking down on her. Then he laughed. "I don't have to worry. A few days away from this and you'll answer my summons. You won't be able to do without me."

"What if I tell Hitty?"

"Your own sister? To begin with, she wouldn't believe you. Whereas Nat would. Letty, you are the one who has much to lose."

"It's all changed," she said dully.

"No it hasn't," he countered. He licked his lips. "It's just grown more delicious."

The heat was insufferable. Madame Blanche's girls hung about the fire escapes like washing set out to dry. Their blouses unbuttoned, sleeves rolled high.

"How's your doll?" Rose asked Angelique.

"Why does she carry dolls about?" Ellie got it in before they could warn her. Angie could be dangerous.

"Delphine's been right poorly," Angie said. She had a small face, delicate and defined with tiny features. A child's mouth. Brown eyes with an odd light in them. One moment she could be singing, sweet as a lullaby—the next whirling about, scissor blades flashing in her fingers.

Sometimes Rose wondered why Madame Blanche kept her on. Angie really only had one customer—Mr. Mackenzie. And sometimes Dr. Grey. He'd come to play with her after she'd misbehaved.

Had a way with her, did Dr. Grey. He had a way with all of them if he wanted to. It was the arrangement set up between him and Madame Blanche. Rose had been here longer than most of the girls. She'd seen the arrangement grow.

Of course it was convenient to have a doctor. Come when they needed him, no questions asked. At any rate, Dr. Grey and Madame were friends.

"Sorry to hear Delphine's been poorly," said Rose. Angie was edgier than usual this afternoon. Sometimes they had to tie her till she got over it. Generally, just shutting her up in her room with her dolls worked. How many dolls did Angie have?

Mr. Mackenzie wouldn't use any of the other girls though. He seemed to think Angie was special. Not that he hadn't been warned.

"I don't want to be responsible should something happen, Nathaniel." Madame always called her best customers by their given names. No one could have gotten away with it but Madame Blanche.

"Now, Blanche, I told you not to be concerned. Angie appeals to me. I tame her."

Blanche had laughed, like distant thunder. Rose could hear the worry under it.

Rose stared at Angie and sighed. How long before she did some real harm? Killed a customer? Or one of them? Shivered, recalling the night last winter. Angie had gotten into bed with her. They often did that—all the girls. For warmth, a bit of comfort. After all, it wasn't as if they had much of a life here. You could hardly cuddle with the customers.

Rose had felt Angie slip into the big bed. The trouble was, Marie was in there too. The two of them wrapped about each other, snug and relaxed, arms entwined. Marie hadn't wakened when Angie lifted the covers.

Rose had raised her head. "That you, Angie?"

"What's she doing in here?"

"Hush. Just get in quiet. Room for all three of us. Here, come on round to my side. I'll hold you."

Rose had put her arms about Angie. Feeling the trembling. She stroked the dark hair, the smooth limbs, until the quivering ceased. Angie's breathing became even. Was she asleep? Did Rose dare rest? You never knew with Angie in the room.

Rose had dozed. Giving way to the exhaustion that the early morning hours entitled them to—after the last customer had left.

Suddenly, there'd been a scream. It was Marie. Angie had crept out of bed and pounced on the girl from the other side. Sunk her teeth into her shoulder—hanging on. A panther, with those strange brown eyes that could turn gold in a certain mood.

Dr. Grey had had to be called. The bite of another human being was perilous he'd said. Word traveled the House like a bad smell. Marie might get sick—worse than sick. Surely Madame would see the sense in sending Angie away?

Madame hadn't. There were those who said Angie's father paid Blanche an enormous sum of money to keep the girl. Certainly Madame retained all of Angie's earnings—except a few pennies for trinkets. Madame managed the rest. Kept Angie in clothes, the necessaries. And dolls.

Mr. Mackenzie brought her dolls too. Perhaps that was why she hadn't done him any harm. Yet.

Rose smiled at Ellie. "You feeling more settled?"

Ellie shrugged. She was a stunningly beautiful girl. Not just pretty, the way some of them were, but the type to make you look twice.

"Oh," said Ellie, running her small finger over the pleat of her high-collared dress, "I think it will take a while."

"You mind the heat?"

Ellie nodded.

"For heaven's sakes, why don't you undo your top buttons? I mean, there's nobody here but us. Take your shoes off too."

"Madame told me to be ready."

"Did she? It's early for a customer—in this heat."

"I believe it's the doctor," said Ellie uncertainly.

Rose laughed. "Gawd—that's just Dr. Grey come to break you in. It's his privilege, you see."

Ellie looked puzzled. "Is he an important man?"

"In a sense he is, love." Rose explained. "He tries you out, you see. Then he reports to Madame. On his idea of what you're worth. What she can nick the customer."

"Oh," said Ellie.

"You had experience, right, love?"

"Oh yes." Bold now. Too bold.

"How did you find us when you got off the ship?" Rose asked Ellie.

"One of the ship's officers—I asked him where I might find work."

"Oh," said Rose, wonderingly. "Then you came here not knowing exactly what sort of work? Right?"

"Not at all." The proud lift of the head. "I knew. I asked him to direct me to the best House in town. It was what I was searching for."

"Well!" said Rose, admiring, seeing Ellie in a different light. Yet something still worried her. A purity? That was nonsense.

"Why did you think you wanted to work in a House?" Rose asked. Persistence. You got the answers if you didn't let them shy away.

"My mother advised it," said Ellie quietly. Her eyes were on Angie but her mind was somewhere else.

"Christ!" said Rose softly. "Your mother wanted you to work as a whore? I must say, that's a new one, eh Marie?"

Ellie held her chin high. "My mother is the finest human being I have ever known. Next to my father, whom I esteem highly." She had a singsong quality to her voice.

There was a knock on the door. "He's come for you," said Rose, surprised at her uneasiness. "I expect it's Dr. Grey. Try to let yourself relax as much as you can. Ask him to go easy on you if you're unused to it. He's not a monster." Though sometimes, she wondered.

Ellie was affronted. "I've been with a man before." Her eyes flashed green fire. Was it anger or terror?

"All right, lovey. Just so long as you know what to do."

Ellie nodded briefly. Apologetic. "Thanks, Rose. I didn't mean to be short. You were just being kind."

"It's all right," said Rose. "You come down and see us later. We'll eat supper together. If anyone can eat in this heat."

She watched Ellie go down the spiral staircase that made you feel dizzy if you looked from the bottom floor to the top. Or vice versa. Said a tiny prayer for her. God, no one had a right to be that beautiful. Perhaps some slob would marry her. Take her away in a fine carriage. Rose had dreams for all of them.

Madame said, "This is the doctor I told you about, child. Compton, this here is Ellie."

Ellie had lied to Rose when she said she'd had experience. She had. Not the sort Rose meant, though. Rose was kind. She shouldn't have snapped at her that way. Mai Tai Wong wouldn't have approved. She brought her daughters up to be polite.

The doctor wasn't so frightening. It was just what she knew she had to do with him. He was staring at her the way men so often stared. She'd even had them follow her down the street when she was still in school.

"Go easy on her, Compton. She's convent reared. Somethin' special in this House. Want to keep her around for a long, long time."

"Well," said the doctor, "we might as well go on up." He gestured with his head, raised his hand, palm side flattened, telling Madame he'd be back. "Looking forward to this," he said.

They had to climb to the third floor. Up under the eaves it was, and hot. The air trapped beneath the sloping roof.

"God!" said the doctor. He strode to the open dormer window and thrust his head out. "You work up here?"

"Madame says she'll move me down if I prove my worth."

"Cunning old bitch," he said under his breath.

"You wish me to help you?"

"Why yes," he said, the slight scowl leaving his face. "I think that would be a good beginning. You can remove my boots."

She began to tug on the highly polished boots. When she had one of them off, he said, "Wait a minute."

"Please?" She knew her way of talking was foreign to him. It was the way all Hong Kong girls talked, the ones of mixed parentage. Singsong.

"Open your dress front," he said abruptly. She began to undo her collar. "Farther than that," he urged, staring at her hand as the buttons came undone. "Low enough for me to get at your breasts."

351

"Now take my foot." He extended the one she had bared. "Place it inside your dress front. I have great sensitivity in my toes—contrary to most people."

The foot was short and splayed and smelled. Sour from sweat. A cheesy odor she associated with infection. She opened her frock and he explored her soft contours, pausing to work around the nipple with his big toe. She felt nauseated, but knew it was only the beginning.

"You got some Oriental blood in you?" he asked.

"My mother."

"And your father?"

"A British merchant." She tossed her head. It was none of his business. If she did her job well, why did he have to know more about her than that?

"I got a right to know," he said, reading her mind. "I have a part-ownership of all you girls."

She looked up at him, startled.

"Surprised you. Madame just sold half her interests out. She's getting old, you see. Maybe will retire before too long."

"What do you wish me to do for you now?"

"Help me get out of the rest of these clothes."

The doctor's clothes were damp from sweat. She helped to peel them off. He scratched his chest luxuriously. "Christ, that feels good. A man gets to itching—this heat. Now, come over here to me."

He placed his hand up under her silk coat. Running his fingers up the inside of her thighs. Exploring until he found the place they all wanted between her legs.

"Not very big, are you?"

The doctor led her to the bed. As he climbed on top of her, he pushed her dress up. Feeling for her breasts. They seemed to please him; he molded them in his hands, bread dough for him to flatten and to pinch. He had raised his body slightly so that he was at an angle to hers, the other part of himself, which had inquired between her legs, entering deeper and deeper.

He seemed to have powers of endurance. Managed to keep up his movements for a long time. At last he expended himself. Lay still and then pulled away.

"Pour me some brandy."

The egg white rolling down the inside of her leg, she got up. Filled him a glass.

"You can have some."

"I don't drink."

"You will this time. I am ordering it. Do you know how fortunate you are to have appealed to me?"

She stared her inquiry, afraid to shake her head.

"I am unlike most other men." He patted his fleshy stomach. "I may be in my fifties, but I have special properties. When I choose a woman, I endow her with something of myself. Never again can her thirst be satisfied. What I have given her binds her to me."

She nodded. He evidently believed what he said. She saw that the key to him was flattery. She stored the information away quietly.

"You have done well. Passed the first tests with flying colors."

"Thank you," she said demurely. "You are a remarkable man."

"Tomorrow, when I can get away, I'll be back. You are to be ready for me. A new dress. Blanche needs to have the dressmaker in. All Oriental clothes—like what you've got there." He pointed to the discarded robe. "The finest—it'll be worth it, for the money it'll bring in. Your name won't do. Not Oriental enough. We have to have something provocative." He thought a while as he did up his trousers, fastened his shirt. "Lotus—that's it. We'll refer to you as Lotus. Lotus Blossom. How do you like that?"

Ellie bowed her head. "As you wish."

"Lotus Blossom, you're a good worker. Catch on fast." Then he frowned. "That doesn't mean you aren't going to need a lot of training. But you'll be worth it to me." He poured brandy, lifted the glass. "Here's to prosperity, Lotus."

She drank the brandy he handed her. Feeling she'd earned it. It looked like it was the only thing she'd earned. Rose's words came back to her. "He gets it on the house."

He left the room without saying a word. Picking up his bag as though he'd just completed a routine house call. Perhaps for him, he had. She laughed to herself. Without humor.

353

Letty got out of bed, slipped into a robe, and went to sit in one of the lemon silk chairs in her morning room. Leaving the snoring Nathaniel.

September! He'd sent for her only once in the past three weeks. She was beside herself. She hated him, but she hated herself more. True to his word, he had implanted a need in her. For himself? Or was it for the way he'd awakened her? His "way" with women? Could there be some truth to it?

It had been ten days since she'd seen him—the longest ten days of her life.

"Letty?"

She jumped, not knowing Nathaniel had come into the room. He was naked under his robe. It hung loose on his body, exposing the thick mat of dark hair that covered almost all his skin. She'd often thought of him as being like a bear.

"You're up early," he said, his walk uncertain, sleepiness disturbing his equilibrium.

"I couldn't sleep," she told him.

He stood staring at her. "You've been restless of late. Isn't there some medicine you're supposed to take? I met Compton at the club last week. He said I was to keep an eye on you—make sure you took it."

She nodded numbly.

He came and stood over her. "He also had another piece of advice."

"What was that?"

354

"He said I should take you more often. That's why I came out here before dressing. I want you to come back to bed."

She would never have known how unimaginative his lovemaking was if she'd not had the other. Compton was right in that respect. He had spoiled her for all other men.

He entered her perfunctorily. The expected performance. Yet she knew, if she moved under him, allowed herself to feel, the stone would drop. The ripples would start. Experimentally, she lifted her thighs.

"Keep still—you're putting me off!" He finished quickly. Pulled out. "You never did that before. Only whores do that."

She had blushed, flame hot. The stone was still there. Waiting to drop. Yearning to be allowed to fall. She got up and poured herself a teaspoon of the medicine. If she couldn't have Compton, perhaps she could have his elixir?

Nathaniel had started his breakfast by the time she got to the dining room. He was reading the newspaper, egg yolk dribbling down his chin. He disgusted her.

He glanced up. "Oh, and another thing."

"Yes, Nat?"

"I am to tell you that if you need anything while Compton's away, you can consult his partner."

"Compton is away?" Spoken with enormous effort. Could she hear his answer over the pounding of her heart?

"Of course he's away. He's gone to that place of his in Vermont. Be away several months. Supposed to get back by Thanksgiving. Hitty's having the baby then, you know."

"Are you sure he's already left?"

"Why do you ask? Are you ill?" He glanced at her from under heavy brows.

"Yes, as a matter of fact, I feel quite unwell."

"Then you'd better see his partner, hadn't you?"

"Yes. Yes, I suppose I'd better do that." Whose voice was it, speaking? Too low to carry the length of the long, gleaming table. But then, Nat wouldn't notice.

"Here's a thing in the paper, Letty, this will interest you. That authoress—wasn't her name Fiona Macleod?"

He caught her attention suddenly, like a kite caught on a tree limb. "What about Fiona?"

"Her ship sank. They fear there were no survivors."

She got up, managed to walk the length of the room and grab at the paper. There it was, in cold print: *Feared lost at sea. Signs of wreckage along the coastline.*

355

"It doesn't say it the way you did. She's alive! I know she's alive."

"Letty, what's got into you? Have you gone crazy? Tearing the paper out of my hands like that!"

She had taken herself up to her morning room to await his leaving. When she heard the carriage drive away, she rang the bell.

"Norah, have Phillips hail me a hansom cab. I have to see my sister."

"Bates will be back in half an hour, madam. Shouldn't you wait?"

"Don't tell me what to do!"

"Very well, madam." Norah's eyes rebuked her. Or was she imagining it? The room was so close this morning. Air—she needed air. She took a second spoonful of the elixir before she left.

She staggered a little on the stairs.

Betsy gasped. "Madam, you all right?"

"Of course." With dignity. What did they think? That she was a hussy who didn't know how to behave? She allowed Phillips to help her into the hired carriage.

"Drive out of the gate. I will tell you where to turn."

"Very good, madam." The cabby jerked on the reins, starting the vehicle to roll. The thin nag obeyed him reluctantly.

Beyond the reach of the staring servants, she gave the driver Compton's office address.

Miss Soames was out of uniform. Her long gray dress was discreet, friendly. "Oh, didn't they tell you? He's out of town."

"I don't believe it." The woman in Letty's body shouted it, her eyes willing the nurse to change the words. "You're just saying that. He's got some other patient in there!"

Before Miss Soames could stop her, she threw open the inner office door. The empty desk. The vacant chair. All in order. It had to be faced.

She gave the cabby the address on Cedar Street. Went up to the front door, knowing in advance what the sign said. Dangling from the brass handle, at a wind tossed angle—but still readable: *House to Let.*

Her last ace in the hole, the card she didn't want to play. Hitty would know. Hitty would have the information. Hitty wouldn't lie.

"Dearest, how lovely to see you. What a nice surprise." Hitty came into the parlor, her body gross—made more ugly than usual by the child within her. From their lovemaking.

"I came—" Letty tried to rise from her chair and found her body to be oddly ungainly. As if she were swimming underwater. She experienced dizziness, not for the first time. Torpor of the arms and legs.

Was she going to faint? She remembered the bottle in her reticule. Should she have another teaspoon?

"Are you all right, Letty?" Hitty's voice echoed from a long way away. "Letty, you're so pale. Oh, I wish Compton were here."

The name had penetrated her daze. "Compton. Where is he?" Why was her tongue so thick? She was acting as though she were drunk.

"You came to see him, didn't you? I'm so sorry—I thought it was to visit me. He left for Vermont on the early morning train."

She'd missed him by one day. She sat hopelessly, the tears pouring down her cheeks. Her mouth drooped while the salt flowed over her lips. Her hand felt too heavy to lift, to brush the tears away.

"Why are you crying?"

"It's Fiona." All of a sudden she had the real reason. It wasn't Compton. She was abandoned, yes. But not by him. By her only friend in all the world.

"Do you have news of Fiona?" Hitty's voice stabbed at her, demanding she give explanation.

"It was in the newspaper. You must have read it?"

"Compton took it on the train. What about Fiona?"

"The paper said that it was feared the ship went down." As soon as she'd said it, Letty knew it was a mistake. Not the information, but telling Hitty. Hitty was too frail to bear it.

Hitty was distraught. All the questions she, Letty, should have been asking came pouring out. "How do they know? It's not true, is it? It's just something they're making up—they print stories every day —to keep people reading."

Letty rose. She patted Hitty on the shoulder, then said heavily, "I don't know. I don't have any answers. I just know I'm not well and I have to go home."

She went into the hallway and told Hitty's black servant, "Your mistress may need you. But please see me out first."

She walked up the staircase to her morning room, closed the door, and walked over to her sewing basket. She took her embroidery scissors and went into the bathroom.

Compton would have approved of the way she was doing it—very clean, so as not to make a mess. Holding her wrists out over the basin. A towel on the floor.

She pulled the scissor blades across her flesh. Awkward because of the way they were linked together. Nevertheless, with persistent jabbing, she was able to start the blood flowing freely. It splashed in scarlet flowers onto the white of the china bowl. How pretty it looked. Too bad Compton wasn't there to see it.

Or Fiona. They might have painted the splotches together. Given them exotic names—for after all, they were flowers. Jungle flowers— wild and untamed. Growing now.

As they increased, she decreased. But it was a clean job. Even when she fell, hitting her head, the towel was there. They wouldn't find her until it was all over.

VI. THE CAGE
October 1888 – September 1889

Sing away, ay, sing away,
Merry little bird
Always gayest of the gay,
Though a woodland roundelay
You ne'er sung nor heard;
Though your life from youth to age
Passes in a narrow cage.

— *from The Quotable Woman*, 1978

I

Henry Porter was coming to see her and Mother about Letty. A little
bit about the baby, which they'd feared for a while might come early.
But she'd weathered it—the shock of Fiona, of Letty. What was wrong
with Letty? Hitty shook her head in impatience. Just because she was
carrying a child didn't mean they could keep everything from her.

"Hitty!" Emma's voice was high with annoyance, "You haven't
heard a word I've said."

"I'm sorry, Mother. I'm afraid my mind was on Letty."

"Why doesn't Henry get here? It's outrageous, the way they are
keeping it all from me. After all, I am her mother. Who has a better
right to know?"

A noise in the hall. Henry had arrived.

"Ah!" said Emma. "At last. I do believe doctors like to have
people waiting for them. It adds to their sense of importance."

She managed a coaxing smile for Henry. "You're putting on
weight! You should go on a diet. That's what we've had to do with my
old dog. Poor girl—she can scarcely waddle."

Henry smiled politely, but Hitty could see he had other matters
on his mind. "Hitty, m'dear. Compton will want a report on how you
are doing. Mother and child well, eh?" It was politeness. Hitty knew
Compton didn't care a fig. If she lost the baby—expired herself—it
would be so much the easier for him.

They went through the amenities. Offering Henry tea—or
brandy?

"Later would be nice. For now, there are things we must talk about." Yet still he fussed. His backside before the fire. "It's hard, you see. Letty has had a complete breakdown."

"I've been expecting it for months," said Emma. Did Hitty imagine it was said with satisfaction? Mother always liked to be proven right.

"What does that mean, Henry?" Hitty pressed for details. "I want to know, for instance, whether we can visit her where she is."

Both Hitty and Emma knew more than they were supposed to. Nathaniel had blurted it out to Emma. Nanette had visited Hitty and wept details. How she'd found her mistress—so fortunate she was in time. "But that place where they have taken her—I had to go along with her in the coach—it is awful. It is a house where they keep poor ladies tied with ropes, madame. I wasn't supposed to see." Hysterical weeping.

"Out of the question," Henry said flatly.

"She's my daughter," said Emma, fierce under her ragged brows, so heavy for her frail face. "I should be permitted—"

"Not now," soothed Henry. "Later, when she's recovered her strength."

"Then you do expect her to get well?" Emma glanced at him sharply.

"Of course she will get well—be back in the bosom of her family in a few months. Dear me, how could you even consider she wouldn't be returned to you?"

"It happens," said Emma darkly.

"Yes, but not in Letty's case. She is strong. A healthy body. All the ingredients to ensure her getting better, overcoming her delusions—"

"She has delusions?" Hitty shot it.

Henry looked at his shoes, his shiny shoes. "In a manner of speaking, yes. She imagines things that are not there. She has already attempted to injure herself—and one of the nurses. I will not try to conceal from you that it's serious."

"When can I visit her?" asked Hitty.

"Not until well after the baby is born. The nursing you plan to do —it could affect the milk." He said it delicately.

"In other words," said Emma, "neither of us can see her for a long time."

"Now, Emma, I don't want to see you upset yourself."

"She's my daughter," said Emma grimly.

"She's your daughter," he assented. "But I have been delegated to explain—"

"Delegated by whom?" Hitty asked.

"By Dr. Prior. He's in charge of your sister. He prefers that the family stay away, give him a chance to cure her."

"Is it the change of life?" asked Emma tartly.

"I'm afraid so." Henry shook his head. "As you know, it takes some women this way."

"I've warned her all her life," said Emma, her mouth snapping shut like a toad on a fly. "Hitty too. We females have to be careful."

Henry lifted his coat, exposing his trousered posterior to the fire's heat. "I learned she was by here to see you the day it all happened."

"Yes," said Hitty evenly. One last attempt. "I have to know," said Hitty, remembering Nanette's tale, "Is Letty having to be restrained?"

Henry smiled. The smile was large and corpulent. It spread over his whole body, pulling at the buttons of his waistcoat. "Now, Hitty, don't ask me questions like that. Even I do not have those answers."

"What do you have for answers?" asked Hitty. Uneasy.

"I trust Dr. Prior. Nathaniel trusts him. Surely that is enough for you?"

She and her mother exchanged glances. Questioning glances.

"I suppose it will have to be," said Emma.

"For now," said Hitty. Warning him. Promising herself. Someday she'd find out exactly what was going on. What they'd done with Letty —were doing to her. If need be, rescue her.

But first, she was having a baby. In about six weeks or more. Or less?

"That's a good girl," said Henry. His smile magnanimous.

2

Compton had promised to get down for Thanksgiving, but at the last moment she received a message sent on the wires: *Snowed in. Trains delayed. Come as soon as I can—Grey.*

Hitty smiled grimly. All along she'd known he wouldn't be here for the baby's arrival. If there were no storms, he'd have manufactured them. Of course there were always storms in Vermont. She realized more and more how much of an excuse Vermont gave Compton to conduct his affairs away from her.

She'd planned a small Thanksgiving dinner here, more for the servants' sake than anything. Tildie seemed to expect it. She awaited Compton, too, by her confident attitude.

As the day wore on the smell of roasting turkey crept under the doors that led from the kitchen area, teasing the house into anticipation. Hitty could hear laughter too, emerging in short bursts from the usually quiet domestics, as though they forgot themselves.

"Lord, Joseph—what you want to say that for?"

"You shore that food ain't ready yet? My mouth's fair turned to water—"

"Hush now. You'll disturb the missus."

Hitty felt lonely. She'd ordered dinner late in the day on the chance Compton might make it after all. The telegram had dispelled all hope of that. She wished she might have had someone over to join her. The Reverend Mr. Evans and Olwen? Her condition made entertaining out of the question.

She sat almost alone. Feeling the presence, the movement, of the child within her. Unreal to her yet. Nevertheless, alive and eager to emerge from her body.

A familiar terror seized her. Usually, it came during the dark of the night. A shadowy thing that claimed her for its own when sleep had left her vulnerable. The nightmare was a corridor that ended in only two possible doors. The one was childbirth, the other death.

The corridor had seemed such a long one at first. Nine months! Would she ever wait it out? Impatient, mulish in her determination to have a child, even in the face of Compton's displeasure. He had lost interest in her now that she had disobeyed him.

His suggestion that another had fathered the child seemed like parceling and string, to do the rejection up in. Something to justify his pushing her away. She was confident he didn't believe a word of it. What he needed to cover up was that she bored him. That marriage had been the means to an end.

Had it been her dowry? The purchase of the Vermont property— it had followed so soon after the wedding. If Compton had funds himself, why hadn't he bought land there long ago? Certainly his coldness when he was at home, the long periods of time he spent away, indicated he had little fondness for her. She felt heavy, with a weight that had nothing to do with her body. She was trapped in a marriage that was very like having the child. Except that this one could only end in a single door. Death—the one conceivable exit.

She reached for her pen and paper—to spill out her frustration in a poem. If only she could write good poetry. "Work hard at it," Fiona had said. "Don't stop writing, no matter how discouraged you get. Persistence, my dear. That's the key."

She heard the sound of someone at the door. Mother's voice.

"I don't want to bother her if she's resting—"

"She just settin' in front of the fire, Mizz Benedict."

Joseph, showing Mother in.

"Hitty, I was on my way home from Nathaniel's—" Once she would have said "Letty's." How quickly matters changed.

"Compton isn't with you? I thought he was expected?"

Hitty silently handed her the wire.

Emma peered at it. "Oh, you'll have to tell me what it says. I've new spectacles, but so cumbersome to carry about."

"The snows have detained him."

"Ah." Like a kitten with changeable interests, Emma had already turned her attention elsewhere. "Now, Hitty, I want to see what you think." She'd seated herself, undone her fur-trimmed coat, and was removing her gloves. "What you think about Nathaniel."

"What about him?" Wearily. Hitty had never liked Nathaniel. He was capable of almost anything with Letty safely away. She realized, with a start, just exactly how she thought about it. "How were the children, Mother?"

"The children were well. Now Hitty, don't be irrelevant. I came here to talk about your brother-in-law."

"What about him?"

Emma's face twisted, all the age lines showing, as cracks in a drying river bed. She seemed ancient suddenly. "Oh, how I miss Letty—" She picked up her kid gloves, making slapping noises with them against her coat. "If Letty had been there, none of this would have happened."

Hitty was aroused now. What was going on?

Emma continued. "I think he's really got designs on that child of John Abbott's." Her eyes looked uncomfortable. "Now, Hitty, please hear me out. I know you don't like me to make accusations. Also, you're very loyal to your sister. That's commendable. But I have this feeling—" Before Hitty's astonished eyes, Emma began to cry.

A rare occurrence. Once or twice briefly, for Oscar. And when the dog she'd owned for years had finally flopped over, its poor heart stopped. Emma had wept. Now she gave way again. Over Letty?

"I had hoped Compton would be here. He would help us get her out of that place. Hitty, I know this is no time for you to become involved. But we have to see she is released. She can't be as bad as they say." The gaze defiant now. It had suited Emma to have Letty's break-down confirm her beliefs in female vulnerability. Now it did not.

"She's being well taken care of," Henry had assured them, his eyes saying he was eager to change the subject.

Emma almost shouted—her voice high with strain. "He hasn't even visited her! Hitty, I don't think Letty's husband cares what's being done with her!" Staring, distraught, shaking her head. "I feel sure he doesn't give a damn."

The expletive, coming out coarse and unfamiliar from Emma Benedict, would have been enough to tell Hitty how deeply her mother felt about this.

Hitty stared back, not quite knowing what to say. At last she asked, "What do you believe can be done?"

Emma shook her head again, her small curls bouncing. "It's for Compton to say," she muttered. "After all, he's a doctor. He knows about these things."

Hitty was quiet. How could she tell her mother how little Compton cared about any of them?

"About Nathaniel, Mother?"

"I can't go on with it, Hitty. Use your imagination. Making eyes at Olivia Abbott. Dancing with her. Holding her as no man should hold a young girl—especially one who isn't his wife! I could tell John Abbott was displeased. He had that nice Virginia Croft there—the pretty little widow everyone says he'll marry. After that unfortunate wife of his goes."

Hitty thought of Letty after Mother had left. She had to get to see her. Where was Letty? Nathaniel, if he knew, wasn't telling. None of the children knew anything except that "Mama is sick."

The odor of roast turkey was making Hitty feel ill. She had had a dull ache at the base of her spine all day. Perhaps it was just that it was Thanksgiving and she was alone.

She rang the bell and asked if Tildie could spare her a moment.

Tildie came, tying on a clean apron as she did so. Her face was shining with sweat. "It be ready mos' any time, Mizz Grey," she said politely.

"I don't want to disappoint you, Tildie, but I think I will retire to bed. I don't feel myself tonight. I'm sorry, when you've gone to all this effort."

"You think we oughta send for the midwife?"

"Gracious, no. I'm just a little weary. My spirits are down."

"I know," said Tildie with unexpected sympathy. "You lookin' fo' the doctor to be heah. Well, I tell you somethin', Mizz Grey, sometimes it's better for the menfolks to be away, time we's havin' chillun. They only gits in the way—fallin' over their feet—havin' attacks of nervousness. So you just hol' tight. You be restin' better soon." Her face was sharp with interest. "You got any pains, chile?"

"No," said Hitty. "Just my back's botherin' me."

"Show me," said Tildie, abruptly.

"I really don't think it's anything—"

"I b'lieve we got to git you upstairs, fetch that midwife."

"Oh, not on Thanksgiving Day," said Hitty quickly.

"Babies don' care when they make their arrival. Just so it suit them." Tildie stalked into the hall, called the black servants. "Joseph, you he'p me see her to her room. Jakes, git you'self going, hitch up that wagon and bring back the midwife."

Hitty was surprised at how steep the stairs had become. Was she really in labor?

The sheets felt comforting. Joseph had the fire roaring in the grate. Tildie brought warming bottles, their heavy sides containing water from her kettles, to ease Hitty's icy feet.

Nellie Parsons, accustomed to being summoned at all times of day or night, agreed with Tildie. "You did right to send for me." She undid her bonnet and cloak, bent to examine her patient with dextrous hands. "It won't be right away, but the child will be born early tomorrow," she said to Hitty, "or my name's not Nellie Parsons."

"Shouldn't we send for Dr. Porter?" asked Hitty.

"Not till near the end, my dear." Nellie had replaced her dress with a striped uniform. Her small bustling form inspired confidence. "Doctors really don't do anything at a delivery, you see. They just like to be seen about—for the sake of the family."

"Oh," said Hitty, who'd been dimly aware of this. Henry had sat talking with herself and Emma while Letty gave birth. What was ahead of her? Hitty gripped the bedpost as a spasm hit her.

Nellie was quickly at her side. "Your first one, right? Now missus, dear, I give you something to pull on. A rag to stuff in your mouth. The more it pains you, the harder you bite. Believe me, it'll help."

The hours passed. Tildie had long ago washed her last dish, polished her roasting pans, hung them in the cave of a kitchen, among the rafters. She couldn't go to bed. Not with what was going on upstairs. Tildie was glad there was a baby coming. She just wished Mizz Grey was a bit younger. That way she could have a large family. Give her something to put her mind on.

"Gawd!" Tildie cried out as the door opened. Terrified. In the shadows, a man standing there.

"Tildie? What are you doing up?"

"Oh Lawd, Massa Grey, doctor—you fair gave me a start. I thought it had to be some bad man comin' through that doorway this hour of the mornin'! We thought you was delayed, suh. Mizz Grey got yo' wire."

"I was." Shortly. "None of us could get through. By the time I could send the message, I was able to reach the train myself. They keep the tracks cleared better than those farm roads."

"You want some'pin to eat, Massa Grey?"

He shook his head. "Just whiskey. And bed. Lord, I'm beat—that's one helluva long trip." He was removing a coat that smelled damp.

"We have to make you up a bed in one of the guest rooms, Dr. Grey, suh. Mizz Grey, she havin' her baby tonight—far as we kin tell. Mizz Parsons settin' up wid her since 'bout seven o'clock."

He was staring at her in the dim light. "That so, Tildie? Well, we thought the child would be due at this time. Dr. Porter been notified?"

"Not yet, suh. Mizz Parsons, she said she thought it'd be all right to let him wait till mornin'. No call to spoil his Thanksgiving. Nor his rest, neither."

"Sounds like things are well in hand." He scratched his head.

She couldn't see his expression very clearly, but she sensed his discomfort. Not that his wife was in labor, but that he was sorrowful he'd come home before it was all over. Well, she'd voiced her belief when she told Mizz Grey men knew they wasn't wanted at a birthing. Nuthin' for them to do. Even a doctor.

"I'll just take this coffee on up to Mizz Parsons. Likely to drop off to sleep, she don't have some'pin hot to keep her awake."

Nellie Parsons wasn't asleep, but she looked worn out. Hitty was sleeping, fitfully, moaning and jumping in her rest.

"Baby takin' its time, eh?" Tildie said.

Nellie Parsons nodded. "Did I hear voices in the hall?"

"Dr. Grey come back down from the nawth. Musta had a hired carriage bring him home. Or else he walked from the station, because the trams don't run at this hour. I tol' him Mizz Grey was in labor."

"Ah," said Nellie. "It's probably for the best he's here."

"Some'pin gonna go wrong?"

"Never can tell," said Nellie. "When they have their first at her age." She nodded at the sleeping woman. "You might ask him, when you're downstairs, if I could have a word with him? At his convenience, of course."

"I'll go tell him right away."

But when Tildie got downstairs, the rooms stood chilled and empty. Compton had gone.

"Compton, for God's sakes—you look all wore out. What you doin' here this hour of the mornin'? All the girls are abed 'cept Rose. She had a late customer. I just saw him leave." Blanche stared at her partner. "You in wet clothes?"

"Don't give me a talking to, Blanche. I just need something dry to wear, a bottle of brandy, and a woman. If Rose is the only one up, Rose it'll have to be."

Blanche stared at him through lidded eyes. "Thought you was up north," she muttered.

"Don't stand there asking me questions. I'm freezing to death," he said angrily. He unlocked the closet behind her desk, picking out a bottle dusty from the cellar that had cradled it.

Behind him, her heavy breathing communicated her displeasure. A business deal was one thing. Invading her privacy, quite another. She hadn't retired yet! Unbeknown to him, she'd invested money in a second house. In New Orleans. Retirement be damned! Angie's father had arranged the transaction. Soon now, she'd be going there to set the place up. Leave Rose in charge here. Rose knew the business as well as any of them. Could be trusted too, which was unusual.

Rose was surprised when she answered his summons. "Doctor, I was just going to bed."

"Blanche said I could come up." He lifted the bottle. "I brought us some brandy. My clothes are damp. Blanche will give you some dry ones for me."

Rose hid her sigh. It had been a long night. Something told her it was going to continue in the same vein. Compton here, at this hour. He hadn't asked for her in years. Prided himself on getting to know the new girls. A "teacher" he called himself.

Rose suppressed a sense of worry. She knew men. She'd find out what was on his mind.

She poured him brandy while he stepped out of his clothes. He spurned the robe Blanche had brought and pulled on the dry street clothing. "I didn't come here to take a woman to bed. I need someone to talk to."

Rose began to breathe a little easier. If it was talk he wanted, he could have all night. If she could stay awake! She rubbed her hands up and down her arms. "Talk? Help yourself. I got time for whatever you want."

He plopped himself down in the only wicker chair the room had. Its cushions were covered in flowered cretonne but gave forth a smell of must. The clothes he'd taken off had an odor too. Warm wool stank when it was drying.

She must be more weary than she thought. It was a sign—when her nose began to bother her. Like she could vomit for the stink.

"—time I talked it out." What was the doc saying? Rose tugged at her reverie. She'd told him she was available to him. She'd better not let him down.

"—realized I couldn't keep away. When I arrived, I wasn't able to stay. What is it about a woman having a child that is so disturbing? I've been present before. The night Sarie had the baby upstairs—patients who've called me in as consultant. Never like this. Do you suppose it could be because I'm married to her?"

Rose gaped at him. "You mean you run out on your wife when she's in labor?"

Irritated. "That's what I've been telling you—I couldn't remain in the house." He put his head in his hands.

She'd never seen him like this before. All the usual arrogance gone. "Are you afraid your wife might die?"

A shudder rippled over his body. "I've never given a damn for women before. In fact, I have suspected I loathe them. My wife—there are times when she actually repels me."

Rose sat quiet. Now he was no longer surprising her. In fact, she might have predicted his words. Pitied the poor lady who had taken him for her husband.

"You knew about my first wife—?"

"Blanche told me—a long time ago."

"We were so young. I never really got used to having her. I was just out of medical school—trying to build my practice. When she

371

went, it stunned me. I felt she'd done it on purpose. To grieve me. Seems like nothing good can come out of associating with a woman. Trouble—always trouble."

She listened quietly. Feeling if she disturbed him, neither he nor she would ever know what he wanted to say. What he felt, deep down. Like glimpsing an animal in the forest.

"—then I had to have more. Money would get it for me. I'd seen that piece of land up there in the north. Seemed an ideal place for a hospital. Thought I could have my old life and marriage too. Worked, for a while. But she wanted a child." He whirled about on Rose. "Why do women always want a child?"

"Not all of us do," she said softly. "It's not up to us. Nature has the final say."

He seemed not to have heard her. "A woman lives her own life. Does as she pleases. A man has to assume responsibilities. Earn his living—even as a little fellow, there's schooling to pay attention to. As a boy, I was never allowed to play." He stared at the fire, lost in his own thoughts. "My Mama died when I was a boy, you know."

"No, I never heard. Say, that's too bad. What did your ma die of?"

"I don't know. They never told me."

"I believe you do know."

He turned around with a movement that showed his intention to strike her. Then suddenly it was all right. He collapsed over on himself, his head in his hands, his elbows sticking into his knees. Weeping. "She died giving birth—" he said in a strangled voice. "She couldn't have cared for me or she wouldn't have given her life for another damned child!" He struck out at the chair arm, smashing his fist onto the wicker back. "She left me when I needed her most. You can't understand that, can you, Rose? A woman dying. It's all she thinks about—what she wants out of it. My mother had me! What did she want with another son?"

"Then your first wife died—" pressed Rose. She had it straight now. Why he did many of the things he did—to women. Punishment. Maybe he'd never understand it himself. To her, it was plain. "So now you blame yourself?"

"No," he said, "I blame women. All women. The irony is—I've made women make it up to me. For all the heartache. For everything they did to me so long ago."

Rose was silent.

He got up at last, stretching like a cat, to refill his glass. "You let one word of this out, you'll have no body left to work with."

"It's all right," she said calmly. "I won't talk. Even to you. You got it off your chest—I suppose it might've done you some good. Me, I've forgotten it." She too stretched. "It's been a long day. You want a bit of lovin' before you leave?"

He shook his head. "It's rest I'm after. You can share a bed with one of the other girls. I'm staying here for what's left of the night."

He lay his length across her bed. Heavy and leaden. She covered him with a blanket, shook her head. How many women had he selected to pay for those childhood experiences? How many more to go?

Hitty lay there, looking down in wonder at the baby she had borne. Her new daughter was red-faced and wrinkled, a thing that had grown in the darkness. The light, sweeping in over the tiny face, as Hitty lifted a corner of the blanket, was shocking. Eyes squeezed tight in protest and a minuscule mouth opened to howl.

Hitty laughed, delightedly. She had thought of herself as aging—they all had. Yet she had given birth to this robust, protesting daughter who would undoubtedly grow to strength and roundness—given such a start.

She opened the front of her robes as the new nurse had urged she do. It felt embarrassing at first, exposing her breasts this way. She tried to remember that women down through time had fed their infants this way. There was nothing "wrong" with it.

She turned the baby's mouth awkwardly to her nipple. Her milk wouldn't come in for a full day, she'd been told. But there was something there that the child would get. Enough to satisfy it. *Her.* Yes, this small creature did have its own sex, personality. She wondered idly what it would have been like to have brought forth a boy. Would Compton have tolerated it less or more?

Sometime during the long night her husband had come home. Tildie, staggering upstairs under a great tray for Hitty, had said, "Leastways I think he came home, Mizz Grey. But time I got the cup o' coffee I done poured for the midwife and back down again, he'd took hisself off. Mebbe it was when I done tol' him he'd have to sleep in the guest room—" Her black face had looked solemn until she'd peered into the bundle in Hitty's arms. "Lawd, you really done it, Mizz Hitty!

What you gonna call the baby? Should have a real purty name, your first un."

Hitty noticed it was the sight of the baby that had induced Tildie to drop the "Mizz Grey," convert it to "Mizz Hitty." Had she done something to satisfy the black woman at last?

The child nuzzled the breast lazily. The nurse left her chair to come over. "She'll have to be encouraged at first." Once more she showed Hitty what to do.

Hitty didn't like Nurse Schmidt. Someone Henry Porter recommended. She'd been with Letty after Warren's birth. An intimidating woman.

"Its seems so cruel to flick at the cheeks—"

"You've got to, Mrs. Grey. That's what I told Mrs. Mackenzie. Of course that last child of hers never had a chance. Born weak. Some are like that."

Hitty closed her eyes briefly, hiding beneath weariness. When Nurse Schmidt left, at nightfall, she and the other nurse could work it out. Surely the other one couldn't be this bad?

There was a knock on the door. Hitty looked up, alarmed. She quickly pulled her nightrobe over while calling out, "Just a moment."

Compton came into the room. He gazed around it as if he'd never been there before. Was he looking for changes in it? He was openly nervous. "So you had the child?"

"Yes," said Hitty, wishing all of a sudden she could disappear and take the baby with her.

"It's a girl, isn't it?" he said awkwardly.

"Yes, Compton, we have a daughter." She fastened him with her eyes.

He motioned peremptorily with his finger. "Nurse, leave us."

She left the room, her back ramrod.

"Who sent her here?" he questioned.

"Why, Henry made all the arrangements."

"Well, I don't want her here." He seemed jumpier than ever. Thrust his hands in his pockets. "Henry been over yet?"

"He was here early this morning. He told me I'd done well. Compton, don't you want to see your daughter?" She started to lift the blanket.

"Yes, yes." He peered. "Looks like any other child."

"Would you have preferred a son?"

"No," he said absentmindedly. "I don't think it matters. But now you have your child, will it satisfy you? Or will you want others?"

"Isn't it a little soon—?"

"I just wanted to point out to you what you've done, bringing a child into this house. It will never be the same again."

"What do you mean?" She was trembling.

"You forget, I've made a study of mothers and children. A family can be very destructive. Childbearing depletes a woman—she grows old more rapidly."

"Compton," she tried gently, "what is it about a woman bearing a baby that so upsets you? If it was only because you lost Missie, I would think you'd show some relief this morning. You seem beside yourself."

"Don't pry into matters that don't concern you," he snarled.

"I think they very much concern me." She was on the verge of tears.

"Well, that's where you're wrong," he snapped. He whirled about on her. "And another thing! You and your mother drop this matter of your sister. Do you hear me? I don't want you meddling."

She was really shaken now. His swift change of subject. Had Letty been on his mind all along?

"None of you understands the nature of Letty's illness. She has succumbed to severe melancholia. Nervous prostration caused by her time of life. I attempted to treat it with sedatives. It seems she was overdosing herself. When I left, I had already transferred her to another physician. Unfortunately there was nothing he could do either. Her illness is progressive insofar as we can tell."

"You mean my sister isn't going to get better?"

He passed his hands over his face. "In rare cases they do. I have promised Nathaniel that I will take her to Vermont in the spring—when the hospital is ready. We are still converting the farmhouse."

"You will take her to Vermont?" Hitty knew it now. This confirmed her sense of horror. About what was being planned for that place up there.

"I've told your brother-in-law we'd do everything in our power for her." He said it slowly, as if needing to hear it himself.

"Nathaniel wants Letty out of the way. Why doesn't he just divorce her? It would be much kinder."

Compton stared at her. It wasn't a new idea apparently. Hitty grasped in a flash of understanding just how much discussion there had been.

"Divorce cannot be considered—for the same reason all of this has to be kept quiet. Not only for the children's sake but Nathaniel is adamant. The Mackenzie name—"

"Ah," she interrupted him, "the good Mackenzie name. Nothing must sully or blacken it. Yet he is the worst rogue of all."

"Don't say that!" He pushed it at her. "It's none of our business what Letty's husband decides. I order you to keep out of the entire affair. Unless of course you wish to further complicate everything."

"For whom, Compton? For you?"

He shook his head. "Hitty, who would have known that the sweet little woman I married would turn into this hard-faced harridan?"

"I am disappointed in you too, Compton. I thought marriage might mean some measure of happiness. It would have been better by far, I believe, to have remained single. Except for the child." She glanced down at the peaceful baby. "Since we are wed, I believe it would be best if we saw each other as little as possible. It is working out that way, in any case."

"I plan to stay in Philadelphia until next April," he said heavily.

She bowed her head. "Of course. This is your house. You will not let me make it into your home. I cannot do what it isn't in my power to do. But I must warn you, Compton, I intend to fight for Letty."

He rose from his chair and stood over her menacingly. "You are a fool! Not only conceited, but a fool. I am warning you for the last time, stay out of this!"

"Talk away," she said softly. "I will never be convinced unless I see my sister for myself."

"When you are recovered, that might be arranged," he said grimly. "I assure you, she won't be a pretty sight."

His footsteps echoed down the stairs—away from her.

She clasped her child to her.

Letty rocked her body back and forth. Her upper arms were still tied by torn sheets to the chair. But today they had freed her hands, her bandaged wrists.

It was a test. Bailey had brought needlework—a soiled bundle Letty remembered seeing long ago. In the morning room of the other Letty. The one who had ruled before she came here—came to live under Appleby and Bailey.

The Letty who lived within her now hadn't been able to be entrusted with needlework. Needles filled with scarlet silk. Canvas the color of pale coffee. What did that remind her of? The Letty holding the needlework stabbed at it. Screaming. A wild banshee noise fled from her mouth to hang clinging under the cobweb-infested corners of the ceiling.

She had failed the test. The nurses, for that was what she was supposed to call them, moved with indolence away from the fire, letting some of the warmth flow into the room, where the tied-up patients shivered.

Then the punishment came. For her scream. The bonds that held her to her chair were jerked backward. A filthy rag was stuffed in her mouth. Now she knew that her whole concentration would have to be on breathing. She stared up at Bailey.

"Goddamned whore! I'll teach you a lesson!"

The other nurses laughed. "Bailey, she don't know what she's sayin'. Why do you take on so?"

"Well, she is a whore—" Bailey rejoined the crowd at the fire.

Letty closed her eyes. It was easier to shut them out. How long had she been here? The other Letty knew, but wouldn't tell. She'd begged, pleaded, entreated. All to no use. Just smiles. If only Compton wouldn't seek her out. If he'd just leave her alone.

"Now, Letty, you know my name isn't Compton. It's Dr. Prior. Can you say that? Doctor—Prior. I am to look after you. Make you well again."

She'd been sitting on his lap the first time he sent for her. It was naturally why she believed him to be Compton. Of course he couldn't be. He had dark eyes instead of blue. Black hair and a beard that was cut quite short and neat into a spade shape. The shape of pubic hair.

She'd shown him how his beard had struck her. He'd seemed amused when she'd lifted her dress. No underwear. It made it too difficult for the nurses to keep them clean. Except when the women patients flowed. Then they wore rags—allowed to become soaked and stiff. Sticking to the hairs, even the skin, so that they had to be torn away. Pulling pain with them. Out of the body that was so often pain-wracked. The medicine they gave them helped. The potion that brought sleep or, sometimes, just dulling insensibility.

Around the fire, they were talking.

"You gettin' time off for Christmas?"

"You serious? Old Appleby never give time off for anything."

"Hush. She might hear."

They were afraid of Appleby—the tall woman with the pinched nostrils. Devout, she was. Prayed all the time out loud. She terrified Letty. She could feel her now, coming with measured tread down the hallway. The nurses caught it too, the cat-soft padding of her feet. They dispersed their huddle about the hearth.

In this whole place, Dr. Prior alone stood up to Appleby. Letty had come to love him for that. The way she loved Compton. Her head ached and pounded when she tried to keep Dr. Prior and Compton separate in her mind.

Appleby shook Letty awake. Pointed to the rag stuffed in Letty's mouth. "You been a bad girl?"

How could Letty answer? Bailey did, for her. "She took to screaming, Miss Appleby. Surprised you didn't hear her. It must a been 'cause we cut her medicine back this mornin'."

Appleby, towering and flat-fronted, a fortress that walked; undoing the wad. Letty's jaw ached—her teeth pained her. She was losing one. First it had been broken. No one would tell her how. Now it was coming away in small pieces.

"What happened to your embroidery, Letty?" Appleby shouted to get her attention. She stared around the room as if the needlework would be discovered sticking to one of the walls. "Bailey, what did you do with her needle and thread?"

"I took it away—what else?" Surly.

"I don't like your tone, Bailey."

Sourness, spreading from Bailey. Funny, how alert Letty had become to the way that feelings smelled. She didn't have to see a person anymore. All she had to do was have her nose free. Up above the covers they tied her into the cot with. Odors pushing through the darkness of the night.

Musky excitement from Bailey. Especially when they took Letty in the closet to relieve herself. Forced her down over the foul commode. "Do it, missus—and not a word, mind. Me and Clark are busy."

Clark. The name meant choking to Letty. Suffocation, while she sat, tied to the commode, listening to them scuffle. At first she'd been appalled she was supposed to let her urine go in front of a man. While they still had her locked away, after she'd first been brought here, it was Clark mostly who untied her. Pushed the pieces of stringy meat through her clenched teeth. Kicked her until she voided in the metal chamber pot. Or, if he felt like it, tickled her bladder, sending streamers of warmth over her body while her yellow water spurted. It was Appleby, he told her, who insisted she yield some fluid. When she became clogged as a drain the other way, Appleby administered castor oil. Holding Letty's jaws until she swallowed it.

Bailey and Clark, using the excuse of Letty's needing to go to the closet to do it. Bailey on the floor, her skirts up over her chin. Clark down on her, his pants around his knees.

Once, Clark had leaned down over her. "Give it to you if you're a good girl, sometime—" Bailey must have heard. She came up behind Letty and pinched her. "You stay away from him. He's mine, you hear?"

The narrow, evil-shadowed closet was an odd place for them to select. Letty had known of other places. She could only suppose Clark and Bailey were limited where they could be together.

It sometimes took restraints to calm Letty down after she'd watched.

Appleby prodded at Bailey with her voice. "You know she's got to be weaned from the laudanum. Dr. Prior wants her alert. Her sister's asking to see her."

Her sister? The other Letty had had a sister. Long ago when she'd been someone else. The woman who had tea in a lemon yellow chair —how vividly she recalled it now. Nice clothes. Limbs free to move about. To lift a silver teapot. An odd life. So remote from the Letty she was now.

Appleby leaned over her, voice raised as if this Letty were deaf. "You remember your sister? Mrs. Grey—she wants to see you."

Grey! Where had she heard that name before? The old ache,

swarming over her body like wasps to ripe fruit. Grey! She was a plum, oozing and swollen, her skin cracked for desire. Hidden in the grass while the wasps consumed. Stingers out and menacing. Sucking her sweetness. Leaving her a limp casing. Empty.

Compton was also known as Dr. Grey! Her sister was married to him. The ache became a stabbing pain. She moved against the restricting cords of torn sheeting, a scream bursting from her, giving vent to her agony. She was so alone! No one wanted her. Not her family. Not Compton. Not Fiona. Fiona had loved her once. Fiona had asked nothing. Given to Letty a last gift, her warning. The old Letty had rejected that gift.

The nurses ran to her. The patients just stared—cow bodies flowing over stiff wooden chairs.

Appleby was hitting her, the horny palms burning her face. Bailey, from behind, was tightening the cruel ties.

A weary sigh from the tower-tall woman. "Into the hole with her till she comes around. Call Clark."

Clark dragged her out of the common room with its warming fire. Down the corridors he bumped her body as he half carried, half dragged her. Such strong arms. They must be beautiful in their hairy maleness. The smell of Clark! It made her want to gag. For pleasure denied.

"Please, not in there. There are rats!"

"Ain't no rats but me, lady. Now you be a good girl and Clark'll come visit ya. You catch my meaning?"

"There are rats! I've felt them run across my body."

"You go to sleep. I bring your medicine. You take it like a good girl—for me? Later, when all's quiet, I come see ya. All right?"

Clark returned. "There you are, missus. You be good now. Drink it down. Remember, if you think it's a rat, it ain't." Holding himself for the joke. Always the joker, Clark.

"Will you hold me? Rock me?"

"Course I will. Now, no more screaming."

In the darkness she found he'd freed one hand. Enough to be reachable. She tasted it, finding its humanness comforting beyond measure.

Perhaps it was Nanny's hand? From long, long ago. When the other Letty had been small. Someone to tuck her into bed.

The blackness was almost entire. Letty put her thumb in her mouth and sucked on it. Inviting forgetfulness. Unknowing.

6

Albert, Amelia, and Polly were to have lunch with their father. It was Sunday, the only day Nathaniel was at home. Clean, combed, their dresses stiff with flounces, they appeared outside the dining room

"Here's Albert. Hello, Albert."

"Hello, Poll. Wonder what's up. Not like the old man to want to see us."

Albert had grown fat. His face seemed to smile even when serious in the wreathing coils of flesh. His wrists were braceleted with wrinkles. A dimpled creature, he was repugnant to Amelia, while she found herself concerned for him. Now that Mama was gone, Amelia enjoyed concern. Not heavy enough to be worry, it increased her stature.

"Albert, you should get more exercise."

"You know I can't, Em. Old ticker won't take it."

"You're getting fat."

"You're turning into a carp."

"Hit you next time I get a chance."

"Silence!"

They froze. Nathaniel's voice dropped over them like a blanket, suffocating individuality, uniting them against their common enemy.

"Squabbling like children! The least you could do to honor your mother's absence is to behave like adults."

Adults. Polly pushed her shoulders back. In June she'd be nine. Next month, Em would be twelve. Albert had become fifteen last November. They were to behave as grown-ups! It was wonderful.

It was part of having Mama gone. Exciting. One never knew what was going to happen. Like today, having lunch with Papa. At Christmas

382

—all the parties. Olivia Abbott asking Papa if Polly and Amelia could stay up late. Olivia was so pretty.

It was nice to be pretty. Polly glanced at herself in the tall mirror as they filed into the dining room. Olivia had made friends with Polly on her last three visits here. They were always coming to stay now. Mr. Abbott knew this very nice lady Polly had learned to call "Aunt Virginia." Olivia said Mr. Abbott would marry Aunt Virginia when her own mother died.

As Polly took her chair, peeping cautiously at Papa from under her lashes, she wondered about mothers and sickness. Mrs. Abbott had been ill for as long as the Mackenzies had known the Abbotts. All of Polly's life. Longer! All that time, Mrs. Abbott had been sick.

Olivia hadn't wanted to talk about it much. She only was willing to, Polly guessed, because Polly brought the subject up. Wanting to know what made mothers sick. Olivia said it was different in different cases. It was exciting having Olivia to talk to. Polly feared the visits would lessen if Mama came home.

Papa carved the roast of beef. Rare and ooozing, the way he liked it. All the food was planned for Papa's tastes now.

Nanette wasn't with them anymore. She had gone to work for Mrs. Frogge, which was silly. Not even Nanette could make Mrs. Frogge look nice. Nanette had cried when she left.

"Are you going forever, Nanette?" Polly had asked her.

"Ah, *cherie*, I wish I knew. If your *maman* was to get well, I'd return in a minute."

"Nanette, did you love my mother?"

"Oh, Miss Polly, everyone loved your *maman*. Until she became ill —so upset at the last. Yes, I still love your mother, *cherie*. I would return immediately if I thought they would allow her to come home." Sighing.

Not everyone loved Mama. Papa didn't. Polly wasn't even sure she did. Admired her, yes. Mama was beautiful. But love? How did one love a parent? Of course one was supposed to. That didn't mean to say one knew how.

A glass beside Papa's plate. He nodded curtly to Taft. "You can refill this for me."

"Yes, sir. From the decanter in the den, sir?"

"What else, Taft?"

"Certainly, sir."

Polly, her lower lip drooping with curiosity, gaped. Too openly.

"Well, miss? What ails you? Did you come down here to stare at your father?"

"No, Papa."

"Then keep your eyes to yourself, miss."

'Yes, Papa." Hiding awkwardness, sudden flushes, under her napkin.

"The rest of you—what's the matter? No appetite?"

Amelia spoke now, her voice clear and distinct as the clock chimes that had just sounded in the hall. "Are you well these days, Papa? We so seldom see you."

He lifted his head, as an animal that scents the wind. "Thank you, Amelia. I am quite well."

Polly felt the hate for Amelia well up in her throat, sticking to her palate. Amelia, so sure of herself. So poised. Always having the answers. Detestable.

Papa attacked his meat. Piling buttered potato and peas onto his fork, spearing a small slice of dripping beef, its blood red staining the purity of the vegetables. He shoved the whole in his mouth and chewed, thoughtfully. His eyes moved over them, taking their measure. Polly felt ill with fear.

Papa roared. They responded at though they'd been hit. "Amelia, why in God's name do you wear those damnfool gloves?"

Amelia gathered herself, raising the fortress walls of dignity. "They are needed to protect my hands, Papa." The voice cool.

"What nonsense is this? Answer me, Amelia."

"Papa, you must surely remember that my hands are still healing."

"I know nothing of the kind. Explain yourself. And while you're doing so, remove those wretched gloves."

Amelia lifted her chin stubbornly. "I'm not sure that you want me to do that, Papa. It may upset your enjoyment of your meal."

He gazed at her, appearing to decide what to do. As he did so, she touched the palm of one hand with the cottoned finger of the other. Exploratively scratched. Unaware perhaps, she was doing so.

"Why do you scratch like that? The whole thing—it's very odd. I don't like it."

"I'm sorry, Papa." The wandering finger stilled.

"This family is acquiring a bad reputation." They were all in it now. "Not right, for Mackenzies." He brought his fist down on the table suddenly, making the silverware and the tumblers jiggle. "Dammit—this family goes way back. We are rooted in American history. Before that, Scottish ancestry—Mackenzie clan, nothing to be ashamed of. But the way you act I'm coming to wish I could disown the lot of you!"

Silence was their best defense. At least Albert and Polly thought so. Amelia cleared her throat, returned Papa's look. Oh, she had courage even if she was hateful. To defy him! It was almost beyond Polly's imagination.

Papa had warmed to his subject now. Perhaps this was what he'd been waiting for. The opportunity to speak out what was on his mind. Why else had he invited them here, pulling them away from the territories they knew best—the schoolroom, the old nursery?

Having dinner with Papa—Papa's guests. It was obvious he wanted them all here for a special reason. Certainly not for anyone's entertainment.

"Your mother is not getting better," Papa began.

They took it in, the information. So seldom given. Any small details with regard to Mama. All they had to go on were guesses, assumptions, gossip among the servants. They never dared ask Papa.

"The doctors know what is wrong with her," Papa went on. "She has had a complete breakdown. Her nerves have gone—her mind is hopeless. They tell me she sits and talks to herself. Sees people who aren't there. It's doubtful whether she'll ever get better." His eyes wandered to Amelia. "This sort of insanity is inherited. You will go without your gloves, Amelia, or I will know the reason why."

Amelia sucked her quiet into her body. "Very well, Papa." She began to unpeel her gloves.

Polly had often seen her hands. They weren't bad when you were used to them. Long stripe marks that never healed. Polly wasn't sure why. It had something to do with the way Amelia scratched them. A joy she allowed herself—when undetected.

She laid the discarded gloves beside her plate. They were noticeable for their cleanliness. Amelia must go through at least six pairs every day.

She took up her fork and without looking at Papa began to use her naked hands to feed herself. Delicately.

"Amelia!" He commanded it. A general at the head of his men. "You come over here this minute—show me your hands—why you're hiding them in those things."

"Very well, Papa." Amelia set down her fork, picked up her napkin, and wiped her mouth. So nicely—as they'd been taught. Nanny had been very particular about manners.

"Christ!" said Nathaniel, half jumping from his chair. "How in God's name did you—" He grabbed the hands, bringing them close so he could see them. At the same time, shoving them away. Revolted.

"I did try to warn you, Papa."

"Warn me? How did they come to be like this? Why aren't you telling me?"

"But I am, Papa. It was when we struck our bargain. I submitted to the lashing, and you said I might wear the dress of my choice to the wedding."

"Wedding! Don't tell me they've been like this since then? Amelia, do you realize how long ago that was?"

"It will be two years ago this summer—"

"I didn't ask you to recite the time!" Explosive. "Has Dr. Porter seen this? Who knows about it? Dammit, your mother should be the one attending to problems of this sort." His eyes swiveled about, looking, they were sure, for Letty. Not finding her, of course.

"Put the gloves back on. You disgust me. Utterly revolt me."

Amelia's nostrils quivered. Ashamed for him. For his stupidity in forcing the issue. She turned away. "I shall need some clean gloves."

"Put those on. Those right there!" Ordering it. His face suffused, his drooping lips shaking as he got out the words. He sat down again, pushing his plate away.

Amelia was beyond dislike. She was loathsome. Polly scowled from the safety of her anonymity. Amelia should be dead. Then Papa might pay some attention to her—Polly.

At last Papa stood up. His hands in his waistcoat, he addressed them. To him, they must be a very large company. Or the message he had saved for the very end was too weighty to be delivered while seated.

"You may wish to know more about your mama," he began.

He had their attention of course. It was the word "mama" that had their eyes alert. Strained faces. What else was he going to add?

"I told you already that your mother is extremely ill. She cannot come home."

"Ever?" asked Amelia. Her lips were pressed together firmly.

Papa rocked back and forth on his feet.

"That is difficult to say, Amelia. But the doctors are dubious. Rather sure, in fact, that she will not come back. For a very long time."

"Not ever?" said Polly, a small open space beginning to appear before her feet. Would she drop in or leap over it?

"Polly," said Amelia with annoyance, "you heard what Papa said. He said 'not for a very long time.' "

Polly stared at her empty plate. When would Taft come to remove it? Bring in the dessert. At nine, Polly found desserts to be more absorbing than meat dishes. Or discussions about Mama.

"Papa?" asked Amelia suddenly. "Exactly where is Mama?"

The question seemed to have startled him. He stared at Amelia, as though searching for words. "In a hospital—"

"I believe you told us that earlier. But what hospital? What is the name of it?"

"Why do you want to know?" His expression was closed now.

"I thought I should like to visit Mama sometime. When I am older. If I had the name, I could remember it."

He appeared astonished. "I wouldn't advise that."

"Why not?"

386

Her response was innocent enough, but it had Papa agitated. "Enough of this. I have an appointment downtown."

"But surely you know where Mama is?"

"Of course I know where your mother is—impudent miss. Now let's have an end to the questions so that I may finish what I was saying."

Amelia seemed to settle back into herself temporarily.

Polly would ask Olivia Abbott to find out. There wasn't anything Papa wouldn't tell Livvie. If anything happened to Mama, Papa would marry Livvie. How old was she, anyway? Polly made her eyes into slits as she counted. If Livvie had been eighteen the last time she was here, she had to be almost nineteen now. Well, maybe she was old enough to get married. But Papa was an old man. Wasn't he?

Papa cleared his throat, stilled them with his eyes. "As I was saying, your mother is being cared for." He licked his lips. "But she can't stay where she is forever. The doctors have a better solution."

Their faces said, "Go on."

"Your Uncle Compton has built a very fine hospital in Vermont. Where he used to visit." Papa was so nervous! What on earth was it?

"Your mother will travel there as soon as the place is completed. She can rest there—good food, country air. But, above all, she will be safe."

"Safe?" Amelia echoed it, puzzled.

He moved his feet, looked down at the floor. "They tell me she has tried to escape—though Lord knows where she'd go to. Poor, demented thing."

Mama wasn't "demented." She was ill. Polly clung to it.

"Up there among the woods and the mountains, they can watch her more closely. At the same time she can have greater peace of mind. The city is no place for the sick." He seemed to have thought it out very carefully. Mama was lucky to have Papa to worry about her.

Polly had a flash of understanding. It would clarify everything. "Papa," she asked, "if Mama isn't to come home again, is that like something happening to her?"

He seemed put off his stride again. Yet less tense this time. "Well, I suppose in a way, yes. You could say that something has 'happened' to your mother. Why do you ask?"

"Because," said Polly, given courage from his attitude, "the maids have always said, if something occurred to Mama, you'd marry Livvie."

He grew slowly pink. "They did, eh? Just like servants—gossiping. Your mother is very much alive." Did he sigh? "It is hardly proper to talk of remarriage when one has a living spouse. No, Polly, I have absolutely no plans to wed Livvie. But I know you've grown fond of her " His half smile teased. Had he meant to say something else and stopped himself just in time?

Amelia smoothed the backs of her gloves, her face cold and remote. Albert toyed with his fork. Why did Albert eat so much when he was so fat? A strange one, Albert.

At last, Taft was allowed to clear the plates. The dessert was a chocolate mousse. Papa didn't have any. Instead, he had Taft bring the decanter from the den and sat, refilled glass in his hand, staring at them. Polly knew, now, he loved Livvie.

Was he even sad about Mama? Perhaps. But Mama was "demented." In a way, Papa deserved Livvie. Hadn't Mama let him down by becoming ill?

Amelia had gotten permission to visit Aunt Hitty. When she had asked her father, he had nodded distantly. "Make your own arrangements."

She arrived at Aunt Hitty's at three o'clock. The black woman came to the door.

"She's expectin' you, chile. She's wid the baby right now. Said for you to go on up to her bedroom."

Amelia was disturbed by colored people. Not used to being around them, she wanted to stare. Knew it was rude. It was annoying to have to decide whether to be impolite or to remain ignorant.

She followed Tildie up the staircase. It was annoying that Aunt Hitty was with her baby. What Amelia had to ask her about was too important to be cluttered up with gurgling and screaming. She wondered, not for the first time, why babies were put into the world. They were nothing but trouble.

Aunt Hitty called out in a firm voice, "Come in." Had her voice always been that firm? "Ah, Amelia dear. Lovely to see you. Do come in. I had meant to be downstairs to greet you, but Felicity needed me."

Amelia came over for a polite kiss. To her horror, Aunt Hitty was nursing the baby. It lay, content and nearly sated, in its mother's arms. True, "it" was a girl. To Amelia, it was a thing. A baby.

Amelia tried not to stare. Worse than wanting to look at Tildie—far worse. She'd never seen a lady's breast bared before. The sight paralyzed her mind, even while she tried to scurry away from it. Amelia looked away, clearing her throat forcefully.

"Have you never seen a baby being nursed before?"

"No, Aunt Hitty." Voice gravelly with embarrassment.

"Well, it's the most natural process in the world, Amelia. Someday you will have babies of your own and then—"

"Oh no!" Interrupting. The awfulness of what Aunt Hitty had said suffocating her. "I shall never have children."

Aunt Hitty's blue eyes were curious, not filled with rebuke, the way so many were when hearing of Amelia's prejudices. "But surely, you will marry?"

"Oh yes. That is my intention."

"Then, dear. Babies come with marriage."

"Not to me." Stubborn.

Aunt Hitty shook her head, glanced down at the sleepy infant. "I'm afraid it isn't al ͭays that easy—the matter of choosing. Sometimes, even if one doesn't want them, the children come." She touched the baby's cheek with a tender finger. "Little Felicity, have you had enough?" She let the nipple nuzzle the tiny mouth. "She's a little pig. And growing so fast. I can hardly believe that she's almost seven months old."

"Don't you have a nanny?" asked Amelia, looking around.

"Not yet. I'm looking for one. I'm afraid I'm very strange, Amelia. I like taking care of my own baby. Of course Tildie helps me, so it isn't a strain."

Amelia knew the whole family considered Aunt Hitty to be a little odd. Amelia could see why.

She almost regretted the decision to come to Aunt Hitty. But there simply wasn't anyone else she could possibly have asked. Although Katie had been her solace when the dark staining began.

"Katie, I am so afraid!" Shaking.

"Saints above, what ails ye? It's only the monthly curse that is on ye."

They supposed she knew. Each thinking the other had told her. Katie perceiving this, suddenly. "Holy Mother, ye mean ye weren't warned? No, I can see that you weren't—what with Miss Petticoat taking over from Nanny. Poor Miss Dove—it was a shame the way she was dismissed. All those years. It makes a body think."

"Katie, what do you mean by 'monthly curse'?"

"It was from the time when Eve first misled Adam. Leastways that's what I was told. Woman has to pay for her sin. Oh, you get used to it, darlin'. Katie'll show you what to do. How to take care of yourself. Now come with me—we'll find rags.'

"Monthly, Katie?"

"On the bell, some women. Others, they come late. Oh, it's the ones who are married suffer over that. Are they with child again?"

Amelia pushing at Katie. "You mean there's a connection between what's occurring now and having a baby?"

"Mother o' God, what I got myself into? Yes, darlin', there is a connection. But don't ask me what now. You've no need to bother your head about it till you're married. They'd have me head if I explained it to you."

Mama should be back. Not because Amelia needed her. Or any of them, for that matter. But because it wasn't right, her being away. Amelia hoped, more than she dared let herself know, that Aunt Hitty would be able to help get her back.

As her aunt poured the tea, Amelia asked, "About Mama? What do you know?"

Aunt Hitty stopped pouring. Set the pot down again on the tea table. "How much have they told you?"

So Aunt Hitty wasn't going to treat her as a child. This much she could see from her expression. Was it relief?

"Just that Mama isn't going to get better, and about Mama being moved to Vermont this summer."

"What did you say?"

"I said Papa mentioned Mama was to be taken up to Uncle Compton's place in Vermont. He didn't say where it was. Just that Uncle Compton was building some kind of hospital. It was why I wanted to talk to you. I thought you'd know."

Aunt Hitty's voice was very hollow. "I'd heard something— Your Uncle Compton doesn't tell me very much about his work."

Amelia realized that Aunt Hitty seemed empty suddenly. She looked so unhappy. She hadn't been that way before the subject of Mama was raised.

"Have you seen my mother since she was taken ill, Aunt Hitty?"

"Dear." Aunt Hitty handed her the cup. "I have tried and tried to see your mother. They wouldn't let me go near her when I was carrying Felicity. Now they give me excuses that it will hurt my ability to nurse my child. But I'm about to wean her. You saw how big she is—" A laugh that was half a chuckle, then the strain returned to her voice. "I haven't succeeded in getting in to see your mama. I worry about it a great deal." She sighed. "And every time I think on it I feel guilty being happy with my little daughter when I think of my poor sister."

"Do you think she's as sick as they say?"

"I don't know, dearest. The day she had the accident to her wrists—" Hitty stared at Amelia to see how much she knew. "She came over here earlier. She wasn't herself, Amelia. I'd never seen her like that. As if her mind was wandering. I would ask her things and she wouldn't answer right away, then she'd act as though she hadn't heard."

"I never saw Mama like that. Ever." The gray eyes probed. Was Aunt Hitty telling all she knew?

"I only saw her that way once. Of course you must understand, dear, your mother and I have never been close. Can you grasp that?"

"Like Polly and me. Or even silly old Albert. We all live in the same house together, but we aren't friends."

"Then you do see? Oh, that helps. I've always admired your mother so, Amelia. Such an amazingly intelligent woman. Talent for painting. That friend of ours, Miss Macleod, felt your mother could become an excellent artist in her own right. Oh dear, I still cry over Miss Macleod."

"She drowned, didn't she?" Amelia's voice was direct and clear. Cutting through Aunt Hitty's soaking emotion. Any show of feelings embarrassed Amelia.

"We never heard anything more. No trace of what happened. If she'd been spared, I feel sure she'd have written your mother."

"But Mama wouldn't have received the letter."

"No, that's right. But, you see, they found evidence of a ship going down. That was in the paper. That was one of the things that made your mother do it."

"Do what, Aunt Hitty?"

"Did I say 'do it'? I meant, go into her breakdown. She was so fond of Fiona. So was I, for that matter." Aunt Hitty blew her nose. "I'm sorry, dear. Is your tea all right?"

Amelia relaxed a little. "Yes, thank you. Can you tell me anything about this place Mama is going to in Vermont?"

"Oh, the town is charming. A person could be very happy there." Aunt Hitty was playing a game now. It was called Hide the Truth.

Amelia cleared her throat impatiently. "But she'll be locked up. She won't see the town."

Her words had ripped a hole in the fabric of Aunt Hitty's resistance. She crumpled. "Who told you that, Amelia?"

"Papa did. He said he'd been informed Mama had tried to escape. That she would be 'safer' in the country. Why would she have to be protected from getting away?"

Aunt Hitty seemed to be trying to make up her mind. At last, she set her spoon in her saucer with a clatter. "Amelia, I am going to be as honest with you as I can. I think you are old enough, and the mere fact of your coming here to talk to me tells me you are mature for your age. Do you think you can be patient with me while I try to explain?"

"Of course."

"Dear, the only one who has the power to get your mother out of that hospital—or any hospital for that matter—is your papa. He was the one who obtained the court order. He went to court and asked a judge to have your mother taken care of. In legal terms it's called having a person 'committed.' Oh, I am sure the doctors had their say. But until such time as your father is convinced that it's all right for your mother to come home, there isn't much the rest of us can do. I know this because your grandmother and I have tried."

"You've tried?" Faintly.

"Yes, dear. We engaged an attorney to make inquiries. We did this without letting my husband know. Now I don't expect you to understand that, but I simply say it because I want to ask you to promise me not to talk about this to anyone."

"Not even to Grandmother?"

"Yes, you can discuss it with her. And of course with me. But not if my husband is present."

"Why can't you tell Uncle Compton?"

"I'm hard put to explain his feelings, dear. He has treated your mother and believes very strongly that she should be kept in the hospital. It's there, you see, we disagree. He is a doctor, and Grandmother and I are just family. It's really your papa though who has the final say."

"Papa doesn't want Mama to come home?"

"I'm afraid, Amelia, I have no other conclusion to draw. What do you think?" Aunt Hitty was treating her like a grown-up.

"I don't know about Papa. I love him very much, but I don't understand him at all. He seems so lonely, but when he and Mama were together, they acted as if they hated each other. Not like when he's with Olivia."

"Olivia?"

"Mr. Abbott's daughter. Do you think they would get married, Aunt Hitty, if Mama were to die?"

"You and I will hope very much that she won't die."

"Yes," said Amelia slowly. "I wonder how well they will take care of her in Vermont. I should like to see her—just to know."

"To know what, dear?"

Amelia smoothed her gloves. "I'm not sure. Perhaps that she's as bad as they say she is. It's like she disappeared. One day she was at home, the next day she was gone. Now I don't believe anyone expects her to come back. Is there any way she could get killed, Aunt Hitty?"

Hitty blanched. "Killed, dear? Oh, I don't think we should have thoughts like that. My husband wouldn't—" Then she stopped.

"You believe Mama's all right, then?"

The veil coming down. The veil of lies. "Of course, dear."

Amelia shivered. "If only they'd let me visit her." She lifted her head. "I just have this feeling, Aunt Hitty. One day we'll get Mama back. When I become a little older, I'll work to make it come true."

"I'm sure you will, dear."

She could see Aunt Hitty didn't believe her. Someone had to have faith it would happen. It just wasn't right, their being able to take Mama away like that.

8

Letty was having pains. Now that she was so heavy they no longer tied her, except at night. Or when she was bad, and they bound her wrists together behind her chair. Her breasts had grown enormous. Her belly groaned and moved about under its own volition.

No, that was wrong. Appleby had explained it. Before they sent her up here to this place. Appleby had had Clark bring her into her office. Told the male nurse to make Letty kneel on the bare boards, before the great ebony crucifix.

"Now leave us!" she'd told Clark.

"Letty, confess your sins to Almighty God and Christ, his Son."

"But what have I done wrong?"

"You stupid, wicked fool—you've been lying down like a whore. I'm not going to ask who did it to you. It's enough you permitted it."

Permitted it? When she was constantly tied? But even as she protested it in her mind, she knew she deceived herself. She had behaved like a loose woman. Done as they asked.

Compton—Dr. Prior. Finally, Clark had filled her with himself in the dark hours. He had twisted her limbs and pinched her inner thighs to make her cry—until she pleaded for him to cease.

"Sinful, evil woman. Now listen to me." Appleby's whisper a hiss. "We are going to have to send you away. We have no facilities to handle childbearing here."

A long time ago someone had told her not to have another child. Who had that been? Henry Porter? Or had it been that strange maid of Cousin Frances'? Well, the cage had come true. She'd glanced at the

394

bars on the windows as Appleby ranted and raved. A cage. For sure, she was in a cage.

"Send me away?"

"Well, you can't have it here, that's for certain!"

She had left them all behind and come to Vermont. To her surprise, Clark and Bailey had traveled with her in the closed coach.

At night, they slept in the bed next to her. Their sweat sour, acrid. Clothes cast aside, to lie naked in the moonlight. Bailey's breasts full and sagging over her rounded stomach, her mouth open to let out her snores. Clark lying long and beautiful the length of the bed. She knew he wouldn't touch her with Bailey there. Bailey'd raise too much of a fuss.

How long had they been on the road? Sometimes Letty slept in the coach. Lay awake most of the night. All of it was upside down, but she knew much of it was due to the medicine they fed her.

"Dose her good, Clark. Won't bother us on the way."

Then she was walking, across the surface of a porch. Into a large room with a comfortable air. A farm kitchen? But when she tried to look about, they pushed her forward.

Bailey? Where was Bailey? And Clark?

"They gone back into town, missus. You be nice now. We settle you in."

They had helped her along the corridor. How long had it been since her head had been clear enough for her to walk unaided? It seemed forever. The other Letty hadn't had it that way. She'd drunk tea from frail porcelain, rung bells for a maid, and let herself know what she wanted. No, that was wrong. She was the Letty who knew what she wanted. The other Letty had had to pretend.

"Well, Letty, how are you feeling?"

Compton! She'd grown weak with surprise. How often she'd spread herself for him, imagining him there, covering her with his seeking hands, his warm, scented body. Now here he was. And she was here too. Or was it a dream? The medicine?

"It's all right, nurse. I'll ring when I'm ready. Mrs. Mackenzie and I know each other. She's a former patient of mine."

The nurse had clucked with her tongue. "Well now, isn't that nice? Sort of like coming home for her, eh?"

"Compton—oh, Compton. Why did you leave me?"

His face kind. Gentle. "Letty dearest. Why couldn't you have had more faith in me? Waited until I came back? We could have talked all this over. You didn't have to try to take your life!" He'd rebuked her like the small child she'd known she was. He was a father to her as well as her lover. He would take care of her now. She could rest in his love.

Hadn't he sent for her?

"No, that's not the way it came about!" His face had changed. Thunderclouds across the sweet skies. "You are here because you got yourself in trouble. Letty, did you have to be so weak-willed?"

"I don't know what you mean?"

"Of course you know. Who was the bastard you let take advantage of you?" He'd passed his hand across his eyes. "Never mind—it's best I not know. I'm familiar with those places. We have you here now. Can take care of you, as long as you agree to behave."

"Behave?"

"Not entice any of the help. We have some young ones. I like to think I can trust them but—oh, Letty—did it have to be this way?"

She had disappointed him. She saw it now.

"Are you very weary, my dear?"

She'd shaken her head. "I slept almost every day in the coach. But, Compton, I'm afraid I'm awkward."

"Leave that to me. Come, sit on the couch." Slipping his hand up under her dress—if it could be called that. "You must be about four months along. Well, we've time we can have together, before you get too large. Now, I must warn you, never to say anything to a living soul. Promise? My loving you depends on it."

"Anything." She'd meant it. Always.

When he entered her, she was momentarily disappointed. He couldn't fill her like Clark. She'd not known he'd be so pencil thin. Remembered him as much more virile. But she seemed to please him. He took a long time until he could reach his own summit. Rasping at her and gasping. Climbing, while her own stone came. Would it drop? It did now sometimes—just for thinking of it—touching herself in the close, heavy darkness. Recalling Clark.

Yet when she'd been dragged into a closet by Clark, she'd remembered Compton. Imagined it was he. How confusing.

Compton helped her to cleanse herself. "Now, you think you can be a good girl?"

"Shall you send for me again?"

"From time to time."

For several weeks, he hadn't touched her. He came to visit her in her room. Stopped to talk to her in the common dining hall where she sat with the others. The ones who muttered. The ones who slapped at imaginary flies—tried to pull their clothes off—touch themselves erotically. The girl who always cried.

Her name was Letty.

"If you can't stop weeping, I shan't come and see you anymore." He sat on the edge of her bed. She was lying there, trying to decide if the pains were close enough together to call for Nellie Parsons.

He had her lean back. Placed his hand on her enormous stomach. A walrus—or perhaps a cow, swollen and gaseous with rot.

"The baby won't be born normal," she said.

"Now, Letty, you don't know that."

"I know."

"Missus—it's over." Wiping her brow.

"The child?"

"Best you not ask. It could never have lived. We've taken it away. But you got others at home, haven't you?"

She nodded, the spilling of her tears bathing her face, her cheeks. She was punished. It was a just reward. Was it enough? That was what bothered her. Must she be flagellated again?

Endlessly?

9

Christmas was a helluva time for everybody. The girls were worked off their feet. Or moped with little to do. Some of the younger ones at Blanche's took to thinking about home. Whether they'd good memories or bad, it was all the same at Christmas. Home was suddenly the place to be.

Many of the customers felt that way also. Some of the regulars were inclined to stay away. Feeling they should be where they'd ought to have been all along. Beside the wife and the little ones. Others stopped by in a surge of gratitude. Ribbons for a favorite girl. Baked goods, dried fruit done up in silver paper. A pint of rum and didn't mind staying to drink it.

Rose opened her door. To signal she was free. It was early in the evening yet, the night before Christmas. She yawned and stretched, then smoothed her dress around her. Madame had given them each a new frock. Not just because of the holiday, but celebration for the year past. Madame, counting the money in her small office, had smiled. Rose had caught a glimpse of her at it through the glass-windowed walls. Walls that allowed Blanche to keep an eye on whatever was going on in the hallway.

Rose patted her hair, tucking an errant strand into her chignon. She felt wonderful. Most, because Madame appreciated her. Rose knew she was getting on—for a whore. The dream that she'd kept alive for so many years would have to take shape soon, or else she'd best kiss it good-bye. That she, Rose, could save up enough money for her own place. Not a House, like Madame wanted. A cottage—somewhere she could call home.

Suddenly she was aware, as the family cat becomes aware, that something was going on. Upstairs. What was it?

She knew without too much scanning of her concerns that it was Ellie. The girl had been too quiet at supper. Pushed away the special dish of pork and rice Tania had prepared for their treat.

Voices in the hall downstairs. Must've come in the side entrance. Coming up the stairs.

"—take care of ourselves, Blanche." Laughter. That could only be the doctor—and Mr. Mackenzie. It would be Christmas had brought the doctor back from that northern state.

"Evening, Rose. May we visit here a minute?"

"Of course," she said, getting out of her chair. With Dr. Grey part owner of the House, he could stop where he liked.

"You want I should fetch you some likker?"

They'd been talking in hushed, rapt tones. Rose was an intrusion. "Oh yes," said Dr. Grey absently. "See if Madame would send up a bottle of the best brandy."

"Some of my own, no doubt." Mr. Mackenzie laughed.

Rose returned with the bottle of brandy. Did she tread too softly on the stairs? But she could scarcely help overhearing.

"—nurses know she's a tendency to do herself harm. It's just a matter of time."

"Thank God. I got a real fever on me to wed that little Abbott girl, Compton. If I wait too long—you know how it is? She's a beauty. Bound to be grabbed by some young fool."

"Don't worry. You'll have your bride."

Rose knocked at the door. "Brought the brandy."

The men were parting on a glass of the liqueur. "One for you, Rose?"

"Not when I'm working. Except when the customers insist."

Ellie was waiting for the doctor. She'd heard he was back in the city. Two days she'd waited. He'd have to help her. He must. Only he would know what to do.

"Ellie?" He approached her like he meant business.

"Ellie—Goddammit woman, how can you be a whore and taste so pure?"

"I'm not!" she wanted to cry. She had let Mai Tai Wong down, getting herself with child this way. It would take all her earnings now, just to keep it someplace. That was what the girls said was the alternative. "But don't do nuthin' stupid, Ellie love. Knitting needles, prodding yourself—you're liable to wind up in a grave."

"Are you cold?" When he asked it, she realized she was trembling

"A little."

"Warm you up. Here, have some brandy."

He probed under her dress while she was sipping. She pretended to an arousal she didn't feel. Dreaded when he came to her sore breasts.

He motioned for her to slip out of her gown. She let it slide to the floor. By now he was erect and ready. But in no hurry. He caressed the inside of her thighs as she stood before him, quivering. With one finger he explored her inner parts, curving it to follow the opening of her body.

"Finish your brandy," he said curtly. She drank it down, feeling it burn her throat, bring quick tears to her eyes.

"Make you cry, huh?" He laughed, then took the glass out of her hand. He was nearly ready. She knew him now, enough to tell.

At last he moaned and gave up his essence. Lay on her briefly. She could feel him content, as if he were smiling. Almost at once, it gave way to briskness.

"Well, that was most satisfying. I see you haven't lost your knack."

She had to speak to him now. She spilled it all out. Not at all as she'd planned. Her hopes that he would help her.

"My dear child. You can't be serious."

"Please." She whispered it. "Please, do something for me."

He fussed with his clothing. "Go to Blanche. It's her province, not mine."

"But you are a doctor—!"

"Not in this situation, my dear." He gave a smug smile.

"You could bring on a miscarriage—" She pointed to the black bag he always carried. "There are potions one can drink, an instrument to pierce—"

"You've had the only intrument I'm going to use," he said sardonically. Shriveling her with his disinterest, his eagerness to be gone. A wave of the hand. "Take it to Blanche. She is used to this problem. Did you think you were the only girl who ever got caught?"

She'd stolen the skewer from the kitchen. In case the doctor wouldn't help her. Now she closed her door. She lay on her bed, and with her limbs opened as to receive a man, penetrated herself.

She used all the inborn will with which Mai Tai and her Chinese ancestors had endowed her. Perseverance in the face of fear—forged in the terrible white hot fires of necessity. She cried out with pain but would not stay the probing intrument till she was satisfied the job had been done.

Her life blood was seeping away. Along with that of the child she was carrying. What did it look like, this thing that she nourished within her? Rose had said, "Oh, they ain't no more'n a speck of flesh and slime when they come that early. But that's no way, Ellie. You hear me? No way at all. It's almost certain death, gal. You gotta have the baby —somehow you gotta see it through."

It had been hatred for them all that had driven her to do this thing to herself. The same hand that had guided the metal skewer wished in actuality to destroy all of them. She turned on the only flesh that might be reached. Her own. The innocent speck that grew within her.

Weakness was beginning to claim her when she heard someone come into the room. "You asleep, Ellie?"

"Rosey?"

Rose was suspicious. She came to the bed, pulled away the blanket. "Oh my Gawd, you been and done it. What's to be done?" Clapping her hand to her mouth and running from the room.

Ellie could hear Rose's voice, shouting, from far away.

Death had steel teeth. Clamped down on her in a way that told her it wouldn't let go easily.

"—take her to the hospital."

"Gawd, not there."

"We got no choice. She's dying!"

Blanche now. Peering down at her with her monkey face. Anger glinting in her green eyes. Her hair brassy, thin with age, brittle fibered. "Why'd ya do it? You coulda come to me any time. I already had plans. Rose, she talked to me about it yesterday. I'd have taken care of you, girl. Allus take care of the ones that need it."

Before she passed out, Ellie knew she'd been wrong about Madame. Old Rosey was right after all. Blanche did care.

She should have had more faith in Rosey. In Madame. They weren't all uncaring. Just some of them. The ones she had made count. The men of honor.

IO

It had been quite a night. Rose lay down on her bed exhaustedly. Catch a few hours sleep before dawn crept in on them. Someone had said it might snow. Well, that would be nice. Rose sought sleepily for visions of sleighs, people flocking to white churches, houses warm with family comfort.

Long ago, there'd been such a life for Rose. In a small town up the Hudson River Valley. Then a sickness had come, bringing all of them to quietness. How had Rose survived, and for what? She'd never known. After it was over, she'd buried her kinfolk with the last of the money. Stayed in the cold house alone, a sixteen-year-old girl with no reason to keep living.

The new young blacksmith had come over for company. She hadn't meant to let him steal any favors. Somehow, with the loneliness, the sweetness of his kisses, she'd heard what she wanted to hear.

The minister and his wife had tried to talk her out of the marriage. "What do we any of us know about him, Rose? He's a stranger when you come right down to it."

But their arguments had lacked weight. She already belonged to him, as indissolubly as if their union had been sanctified. The church blessing was merely an afterthought.

Which, as it turned out, it was. After he'd failed to find work in New Jersey, they ended up in Philadelphia. The money had disappeared as fast as snow in April. Rudie liked his liquor. Became abusive when the mood was on him. Once he threatened her. "I don't have to stay with you. You ain't nuthin' to me. Just a whore."

Not that she began right away at Blanche's. There were the hateful other jobs. Long hours over a loom. A maid in a tavern. Finally one of the girls that worked there whispered, "I know a place we could make twice as much. Want to give it a try?"

She had to hand it to Blanche. Raggle-taggle as Rose must have looked when she first came applying for the job, it was a wonder that Madame had been able to see beyond the taut skin and the scratched hands, the tousled hair, the gaunt cheeks.

Angie slipped into the bed. She insinuated her slight frame into the curve of Rose. The older woman placed her arms about the girl protectively. Angie was nothing but a kitten. Sharp teeth, but meant nothing by it. Rose pulled the slender body closer. Emulating concern, tenderness.

Angie smelled strongly of blood. That was strange because, insofar as Rose knew, she hadn't been one of the ones to gather about poor Ellie. Perhaps she was in her monthly? But that couldn't have been right, or Madame would've sent Mr. Mackenzie to one of the other girls.

Mr. Mackenzie. Rose came awake at that. Couldn't recall seeing him come downstairs. All that commotion going on. You'd have thought he might have inquired. Though, like most of the customers, he was naturally cautious.

She whispered to Angie, who was feigning sleep, her breath coming regular though her limbs were still tense, "You entertain Mr. Mackenzie this evenin', love?"

At once, Angie sat up. Curling away from Rose. "He was up earlier. What you want to know for?"

"Nothing, nothing." Rose tried to sound soothing. She wished now she hadn't said anything. Yet something was going on. Earlier she'd thought her innate sense of disaster stemmed from what had happened to Ellie. She had tried to dismiss it, but it had hung over her, like a rock perched on a hillside, waiting for something as light as the scrabbling feet of a bird to decide it to fall. Try as she might, she hadn't been able to get rid of the uneasiness. Why did Angie smell of blood?

Then she caught the other whiff. The one above all others that they dreaded. Fire.

"Gawd—I smell smoke. Angie!"

"No you don't, Rose." Angie's thin, groping arms had reached for her, trying to pull Rose back down in bed. Surprised at first, then annoyed, Rose pushed her off. Or tried to. The girl was astonishingly strong. Finally, she had to use subterfuge.

"Where's your doll, Angie? You don't want to sleep without your doll, do you?"

"He promised me a doll for Christmas. Said he forgot."

"Who forgot, dearie?" The smell was stronger now. Not Rose's

403

imagination. She leaped from the bed. "C'mon, Angie—let's go see where your dolls are."

It was curling on the staircase. In the dim light of the guttering candles, she could see it billowing from the upper landing. Smoke!

Rose screamed with all her might, "Fire—we got fire!"

Angie was behind her. "My dolls! My dollies are burning up, Rosey!"

Mad. She was insane. Blanche should have committed her years ago. Or insisted that riverboat gambler who'd fathered her take her back.

Flames were shooting out from under a doorway. It would have to be Ellie's room. Had the fire begun in there? A candle left burning in the flurry of concern over Ellie's condition? Rose saw with stinging eyes the doorway to the next room was open. Angie's room.

Rose staggered to the entry. Angie was dancing about the engulfed room, a doll in her arms. Rocking it. Singing between spasms of coughing.

"Angie, for the love of Gawd. C'mon, we got to get outta here."

Then she saw him. As Angie unthinkingly danced, a marionette witch suspended on wires of her own illusions, Rose stared at what was left of Nathaniel Mackenzie.

Lying statuesque, stark naked. The mattress red from his already coagulating life blood. His throat had been slashed from ear to ear.

Angie had a knife now, and was waving it over the doll's head. "You be wicked, I punish you. Like I punished him."

Rose stifled a scream. She hurled herself on Angie, trying to drag her toward the door.

Angie whirled the knife around. "Leave me be!" Pettishly.

"Angie, we gotta—" Not able to breathe.

The door. Rose held Angie by the wrist, conscious that the knife was stabbing and stabbing at her arm. Suddenly Angie pulled away, backing into the flaming interior.

Much later, Rose saw Blanche hovering above her head. Rose came to slowly.

"Where am I ?"

"In the hospital, Rose. I got to know. Did Angie kill him ?"

"Mr. Mac—" The words didn't come out. Rose was saying them in her head clearly, but her tongue was thick and stiff as a piece of old leather stuck between her teeth.

"Did Angie kill Mr. Mackenzie? I know you went in there, Rose. We found him after the fire was put out. Not much left to tell him by. His gold watch fell through a crack clear to the ground, or it'd have been melted. Rose, I know how bad hurt you are, but you gotta tell me.

For the sake of all the times we been together. Did she kill him?"

Rose exercised enormous effort. She was so tired. They had to leave her alone. From a great distance she heard Tania.

"Madame, you shouldn't feel responsible. Come on back to where we're staying. We can't do no more here. Poor Rosey."

Madame left. But not before she planted an awkward kiss on the forehead of Rose. Rosey, mother to them all. Far from pain now.

A nurse, coming over to Rose's bed, pulled the sheet up, covering the dead woman.

II

"Letty should be here!" Mother had said when they all gathered about the dining table after the funeral. But it wasn't as easy as that.

There had been papers to sign, attorneys to plead the case in court. Hitty wondered how she had stood it all. Yet, thinking back, she knew. Someone had to see to it. To right the wrong. At times when Hitty faltered, she saw Amelia's face before her.

"Mother should be at home. Isn't there something you can do, Aunt Hitty?"

She didn't know what she would have done without Paul Schwartz-kopf. At first he had been obdurate. As Compton's partner, he would be reluctant to intrude. Another physician would be in a far better position to assist her.

"You are the only one who can get us the information we need," she had persisted. "Just because you are his partner you would be justified in going up there, to see what sort of facilities he is offering the patients you send him."

Dr. Paul's young face had looked unhappy. Thoughtful. When he had said "We-ell," in that slow way of his, Hitty knew she had won. "I can try. Make my report to you. If it would help to ease your mind? But remember, she is officially your husband's patient—"

"We can have him removed—now." Now that Nathaniel was dead.

He'd gone without telling her. Perhaps it was for the best. After all, she was Compton's wife. She was also Letty's sister. Hitty bided her time—playing with Felicity. The little girl was walking now, practicing her words. Such a joy to be with her.

Finally, he returned. He came to her house directly from the train. His usually pleasant face was stern and grave.

"Mrs. Grey, there are some very ill people up there."

"So we have understood." She waited for him to come out with the reason for his anger, his tense, white face.

"Some of them are hard to control without heavy doses of sedation."

"My sister—" She said it carefully, studying his expression. "You found her to be like that?"

"Your sister has been treated that way. We could try another method," he said cautiously.

"What are you suggesting?"

"If we could get permission to have her withdrawn from your husband's care, we could bring her back here. Under supervision, you understand—"

"Another of Dr. Prior's places?" Hitty felt herself stiffen, prepared to be disappointed in him.

Quickly. "No, not that at all. She could live in her own home. With dignity." Had he emphasized that point? "If her servants are loyal, as you've suggested—if one maid in particular could be selected as a companion. I think under supervision—"

"Supervision?" Her alarm flaming up again.

"Yours and mine, Mrs. Grey."

"Ah." She understood.

"When a patient has been under such heavy amounts of sedation, it is sometimes difficult to persuade them to turn to a life without it. We shall have to wean her slowly. Very slowly. It is going to be a struggle. The hardest part will be the first few weeks. It may turn out to take months. But I believe that if she is surrounded with kindness, she will want to come out with it. Eventually."

Polly and Amelia were waiting for Hitty when she arrived. Albert joined them minutes later, closing the parlor door behind him.

"We tried asking her to have lunch with us today, Aunt Hitty, just as you suggested. But she won't have anything to do with us." His round, slightly petulant mouth was twisted with hurt.

Letty uncovered private angers in all of them. How well Hitty knew it.

"Mama said she'd come up to the schoolroom to hear how nicely I read," Polly complained, "yet when Miss Pettigrew sent me down, Nanette told me Mama wasn't feeling well. Is she ever going to be better, Aunt Hitty?"

"Dr. Schwarzkopf feels your mother is making progress," said Hitty, trying to believe the statement. He had only half said it. "We know so little about what goes on in the mind, Mrs. Grey."

Still, Letty was at least at home.

"—with you all again, darlings," Hitty reminded them. They

glanced up, hopeful. Until they remembered the reality of having Letty here, at home. Was she upstairs? Or was she still in some other place —Vermont perhaps?

In the darkness of the night, Hitty had asked herself if she had made a mistake in moving heaven and earth to bring Letty back to Philadelphia. As Compton had accused her.

"Meddling hussy! What do you know of illness?"

"She is my sister, Compton."

"Which merely underlines my point. You cannot see her objectively."

"Nevertheless, I owe her my caring. She should be near us, Compton. Now that Nathaniel's gone, the children need her."

"She is one burden those children don't need."

She had put it to him then. "Why do you dislike her so, Compton? I should think that would stand in the way of your being able to treat her."

He'd looked as if she'd struck him. "You Benedicts! Pushy, unnatural women—wanting to have your way with a man. Reduce him to less than his real stature. Demolish his pride. You none of you deserved to be married. I see that now. What a fool I was."

"Let us speak frankly, Compton. I have only to look about me to be able to see how much my wedding endowment has permitted you to do. This building, for instance. It is hardly recognizable as the one we visited on our honeymoon. You were no fool, Compton. If anything, I was the fool. But I'd led a very protected life. I wanted to marry. I doubt if my parents could've talked me out of it even if they'd wanted to."

He glared at her. "What makes you think I used your funds to build this hospital, Hitty?"

"Let's just say that both of us have gained. You have your treatment center. I have our daughter."

"Your daughter."

"If you wish to think that, that is your business. Now, we have a carriage waiting and are anxious to be on our way home. I trust someone has gone to ready my sister?"

"So you can be together again with your lover, the good Paul Schwarzkopf?" he'd hissed. His eyes were lidded, his face reptilian.

"Compton, if anyone is ill in this place, it is you." She'd put her hand on the doorknob, to move by him.

"Don't think you can go unpunished, Hitty. Someday our daughter is going to hear just how disgusting her mother can be."

"*Our* daughter, Compton? I thought you were so sure she was born as the result of an affair?"

Hitty left the children and mounted the staircase to Letty's suite. Unshared now. Perhaps, in spite of the aura of tragedy that convention coated Nathaniel's death with, it was a blessing. Hitty stopped herself, seeing how far she'd come to doubting, now, that Letty should be at home.

Nanette answered her knock. Nanette was imbued with cheerfulness. Where did she get the patience? Brushing Letty's hair, which had at last begun to grow back, rubbing her shoulders, coaxing her to eat.

"Oh, Madame Grey, it is so nice you are come. Madame Letty feels a little better today."

If she did, it wasn't noticeable. Letty, sitting with her feet on a stool, gone dull with age. Letty, her hands quiet in her lap, enclosed by one of the lemon silk chairs.

"Dearest, how are you?"

The opaque eyes moved with infinite care to take in Hitty. They fell upon her with a glance that was heavy, dismissing. "Hitty, I didn't know you were coming to see me."

An accusation? Hitty found it hard not to take it so. She pressed her lips to Letty's forehead. "Yes, you did. Nanette told you."

"You shouldn't have come." It was always the same conversation, though sometimes with different phrasing. "I ought to be left alone."

"Now, dearest, you know that isn't true. It's good for you to see people. We were hoping you'd join us for lunch today."

Silence.

"Letty, those flowers are lovely. Did Mother send them?"

Silence.

"Have you been trying to read?"

Silence.

Through it Nanette moved with solid reassurance. "Madame talked today of having some new clothes. For the fall season, right, madame?" Coaxing her as if she were a small child.

"She did?" Hitty played at being pleased.

As expected. "No. I need no new clothes. Nanette is quite mistaken."

"Ah, madame, you will soon be pretty again, *cherie*. A little time. The hair is already growing back—but madame must try to have better appetite."

"I am waiting to die."

Hitty stared at her. Had there been any change in Letty at all? She went back in memory to the day she'd first seen her—the day they fetched her away from Grey Home.

Shock. This wasn't Letty! Not their beautiful, handsome Letty? This woman who had sat, drugged still, in the high-backed chair before the window. Staring at nothing.

Letty? Hitty had had to look twice. The cheekbones, always molded with fine lines, were hollow. A gaunt, pallid woman who better bore the designation "female." She reeked of carbolic—she who had exuded lavender. Her hands crisscrossed with sharp cuts, the flesh about them angry and puffy. Her mouth gone sour and thin-lipped. Her hair in jagged cuts, close to her neck. It gave her a boyish appearance, but not one that was pleasing.

Neglected. Letty looked utterly neglected.

Now the hands were healed—Nanette had rubbed healing salves into their coarsened skin daily. The hair was cut again, but with tenderness, so that now it had a desire to curl, framing Letty's face in curious tendrils that seemed to wish to peer at the face they surrounded. Asking why no levity, no joy?

Hitty felt the weariness. It seeped out of Letty and spread across the space between them. There was anger in it. Bright, flashing anger. Hitty doubted whether Letty had any idea of its existence. It lurked in whatever recesses of Letty there were. Bat-haunted, unforgiving towers filled with some lonely pain.

Something Letty couldn't forgive herself for? Hitty groped at the notion, trying to transform it out of tenuous wraithing mists into an idea that had substance. It eluded her; oil floating blue gold on water, shimmering away down a drain. Evading capture. Yet she'd glimpsed it. Letty, unable to forgive herself.

Hitty did the best thing she could. She withdrew herself, seeing the necessity to safeguard what little strength she had left.

As she walked on down the stairs, she had to ask herself, was this anger she felt in her sister directed toward herself alone? Or toward all of them? Perhaps Letty hadn't wanted to be brought back home? The thought was so startling that Hitty stopped, midway down the staircase, shocked. For if this were the case, then she—Hitty—was to blame. Mistaken in her rescue efforts. The enormity of the thought consumed her.

Hitty's self-confidence was as fragile as Felicity. A pale child who needed to be sheltered from the lashing force of deeply ingrained fears. Even Mother—especially Mother—had given lip service to the concept that men were always right. When wrong, they shouldn't be told so. Hitty had built her strength by flying in the face of that tradition. Timidly at first, quaking at every footfall; but persistently, until she was able to claim her sister.

She corrected herself. Claim the outer shell of Letty. With anguish, Hitty realized that might be all that was left.

410

12

Taft hovered at the bottom of the stairs. "Mrs. Grey, there's a lady to see you."

"To see me?" Hitty shouldn't have been surprised. Since she had assumed control of the affairs of the Mackenzie household, she was frequently approached by people on varying quests—new uniforms for the maids, when the seamstress should come. Very occasionally it was ladies of their acquaintance asking after Letty, though most of them had given up by now.

"It's Miss Macleod," Taft said, as though the name pained him.

Hitty's mind went blank. "Miss Macleod? I know no one by that name—"

"Oh, yes you do!" said a very English voice.

"Fiona!" It was all Hitty could manage.

"Have I been gone so long? I thought I must have offended the lot of you—every letter to Letty returned and I didn't have your address. What is going on? Am I welcome?"

"Are you welcome!" Hitty drew Fiona to her. The clouds had opened up and delivered exactly the right answer to Hitty's prayers.

"What do you mean, you thought I was drowned?" Fiona protested, while Hitty tried to explain.

Above them, from the parlor wall, the cool, distant figure of Letty looked down. Letty at eighteen—before everything.

They exchanged information. Felicity's birth for Fiona's rescue. "Indians, terrifying my dear, but they saved us. I thought sure they were going to kill us, but they ended by taking us to another tribe. Then so on and on until we made it to a coastal settlement. But where is Letty? Did I arrive on a bad day? Is she away or something?"

"She's been ill," Hitty began. "It's been rather awful."

"What kind of ill?" Instantly Fiona's plain face was alert. The brown eyes keen, perceptive. "Where is she? Is she in her room?" She started to rise, had to be stopped.

"I wish I could give you an explanation. It's been a breakdown. She—she tried to slit her wrists and—"

"Letty? You are telling me this about Letty?"

"I'm afraid so." Faltering. "We've got her back at last. Nathaniel had sent her to a dreadful place."

"That man!" said Fiona.

"Save your breath on him. He's dead. In a fire."

"Good riddance!" said Fiona heartily. "Oh, I'm sorry for him, but not for the rest of you. He was a beast."

"The children were told he died a hero."

"Who thought that up?"

"It was a tenement fire, you see. He was inspecting some rental property when the blaze broke out. He died attempting to save one of the poor tenants."

"Ah," said Fiona knowingly. "I'll remember that when I see the children. Did they take it hard?"

"Mostly Amelia. She was devoted to him, though I'll never understand why. The way he punished her—"

"It's often the way," said Fiona sagely. "Spoil the brats and they'll end up detesting you. Now, go on about Letty." Her lips had gone tight.

"After Nathaniel's death, we went to court and had the committal orders nullified. We brought Letty back here."

"Couldn't your husband have helped?"

There! It was out. The reason for her shame. It was Compton she was shielding. Herself, stained with Compton's guilt.

Hitty said evenly, "Letty was confined in my husband's hospital."

Fiona stared at her. Saw it all slowly. Putting the pieces of it together—even down to the bottom of the jar. "Well," she said at last, "now that it's over, how is she?"

"I wish I could tell you she's better. In fact, I am starting to ask myself if we did wrong bringing her here."

"No!" said Fiona vociferously.

"You haven't seen her." Uncertainly.

"I don't have to." Fiona shook her head. "By heaven, Hitty, I may not know your sister well, but I know people. What's more to the point, I know men—what they are able to do to women. Can I go up and see her?"

"I don't know if that's wise," said Hitty.

"Let me have my tea first. Then I want to go up alone."

Fiona had come back. Letty knew it was a dream. Part of the reality that had begun to intrude on her vision again, as she became free of the deadening fogs.

When she had been with Compton, she had been able to ask for the medicine. Its honeyed secrets helped her to snuff out the sharp edges of existence. Stilling awareness. She hated her sister and the new doctor for what they were doing to her. After a while, when she discovered that no one was going to relieve her of her misery, she became vindictive. She would defy them all. Deliver herself up to unknowing.

It was Nanette who had stopped that. "Please, madame. Now that we have a chance to make you well again, would you disappoint us?"

"No one asks me if I want to get well, Nanette."

"Madame! That is no way to talk. I do not know what I would do if madame did not get better. Always, I am heartbroken over madame. You see, I took the bundle of clothes to that place. I saw where it was they were asking you to live."

Letty nodded. Her face stony.

"Listen to me, *cherie.* I talk to you like a child, even though you are always 'Madame Letty' to me. This I know, madame. Not in all the years I've worked for this household have I seen madame *hystérique.* It is only one problem madame had. She was very, very unhappy. And why? Monsieur Mackenzie, he was very unkind to madame. Yes, you can shake your head, little one. But Nanette remembers."

"My husband tried his best—" Letty said it through tears, falling like quiet rain on a parched land.

"Poof! I am going to speak frankly. Madame has to hear this."

"No, I mustn't hear anything bad of Mr. Mackenzie. It is I who have been a disgrace to the family. He was right to send me away, even if the place was dreadful. I deserved it."

"Never, madame. It is my belief that this place you were taken to has convinced you that you were sick."

Letty opened her eyes at that. She managed to say cautiously, "Why would you think such a thing? The doctors—"

"And who was the first doctor? Dr. Grey, *n'est-ce pas?* Madame, Nanette knows men. I am not French for nothing. I have seen what he did for madame."

Letty peered at her under lowered lids.

"Madame was so lonely. I remember how much care you would take, with your dress, your hat. 'Nanette, we have to redo my hair.' You dressed as for an assignation, *petite,* not for a doctor's appointment."

Letty buried her face in her palms.

413

"But it was his fault. He took advantage of you, madame. Then, when he had you trapped, he went away without a word."

"How did you know?"

"Madame herself told me—after I had found her in the bathroom. Oh, it was not the blood that made you pass out. It was the medicine. Dr. Grey was drugging you, madame."

"No, no. You are mistaken."

"I have discussed this with Dr. Schwarzkopf. There is a doctor you can trust, madame. Many times I have said to the good Lord, he has blessed us in this man. Why do you think we have removed all the 'medicines'? We are resolved madame should not longer remain drugged."

Letty stared at the girl. Could she believe her? Even as she questioned it, she knew beyond a doubt that it was true. How else to account for the shadowy world in which she had existed for so long?

"Madame was persuaded she was sick. After I saw that place where they had taken you, I knew that they were in fact holding you a prisoner."

"But why? What had I done?"

Nanette's face became old-wise. "It was a convenience to have madame put away. It was common knowledge among the servants that Mr. Mackenzie wished to marry Miss Olivia. Even the children heard the talk."

"But, Nanette, if that were the case, why didn't he just ask me for a divorce?"

"That I do not know." She shrugged. "Perhaps he wished to avoid scandal. He was very proud. I often thought about you, *petite,* and I wondered if they were not making it most easy for you to wish to die."

"If I had died, he would have had access to my money," said Letty slowly. "If he divorced me, by the terms of my father's will and the trust he set up, the funds would have gone to take care of me. The other way, he could have claimed they were for the children. Not that Nat needed more money." She shivered. "I came very close—" she said, remembering.

"These things we may never have the answer to, madame. But it was not for madame's good that she was locked away. Madame tortures herself for something that was not her fault."

Not my fault. Letty pondered the words, but they were merely words. She was as guilty as if she'd been condemned by judge and jury. Until Fiona walked into her room.

Letty was crying. It was as though a dam had burst.

"Mercy on us!" Fiona said. "I didn't know I looked that frightful. I thought you'd be pleased to see me."

"But you can't be here. You were lost at sea."

414

"No, I wasn't. I already went through all that with Hitty."

"Why did you never write?"

"I did. The letters were sent back. I wrote three times. Once, to say I'd reached California. Once, to make sure the first letter had arrived. Another time to let you know where I could be contacted."

"I believe you," said Letty slowly.

Letty was becoming confused. Was Fiona talking to her? Or was it the wish to conjure up Fiona that was speaking to her? She got out of her chair distractedly and walked to the window, staring out at the late summer garden. If Fiona was real, she wouldn't allow Letty to ignore her.

"I don't see any of your paintings around." The voice accused. "Look, I've got some wonderful sketches in my valise. When I'm unpacked, I'll bring them over to show you."

It was another woman Fiona was talking about. Another Letty. This one, her eyes fastened on the garden, was the second Letty, the one who'd been locked up. Did anyone actually know what this bold, shifty-eyed Letty had done? Dirty. She was filthy.

"What are you so wrapped up in?" Fiona came to the window and stood beside her. She put her arm lightly about Letty's shoulders. "You still have roses out in flower, I see." The practical, no-nonsense voice, comfortable as old shoes.

"Yes, there are a few flowers left." Politeness had tricked Letty into answering. She munched on her lower lip. Seeking escape. She didn't deserve concern.

A question turned her. She asked Fiona because she had to know. "Aren't you staying here? It's all right, you know. Nat's gone now."

"I'll stay with Hitty for a few days. She's asked me to go back with her. I've got my luggage downstairs. Not that it's much. You know the way I travel." Fiona smiled at her.

Letty didn't smile back. "Hitty? Why would you choose to go with Hitty? It's not fair. You came to this house first. You are my friend." She pouted.

"Of course I'm your friend. That doesn't mean to say I can't have others. Look, I'll come back—stay here if you wish. But I can't if you're going to insist on moping about in here. They tell me you don't come downstairs for meals. The children never see you. Your painting is gathering dust. You should be ashamed of yourself."

This was a different Fiona. A scold who was going to be harsh with her, demand that she go on with "life as usual." No holding herself back—armed with excuses, fears.

"I haven't been well," Letty said with a whine. "Didn't they tell you? I can't do things the way I used to." Her eyes sought Fiona's, but covertly.

415

"I'm glad you said 'haven't been well' because I was afraid you were sold on the idea you were still unwell. All that's in the past, you know."

"No!" said Letty, astonished at the strength, the bitterness in her own voice. Shouting to defend herself. To maintain her position, however precarious it might seem. "That's what none of you seem to realize. It isn't in the past. I am what I am."

"Tush!" said Fiona cheerfully. "All right, have it your way for the moment. If that's true, then you are still the person I had a lovely visit with before I boarded the ship. If you weren't that person, you wouldn't even remember me, would you?"

"Please, just go away for now."

"All right. I'll come back tomorrow. In the afternoon. I have to have my tea, you know. That cook of yours makes the best tea I've drunk since I left England."

They none of them understand, Letty thought. Perhaps I should end it all. I have hidden the pair of scissors where Nanette won't think to look. I could do it in the night. Norah sits in the room next to mine. But I've learned to be very cunning.

It would serve them right if they found me dead in the morning.

But what if I only half succeeded? Would they send me back to one of those places? Compton's derisive eyes again. He treats me the way he does because he knows what I am. I am a slut—a whore. That's what Bailey called me. I was so bad, Compton had to leave me. And Nat. Nat accused me of behaving like a loose woman in bed.

Letty hid her face in her hands, willing the tears to come. The desert was dry. The heat of her disgrace consumed her, separating her from others—the ones whose love she needed. The sinful Letty wouldn't permit it.

Fiona was taking tea with Letty in the parlor.

"We first met in this room," said Letty, remembering.

"Yes," said Fiona. "It was nice. But don't let's live in the past. We've moved on from that first meeting."

They sparred. Letty came out of her shell to fling a challenge to Fiona. Fiona ignored it. After tea, they walked in the garden.

"We painted under this tree," said Letty. She was deliberately sticking to her point—that she was the other Letty, the one who had waved good-bye to Fiona and disappeared into Compton's arms.

"We'll paint again. Tomorrow, if you like," said Fiona.

They cut roses. Letty produced the hidden scissors from under her shawl, furtively dipping into the pocket of her dress. She peeped at Fiona to see if there was any reaction to the scissors. Fiona took it as a matter of course that Letty should produce this bountiful wealth of a pair of scissors.

"How convenient, Letty. You have a scissors. You cut and I'll hold. Oh, but they're so prickly!"

They arranged the flowers in the vase room. Letty had always liked this closet of space. Rows of containers to choose from, all lined up in neat rows on the overhead shelves. A table for work. Scissors hanging from hooks on the walls. Pairs and pairs of them!

"Which vase do you want, love?" Fiona's practicality snapped her back. Away from the scissors.

Letty pointed to a rose bowl of fluted Venetian glass. Fiona reached for it. Together, they placed the flowers in its depths.

It was after supper and quite late when they finally spoke of what needed to be aired.

"You don't know what it was like," Letty began.

Fiona sat back in one of the lemon silk chairs, her eyes narrowed, not looking at Letty. "Remember what I said to you when I met him?"

"Who?"

"Hitty's husband. Isn't he the one you want to talk about?"

Letty let her eyes fall, seeking some object of comfort on which her attention might rest. She felt naked, alone.

"Remember, I said he reminded me of that friend of my father's?"

"Yes." So Fiona wasn't going to leave her solitary and abandoned after all. "You said something like that."

"What I was trying to say to you, love, was not to trust him. Hitty's husband. Fact was, he impressed me as a real snake."

Letty sat up in her chair. She said slowly, "How do you know?"

"Oh, my dear. I'm not a child. I've got eyes—a mind to perceive with. Besides, Hitty and I have discussed it. He's quite dreadful."

"He is?" Then, with a rush, "You and Hitty talked of Compton? How much does she know?"

"Not enough to embarrass you. Enough to let you know she understands. She'd like to get through the barrier between you, you know."

"She would? I hadn't seen that. Hitty and I have never been close."

"You could always begin. It's never too late. Try, for starters, seeing that the reason you're here—back home—is entirely due to Hitty. She was the one who wouldn't give up."

"If she knew, she wouldn't have wanted me back. I mean, knew all."

"That may be. Again, she might surprise you. The fact is, she cares."

"She wouldn't—if she really knew."

"Do you ever think of Hitty? No. You're bogged down in your own troubles. Hitty is far more alone that you are. Yet she manages."

"Hitty hasn't had a breakdown."

"She could. Don't forget, she's married to that bastard. He makes a practice of getting people to trust him, then using them when they're vulnerable. Knowing what you do, you could help Hitty if she needs you—or if Felicity needs you. Nobody's completely safe, not ever, in life. I should know." Fiona gave a short laugh.

"You are so strong. In spite of what you've been through."

"Look, there's one thing you need to get straight. You don't become strong before you have experiences. It's having a basketful of heartache that forces you to develop muscle. Oh, you may have the potential to be somebody. But how do you know? It's when you get hit in the face with a wet mackerel that you find out where you're going."

Letty said sadly, "It's too late to be strong. I made a mess of it all —long ago. They never told you I tried to take my life?"

"We've talked about it already. All right, you don't remember. You want to think I'm an ignorant woman who doesn't know what it's all about. But I do know. Sometime I'll tell you stories that will make your hair curl."

"Things that happened to you?"

"Things that happened to me."

"How did you go on?"

"Simple. You just go on."

"It's impossible to 'just go on.' How can you when you can't forget?"

"Oh, I didn't say you would forget. Or that it was even possible —which it isn't. Not the worst of it. But if you go on, fill your mind with other matters, let your life take up the slack, it softens. Like the cut fingers and bruises we had as children."

"A serious illness, like Albert had as a child—it can change your whole life." Letty persisted.

"Change it, yes. Not stop it. Which reminds me, someone's got to take a hand with that boy. Your own problems are so large, you haven't had a good look at your children lately. Any of them. Yet who's going to set them an example, listen to their troubles, if you don't?"

"I'm not up to it." The room was closing around Letty. She hated Fiona. For asking her to emerge, to assume responsibility. Didn't she know it was impossible?

"Of course," said Fiona, "they've grown up whether they had you or not. But your own experiences, the things you've had to overcome and move ahead from, they could make you into an exceptional mother."

"I don't follow you."

"I don't expect you to—all at once. Little by little, you are going to find how much larger your understanding has become. Suffering can teach us about forgiveness. After all, how can you condemn someone else when you know you've made a perfect idiot of yourself?"

It made sense. Yet Letty wasn't ready to commit herself. "I feel I've been too awful to be forgiven."

"Ah," said Fiona. "Self-forgiveness isn't easy, is it? When you find out how it's done, let me know, will you?" Her eyes clouded. "We've all done things, Letty. Those of us who haven't never know what's around the corner. Life is a long job. It goes on from day to day, and sometimes it seems as if the troubles it brings are never done. But cheer up, when they are, you'll be dead. Doubtless that will bring fresh worries."

Letty laughed—a clear sound that hadn't been heard in these walls for a long time. Nanette, hovering in the bedroom, set down Letty's silken nightgown and ran to the door.

"Nanette," said Fiona, "I think we should have Bates drive me back to Mrs. Grey's. I'm turning your mistress over to you."

"*Pauvre petite,* she hasn't smiled since I can remember."

"She's going to smile much more now. She's found out she can." Fiona pressed her lips together and shook her head at Letty. "You and I have what it takes, girl. I'm an old busybody that few people want to see coming for a lengthy visit. But I'm tough as a boiling fowl. Even the natives couldn't stop me, though they frightened me half to death. You've been to hell and back, and one of the odd things is that few will ever suspect it. Even if you shared it with them, they wouldn't have been in your shoes to know. Only the few who have been there can know. Those will respect you—as you will respect them."

"Respect?"

"Yes, m'dear. That's what I said. It takes a tremendous amount of courage to come back. You're partway there. Tomorrow, you'll start the next phase."

"I will? How?"

"Heavens, woman! By rejoining the human race—having breakfast with your children—going out in the carriage. When was the last time you visited your mother?"

Letty's face closed up.

"I never said it was going to be easy. Good night, love. Invite me over for tea again soon, will you?"

When she had gone, Letty rose from her chair. She gazed up at the picture of Clemmy. Why hadn't she seen it before?—the style was pretentious. The artist had painted without depth. Letty reached into one of the desk drawers, wondering if the sketch pads she'd filled would still be there.

They were. Stonehenge in all its tentative lines. Would she do it differently today? She became excited at what she might do, given paints and paper. It was wearying. It was easier to pull the coverlet of defeat over her. Then she didn't have to try.

Fiona said she'd have to live with it. That there was no going back. No erasing what had been. Time was the only ally—and persistence. Courage? A quality she'd never been able to boast of.

She pushed her sketches back into her desk, glanced again at the portrait of Clemmy. She'd be like that artist—draining his creativity into a narrow stream. Not wild and gushing—life energized.

Was that how she'd been? Opening her loins in answer to a call?

A reply that condemned her because she was a woman. Women didn't respond that way unless they were whores.

But what of the men who issued the invitation? Who lured and begged and seduced, using all the weapons in their armamentarium? Were they blameless?

She sat again in one of the lemon chairs. There was no escaping the censure of society, no matter which way she reasoned her own role. Society was herself. Its rules and mores had gone to make up her being, its judgment had become her finger, pointing censure.

Could a caged bird survive flight? Where once she had felt walled in by life, then later literally bound by bars, now she saw her restricted existence as providing security.

She might emerge. A butterfly, its wings wet and crumpled, to face the heat of the sun. It would have to be in her own time, though. Not for the beseeching eyes of Hitty. Not for the clarion call of Fiona. Duty to her children? She could fulfill this quietly, unobtrusively. In no way need responsibility commit her to further than today. Need it?

Of this last, she wasn't so sure. She promised herself to think about it. As to the other—flying beyond the cage—it was enough to know that there was a door.